THE FINAL ADJUSTMENT

TOM PEAVLER

iUNIVERSE, INC.
NEW YORK   BLOOMINGTON

The Final Adjustment

iUniverse books may be ordered through booksellers or by contacting:

iUniverse
1663 Liberty Drive
Bloomington, IN 47403
www.iuniverse.com
1-800-Authors (1-800-288-4677)

ISBN: 978-1-4502-5531-8 (sc)
ISBN: 978-1-4502-5532-5 (ebk)

Printed in the United States of America

iUniverse rev. date: 9/16/2010

THE FINAL ADJUSTMENT

The day like most of the recent others had been boring. Things had gone so well recently that he found himself with little to do. For more than two years, all of the cars on the North American continent had been manufactured in Perdido. He loved the time he could spend with his family, but in some strange way he missed the excitement of the days when things had looked so shaky. He had just read the latest financial report that had lain almost unnoticed on his desk for the last two days. He smiled as he remembered the prediction of Juan that he would one day be the richest man in the world. That prediction had come true almost two years ago. With the dissolution of America's Big Three automakers, the Japanese had been ready to step in and fill the void. The percentage of each unit sold by all of the Japanese manufacturers far exceeded the profits they could have earned if they had settled for a flat sum. For Juan, who had negotiated the agreement, it had made him one of the 100 richest men in the world.

There had been no serious attempt by either the Big Three or the oil companies to interrupt the status quo for more than 14 months. A couple of half-hearted attempts by Juan's brothers had been easily thwarted by Hans shortly after they had discovered that Diego's brag that he had successfully assassinated Juan was false. Only a short delay from the patent office in transferring Tink's patent to Charley had slowed the complete take-over of the automobile industry by Charley and the Japanese. The European carmakers had followed suit in less than a year and moved their entire operation to the growing outskirts of Perdido. Millions of Americans in used cars continued to wend their way southward as the price of gasoline became prohibitive for the average citizen. To Charley, every passing day seemed more boring than the one preceding. His only real happiness came in the time he could pass with his daughter and granddaughter. Alice could sense his unhappiness, but she was powerless to improve on the moods which came over him with ever increasing frequency.

Billy had never really conceded that he would never be able to return to his former home in Chicago. He shared his father's dream that some day they might be able to return. Unlike his father, he had never shared that thought with his wife. He feared that she would not share his dream, for she seemed far happier in their present situation than Charley or Alice.

Juan knew of Charley's dream. He remembered distinctly what Charley had told him of the Ozark lake where he and Alice had disposed of the car in which they had attempted to make their escape to Mexico. Charley had never mentioned it directly again, but it was evident to a man who was able to read and analyze the moods and actions of others that the idea of returning to the States was never very far from Charley's thoughts. He knew that he would never leave Perdido to accompany his boss if he ever decided to take the big step. He knew he could run the corporation without Charley's being there. Charley was rarely involved in any of the major decisions. Juan had long since taken over the role of decision maker while Charley had become nothing more than a consultant. Charley was also aware of the new pecking order within the corporation, and although he was relieved that he no longer faced the major decisions, it added to his frustration of being the richest man in the world with nothing really to do with all of his free time and money.

Charley sat at the breakfast table with Alice. They were sipping at their second cups of coffee when Charley looked up from his morning newspaper and asked Alice, "Did you see this?"

"What was I supposed to see?"

"The Mexican government is sending a huge group of regular army units here to Perdido."

"Why, love?"

"Seems like there's a rumor goin' round that there might be an invading army headed here from the States."

"What kind of army? Regular U.S. Army?"

"No, more like one of the so-called militias, but the rumor says they number in the hundreds, maybe even thousands, and that they appear to be well armed."

"Should we be alarmed?"

"I think concerned might be a better word for it. I'll have to have a chat with Hans to see how much cause there is for alarm."

"Where is Hans today?"

"I haven't the foggiest. He's been so bored recently that I haven't even thought about what his present daily routine might be. I'll put in a call to Billy and Juan and see if they know where I can get a hold of him."

He got up from the table and went to a phone to make calls to try to find Hans. Neither Billy nor Juan could give him any real information on the whereabouts of his main man in security. It was Terry who told him that he thought Hans would probably be at a recently opened cantina in the suburbs of Perdido. He hung up the phone and went to tell Alice that he would be leaving soon and not to expect him back before much later in the afternoon. He dressed hurriedly and sent word to his driver and bodyguard that they would be leaving soon.

As he got into the back seat of the bullet-proof limo, he gave the driver the name of the cantina and the general direction of its location. He said nothing else until they arrived at the cantina. He told the driver to wait until he returned no matter how long that might be. The bodyguard preceded him into the air-conditioned silence of the cantina. No more than a dozen patrons were inside. Three sat at the gilded bar while the others sat in small groups. Hans was the only one sitting alone at the table that was fartherest from the bar. He tensed as he saw two men approaching his table, but he relaxed when he recognized Charley and the guard.

"What brings you here at such an early hour? You've never been known to have an early morning thirst."

"I just wondered if you'd read this morning's paper?"

"You mean the part about the approaching army from the North? Yeah, I read it. So what?"

"Do you see any cause for alarm?"

"Not really. We've had other groups try before. This time we have the support of the whole Mexican army."

"Do you intend to become personally involved in this?"

"If I need to be. Why do you ask? Are you really worried?"

"I guess I am, a little bit."

Charley turned toward the guard and told him to sit at the bar and have a drink. He wanted to discuss some things with Hans privately.

"So what do you want to discuss. I've a hunch that it really has very little to do with security here in Perdido. Am I right?"

"As usual, you're right. I don't know if you're ready for this, but here goes. Alice and I are seriously considering leaving Perdido for good."

"And where, might I ask, are you considering as your new residence?"

"Back to the States. Do you think that's crazy?"

"Does it really matter what I think? Why do you even care what I think? I've known you long enough to know that when you make up your mind to do something, it matters very little what anyone else thinks."

"That's true. Probably the influence of a bloated bank account. I'll get right to the point. If Alice and I go, would you be willing to go back with us? I know you're bored with what's been happening here recently, and I can almost guarantee you that if you go back with me that things will not be boring."

"Who'll be watching things here if I leave? Will Terry go back with you?"

"I don't know. I've never really discussed it with him. He seems to like it here. I'm not sure he'd be interested in going back. The only one I've ever even mentioned this to is Juan. I know that he can take care of the business end of things here. I think Billy would like to go back, but I'm not certain what Luisa thinks about the idea. I think she'll probably go along with it even if she isn't crazy about the idea."

"Do you have any time frame in mind?"

"Not really. I think as soon as this latest threat from the North is over, I'll start making some plans to leave."

"Do you have a concrete idea of where you would like to settle?"

"I have a pretty good idea. The place has no name. It isn't in any city or town. It's a place in the Ozarks where Alice and I dumped one of the cars that we were making our getaway in. We pushed the car into the lake and kind of made a vow that we'd come back some day and see what the place looked like in the light of day."

"And that's it? Just some place you've never even really seen? Now that does seem a little crazy."

"More than a little. Still, are you willing to spend the rest of your life here in Perdido in relative safety, or would you like to have a go at returning to the States?"

"I don't usually have to make this kind of decision before I've had my second drink in the morning. Can I have a little time to think it over?"

"Of course. Take all the time you need."

"Okay, that's enough time. Yes, I'll go with you. I don't suppose there's any reason to even discuss money, is there?"

"Not even a consideration. Name your own price."

"I don't think this approaching group from the North will take more than a couple of weeks. How much longer than that will it take you to be ready to move?"

"I can't say. I'm going to let Juan see how much of the land around the place I want is available. Some of the land might not be for sale, but I think with the money we have to offer, we can be assured that we will have no close neighbors."

"I don't think I can protect you from the whole population of the United States all by myself. I'm flattered if that's what you think. How much of the security we have here could I count on taking with me back to the States?"

"As much as you think necessary."

"Really? But how will I have any idea how much that would be if I've never seen the place I'll be trying to defend?"

"I never even thought about it. Would you be willing to make a sneak preview trip with me to get a look at the place? Just the two us? I might not even like the looks of the place in the light of day."

"You'd be willing to risk everything you have here just to go back and get a look at this place? Well, if you're willing to take that risk, count me in. Tell Juan to start his inquiries immediately and I'll try to make whatever arrangements we'll need for a look-see at this Garden of Eden of yours."

Charley nodded and motioned for the guard to head toward the exit. Outside he signaled for the driver to bring the limo around to pick them up. Once inside the car, he told the driver to head for the plant. He was certain that Juan would be in his office in the plant. The guard at the main gate recognized the limo and Charley's driver and waved them through. The guard accompanied Charley to Juan's office and waited outside the door. When Charley entered, Juan looked surprised when he saw Charley standing in his doorway.

"I wasn't expecting you. Anything wrong?"

"No, nothing wrong. Have you got a little time?"

"Sure, sit down. I don't have anything very pressing today. What's on your mind? Does this have anything to do with the article in today's paper?"

"Not directly, no. Do you recall a conversation we had a couple of years ago when I told you that some day I was considering a return to the States?"

"Yes, vaguely. How does this concern me?"

"I want you to begin looking to see how much of the property around the lake I mentioned might be for sale."

"You'll have to show me on a map exactly which lake you're talking about and for sale at what price."

"I have a map in my office. Give me a minute and I'll go get it. As for the price, whatever it takes.'"

He left and went to his own office and returned with the map. Juan hung up the phone when he heard Charley tap once again on the door.

"You sure you're not too busy for this? I could come back later."

"Never too busy to accommodate the man who's made me rich."

"Let me ask you something. If I do decide to leave, are you sure you can manage everything if I'm not even close?"

"Would you think it presumptuous of me to remind you that I've been making most of the big decisions around here for the past two years?"

"No, that would be a statement of fact. But I've always been close by if anything should go wrong."

"I assume you'll still be only a phone call away."

"I guess that's right. Do you have any connections at all in the States that might give you a hand in finding out if any of the real estate that I'm interested in might be for sale?"

"Yeah, I have a friend or two that might be able to help. I'll try to get on it right away."

"Not really. I'm not leaving until this deal with the American militia is over. I hope that whole thing has been really exaggerated."

"I hope so, too. What does Hans say about it?"

"Not much, but he doesn't seem too worried. As soon as this latest deal is over, Hans and I are going to make a secret trip back to the place that I want you to buy. I can tell by your immediate reaction that you think a trip of that type is far too dangerous."

"Of course I do. What does Hans think about the idea?"

"He's willing to take the risk, so I guess he doesn't think it's too risky."

"Tell me one thing if you can put it into words. Why do you want to go back?"

"It's hard to put into words. I have everything that any man could wish for. I have a good wife and family, a glorious house with all the comforts that anyone could imagine, more money than a king could spend in 10 lifetimes, more free time to do anything I want to do in the way of recreation, and although it was never one of my goals, I have that thing called power."

"I wouldn't argue with a thing you just said, so why risk it all to return to a place that scorned you?"

"Like I said, it's hard to put into words. Maybe it's the challenge. In a way I've been told that I never could come back. The oil companies, the Big Three, and the American government have all told me in no uncertain terms that I will never be able to return. I guess I'd just like to show them that they're wrong."

"Yeah, I think I understand that. Since practically every car in the world is now manufactured here, and you are recognized as the richest man in the world, they're aren't many challenges left here."

"That pretty well sums it up. I'll check with you again in a few days to see if your connections can tell you anything about what I hope to buy."

****

Three days passed before Juan had an opportunity to talk with Charley concerning what he had learned about property in the Ozarks. It was the middle of the afternoon when Juan had some free time. He called the extension of Charley's office, and when Charley answered, he asked if he was busy. When he said he was about to leave, he asked him to stop by before he headed home. In about 15 minutes he tapped on Juan's door.

"Do you need something?"

"No, not really. I put out some feelers about the property you wanted me to check on."

"And what did you find out?"

"Property values there are sky-high. I know that's of no real interest to you. You can afford anything you really want. I also learned that much of the property there is owned by people closely associated with the Mafia. I'm not sure they could be persuaded to sell, no matter what you offered them. As far as I could tell, the Mafia connections are not related to the family of your brothers."

"Anything else of interest?"

"Perhaps. Unlike most other lakes in the area, this one is not completely under the control of the Corp of Engineers. People are allowed to build their own private docks there on the lake. The dam there does help provide electricity for that region. There is actually a small community right there on the edge of the lake. There are several real estate offices right there in the small community. You could check with them to see just what might be readily available."

"Thanks. Hans and I will probably be leaving for an exploratory within a week. I'll let you know when we're ready to take off."

When Charley arrived at his home, he went to his study and put in a call for Hans. When he answered, Charley asked him to stop by for the evening meal and some conversation. Hans knew Charley was reluctant to discuss any important business over the phone, so he merely agreed to stop by for dinner.

Charley then looked around the huge house he'd never really gotten comfortable in. He wanted to share what he had learned with Alice, but she didn't seem to be anywhere in the house. He checked the nursery last, and when he found no one there, he surmised that his wife and daughter must be in the garden. He was right.

"What you guys doin' out here?"

"Just watering some of the flowers. You're home a little early. Anything special going on?"

"Not really. I invited Hans to stop by for dinner. We're goin' to have a chat after that."

"A chat? About what?"

"I think maybe he and I are gonna make a little trip in the near future."

"A trip? To where?"

"Remember that lake where we dumped the Buick on the way down here? Well, we're gonna go see if we can buy that lake."

"You're kidding, right? You can't buy a whole lake."

"Probably not, so I'll just have to buy all the land that surrounds the lake."

"And what if some of the land there is not for sale?"

"That's why I might need Hans. He might have to make those unwilling to sell an offer they can't refuse."

"You're kidding again, right?"

"Maybe, maybe not. I'm serious as a heart attack about returning to the States. Have you changed your mind about returning?"

"I know we jokingly discussed this from time to time, but I guess I didn't realize that you were that serious. Why the sudden urge to leave? Are things going badly with the business?"

"No, that's part of the problem. Things are goin' too smoothly with the business. They don't really even need me at the plant any more. I sign a few check and okay a few details, but there's really nothing to what I do that a dozen guys there at the plant couldn't do."

"Are you sure? I think just your presence alone there helps things run smoothly."

"Of course you think that. You're my wife, and you're supposed to think that. So now, I gotta know. Would you risk your life and that of our daughter to go back to the States?"

"Charley, I risked everything I owned to make the trip down here with you. You had nothing but a dream back then, and still I risked everything with you. If you think for a minute that I'd not follow you anywhere now that you have billions, you certainly don't know the real me."

"Then you'd go along just for the money?"

"No, it just means that now I have a billion times more reasons to love you. What about Billy? Have you discussed this with him?"

"No, but I know he wants to go back home. I'm not sure what Luisa would think about the move."

"I know she'll think it's a crazy idea, but like me, she loves her man enough to follow him anywhere. What would you like for dinner?"

"Doesn't really matter. How about burgers and fries?"

"Does Hans have a taste for things a little more fancy?"

"Yes, but with what I pay him, he can afford to buy anything he wants to eats. Tonight I'm pickin' up the tab, and he who pays the fiddler, names the tune."

Hans arrived precisely at six. Alice greeted him at the door and invited him into the dining room. She apologized for the simple fare that would make up the meal, but he assured her that he had very little appetite and that anything she had chosen to serve would be great. He gave her his hat, and she asked him if he would like to check the pistol she knew he carried. He declined and she led him to the table where Charley was already seated. He sat down next to Charley, leaving the other end of the table to Alice.

Charley asked, "Would you rather talk before we eat or after?"

"Let's eat first. Sometimes unpleasant conversation causes me to lose my appetite."

"And what makes you think our conversation will be unpleasant?"

"Just a hunch. Am I right?"

"If you think the trip we talked about earlier is unpleasant, then you're right. If not, you are wrong."

"I see

"Have you discussed this with Alice?

"Yes."

"And?"

"She isn't crazy about the idea, but she has agreed to go if we can provide adequate security."

"What have you learned from Juan?"

"There is a small settlement close to the town. In the town there are several real estate offices who could direct us to people who have property nearby for sale."

"Anything else?"

"Yes, much of the property close to the lake is Mafia owned. Prices for the real estate are sky-high, but not out of my price range. None of the Mafia-owned property is connected to Juan's brothers. It seems that most of the housing there is mostly for weekends only. Very few full time residents."

"How soon will you be ready to make the trip, and how long do you anticipate that we'll be gone?"

"I'll need about two days to get everything ready. I'll have to delegate a few things, and I'm sure you will, too."

"What means of transportation do you think we should employ to reach our destination? Air would be faster, but I'm not sure it would be the safest."

"We could take my private jet. What do you think would be unsafe about that? The plane is in great shape, and I have the utmost confidence in the pilot."

"I'm aware of that, but have you considered where we could land the plane. I'm pretty sure there aren't any airfields close to the place you describe with a runway long enough to accommodate the landing of a jet aircraft."

"You're right. I hadn't even considered that. What would you recommend?"

"I think the only way to go is by car. With the battery powered new ones, we wouldn't have to stop for gas, and we could take enough food with us to avoid being seen in restaurants."

"Why not a commercial airline? That would save a lot of time?"

"Too many people watching at the airport both here and there. If we're spotted getting on a plane, there might be an unhappy welcoming committee waiting for us when we arrived. I couldn't even get on board a flight without setting off the metal detector with any weapon I might carry for our protection. I think it would also be wise for the both of us to use a disguise. Have you ever used one?"

"No, you'll have to help me with that. What else will we need?"

"Well, I think we'll need some really good phony ID's. You know, things like driver's licenses and social security cards, maybe two or three major credit cards. I can have all that for both of us in a couple of days. Do you want me to set up for the loan of the car we'll be using?"

"Yeah, go ahead. Let's plan on leaving in three days. There's no real hurry. I'm sure I can have Billy and Juan ready to handle about anything that might happen while we're away. Can Terry cover for you?"

"I think so. The word I have is the invasion by this so-called militia won't happen in less than a month. I'm certain we won't be gone that long. Besides, the Federales are already in place. Do you plan on really buying anything while we're there, or is this just a scouting expedition?"

"I'm not really sure. I don't know much about buying real estate. I'll have to let Juan give me a short course in how it's done.

If I see something I really like, I'd like to just go ahead and buy it if it's for sale."

"How about finances? Are you gonna take that much cash with you?"

"No, but I really hadn't thought much about it. I haven't really had any money in my pockets for years. You know, I just sign for about anything because everybody knows I'm good for about any amount."

"That's because they know who you are. Up there, we're hoping that nobody will know who you are. If they do, I'm afraid we could be in a world of hurt."

"What would you suggest I do about having the where-with-all to pay for something if I should decide to buy?"

"Have Juan open up an account at one of the local banks. Put the account in the name of some corporation that is supposedly trying to develop or re-develop some of the local property. He can come up with a cover story that will match up with the phony ID's we'll be carrying."

"How will I explain your presence along with me?"

"Just a business associate and a member of the group that is trying to buy up any promising property we come across. I'll drop by tomorrow, and I'll try to get you fitted with a disguise. I've got a couple of ideas. I think some horn-rim glasses, a stylish hat, and some facial hair might be enough to get you by."

The next day Hans stopped by Charley's house and brought with him the basics for the boss's disguise. Alice could not restrain a laugh when she saw her husband decked out in the manner that Hans had prescribed. She found the disguise of Hans equally laughable, but she said nothing.

Hans said, "Don't worry about what those who know us around here think of our disguises. It's only because they know what we really look like that makes our appearance seem ridiculous. If you dare, and I think you should, why don't we take a little run down town here in an unmarked car and see if the locals recognize either of us. Are you willing?"

"No other guards?"

"Don't you think I'll be enough? I was all you had in Japan."

"Yeah, that's right. Where shall we go?"

"How about Walmart and a really fine restaurant for dinner. If we can get by in those two places, I think we'll surely be alright in the Ozarks."

An hour long stay in Walmart and 45 minutes in the *Casa de Oro* restaurant did not seem to arouse any suspicion on the part of the locals. When they got back to the house, Alice laughed again, but she put on a more serious attitude when she was informed of the success of their venture. Hans left in what seemed to Alice to be a big hurry, but she said nothing. Charley went to the phone and called the plant to be sure that Juan was in his office. When he answered the phone, Charley told him not to leave the plant until they had time for some conversation. Then he took off the disguise, dressed again in his normal style, and sat down at the table to have a cup of coffee with Alice.

"He was right. You certainly don't want to be burdened with the amount of cash you might need. How much do want deposited, and what will be the name you wish to have as the man who will control the deposit?"

"Do you think a million would be enough?"

"Certainly not. I can see you have no idea about real estate. 5 million at least, but I would feel a lot better about things if you had 10 million at your disposal."

"10 million, it is, then. That's a good round figure. Is it usual practice to pay the asking price in a lump sum, or should a buyer merely make a large down payment, you know, earnest money, as it were?"

"I think 10% to 20% should hold about any property you look at for at least 30 days. If you put up more than that, you'll look like a real amateur. Also, if you can, buy some property from more than one real estate agency. The properties don't even have to be adjoining. Sometimes, if you can surround a reluctant seller with property all around him, he can be more easily persuaded to sell, especially if he doesn't like his new neighbors."

"Thanks for the advice. Call me tomorrow and tell me the name of the bank we'll be using to buy the properties. Check with Hans and see what names we'll be using and what will be the name of the corporation trying to buy up the land."

"Will do. Will I see you again before you take off?"

"Probably not."

"Well, if not, let me wish the both of you the best of luck. Be careful."

"You can be certain of that. As soon as we get settled, I'll give you a call and tell you where we can be reached should anything of real importance happen while we're gone."

"Adios."

****

The trip to the Ozarks took almost five days. They alternated driving with Charley taking the lion's share. Charley had gotten used to the disguise he was wearing although he still hated the way he looked. It was the longest period of time that Charley had ever spent alone with Hans. He had wondered if they would share any casual conversation along the way. He remembered that Hans had preferred to sleep on their long airline flight to Japan and dreaded the thought of days with only the car radio for companionship. He was surprised and pleased to find that Hans really could be an engaging conversationalist. He even shared some of his boyhood memories in the days long before he had chosen the type of work that had led him into Charley's direction.

Upon their arrival, they checked into what looked like the best of the half dozen motels that the village offered. They went directly to their room to freshen up and make sure that their disguises were in good order. Charley assumed the leadership role in asking the clerk where they might find the real estate offices.

The first one they chose to visit was the closest to the motel. The office itself was small with only two people in the office, a man dressed casually and a young woman who sat behind her desk at a computer. The man looked up as Charley entered alone. Charley introduced himself as Mr. Ralph Swanson, the chief purchasing agent of the Golden State Development Corporation of Fresno, California. The man did not seem overly impressed and remained seated while Charley tried to explain the purpose of his visit. His interest seemed to grow when he was told that the corporation might be interested in buying complete tracts of land around the lake as well as selected sites already fully developed or partially developed.

"Well, we certainly have some of both. We're not the biggest, but we have some very nice locations that fit what you've described. Would you like for me to show you some of what we do have?"

"Sure, my partner is still in the car. Want to take our car, or you want to show us around?

"Let's take my van. I know where we'll be goin' and some of the roads around here are pretty rough."

"Sounds good. I'll tell my buddy to join us."

They got into the large van, and Charley introduced Hans as Tim Worthy, one of the traveling secretaries of the company. They traveled about two miles before they came upon a large two story log cabin that had an upstairs veranda that provided an excellent view of the lake.

"How much land goes with this one?"

"Almost an acre. How do you like the looks of this one?"

"From the outside, it looks pretty good. Is it presently occupied?"

"Well, yes and no. The couple who bought it about a year ago is several months behind on their mortgage payments. They've already started the moving out process."

"How much are you asking?"

"It lists for a million five, but I think we might be able to do a little better if the right prospective buyer came along."

The man looked closely into Charley's face to see if he had blinked when the word million came out of his mouth. When he got no reaction, he asked if they would like to look inside since the owners were not there. They agreed to take a look.

Once inside, both Charley and Hans pretended to be interested in the things that most prospective buyers would be examining. After some 30 minutes inside the house, Hans was the one who asked, "How much down would you require to hold the property for 60 days?"

"Ten per cent of whatever we agree upon the asking price. Are you guys really interested?"

"Yes, I think so. I'll have to call home base tonight to make sure the check will clear. We do so many transactions on a daily basis, and the money comes from so many diverse funds that we have to make sure before we write anything really large. If we wrote it on the wrong bank, it might prove to be embarrassing. How long will it take for you to be ready to transfer the deed of ownership to us?"

"I think a couple of days after your check clears. Would that be satisfactory?"

"Yes, are you busy now, or can you show us what else you've got?"

"Never too busy to do business. Can you tell me what you'd like to see?"

"What's the closest thing you have to this property in your listings."

"Oh, I've got two or three which border on this one, but I'm not sure you'd be interested any of those. They're not nearly as nice as this one."

"Doesn't matter. If the location is good, we can always upgrade whatever is located on the property."

The man showed them three more properties, and he had been honest in his assessment of their relative value when compared to the first one he had shown them. Two were average and the third was a dump, a veritable eyesore which the man had been reluctant to even show them. He was surprised when Charley showed interest in all three and priced them carefully. He asked Hans what he thought of each, and in all three cases, Hans had agreed that the corporation would probably agree to their acquisition since they bordered on the original.

When they returned to the office, Charley told the man he would be there bright and early next morning with checks totaling 10% of the asking price of all four properties. He asked if the man had other properties, even in the general vicinity of those they had visited. The agent could not believe his good fortune. His eyes seemed to light up like a cash register when he thought of what his commission already was and what it might be if these gentlemen were really on the level about purchasing even more properties. He asked if these other properties had to be adjacent to the ones they had visited. Charley told him no, but we wanted to know if any of the other agencies in the village might have properties either directly adjacent or in close vicinity. The agent promised to check the listings of his competitors to see if they had anything that might interest them.

Later that evening, they returned to their room. Charley was satisfied that they had made a good beginning. They went out briefly for burgers and fries. Hans would have preferred something a little fancier, but Charley was tired of the disguise and really wanted only an order to go so he could get out of what he considered an outlandish costume.

The next morning they were at the office of the real estate agent when it opened. The man   greeted them warmly and asked if they were ready to do serious business. Charley just nodded and took a seat opposite the man's desk.

"Before we start making out checks, I think we're gonna have to do a little dickering on some of prices of those last three pieces of property that we looked at. My company thinks they're a little too high, and I'm inclined to agree. Do you have any wiggle room?"

"Perhaps. How much reduction are you talking about?"

"Somewhere in the neighborhood of 5 to 10 %."

"Let me make a couple of phone calls, and I'll be able to tell you in about an hour. Will that be all right?"

"Yeah, have you been able to find out if any of your competitors have any property we might be interested in?"

"I haven't had a chance to take a complete look, but I have a couple you might be interested in. They are directly adjacent to the most expensive one that you liked so well. You know, the first one we looked at."

"And who holds title to these?"

"Missouri Land and Title. They're about a quarter of a mile right down the road. You'll see   the big sign they have out front. They're a little larger than we are. They may have several more that I don't know about. There's been a lot of turnover recently."

"We'll mosey down that way and check them out while you find out if you have any leeway on the asking price of those other three."

They left and went directly to the second real estate office. It was indeed a little larger and fancier than the first. The agent there seemed to be expecting them, and there was no doubt in Charley's mind that the first agent had called ahead to inform them that potential buyers were on the way. He shook the hand of both men and asked them to have a seat. They sat and briefly explained what they were interested in. The agent smiled and said he did indeed have two properties that bordered on the one that Charley had described to him. He offered to take them immediately out for a look if they were interested. Charley declined, saying they had other business to take care of at that time, but that they would like to see what he had early that same afternoon. Then they returned to the office of the first agent. He was smiling as they walked through the door.

"Gentlemen, I think I have some good news for both of us. The people who own the properties you paid down on have agreed to take 8% off the asking price. Do you think we can agree to that price? It will save you quite a lot on the total."

"Probably. I'll have to make a couple more calls, but I think we're on the right track. How long before you'll know for sure?"

"By early afternoon.

"We have an appointment with the other agent to take a look at the properties you mentioned. Is that outfit really on the up and up? I didn't really like the look of their agent."

"Yeah, I know. He doesn't look like anyone you'd buy a used car from, but as far as I know they've never been involved in any shady dealing. I'll start the closing procedure as soon as you give me the okay. How will you handle the financing of the rest of the deal?"

"A certified check should take of it, if you have no objection."

"Of course not. It's just a little unusual to take care of it all at once."

"That's the way we do business. We always say strike while the iron is hot. When we see something that we think is a good deal for us, we jump on it."

"I know, but that is a lot of money."

"Not to us. We do bigger deals than this every day of the week. I'm surprised that you haven't heard about us."

Charley left and went outside and joined Hans who had remained in the car. He produced a cell phone and went through the motions of making a couple of calls in case the man happened to be watching through the window. He then went to the bank nearby and had them draw up a certified check for the new amount they had agreed on. That done, they returned to the office and told the man to start the closing procedure and gave him the check.

The agent in the second agency dropped what he had been doing and could hardly wait to show them the properties that were adjacent to the first one they had purchased. Charley feigned little interest at first. He told the man he thought both were terribly over priced and that his company probably wouldn't go more than 80% of his asking prices. He then asked the man if he had any other properties in the vicinity, even though they did not border on these two. He said he had several and offered to show them now if the were interested. Charley said they were ready now to take a look at whatever he had.

Though none of the other properties they looked at that day had any real value in Charley's overall plan, they showed substantial interest. When they returned to the office, Charley put up 10% of the asking price on four smaller locations. Hans had remained silent throughout nearly all of the business transactions He mere nodded assent when Charley asked him if he thought the properties were worthwhile.

Later that evening at the motel, Hans appeared a little more nervous than he had at any previous time since they had begun the trip.

"What's the matter, Hans? You don't look quite as confident as you did yesterday. Is anything wrong?"

"I'm not sure. I just got a creepy feeling. It's hard to explain, but sometimes in my line of work you just get a feeling that something is about to pop."

"Does it have anything to do with anybody we met today? I didn't see anything out of the ordinary."

"I'm not sure you'd really see anything out of the ordinary if it rented space in your rectum. Sorry, Charley, it's just your line of work and mine are vastly different. Most of my adult life has depended on not only noticing things out of the ordinary, but also just a gut feeling that something is about to go down."

"You didn't care much for any of those last four places I bought today, did you? Why not?"

"They're too scattered. There's no way I could possibly defend all the places you've purchased, even if you let me bring our whole security force down here, and I don't think that's gonna happen."

"I'm not sure how much security we'll be able to bring with us or how much we'll need. Some of the properties on the fringe of where I'll be will just serve as a buffer to slow down anyone who might try to attack us."

"My God, maybe I've misjudged you. What exactly do you plan to do after you've gotten moved in down here?"

"I'm not really sure. Maybe I'll just go fishing. They say the fishing here is excellent."

"I'm more worried about hunting than fishing. I'm afraid you may be the game being hunted."

"Nothing new about that. I've been hunted by the best for years. How long do you think we can hang around here before things get too dicey?"

"I'd say that anything longer than a couple more days would be too risky."

"Why? What are you most afraid of?"

"I'm afraid we're gonna attract too much attention just by the number of properties we've paid down on. Somebody might get real inquisitive about why a California Land Company has suddenly taken such an interest in a place like this. They might even think there's a huge discovery of some natural resource like oil or uranium."

"Who do you think would be the first to notice?"

"Doesn't matter who's first. Word gets around and it's a small world. People are gonna want to know why the type of stuff we're buying has suddenly become such a hot commodity."

"Maybe you're right. I intend to buy a whole lot more of these properties before I even think about moving down here, but I don't have to get them all at once."

"Do you even have a time frame in mind about moving down here?"

"Not really. I know there'll never be a time when it's completely safe, but I have a vague plan that has to include a nice buffer zone around me. That zone around me will include a high fence wired to be electrical, full time human guardians, attack dogs, and motion detectors which will link up with a central control system which is manned 24 hours a day. What do you say to that?"

"I say you've learned a few things from yours truly. How many guards are you willing to hire to protect you?"

"As many as you think necessary. Don't forget that cost is no object. How many do you think it would take?"

"That depends on the size of the perimeter they'll be trying to defend. Where are you gonna house this small army that's gonna protect you?"

"I'm not sure, but once again, when you factor in the amount of money I have to spend, nothing is really impossible."

"True, but there are logistic considerations. Things like how far away from your own house will these guards be quartered. Also will these guards be single men or married men with families?"

"Which would you recommend?"

"No doubt in my mind, I'd take the married men with children. If you were gonna attack someone, I'd take bachelors. They're more willing to take risks, but for defensive purposes, no one fights harder than a man with a wife and children."

A slight tapping at the door interrupted their conversation. Hans opened the door cautiously and asked who it was. The man asked if he could come in. Hans asked the nature of his business, and he replied that it was concerning the purchase of properties. Hans opened the door very slowly, and the man stepped inside the door. Once completely inside, Hans spun the man around, pushed him to the wall, and frisked him thoroughly. The bulge underneath the man's suit coat revealed a snub-nose .38 revolver. Hans removed the weapon and tossed it onto the bed out of the reach of the visitor.

"Who are you, and what's the idea of bringing a loaded weapon into our room?"

"My name is Clark, and I come here as a personal representative of some very important people."

"Really? And just who might these people be?"

"I'm not at liberty to divulge their names, but they represent a very powerful organization, one that becomes very curious about anyone who might be thinking about becoming one of their neighbors."

"Do tell. I never really believed there was such a thing as the so-called organization you're talking about. Maybe I was wrong."

"All these people really want to know is why your company's sudden interest in all the property you've paid down on the last two days."

"The only thing you can take back to these powerful people is that the land is being purchased by equally rich and powerful people who are equally concerned about the type of neighbors they might have. Some of these people who sent you here may be wanting to sell the land they now have."

"I doubt it. They've been here for a long time."

"Well, nothing lasts forever. There're changes in everything."

The man made a sudden move to grab at Hans, but Hans pushed him aside. They struggled until Hans gained enough leverage with his left arm to pull his own pistol with his right hand. With the barrel of the gun he struck the man across the forehead, and he slumped to the floor. Hans stepped back and waited to see if the man was conscious. He lay motionless, and Hans stood over his body, still holding his gun.

"I think you may have killed him, Hans."

"I didn't mean to, but if he's dead, he deserved it. It was foolish to come here into our room carrying a pistol and then making a grab for me."

"I'm sure he didn't know it was you, Hans, or he wouldn't have tried anything that foolish."

"Probably not, but it was foolish anyway. You don't go into the other guys' home base and try something like he just tried.

If the people who sent him here are that stupid, we don't have a whole lot to worry about."

"Maybe they're not that stupid. Maybe he was just one of their more stupid employees."

"People who hire people like that are just as foolish. You have to know how one of your operatives will react in almost any given situation. The people who sent him should have known that under pressure he'd do something foolish."

"He still hasn't moved."

"I'll check and see if he has a pulse."

He didn't. Hans stepped back from the body and slowly shook his head. Charley sat down on the edge of the nearest bed and said nothing for a brief moment.

"Well, what are we gonna do now?"

"We'll have to dispose of the body as best we can. We don't want some Barney Fife type to come in here to investigate a murder. If the Mafia really is as well entrenched around here as we've been led to believe, they probably ignore lots of complaints about missing persons. We'll just have to see that this guy is missing."

"How do we go about that?"

"How did you and Alice get rid of the car that you'd been riding in on your first trip down here?"

"Like I told you, we dumped it in the lake."

"Doesn't that give you any idea how we might be able to dispose of a body?"

"But how...."

"Don't worry about how. Leave that to me. Remember, I got rid of two busloads of bodies that haven't been found yet. It's early. We'll have to wait till everybody around here is fast asleep before we try to move him out of here."

It was about 2:30 when they put the body into the trunk of the man's own car. The blow that Hans had given the man had left no trace of blood. The body had been wrapped in the spare blanket that came from the closet of their room. Han's removed the man's car keys before they wrapped the body. He handed them to Charley and told him to find the spot where they had drowned the Buick or to find one that was similar. He would follow Charley in their car at a safe distance.

At about 4 a.m. Charley found a place that he thought resembled the one that he and Alice had used. It was hard to tell in the dark. He parked the car at the edge of the road that led down to the lake. It was a drop of more than sixty feet into the dark water. Hans was three minutes behind. He pulled in behind the other car and hesitated before he got out. Then he approached Charley who had remained behind the wheel of the other car. He rolled down the window and said nothing.

"Well, looks like this is your area of expertise. You're one up on me at disposing of cars. I've gotten rid of lots of bodies, but I can't recall drowning any cars."

"Nothing to it, really. We just put the car in neutral and give it a good hard push. Gravity will take care of the rest. If this really is where we dumped the other one, the water here is definitely deep enough to keep the whole thing covered up. We don't even know how big a search will be made for the guy when he turns up missing."

"How about noise? Will the splash the car makes when it hits cause anyone to become curious?"

"I don't think so. As I recall, we were really surprised that there was hardly any noise at all when it hit."

"Well, then let's do it."

They straightened the wheels of the car so that it pointed directly into the lake. Both men then pushed and then watched as the car gathered speed before leaving the road and sailing several feet out into the dark water. Charley had been right. What little sound the impact of the car made was almost undetectable. Both men then returned to their own car.

"What do you think we should do now? Should we go back to the motel, or should we just head on back home?"

"Of course we have to return to the motel. If we were to make a run for home now, even the local yokels of a police department here could probably put two and two together and make us prime suspects. Let's just continue to drive around these lake front roads until well past daylight. If anyone asks what we were doing out at this time, we can say that we were scouting properties that we're interested in buying."

"Won't the police come and question us?"

"Probably. The people who sent the man will eventually tell the police that the man was probably sent to contact us on business. He won't even be considered missing for at least a day or two."

"And in the mean time?"

"We just go on with business as usual."

"What do we tell the police when they do come to question us?"

"We tell them the man did come to see us. We had a lengthy discussion about various properties, and that he left here sometime after midnight."

"Do you think they'll buy it?"

"I don't see why not. There are no witnesses to the man's demise. If the car doesn't suddenly float to the surface and they find the body, I don't see how we can be held accountable for the man's disappearance."

Later that same morning, they visited two other real estate offices. Charley was nervous, and for the first time Hans did most of the talking. Both agents were eager to show the men what they had available. Word had already spread about the California company that had been gobbling up local real estate at an amazing pace the last two days. To lend credence to their story about why they had been out driving around so early that morning, they put down money on several properties from both agents. That left only one agent in the community that they had not visited. They planned on seeing him the next day before starting back for home.

They purchased three more properties from the final agency the following day, and by the end of the day they had returned to the motel to pack and get ready for an early departure the following day. The next morning a squad car pulled up, and two officers got out and approached the men as they were loading suitcases into the trunk of their car. Once again it was Hans whose calm nerves let him do most of talking.

"How you guys doin' today? Looks like you're about to leave us."

"That's right, officer. We've done about all the business we can do at this time. I'm sure we'll be coming back fairly soon. We're not completely finished here, but we've got some other things we have to attend to back at home base. Is there anything we can we do for you?"

"Just a couple of questions, if you don't mind. We got a missing persons report today, and we heard maybe you'd seen the man that's missing."

"Sure, what did he look like?"

"He looked pretty much like this photograph. It's a pretty good likeness. Have you seen him?"

Hans looked the picture over carefully and then held it out in front of Charley. He turned his head from side to side and then nodded.

"What do you think, partner? Is this the guy came knocking on our door the other evening? I think it is. What do you say?"

"I agree. I think that's him. What do you guys think? Has something happened to him?"

"That's what we're tryin' to find out. The man he works for is worried. He says it's not like him to just take off."

"Is the missing man in real estate? We talked for quite a while, but he never did really say what line of work he was in."

"Did the guy seem okay when he left? Was he on foot?"

"Yeah, he seemed alright to me. He left us in the car he drove up here in, officer. That's all I really know."

"You guys takin' off pretty soon?"

"Yeah, about as soon as we can get our stuff loaded. We've sure have enjoyed out little stay here in your community. We look forward to coming back sometime real soon."

"Can I ask you one more question?"

"Sure, fire away."

"Why is your company so interested in buyin' up so much of the land around here."

"That I couldn't say. We we're just told by our bosses that they wanted as much of the properties around here as we could get. I'm not sure what's made this buying spree necessary. We're just doing our job. Is there anything else we can tell you?"

"Where can we get hold of you guys later if we have some more questions?"

"Here, let me give you one of our business cards. If we're not there when you call, our boss will tell you how to get in touch with us."

"Okay, guys have a good one. Drive carefully. Some of the roads around here are not the best."

"Yeah, we noticed. Thanks, officers."

The officers got back into their vehicle and drove away. Charley was in a hurry for them to be on their way. Hans wanted a walk-through to make sure that they had left nothing behind, but Charley remained seated in the car while Hans made his last look around.

The trip home took two full days, even by driving straight through. Charley was afraid that they might be pursued as they had been when he and Alice had made their first trip to Perdido. Hans was more relaxed and tried to ease Charley's mind. He reminded him that the only person who could have directed the police to them was probably Mafia related. That did little for Charley's nerves, for he knew that Mafia people, like big oil, had the potential to control whole police forces, many of whom were much larger than the tiny one they had just met.

"I can't wait to get back home again. I'm beginning to think the whole idea was a big mistake."

"I thought so when you first brought the idea to my attention. After seeing the place, I still don't see why you or anyone else would want to live there."

"I'm not really sure myself. I told you once it's hard to put into words. I guess maybe it's just my showing them that they can't stop me from doing what I want to do. That may seem childish, but that's the way I feel. They tried to keep my carburetor off the market, but they failed. They tried to have me arrested on phony murder charges and failed. They tried to extradite me and failed. They tried to keep me from doing business with the Japanese, and they failed. Now I'm sure they'll try to keep me out of the country. That's my next challenge."

"I guess when a man has as much power and money as you have, there are very few challenges left in life. Well, if you're that determined to do it, count me in. Do you have any idea how much man power you're gonna have to have around you to provide any real security?"

"Not really. You'll have to fill me in on that later on. Don't forget, that anything that seems almost insurmountable, really is no problem, if you have enough money."

"You don't have to tell me that. Remember, I worked for the oil companies. I saw them topple whole governments with the money they had. I know what money can buy. Do you plan to hire a lot of Americans for security here, or will you bring mostly Mexicans that you have already learned to trust?"

"What would you recommend?"

"Mostly Mexicans, I think. You've improved the lives of lots of those people. I don't think you'll have much difficulty in finding plenty that would follow you almost anywhere. Where will you house all those people, in the houses that are on the land you just purchased?"

"I don't think so. I'd rather tear all those down. Besides they're too scattered out to bring them all to bear if we should be attacked in force."

"Once again, you're starting to think a lot like me. Congratulations."

When they got back, Charley made a brief stop to tell Alice that they were okay, and then he went directly to his office. He carried with him a map and also the location of all the properties he now owned. There were several gaps he needed to fill in before he could ever really consider making his move. He needed to talk to Juan. He went to his office and found him busily engaged in telephone conversation when he knocked and entered.

"Hope I didn't interrupt anything important."

"No, just some routine stuff. How did everything go? Were you able to get what you wanted?"

"Some, but not all. We had to leave a little earlier than I would have liked."

"Why? There's nothing really pressing going on here."

"How about the militia that's supposedly headed our way? What have you heard about them lately?"

"Still about two weeks away from the latest intelligence report. Terry will be glad to see that you're back."

"We're glad to be back."

"Why are you back so soon if you didn't get done what you set out to do?"

"Someone, Hans thinks the Mafia, sent an armed man to our room to threaten us."

"I can't believe that frightened Hans into leaving a minute earlier than you guys planned on leaving."

"You're right. Hans killed the guy with a blow to the head with the barrel of his gun. We disposed of the body, but the local police did come our way to investigate. We don't know if they really believed our explanation or not. We decided it was no time to hang around."

"Will you be going back soon?"

"I'm not sure. I've got things started, but I may not be able to get by without somebody else going back to finish what I've started. Here's a map of the entire area. I've colored in the properties we now control. As you can see, there are still lots of holes to be filled in. There's a totally undeveloped area about six miles from the lake. I haven't shown any interest in it yet, but I think it would be wise to get control of it. Hans thinks so, too, but he thinks the whole concept is pretty crazy."

"I think Terry can fill Hans in on the progress of the militia. The American government still denies its existence. But the report we get is that it is still in its formative stage in rural New Mexico."

"Do you have any people around here that you would trust to take a return trip to Missouri to try to finish what Hans and I started?"

"I have some that I trust, but I'm not sure any of them have the expertise to accomplish what you want. On the other hand, I have extensive experience at land acquisition. That was my main job in the corporation I worked for before I joined up with you people. It was my success at this type of work that led to my rapid advancement within that corporation."

"That, and no doubt your father's influence."

"I'd be a lying fool if I didn't credit some of my success to that, but that alone could never have gotten me to where I was."

"I never doubted that you made it on your own. Are you telling me now that you'd be willing to go down there and try to finish up what Hans and I started?"

"If you needed me to. All you have to do is ask. Will Hans be accompanying me on this trip?"

"I don't know if he'd be willing. We'd have to wait and see if the body of the man Hans killed has ever been discovered."

"How long would you be willing to wait?"

"Until Hans thinks it would be safe."

"Let me take a closer look at the map you brought. Can you explain to me what your plan really is?"

"Sure, I want enough land that I can use a lot of it as a buffer against any kind of attack that Hans might foresee. I'll need enough room to house a lot of security that I'll be taking with me."

"Can you point out exactly where you think your headquarters will be? I'll have to know at least that much so I can concentrate my efforts on the properties closest to that point."

"Here, it's this one. It's a huge log cabin style, two stories, with a veranda upstairs that provides a beautiful view of the lake itself. I already have money down on this one and a couple more that are adjacent."

"It doesn't seem nearly as elegant as the one you're living in now."

"It isn't, but that's not the point. I'm not trying to move up."

"So, what is the point?"

"I'm not really sure. I just know it's what I want to do. I tried to explain it to Hans, but I don't think he understands even after my explanation."

"Why does he think you'll be moving?"

"Because people like me have so much money that they find very few challenges left in life. He may be right, but I think it goes deeper than that. I don't want you or Hans or any of the people I count on leaving here until the business with the American militia has been settled."

He left Juan's office and went to find Terry. He hoped for more exact information about the progress of the American Militia.

When he located Terry, he got right to the point. Exactly where was this American force? How many were there? How well were they armed? What was their goal? Terry produced a map of the Southwestern United States. He pointed to two counties in New Mexico. He said the latest report was that they now numbered about 1300. They had automatic weapons, a few mortars and bazookas, but no aircraft of any kind. Their only stated goal was an attack on the Japanese car making industry. The Japanese had been given most of the blame for the demise of the Big Three.

Hans was worried that he wasn't getting all the information that he needed to adequately prepare for the invasion they all knew was coming. It all seemed too simple. He feared they might be lulled into a false sense of security by the openness of the preparation of the militia. They made no pretense of the fact that they were planning an attack on the car industry in Perdido. If the enemy force was no larger than what he had been told, and if their weapons did not include any aircraft, he really had nothing to fear. It was the unknown that was frightening. Also in the back of his mind was the thought that this might be another human sacrifice similar to the previous one. It might be a ploy by the U.S. government to use massive force as retaliation for the slaughter they must know would ensue if an attack like this was launched against a well-entrenched enemy. He considered sending out a force large enough to turn back the Americans long before they could reach Perdido. With the help of the Reales from the Mexican government, he could put ten thousand men between the attackers and Perdido. There was no way the attacking force could ever hope to reach Perdido without air transport. That was what was so frightening. Without the element of surprise and with only land-based transport, how could the leaders of this expedition ever hope to even reach their destination, let alone launch a successful attack against the Japanese? It made so little sense that it was frightening. He had no choice but to confide his fears to Charley.

"What the hell are they up to? I can see how a small group led by the brothers or a group of mercenaries with air transport might think they had a chance to do us quite a bit of damage, but this thing they're lining up for is suicide. There must be more to it than what we're being led to believe."

"I agree. Here's what I intend to do. I'm gonna have Juan see if he can use any of the influence his father used to have with the Mexican government."

"What exactly do you want him to do?"

"I want him to see if the Mexican ambassador to the U.N. might be willing to make a speech to the General Assembly."

"What will the speech be about?"

"It will tell the world that there is a large force on the northern border of Mexico poised to make an armed assault on this country. This is being done with the full knowledge and cooperation of the U.S. government. Mexico is prepared to defend its territory if it is invaded, but it is asking the rest of the world to condemn any aggressive action taken by the U.S. Mexico will do its best to see that our country is never overrun by Americans as it was when they stole much of our land in the War of 1847."

"Do you think Juan has enough pull to get him to deliver such a speech? It's almost like a declaration of war."

"I don't know. I guess there's only one way to find out. I'm sure he'll give it his best shot."

Juan indeed had enough of his father's influence to get the speech he wanted delivered to the General Assembly. It was given with such conviction that the ambassador got an ovation when he had finished. It was clear that America had fewer friends now than it had in former years.

The speech had the desired affect. In less than a week, reports came to Hans that the group was dispersing. Their number had shrunk to less than 800 after it had ballooned to almost 1500. Several of the leaders had withdrawn their support. An international outcry against the United States rang out with the charge of naked aggression. It seemed the eyes of most of the countries of the world were focused on New Mexico and what had been a growing band of warriors, poised to take on the whole of Mexico.

Terry seemed pleased that the threat from the North had greatly diminished. Hans, on the other hand, felt a sense of disappointment. He had already constructed several plans to deal with the aggressors no matter what their battle plan might be. He saw it slipping away with each passing day and wondered if his expertise in these matters would ever be needed again. He was reasonably certain that if Charley followed through with his plan to return permanently to the States, he would see plenty of action, but not on the scale which had suddenly diminished.

A month passed before Charley decided that it was time to make further acquisitions. He wondered if there was any way that he could accomplish that without risking his own life. He knew that Hans would be willing to make a return trip, but he wasn't sure his own nerves could hold up under another confrontation with the people who would actively oppose his presence. It was time to take some sort of action. He went to Juan's office for a chat.

"Juan, I haven't had a chance to congratulate you on getting the ambassador to deliver that speech to the General Assembly. It sounded a lot like what your father would have written."

"I'll take that as a compliment since I wrote the speech myself. What have you decided to do about things back in Missouri?"

"That's what I really came to talk about. I need a completely honest answer. I don't think my nerves are up to another trip right now. I know Hans isn't afraid to go back, but I'm just not up to it. Would you be willing to make a trip back with him?"

"Sure, what exactly would you have me do?"

"One of the things that you say you do best. Acquire all of the land that's for sale at this time and better yet, get some of the land close to what I already have that may not be for sale. I have an idea, but you'll have to tell me if it's a good one."

"Okay, what's the ideal?"

"Well, you know we bought up several properties under the name of the Golden State Development Corporation. Is there any way we could purchase a lot more land under the name of another dummy corporation and then later consolidate all we have purchased to my own corporation. I don't think the locals would be nearly as nervous if they thought there was a lot of interest from more than just one group of buyers."

"I think that's an excellent idea. There would be absolutely no problem. I'm not afraid to make the trip as long as Hans agrees to go with me. After that rescue job he pulled when my brothers grabbed me, I think I'd go about anywhere with him. When would we leave?"

"I don't know yet. I'll have to talk to Hans. He may nix the whole idea, but I'm guessing he'll go along for the ride. He seems disappointed that the Militia thing from up north seems to have fallen through."

"Well, let me know as soon as you find out. It won't take me long to get ready."

Hans was ready. He would have left that same day, but the problem of shifting several million dollars into an account that would let Juan buy up anything available would take a day or two. He planned on using the same disguise he had used on the first trip, but then decided against it. He didn't want one of the real estate agents to remember that he had been working for a different company on the first trip. He wasn't sure that Juan would need any disguise at all. Only his brothers might recognize him, and they would not be close.

****

Two days later they began their trip. They checked into a different motel this time when they arrived. There was a much smaller chance of someone recognizing Hans at a different motel. They waited until the following day before starting the round of the real estate offices. This time Juan carried a business card that said he represented the Florida Dreamland Corporation.

For more than a week, they were wined and dined by all of the real estate agents. They purchased everything that was for sale and even managed to buy several others that had not even been listed. The prices they were offering were too much for most of the owners to resist. While Juan had been busy on one rather long transaction, Hans had managed to slip away long enough to find out that the police had never discovered the whereabouts of the missing man they had deposited into the lake. He knew that Charley would be glad when he got that news. He would also be glad to know that he now had what he would consider a sufficient buffer around his new abode.

The first new chore for Juan when he returned home would be to hire a local construction company to begin the demolition of all of the houses on the land they had purchased except for the one that Charley was planning to occupy. Juan did not feel that it would be necessary for him to be there personally to supervise the demolition. He delegated the authority of finding the right company to begin removing the houses. The man he chose was one he had great faith in, and with Charley's approval, the man and three of his best men took off with work orders that would allow a company to begin the destruction of many nice looking houses. If anyone became curious about why these houses were being destroyed, they were to answer that much of the property was to become part of a wildlife preserve. The man was to report daily to Charley to tell him how the project was progressing and also to report if there seemed to be any negative reaction from anyone in the immediate vicinity.

The reports which Charley received over the next two months were that the only reaction from the natives was one of curiosity. They couldn't help but wonder why several expensive houses were demolished, only to be replaced by ones of lesser value. No one as of yet had issued anything in the nature of a complaint. The price paid for the properties by the companies that appeared to be rivals had caused the value of the surrounding properties to skyrocket.

Now began the process of recruitment. It was time for Charley to find out if there were enough of those he trusted to begin the migration to the States. He was smart enough to let Hans and Terry recommend those they thought could be trusted.

Each of the security chiefs was asked to recommend at least a dozen men. These choices were to be restricted to family men who would be willing to move with their wives and families on a permanent basis. After the complete list had been compiled, Charley had an independent detective agency run a security check on the men, just to be certain there was nothing in their backgrounds to fear. Later the security demands would force Charley to have more than 200 men surrounding him for adequate protection. What the men would be doing when they first arrived would be nothing more than clearing brush and building high cyclone fences around those properties that Charley had designated as his buffer zone.

It would be a ticklish situation. Charley and Juan took separate cars back to Missouri, each with five of the men who had agreed to migrate. Both men carried with them checkbooks of the "rival" land companies. This was largely to purchase the building materials for the fences around the properties. Also, the houses which had been built for the workers were only rough finished and would require some finish work before the wives and families would arrive.

Charley came back in the same disguise that he had worn before. He was relieved that the police did not come to question him when the news of his arrival had surely reached them. This could only mean that the body of the man in the car had never been discovered. Both men were able to purchase even more property at the inflated prices that had become commonplace. It was two weeks before they were back in Perdido and ready to make another trip in a few days. All of the men had instructions to report directly to Charley if there were any problems. There were none.

Each of the five man groups was assigned to work with each other. It was deemed far too dangerous for any of the men to work alone. Each group was assigned a number of projects within the framework of the properties that had already been purchased. Mostly their main function was the demolition of houses and other buildings on those properties. In little more than two weeks there would be many more workers to begin the construction of the houses that would become the homes of the migrating men and their families.

Charley thanked God for the foresight of Hans and the connections of Juan. Hans had warned Charley that the men might be challenged to show that they were legally in the United States. Workers' identities and work permits had been forged through the connections that Juan still had, thanks to the reputation of his father. This time a larger group would be making the long trip to the Ozarks.

Hans had recommended that the next load of workers should be delivered by bus. This group would include as many skilled carpenters and other necessary craftsmen as they could locate. House building, rather than demolition, was to be the new order of the day.

"Charley, what do you hear from the ten we already delivered? Have they run into any problems with the locals?"

"Nothing serious. There seems to be more than a little natural curiosity, but I guess that was to be expected."

"No doubt. Does the fact that all of the men working there are Mexicans seem to make any difference to the locals?"

"Not that I've been able to learn. The men have money, and they're spending it, and that goes a long way toward making newcomers welcome. When will the next group be leaving?"

"In less than a week. I'll have about forty more ready to go by then. They're getting antsy to take off, but I think they need a little more orientation before we let them make the plunge."

"Do all of the men have a least some proficiency in English? It's been my experience that local populations are a lot more easy to get along with if the people they're dealing with can communicate with them."

"Yeah, all of them can speak at least some. That was one of the qualifications we insisted on when we started recruiting this group."

"Where are you getting the building materials for the new houses?"

"I left that up to Juan. He's dealing strictly with the locals as much as he can. He's getting free delivery on all of the stuff because of the volume. We don't have any trucks of our own down there yet. I have a whole fleet set to take off in less than a month. We'll need those vehicles to move materials from site to site. That will speed up the building process a lot when they get there."

"I wish there was some way we could get a stash of weapons down there. If push came to shove, everyone down there could easily be wiped out if anyone found out the true nature of their being there."

"True, but the men realized the risks when they chose to make the trip. Nobody forced anybody to sign on for this caper."

"How would it alter your plans if all or most of that group were to be wiped out?"

"I don't know. I haven't even considered it, and I hope I never have to. It would certainly mean a long delay before I tried again."

"But you would try again?"

"Probably, if it was my decision alone, but I think Alice would have to agree before I'd make another attempt."

"You know Alice would go along with you on anything you decided."

"Yeah, I think she would if it was only her and me, but now that we have a daughter, she might not be as willing as you think."

"I suppose not. Do you intend for me ride the bus down with next load headed that way?"

"No, I want you to run interference for them in a car which will have license plates that will give you immunity from being stopped and searched. It's Juan's idea, but I think it's a good one, don't you?"

"Yes, I do. Since we can't legally be searched, can't I take a few weapons along? I'd feel a lot safer if I had something more than the pistol I carry."

"I hadn't thought of it, but I suppose so. Where will you stow them when you get there?"

"Don't you worry about that. I'll find a safe place. Since you seem to have everything so well planned out, I'm beginning to get a little antsy myself."

"Yeah, me too. I wish I was goin' back with you, but there's too many details that I have to take care of here. We've hit a snag on a property or two that I was sure we had locked up. Juan says it's just a matter of time, but I don't want to take off until those items are settled. One of those properties is directly adjacent to the one where I intend to live."

"Yeah, that's too important to leave hanging in the air. You'll definitely need all of the properties next to yours if you ever hope to have any real security."

"My feelings exactly."

"Give me at least two days notice before you intend to take off."

"Will do."

****

Ten days later Charley told him that he was ready to begin the next trip. He had purchased a late model bus of the Grey Hound type. It had more than enough room for the men to take whatever they would need. Hans was to lead them in an older Lincoln Town Car. The car was sporting diplomatic license plates, so Hans had stashed several automatic weapons in the trunk. The trip was to take about four days with the men sleeping on the bus at designated rest stops.

As the trip was almost over, a squad car turned on its flashing lights behind the bus. Hans noticed this and made a turn-around as quickly as he could. He got back to the bus and got out of his car. He crossed the highway and approached the officer who had made his way to the door of the bus.

"What's the problem, officer?"

"I'm not sure that it's really any of your business."

"I think you're wrong. I'm responsible for all the people on that bus."

"Oh, really? And just who might you be?"

"My name is Jeraldo Lopez. I work for the Mexican Embassy."

"Do you have any identification that will verify that? I'll need to see it if you do."

"Of course. I have it right here in my wallet."

The officer looked closely at the card and the papers that were attached to it. Then he nodded his head as if to say that he found everything in order. "Just what is the business of these people who are on the bus?"

"These men are part of a large work force who will be here in the United States for quite some time. They are all legal. They have work papers that are all in order if you would care to examine them. I'll have each one of them leave the bus and let you examine all their papers as closely as you want. I'm sure you'll find that they are all in order."

"No, I guess that won't be necessary. What type of work will they be doing?"

"Building houses, I believe. Can I ask you now why you stopped the bus?"

"Nothing more than the Mexican license plates. We already have a bunch of Mexicans working at a few places around the lake, and the locals are worried that they're gonna be overrun by even more."

"I'm sorry to tell you this, officer, but stopping someone for no other reason than a Mexican license plate would probably qualify as racial profiling. These men are all here legally. They have met every qualification that your government demands for them to come to this country and work. They are not to be confused with the illegals who slip into this country. I hope we won't have to pursue this matter any further. I would hate to have to file charges of harassment if we are going to be continually bothered for nothing more than the color of our skin."

"Okay, I'm satisfied you're alright. I won't bother you any more, but I can't say there won't be others who find what's been going on at the lake a little bit strange. We don't see foreigners of any kind very often around here, and lots of people who've lived around here for a long time have suddenly sold out, and it looks like others might be about ready to leave. That's strange. People are worried that property values will hit bottom if they're surrounded by Mexicans. Right now property values are sky high, but people wonder why. There afraid if they don't sell now they won't get a fair price for what they own."

"I see. Mexicans show up, and there goes the neighborhood. That's not a very friendly attitude. I thought this country was the land of the free. Maybe that doesn't apply to Mexicans"

"I'm sorry, but that's just the way things are. People are frightened by change. They like to keep things the way they are. I think that's only human nature."

"You may be right. Can I tell the driver that it's alright to go now?"

"Sure, go ahead."

He tapped on the door that had remained closed during their conversation. He told the driver to follow him as soon as he could get turned around and headed back toward their destination.

When they arrived at the agreed upon site, they were met by the first ten. There was a lot of backslapping and noisy congratulations shared by both groups. Hans waited until the noise had subsided before he tried to address the men. Then he told them that their work for the day was finished and that they would all meet at this spot tomorrow to get their individual assignments.

"*Señor* Hans, by any chance did you bring along any tequila? I think tonight we have an occasion that calls for a little celebration."

"It just so happens that I have a case of Cuervo in the trunk of my car. Two things I want you to remember, though. Even though we are in an isolated place, noise carries a long way in this place. Keep the noise down. Also, a hangover will not get you an excused absence from the work to be done tomorrow."

"Then you won't be spending the night with us?"

"No, I'm headed on in to town. I'll be staying at one of the local motels. I'll meet you guys again at 7:00 tomorrow morning."

****

There were no ugly incidents for the next two weeks. Several trucks had arrived that made the jobs to which the men had been assigned much easier. Also a couple of bulldozers had made their way to the various sites, making the job of demolition much easier.

In Perdido, Charley pondered the advisability of taking the next step. That would be the actual move back to the States. He had decided earlier that he would not risk the safety of his wife and daughter until the situation became clearer. That would mean that the locals had accepted his presence there, and that neither the oil companies, former auto-makers, nor Juan's brothers were a present threat.

Charley had also decided not to even ask Terry to accompany him on the final trip back. He had come to the conclusion that Terry would be a stablizing influence if he were left there in Perdido with Hans protecting his interests in his new locale. He was certain that Juan could take care of all the business interests, and he had no reason to doubt the honesty of his CEO. Still, Juan had the same blood coursing through his veins that had made his father the rich and powerful man he had become.

Charley had decided to leave nothing to chance. He had long ago put billions of dollars away in accounts that could not be touched by anyone but himself. Some of these were Swiss accounts, while others were off-shore banks which had the reputation of being able to hide huge sums of money from even the most thorough searches by government agencies. Juan still controlled about one fourth of the liquid assets of the corporation, but he had never been put in position to do Charley any real harm should there ever be a parting of the ways. The alcalde would have been proud of his caution. He was certain of that.

Hans was displaying a nervousness that Charley had not seen in him since he had been their prisoner, locked in the alcalde's study.

"What's the matter, Hans? Do you know something that I don't about what's goin' on down there. I've been around you for quite a while now, and I think I detect a lack of certainty about you recently. Come on, tell me."

"You know, around here there is a certainty. We know who our enemies are and from what direction they might attack us. Down there, we can't be sure who the enemies are, and we have no idea where they might try to hit us."

"You still think the whole idea of settling down there is crazy, don't you?

"Not crazy, but it's certainly more risky than staying here would be. Even I've turned down a few assignments that I considered too risky."

"You're not backing out on me now, are you? If you are, I'll have to re-think the whole idea of the move."

"No, I'm not backing out. I'm just warning you that you're going to find out sooner or later that this move is not going to be the bed of roses that you've imagined. You've made too many enemies along the way to ever be able to relax up there."

"Well, I guess I've long since given up on ever being able to relax, so it really won't matter whether I'm tensed up here or there."

"Yeah, I know, after a while you get used to a certain amount of tension. Still, I'm beginning to wonder if I still have what it takes to do the kind of work you pay me for. You only have to lose a little of your edge to become a victim in the games we play."

"Do you think you've lost your edge?"

"No, but there's really no way to be sure until you're tested. When you flunk the test, then you know that you've lost your edge."

"Have you ever wondered just what kind of end you'll have, or do you see yourself dying a peaceful death?"

"I never think about such things. I usually have too many other things on my mind to give thoughts like that any brain room."

"When will you be ready to make another run?"

"Any time you're ready. Are you sure you want to run the risk of a return right now? It might be better to wait until those crews already there have better security lined up. I could escort another bus load down and then come back for you if you're willing to wait."

"No, I think now is as good a time as any. I'm ready, and no matter how long I wait, there's never really going to be a right time to go back down there."

"I guess not. Have you discussed all this with Alice?"

"Of course. She knows it's risky, but she's been in a lot of risky situations before. One thing for sure, if they do get to me, she won't have to worry about money."

"True, she'll be the richest widow around, but I think she'd never be happy if you aren't around to help her spend the money."

"Why Hans, I never suspected that you had a romantic bone in your body. I think you're right, but she knows that I'm not really happy here, so she's agreed to support me in any decision I make. Neither of us can imagine what life will be like when we get set up there. I think that's really the beauty of it. We know exactly what life here holds for us, and after a while that gets boring, no matter how much money you have."

"I think maybe now you know how I first felt when I went into this line of work. It wasn't just for the money. The money was great, but it was more than that. That feeling of not knowing what's going to happen next was what I consider the deciding factor."

"Funny how you strive for a thing like security, and then when you get it, you find it's not what you hoped it would be. They said be careful what you wish for, because you might get it."

****

Back in the Ozarks, the men were working continuously to demolish the houses and cabins which the previous owners had left when they had abandoned the area. The men worked in groups of five to ten, depending on the size of the dwelling they were trying to remove. More equipment had arrived, making the jobs of removal easier.

One day, one of the men had traveled a short distance from the house they had all but completely torn down. He had stepped into a wooded area to relieve himself when he heard the sound of human voices. It was not a usual occurrence. Mostly the men never heard the sound of any voices other than their own. The first voice he heard seemed to be that of a youngster, and the second seemed to come from someone much older. He stepped in the direction of the voices to see if he could understand what they were saying. His knowledge of English was limited, but he hoped to be able to go back and tell the others what he had heard.

"I'm not really sure we're on the right path, sir. Are you?"

"Of course I'm sure. We've been over this ground a lot of times."

"Yes, but there's a fence I never saw before across one of our trails. Two of the cabins we used to pass aren't there any more."

"I'm not really sure about the fence, but people do move out, and sometimes they take the cabins with them or sell them to somebody who moves them."

The workman hurried back to tell the others what he had seen and heard. They did not seem to attach any real importance to his report. One suggested it might be a father and son out for a hike. Others just told him it was time to go back to work. Then all conversation ceased when they heard the sound of several voices. Gradually approaching from the right of the house that they were about to totally demolish came the man and the boy. Following behind them was a group of youngsters numbering about twenty. None of the men recognized the uniform of the Boy Scouts. The leader of the work force walked toward the man and the boy.

"How come you guys are tearin' down that house?"

"It's our job. That's what we get paid to do."

"Why would anyone want to tear down a perfectly good house like that one? It's only about four years old. I know the people who used to live there. They told me they were moving, but they didn't say anything about tearing the house down."

"All I know is that the new owner didn't want the house. He just wanted the land, so that's why he's having us tear it down."

"Is he going to build a new one in its place?"

"I don't know, mister, we just get paid to do what he tells us to do."

"Who is the new owner? Does he live around here?"

"Not yet. He will soon, but not now."

"What's the new owner's name?"

"I don't know. The land belongs to a big corporation that develops land. They are based in California, I think. Where are you taking the boys?"

"Down to the Lake. We're just on a nature hike. I see several new fences in this area. Who ordered those?"

"The same people who own the land. We have been instructed to put the fences up but not to block the way of anyone who wants to get down to the lake."

"Okay, I guess me and the boys will just hike on down to the Lake. We heard what sounded like it might be a series of small explosions. Are you guys the only ones working up here?"

"No, there's several other groups doing about the same kind of work that we're doing in this area."

"Are they hired by the same company?"

"Couldn't say about that. They may be. We hear them, too, but that's all we know."

The troop continued on their way and the men then resumed putting the finishing touch on what was left of the house. Later that evening the leader thought it might be wise to report the incident to Hans. Soon afterward, Hans decided to relay the incident to Charley. He did not show any real surprise or alarm.

"Don't worry about it. That whole area is open to lots of different kinds of recreational activity. Hiking is one of them. Doesn't sound to me like the guy was in the area to do any spying. Just sounds like a scoutmaster taking the kids for a hike. Unless this same guy shows up again, I wouldn't worry about it. We're bound to run into some of the locals eventually."

"Okay, I'm gonna make the rounds now of all the groups and see if they've seen anybody who fits the description of the scoutmaster. If not, I'll rest easy on this one."

None of the other groups reported that they had had any contact with anyone fitting the description of the scoutmaster. Hans told the leaders of each group that if anyone like that showed up, they were to contact him immediately. He wasn't completely convinced that this wasn't a clever ruse to get close to one of the groups to see exactly what was going on. He was starting to feel the pressure of this new job. He hadn't felt this much pressure since his surrender to the alcalde. He wanted more troops, more weapons, more fences, more barricades, and he wanted them all in a hurry.

****

Later that same week, the scoutmaster was attending a Lodge meeting in his hometown some thirty miles from the lake. After the business of the lodge had been conducted, the scoutmaster was relaying the story to his fellow lodge members during the social hour. At least three and possibly more showed a keen interest in his account of what had happened. They hadn't heard of any California based Land Development Company ordering the destruction of any of the houses built around the lake.

"What did these guys that were tearing down the Winston place look like, Arthur?"

"Well, I can't be for sure, but they were all dark skinned. The leader I spoke with had a foreign accent. I think it was Spanish, but I'm not an expert on languages."

"Mexicans, do you think?"

"Could be. I heard some rumors quite a while back that there were gonna be a lot of them headed our way. Do you suppose the authorities know what's goin' on? Do you think we ought to report this to the Park Department or the local police?"

"Couldn't hurt. Maybe they know the score, and maybe they don't. The local police don't have one hell of a lot to do most of the time. About the only real thing they've had to investigate this year was that guy who just disappeared. They never did find him. They looked for him for about two weeks and then just gave up."

"That was strange. You know he worked for some pretty big shots back East. I heard they were offerin' a reward to anybody who could tell them what had become of him. They just couldn't believe he just rode off into the sunset. You know, it's kinda funny. You said the guy you talked to said this operation was coming from some Land Company in California. Well, one of the deputies I know said that the last people who saw this guy worked for some California Land Development Company. Do you suppose there could be any connection?"

"I don't know, but I do think you ought to report what you saw and heard to the authorities."

"You're probably right. I'll do that first thing tomorrow morning."

"You can tell us next week what they have to say, Arthur."

True to his word, Arthur did report to the local authority what he had heard and seen while leading his troop on a hike.

"You say these men all looked like they might be Mexicans. Did any of them look like either of these two?" He held out two pictures that he had taken of Hans and Charley.

"Naw, they don't look anything like that. Those guys sure don't look like Mexicans to me."

"No, they don't. Say, Willis, wasn't that other guy that came around later tryin' to buy up property, didn't he have a Mexican look about him?"

"You mean the other one, the guy who said he worked for a Florida Land company? Yeah, he looked more like a Mexican to me than those other two."

"Was he here at the same time the first two were?"

"I don't recall for sure, but I think he came along quite a bit later than they did."

"You don't suppose there's any connection between two land companies battlin' it out that have could have caused the guy to disappear?"

"It's possible, but from what I hear this guy that disappeared was pretty well connected with people who have nothing at all to do with Land companies, if you know what I mean."

"Yeah, I've kinda heard rumors that he might have mob connections. Have you guys just given up on ever findin' the guy?"

"The case is still open. We're callin' it a missing person thing, not a homicide. That's all we can do until a body shows up."

"I think it might be a good idea if some of you guys would go down around the old Winston place and see if you can get a better line on what's goin' on down there."

"Well, it's getting pretty late in the day for something like that now. We'll maybe take a run out there early tomorrow morning for a look-see."

The next morning two of the deputies made their way to the spot where the scoutmaster had directed them. They watched from a distance after leaving their vehicle out of sight. They observed the dark skinned workers and also one man with a much lighter skin. After about thirty minutes, they began their approach toward the men. Hans was the first one to observe their approach. He walked in their direction to meet them halfway.

"Good morning, gentlemen. Is there anything I can do for you?"

"Just the answer to a few questions. Who are these guys that are tearin' down what's left of the Winston house?"

"Those guys are a work detachment from Mexico. They were sent here for the specific purpose of removing several houses from property recently purchased by a large Land Development Company."

"From Mexico? Why from Mexico? We got lots of people around here who could do the job just as well or better?"

"Quite possibly, but my question to you is would they work as cheap as these guys? These guys are makin' a lot more money here than they could make in Mexico, so they're happy. The company doesn't have to deal with any labor unions or pay any overtime, so they're happy."

"Are these guys all legal?"

"Yes sir, they are. I have a copy of all their papers that let them work here. They have green cards as well, if you want to look."

"Are you the one in charge of this operation?"

"I guess you could say that. I'm not the head of the Land Company, just one of their crew bosses."

"Are there other work groups here in the vicinity?"

"Yes sir, there are several. You can probably hear them at work if you listen close enough. It's my job to go from site to site to see how well each group is doing. I was just about to leave to check on another site. You can go with me if you like."

"Exactly how many groups are working here?"

"Several, I never really bothered to count them. The number changes as we finish some jobs and move on to the next ones.'

"Are all the groups the same size?"

"Not exactly. Some are larger because the buildings they're having to remove are larger."

"How long do you think it will take for these groups to finish getting rid of all the buildings the owners want removed?"

"I couldn't give you an accurate answer on that one. I'm not sure the company has actually finished purchasing all the property they want here."

"Okay, I guess that answers about all the questions we had. We may come back and see you again some time."

"Come again any time. You guys have a nice day."

When they got back to their squad car, the deputy said, "What do you make of that? The whole thing sounds kinda screwy to me."

"Yeah, me too. I can't put my finger on what it is exactly, but something just doesn't seem right. All these Mexican workers, tearing down perfectly good houses that they could sell for who knows how much money. Also the guy we talked to. He just doesn't seem like the type to be the foreman of a bunch of Mexicans. I guess there's really nothing suspicious, but I'd still like to know more about what's goin' on"

"Me too. Wanta head toward where we heard that other noise comin' from, or you wanta head back to the station?"

"Let's head on back. If anything funny is going on, he'll beat us to the next site and we'll find nothing. We'll check around again tomorrow. Did you hear what he said just as we were leaving?"

"What do you mean?"

"Have a nice day. That's California bullshit. I used to hear it all the time when I watched CHIPS on TV."

After work was concluded, Hans put in a call to Charley. He told him about his confrontation with the local lawmen. Charley was relieved to know that as far as Hans could tell, the missing body was still missing. Hans said he was going into town later that evening.

"I think I'll just go into one of the local taverns and see if there's any conversation going on about what we're doing."

"Good idea. Call me back tomorrow if you hear anything I ought to know."

When Hans arrived at the tavern, he seated himself close to a group of five who were sitting at a table away from the bar. He ordered a beer and left the barmaid a generous tip. Then he relaxed to see if he could overhear any of the conversation from the closest table. It took him only a minute or two to realize that his presence had not gone unnoticed. A short time later, one of the five got up and walked over to Hans' table.

"Mister, can I ask you a question or two?"

"Sure, sit down. I'll buy you one. What are you drinking?"

"Budweiser."

Hans signaled to the barmaid, and she stepped lively in his direction He ordered the man a Bud and then turned his attention to the man.

"What can I tell you?"

"You're the guy who's in charge of all those Mexicans that we hear are tearing everything up down by the lake, aren't you?"

"Yes, I am. What else can I tell you?"

"What's really going on down there?"

"It's really not as complicated as some people make it out to be. I work for a large land development company that's based in California. We hire a lot of Mexican labor because they work a lot cheaper than the help we can get out here."

"Why are they tearing all those houses down when they could be sellin' them for lots of money?"

"Those houses just don't fit in with what the company has in mind. They're into subdividing the properties into much smaller units. They think the houses that are already there would just be in the way of their new subdivision. Some of the properties they own cover several acres, and they think there's a lot more money to be made by building lots of houses on smaller pieces of ground. Folks on both coasts are in a really crowded situation.

They'll pay almost any price for a little piece of peace and quiet. Why don't you invite your friends over to my table and I'll buy a round?"

The man finished his beer and returned to his own table. He told them of Hans' offer, and all but one accepted. They single filed slowly over to the next table and seated themselves. Each man introduced himself with a first name. Hans told them his name was Gerald but they could call him Jerry.

"Well, guys, I already told your friend here as much as I could about my business here in your area. I love this place. I wish I could settle down here, but I'm afraid I'd never be able to afford what the company is gonna ask for a piece of ground here."

"Why is this land suddenly so valuable? Did somebody hit oil, or is a gold mine that's suddenly made it so pricey?"

"Neither, just a good gamble by people who have lots of money and think they can make a whole lot more."

"I suppose they know what they're doin', but greed is a terrible thing. Why is it that people like that who already have millions can't be satisfied?"

"I'm sure I don't have the answer to that one. Are the people around here really concerned that the changes will somehow not be good for them?"

"I'm not sure all of them feel that way, but there is some worry that a lot of Mexicans might be movin' in. I know they wouldn't like that. How long will those working for you be here? Some are afraid there'll be marijuana for sale if they're around for very long."

"Yeah, I understand that. I can't say some of the men don't roll a joint once a while, but they won't be in contact with the rest of your people. I'm pretty sure as soon as our work is finished here, they'll all be on their way back to Mexico."

"Well, the folks around here will breathe a lot easier as soon as they take off. We're not really a prejudiced bunch, but we don't cotton much to people who don't speak our language."

"Tell the folks to relax. These guys all speak English. What's got all the locals so up in arms recently?"

"Well, right after those two land companies first came down here to buy up land, one of the guys who works around here just disappeared. The police are just callin' it a missing person thing, but most everybody else thinks the guy is probably dead. People around here didn't like the guy, but it makes them nervous for a person to just disappear."

"I can understand that. Why didn't they like the guy?"

"There was talk that he had Mafia connections. We know some of the property around here is owned by the mob, but they stay to themselves and don't threaten any of the locals. This guy, though, he liked to throw his weight around. He got into several fights and gave a couple of guys a beating that sent them to the hospital. I'm sure if you'd met him, you wouldn't have bought him a beer."

"Anybody besides me still thirsty? I'm still buying."

"Not me. I got to get home before my old lady turns me in as missing."

The rest of the group followed his lead, got up from the table, and headed for the exit. Hans finished the one he had been drinking and decided to have one more for the road. When he got back to camp, he decided to go ahead and call Charley. It was late, but he was certain Charley would rest easier if he knew that the only real problem they might have to overcome was the local prejudice against Mexicans.

He was right. Charley asked if he was ready for the next load of workmen. He acknowledged the fact that he would feel a whole lot safer as soon as they had sufficient numbers to ward off any attack by the locals or the mob. Charley told him that the largest bunch yet would be leaving Perdido tomorrow and would be arriving in about three days. This news was so good that Hans decided to finish off all of the 6-pack he had taken back to camp. Better than a sleeping pill, he thought.

The Final Adjustment

****

As dawn broke the following day in Perdido, Charley was already up and about. He had several things on his mind, and he was anxious for an early start. He left Alice sleeping soundly and quietly fixed himself a pot of coffee. He turned the TV on to catch some of the morning news and relaxed briefly in his easy chair. The morning paper had not arrived yet, but he seldom read anything it contained except a cursory look at the financial section. Later in the day he hoped to get an update from Hans about the situation in Missouri, but the first thing on his mind was a chat with Juan concerning the overall situation of the finances of the corporation.

The stock market worldwide seemed to be on a severe downturn, yet he couldn't help but notice that his own corporation's bottom line continued to climb at a surprising rate. He wanted to know if Juan could explain why this was so. He knew that Juan was not an early riser, so he saw no need to rush to his office to await his arrival. He had not been in contact with Billy for several days; it might pass the time a little faster to check on his son and his family. He missed the almost constant contact with his granddaughter. He feared they might not be up yet, but he decided to go ahead and call anyway. He was relieved when the phone rang only twice before Billy answered.

"Hi, son, it's just me. No, there's nothing wrong. It's just that we hadn't had a chance to talk much and I was kinda curious how things were going."

"No real problems that I'm aware of. What's the latest word from the Ozarks? Have you heard anything from Hans?"

"I plan on having a chat with him sometime later today. I'll be out to the plant for a talk with Juan later this morning."

"Why? Is anything wrong?"

"I don't think so, but there is something I'm curious about."

"What would that be?"

"Have you noticed that stock markets all over the world have really taken a hit recently?"

"Yeah, so?"

"Well, have you also noticed that our stock continues to go up while most of the rest of them are sinking like a rock? I wonder if we should be worried. I want to know what Juan has to say about that."

"Well, if you find out anything, I'd like to know, too. Give me a call back later today if you get to the bottom of it."

"I will. How's the wife and my granddaughter?"

"Both doing well, Dad. When are you and Alice coming over to our place for dinner?"

"I don't know for sure. I'll have to ask Alice about that. Would tomorrow night be alright?"

"Sure, dad. Just give Luisa a call and let her know you guys are coming. She'll fix up something really great if she knows ahead of time that you guys are coming."

"Okay, I'll have Alice give her a call. I got to be on my way. You have a good day."

"You too, dad."

Charley arrived a little after nine at the plant. He could see surprise written on Juan's face as he knocked and entered his office.

"*Buenos dias, señor.* To what do I owe this unexpected pleasure?"

"Oh, just a little info, I guess."

"In regards to what?"

"Have you noticed that recently our stock seems to be going up while most of the rest of the markets are spiraling downward?"

"Of course I've noticed. I'd be a poor CEO if I hadn't. What do want me to explain?"

"Just that. Why doesn't the down turn affect us?"

"There may be more than one reason, but if I had to put my finger on the main one, it would be this. Months ago while the Japanese were swallowing up all of America's Big Three, I invested heavily in their stock. They needed a lot of capital to buy out the American car market. I got the stock at a bargain, so every time they make money, we collect both ways. They pay us a percentage of the price of every car they sell, and as that increases their bottom line, it also does wonders for our own. Is that a satisfactory explanation?"

"Yeah, I guess I ought to keep closer tabs on just what we do own. We've done so well that I never even bother to consider what we do own."

"We have everything from Brazilian gold mine stock to NASA. I do agree that you should take a long look sometime at what's ours. If something should happen to me, I think it would be a good thing if you knew what we own before you turn it over to the new CEO."

"You're right, as usual. I don't have time for it right now, but if you'll compile a list of our assets, I'll take a look at it the first chance I get."

"I'll assign one of my secretaries to get right on it. I'm afraid it will always be only a partial list since our assets grow at a rate that even we cannot keep up with."

"That's okay, just let me see what we do have at any given time. Have you sold any of the companies that we purchased recently?"

"Yes, those that don't show much promise have to be dumped."

"I guess I did know that. Well, that's really all I wanted to know. I'll be on my way now."

"Stop by again sometime when you're not so busy."

****

It was late Friday afternoon, and Hans stood amazed at the progress all of the crews were making. The weather had turned off unseasonably warm, and most of the men were working without their shirts. Some of the men sang while they worked, and he liked to listen. When he called the workday to a halt, the men gathered around him. He asked them if they needed anything from town. The almost unanimous response was "beer." He smiled when he thought the response would probably be the same with the other groups. He decided it was time for a party. He would assemble all of the other crews here with this one so the men could share in the celebration.

He drove to the tavern where he had talked to the locals several nights before. He had driven one of the trucks which were now a part of the clean-up procedure going on at most of the work sites. He started toward the bar but was intercepted by a local before he got there. He tried to get around the man, but the man continued to block his way.

"Mister, I need to get to the bar. Would you excuse me?"

"No, I think we need to talk."

"About what? Do I know you?"

"No, but we're about to become better acquainted."

The man aimed a roundhouse right hand punch at Hans. Normally it would have been easy to avoid such a punch, but as he tried to sidestep the blow, another man impeded his attempt and the punch struck him a glancing blow on the side of the head. The shock only lasted for a brief instant. He kicked the man who had held him in the shin and simultaneously countered the punch with one of his own and gave a kick to the scrotum of his assailant. This gave him just enough time to get prepared for three others who were about to join the fight.

These three he could tell at a glance were not professionals. He thought about drawing his pistol but decided it wouldn't be necessary. He charged the first assailant and sent him sprawling with a head butt to the chin. He turned to the one on his right and gave him a spinning back kick that sent him unconscious to the floor. Then he faced the final man still standing.

"Do you want some of this?"

"No, I don't," he said as he scrambled toward the door.

He walked up to the bartender and asked, "What's this all about?"

The bartender shrugged and said he didn't know. Hans made a menacing gesture toward the man and he tried to retreat, but Hans cut him off. "Now one more time, what the hell is this all about?"

"I really don't know. I heard them talking about trying to beat some guy up who was in charge of all the Mexicans. I remember you from the other night. When you came in, you asked a bunch of guys at a table to join you and you bought a round of beer. There was only one guy at the table who refused your offer and stayed at his own table. That guy was the one who got the others to agree to try to rough you up. Really, that's all I know."

"Was he the one I spoke to before the others tried to jump me?"

"Yeah, that was him. He thinks he's pretty tough. I was glad to see you take him down. He's started more than one fight here in my place. The other three have never caused much trouble, but he's the instigator."

"Okay, I think I got the picture. He's made the others think that in some way the Mexicans working for me are some kind of threat to the local community, right?"

"I guess so."

"How do you feel about it?"

"I don't know. It's no skin off me."

"Now, how about a little discount on some beer I need to take back with me?"

"Okay, how much beer do you want and what kind?"

"I'd like about 30 cases. Do you have any Dos Equis or Carta Blanca?"

"No, we don't get many requests for that Mexican stuff."

"That doesn't surprise me. Okay, let's make it 15 cases of Bud and 15 more of Bud Light. I think they'll be happy with about anything I bring back. They can't complain about the price. It's all on me."

"How about $180? That's only $6 a case?"

"Sounds like a bargain. I'll take it. And by the way, if your trouble-making friend has any thoughts about coming out to where we're working to cause trouble, tell him we'll be waiting for him and next time I won't go so easy on him."

"Okay, will do."

When Hans returned to camp, he found everyone anxiously awaiting his return. He had already decided not to mention the brawl at the tavern. He would wait till later when he was warning them about the potential of some strangers coming to make trouble. He didn't want to dampen the enthusiasm of the men. They needed a break from the exhausting work they had been doing for several days.

"Okay, guys, gather around. First, the bad news. No Mexican beer. Now, the good news. Lots of American beer, and I picked up the tab. Drink until it's all gone, but remember we still have work to do tomorrow. Hangovers won't be an excuse to sleep in."

The men gathered close to the truck, and Hans left them to make a call to Charley. When he picked up the phone, Hans wasted no time in small talk before relating the incident at the tavern.

"What do you think will happen next? Do you think they'll try to make an attack on the sites where the men are working?"

"How the hell can anybody predict what a bunch of rednecks are going to do? I don't think the four I tangled with would try it alone, but one of the four is known as an instigator. He might try to raise a much larger group and come looking for us."

"Are you guys ready for that kind of action?"

"We can be, if we have any advance notice that they're coming. I'm going back into town early tomorrow morning to have another chat with the bartender. I think if I offer him enough money, he'll become our eyes and ears. I'll let him have my phone number and promise him a good chunk of change if he reports anything of value to us. He didn't look too prosperous, and I know he doesn't like the guy who started the fight tonight."

"Call me back tomorrow night and keep me advised."

"Okay, will do."

The next morning Hans went back to the tavern. The owner was just about to open the doors. He let Hans in and retreated behind the bar.

"What can I do for you? You surely don't need more beer this early in the morning, do you?"

"No, I don't. I have a little business proposition for you. You wouldn't have any objection to making a few hundred bucks on the side, would you?"

"Not unless I have to do something illegal. What's your thing?"

"My thing, as you call it, is to have you call and tell me if you hear anything more from any of that group I tangled with last night. If you pass on even one piece of advance warning that they're planning to hit us, you just made yourself a thousand bucks cash. Interested?"

"Sure, all I gotta do is just call you if I hear they're gonna try something, and if they do, you're gonna give me a grand, right?"

"Right, do you want to shake on it?"

"Sure."

"Well, here's a hundred just for what you told me last night."

"Gee, thanks mister."

****

It was two days later when Hans got the call. He didn't recognize the voice at first, but by the time the bartender had begun his second sentence, he knew and hoped the reason for the call would be of some importance.

"Slow down, man. I can barely understand you. Now, say again."

"It's gonna be tonight. I heard them talking, and the guy who jumped you said there's gonna be at least a dozen men in on this thing. They're gonna have high powered rifles, and I know for a fact that some of these guys aren't afraid to use them."

"Okay, hold on. Don't hang up yet. Did you hear at about what time they're gonna be here. Do you have any idea what direction they'll come from?"

"I heard him say something about after midnight, but I didn't catch from what direction. What are you guys gonna do when they show up?"

"You don't have to worry about that. We'll take care of the rest. If they show tonight, I'll stop by tomorrow to give you what I promised."

"You guys be careful and good luck."

Hans hurried back to camp, but he didn't tell the crew anything about what might happen that night. He gathered the men and told them that he would be setting up some guys on guard duty for the night. When they asked why, he just shrugged and said it was merely a precautionary measure. He'd heard a rumor in town that a bunch of drunks might be headed their way sometime during the night, and he wanted to be ready if the rumor turned out to be true.

He asked if any of the men had had any military training. Six men raised their hands, and he led them away from the group for a little private conversation.

"Have any of you men ever used a sniper type rifle? I have several and I could give each of you a short course in how to use one if need be. These guns all have scopes that let you see in the dark. Follow me and I'll take you to where the guns are hidden."

"But why? If this is just a case of a bunch of drunks out to make a little noise, why will we need scoped rifles?"

"I didn't want to upset all of the men, but I have a hunch we're to be assaulted tonight by men who'll be carrying some pretty high-powered weapons of their own. These are not just run-of-the-mill drunks. They're red necks, the kind who hate foreigners, you guys included. If any of you are too frightened by the prospect of having to defend yourselves, I'll go back and try to find somebody else."

No one spoke up, so he headed in the direction of the weapons he had hidden away. Ten minutes later, he stopped and picked up a shovel which was hidden in some brush. He gave the shovel to one of the men and told him to dig under a tall pine tree. After the shovel had been passed to each man, the last shoveler struck something solid. Hans took the shovel from him and finished the dig. Now the men could see the outline of a large wooden case. Hans opened the top of the case and began removing the contents. None of the six rifles had been assembled. It took him almost thirty minutes to completely assemble the weapons and attach the night scopes. He showed the men how to load the weapons and then led them back in the general direction of their camp. Along the way, he positioned the men in six different locations.

"Now men, all of this may be completely unnecessary. What I heard may be nothing more than a lousy rumor, but in case it's not, I want us to be prepared. I know for a fact that there are those who resent us and certainly don't wish us anything good. Now, here are the rules of engagement. You are not to fire your weapon unless you are fired on, or unless I give the word. Be absolutely sure what you're shooting at. The last thing we want to happen is to fire a shot in the dark and kill some innocent person who just happens to be wandering our way. I hope we don't need to fire a single shot, but we gotta be prepared to defend ourselves if necessary."

There was no response from any of the men. They were told when they agreed to take this job that there was a certain element of danger. They had been kept so busy recently that the thought of danger had hardly crossed their minds. Hans checked the demeanor of each of the men before he started back to the base camp.

The men in camp sensed that something was not right. Hans offered no explanation as to why none of the men who had followed him off had not returned to camp. Most of the men drifted off to an uneasy sleep, but Hans made no attempt to sleep. He checked his pistol to make sure it was fully loaded and opened a new box of ammunition. He sat in his truck and waited.

At about 1:30 Hans heard two shots. They seemed to come from about where he had stationed the man fartherest from the camp. It seemed to him that shots had come from two different directions. None of the men stirred, but he slipped silently from his truck and headed in the general direction of the two shots. He found at his last checkpoint his man standing behind a large tree. Before he could even ask what had happened, the man said. "I didn't really mean to shoot the guy. I just wanted him to go away after he shot at me. He's laying over there. I'm pretty sure he's dead."

"Don't worry about it. If he took a shot at you, he got what he deserves. Follow me. We gotta round up the others."

He took all of the men who had been standing guard and took them to the place where he had first hidden the weapons. He had every weapon reburied and covered in a way to conceal the digging. Then he told the men what they were to say if and when the authorities were to come asking questions.

"Men, what happened here last night might be just the beginning. There are people close-by who don't like you for the color of your skin. Maybe the guy who we left lying dead out there was just after me. I don't know. I had a fight with a few of them the other night when I went into town to get you guys the beer. I heard they might come after me. That's why I had you people stand guard last night. Now when they come asking questions, our stories must all be the same. Here's our story. We heard two shots in the night, but we thought it might be a couple of guys out jack-lighting for deer. We didn't find the body until a lot later after daylight. We don't know anything else. I'm headed into town now to inform the police we have found a body close to where we're working. Now let's all get to work."

They scattered as he left for his truck. He drove to town and went directly to the small building that doubled for a courthouse and jail. The sheriff and one deputy were the only ones there. He tapped on the door and waited for a response.

"Come on in. It isn't locked. What can we do for you?"

"I've come to report what I think may be an accident."

"Go on."

"Well, close by where my men are working, we found a body. It's a man. There's a lot of blood, so we think maybe he was shot. We didn't touch anything. We left the body just like we found it. It's pretty certain the man is dead."

"Can you take us to the spot? We'll follow you."

He went back to his truck and led the squad car back to the base camp. Only a handful of the men were still there. The rest had already left for their own designated work areas.

"Where's the man who discovered the body. We need to talk to him first."

"He's right over there. I'll go get him. You guys wait here. I'll be right back."

He walked to a spot about 100 yards away to get the man. He told him not to act nervous and not to volunteer any information, just to answer their questions and nothing more.

"So, are you the one who found the body?"

"Yes sir, I am."

"Can you take us to where you found the body?"

"Sure, it's quite a walk, but there's really no good road to where I found the body."

"What were you doing that far from this camp?"

"I don't usually work with this group of men. My regular camp is a lot closer."

"What were you doing out away from the camp?"

"Just taking a crap. We don't have any restrooms out here. We just go out in the woods and do our business."

"Okay, lead us to where you found the body."

The squad car followed Hans' truck to a spot where the road ended, and all four men dismounted and headed to where the man led them. About thirty yards back in the underbrush, the man stopped and pointed to the body.

The sheriff knelt over the body briefly and shook his head. "You were right. He's dead all right."

"We thought so, just from looking, but we didn't want to touch anything. Everything is just like he found it."

"Do any of the men have guns?"

"No, they don't, but I do. I have a pistol and a permit to carry it. Can you tell what kind of bullet he got hit by?"

"Not really. He'll have to be examined by a coroner. We don't have one there in our town. We'll have to take the body about 50 miles to get an official report from a coroner. In the mean time, I'm gonna ask you to give me your pistol. We'll give it back to you as soon as we can find out exactly what kind of gun was used."

"Okay, here it is." He reached inside his jacket and produced the pistol and handed it to the deputy handle first. "Take good care of it. I've had it for a long time."

"Don't worry about that. We know how to take care of things."

The sheriff made a call on his cell phone for a pick-up of the body. They hung around waiting for the vehicle to arrive, but they made no further attempt to interrogate either of the two men. They strung out a crime scene banner and asked Hans to remind his men to stay away from inside the yellow marker.

"Well, boss, do you think they believed our story?"

"Doesn't really matter whether they believe it or not. If they don't, they'll have an awfully hard time proving otherwise. Let's get back to camp and see if anyone else has been around to question any of the other men. The only thing we have to do is make sure that our story is the same to no matter who's asking the questions."

It was late in the day when the sheriff returned with several men whose duty was to search the immediate area for any clues to the death of the man. His identity had been easily established, and for certain there were few tears shed by those who knew him. The sheriff had already established that the man had been part of a group that had attacked Hans earlier in a tavern. This they had decided was a possible motive for Hans or one of his men to have been the one who had fired the fatal shot.

Hans had an alibi. At least a dozen of his men would swear that he had never left the camp for a minute that night. However, one of the crime scene search crew had found an empty shell casing from the victim's own rifle close to where the body had been discovered. This seemed to indicate that he might have fired one shot at the man who had killed him. It was enough for the authorities to question all of Hans' crew several times, looking for a hole in their story.

The sheriff complained to one of his deputies, "It's just a little too pat. The story we get from all the men seems to me like it's been well rehearsed. Every point in their version of what happened is identical."

It wasn't until the second visit from the State Police that Hans thought it prudent to inform Charley of the situation. Not a single man from the crew had deviated a bit from the story that they had told to the local police.

"How much trouble do you think you're in, Hans?"

"As long as the men hold up under the questioning, we aren't in any trouble at all. If they should stumble onto the cache of weapons that we buried, it would really make things hard on us. I'd like to remove them completely from the area, but I'm afraid the area is watched too closely for that, even at night. The longer this drags on, the less chance there is that they'll ever find out what really happened. If the guy that got shot hadn't been such an asshole, I think the locals would have made a more thorough search and might have found the rifles."

"Don't let another day go by without letting me know what's going on. Sometimes I go almost crazy just sitting here wishing I knew what's going on down there. I'm tempted to make the trip and see for myself."

"Don't. Your being here just might complicate things. I've got enough to worry about without having your personal safety on my mind. There isn't a single thing you could do here that would make things go any better. I'll try to do a better job of keeping you informed. Always consider that no news is good news. I'll always let you know if we run into anything that's a real threat, okay?"

"Okay, but Alice is getting really jumpy. She wants to know when we might be able to start the big move. Got any estimate?"

"Not really. I'd say at least two months. It will take that long to clear all the properties you guys bought and to fence it off. The men are working hard, but there's a limit to human endurance. I gotta say you sure picked a good group of workers. These guys never complain about the long hours or the hard work. They're only a little spooked when the authorities come around asking questions."

"I can't take much of the credit for picking the crew. Billy and Juan had a whole lot more to do with that than I did."

"How's everything on the home front?"

"Same-o same-o. Every day I get a little richer and a whole lot more bored. Everything seems to go like clockwork. Juan and Billy seem to be able to handle anything without even contacting me. Terry hasn't had anything to do for so long that I'm afraid he might not be able to handle a real emergency. I wish you could be in two places at once. I'd feel better if you were here with us, but I know you're needed a lot worse down there."

"Don't underestimate Terry. Sometimes he's on top of things a lot more than you realize. He just doesn't want to worry you with small details."

"Okay, I got a call-waiting on the other line. I think it's Alice, so I gotta run. Please keep me better informed if you can."

"Will do."

Interest in the case was beginning to wane. The locals had long before lost interest, and the State Police had not been able to develop any new leads. They suspected that Charley and his crew knew a lot more than they were telling, but they could never catch anyone in any discrepancy to the story they told, and neither the locals nor the State seemed anxious to spend any more money on the case.

****

A month passed. Everything from expensive mansions to cheaper weekend cabins was disappearing from the landscape. Another crew had arrived and was making great progress at fencing everything that Charley had been able to purchase. Several new properties had been acquired when the owners did not like being crowded by people they didn't know. Juan kept a close eye on the ever-expanding limits of what Charley now controlled. He was always ready to make an attractive offer to the owners on the periphery of land controlled by the two land companies that Charley had used to front his ownership. He kept Charley informed any time he made a new acquisition. Sometimes he had little else to do. The complete monopoly of the automobile industry had left him with time on his hands. None of the Japanese carmakers seemed to want to put their competitors out of business. There was plenty of business to go around, and the Americans had not lost their taste for the automobile and lots of travel.

Six weeks passed. The authorities had decided to give up on solving the mysterious death of the man whose body was found so close to Hans' work camp. They had decided to leave the case open in case there should be further evidence come to light in the future.

When Charley heard that the heat was off, he made up his mind that he would start the big move in about two weeks. Hans would have liked for him to give it a little longer, but Charley's patience was at an end. Alice was not as anxious to go, but she could see that there was no way to delay her husband any longer. She sometimes wished that she had discouraged him when he first broached the move, but it was too late now to tell him she had changed her mind.

Three large moving vans carried what Alice considered the bare necessities for their new home. Charley would have preferred to leave most of what she insisted had to be included in the move. After all, they could certainly afford to replace anything they left behind. Somehow, in a short period of time, many items had acquired nostalgic qualities that she felt gave then a place in their new home.

The three vans did not travel together. They did not even leave Perdido on the same day. Hans had persuaded Charley that they would attract much less attention if they arrived on three separate days. Therefore, the first to arrive had to carry the most essential items in the move. Nearly all of the baby's things, living and bedroom furniture, and a few cooking utensils made up the first load.

Alice fell in love with her new home before she ever saw the inside of it. The second story porch which gave a person a great view of the lake made whatever else the rest of the house contained totally unimportant. She knew that this place could not compare in luxury to the one she had left behind. She also realized it would take a long time to get the feeling of security that Perdido had provided since the birth of her daughter. The feeling was a mixture of fear and excitement she had not felt since the early days in Mexico.

Charley was certain he could be happy here if somehow a sense of security could be maintained. He tried to imagine what might be the most imminent threat. It might be the resentment of the locals, or perhaps the de los Santos brothers when they discovered his whereabouts. He was certain the oil companies had never forgiven him, nor had the Big Three automakers and all their unemployed workers. It was an impressive list of potential enemies. Hans had tried to warn him that it would not be easy.

The only people he felt he had any chance of taking off the enemy list were the locals. He knew that money could smooth a lot of things. These people, unlike the others, had no real reason to hate him, so if he proved to be a generous man to the locals, he was convinced that they would accept him. He called Juan to ask him what he thought would be the most impressive thing he could do to win the support of the locals.

"Hey, Juan. How's it going? Is everything still okay there?"

"Just like you left it. No problems that I'm aware of."

"I have a question or two. When you were acquiring land in South America for the company you used to work for, did you make any enemies with your acquisitions?"

"Of course. You're bound to make a lot of people unhappy when you upset their lives. There's no way around that. Are you upsetting people now?"

"I've already upset a bunch of people by buying their property or their neighbors' property. Here's my question. Did you try to appease these people in any way? Your company had millions, so did you use any of that money to try to change their attitude toward your company?"

"Yes, we did. The company thought it was money well spent. We often had the threat of a public uprising if we were too heavy-handed with the locals."

"What were some of the ways you used the money to win their support?"

"Lots of things. We built hospitals, schools, roads, and playgrounds. We even had a program for young doctors to come and open clinics for those who could not afford medical care for themselves or their children."

"What would you recommend that I start off with, if I tried to win some local support?"

"That depends. Look around and see what the needs are. Whichever is greatest is the place you should begin."

"Yeah, that makes sense. It'll probably take a while for me see what they need most since I won't be in a position to chat much with the locals."

"True, but you can read the local papers and listen to the local radio and TV shows to see what they're most interested in. I'm sure if you give it a shot, in less than a week you'll know what they're wanting."

"Do you think I should try to make my gifts anonymous? Is it too early to let these people know who I am?"

"Sooner or later they're going to have to know. I think the sooner the better."

"Okay, that's really all I wanted to know."

Charley had Hans begin to pick a copy of the local newspaper. It only came out twice a week and contained more local gossip than anything else. It didn't take long for Charley to see what the biggest concern in the small neighboring town was. The town had been growing for some time now, but the local sentiment was that it would grow much faster if it had schools. The children were bussed almost 20 miles every day to the nearest town with schools. It was a long ride for the kids, especially the younger ones. Most everyone knew that they had an insufficient tax base to build and maintain any sort of school system of their own, still they complained of the status quo. Charley decided it was time. The local town council meeting was scheduled for the following Monday night. He decided to attend the meeting.

Hans was not in favor of Charley's decision. He thought it was too soon and too dangerous. He wanted to go along to the meeting but Charley said no. He didn't want the people to think that he was afraid of them.

He entered the small building where the meeting was to take place. He introduced himself as nothing more than Charles Johnson. Only two of the five-member council were there when he entered. He told them he was a new member of their community and he would like to address the council with some information that might be of interest to the community. None of the council seemed to attach any importance to the name of the stranger.

The regular business of the council lasted no more than 45 minutes. Charley waited patiently until he was asked if he was ready to make his pitch.

"I hope you haven't come here tonight with the hope of selling us something. I'm afraid our treasury is about busted."

"On the contrary, I have come here tonight to help you in that regard."

"Oh really? And just what form will this financial assistance take."

"Well, correct me if I'm wrong, but I read in the local paper that many of the local patrons are unhappy about the long bus ride their kids have to make every day to attend school. Am I right?"

"You're right, but I don't see what we or you can do about that."

"How much money would it take to build a school here?"

"A lot more than we can ever hope to raise. We just don't have a large enough tax base to build or maintain a school."

"But give me an estimate at least of what it would cost."

"Okay, I think in the neighborhood of 15 million dollars if you mean for all 12 grades. Is that what you mean?"

"Yes, that's it. What would you say if I told you that I will personally donate 15 million dollars toward the building of such a school?"

"Talk is cheap, Mr. Johnson. Where are you gonna get that kind of money?"

"I think maybe I'd better give you a little bigger introduction. I can see from your reaction that you don't realize who I am. I am the American who was forced to go to Mexico to produce the carburetor that eventually put America's Big Three out of business. I wouldn't be bragging if I told you that I am considered one of the richest men in the world. Since I've recently taken up residence nearby, and since I have a young daughter, I certainly don't want her taking long bus rides every day to get to school."

There followed a short period of stunned silence. The men at the table looked back and forth at each other and seemed reluctant to look at Charley. Finally it was the leader who had the courage to speak.

"Well, Mr. Johnson, welcome to our community. If your offer is a serious one, we accept. How long would it take you to raise that amount of money?"

"Just long enough to write a check. I could write it now if you could tell me who to make it out to."

"Now hold on. You're going way too fast. We'd first have to hire an architect and then try to get bids from the builders before we could seriously consider your offer."

"I have considerable experience in these matters. I've been responsible for building most of the structures where the vast majority of automobiles are produced. For my people, this would be a very small project. Does the town own property where the school would be built, or would that be an additional expense?"

"No, we have plenty of ground. It would probably take a vote of the people to decide exactly where the majority would like to see one built. Are there any strings attached to your generosity?"

"Only one. I don't want my name mentioned as the donor of the money. There are lots of people who resent what I have accomplished."

"How else can we explain where the money comes from?"

"How about this? What if one of you were to win the Missouri lottery? We can give out that the money will go for civic improvements."

"But how about the taxes on the winnings? That alone would take millions."

"No doubt, but don't worry. I can take care of that as well. If you have a better idea of how to explain the windfall, go right ahead. I only ask that for the present, my generosity is known only to you five."

That same night Charley placed a call to Juan. He knew that it would take a lot of cooperation from his CEO to pull off what he had begun that night.

"Well, it's started. Tonight I met with the council and promised them 15 million dollars toward the building of their new school. I'll need some help on this to get it going. I'm gonna need an architectural firm to draw up the plans for the building, and I'm gonna need the best construction crew available. I'll leave it up to you to find them for me."

"Do these people know who you are?"

"Only the council members. They promised not to mention where the money comes from."

"Yes, but they'll have to explain it some way. They can't just say they found the money."

"I suggested winning the lottery, but I kinda left it up to them. I'm sure they'll come up with something. The people of the town won't really care where it comes from as long as it isn't coming out of their pockets."

"You're probably right about that. Is 15 million the top of what you're willing to spend on this project?"

"No, whatever it takes. I want a state-of-the-art complex. It will be large enough for grades one through twelve. It will also include a separate building for pre-school and kindergarten. The high school will include a regulation size gymnasium and an Olympic size swimming pool."

"Okay, but I'm afraid you're looking at a lot more than 15 million."

"How soon can I expect to see the architectural firm here to begin drawing up the plans?"

"I think I can probably get them there in two weeks if you're not going to squawk about what they cost."

"I'm not in that big a hurry. The town will have to vote on the site where they want the school built. That will take some time. Just be sure you have someone lined up as soon as we know where they'll be building. I want the best. I want this thing to be the envy of every other school district in the state. Money is no object."

"Okay, I'll get right on it. I'm not really familiar with many construction companies in that area. Should I try to get a company close to the site?"

"Yeah, that would open up a lot of jobs here for a while, and usually some of the workers decide to stay and become part of the community. Don't limit the architectural firm to this area. I want the best, no matter where they come from. I'll call you again in about three days to see what progress you've made. I'm counting on you."

"Okay, I'll try to have something by then. *Adios*."

****

The local paper ran banner headlines. An elderly gentleman who wished to remain anonymous had died and left the town a huge fortune that he hoped would be used for the building of a school. There were no further details on the man or the amount of money. It was announced that an election would be held in two weeks to decide the exact location of the new school. It was hoped that the school would be finished in time for the following school year.

Charley was pleased with the site the people had chosen for the school. It sat upon a small hill which gave it a commanding view of the area around the town. It also had the advantage of enough ground for athletic fields such as soccer or football when the school should have enough students for those sports. Until that time, Charley was sure that the school would have enough students for both girls and boys basketball teams. He would insist that the architects include a small practice gymnasium so that both girls and boys could practice after school simultaneously without conflict.

The town council held a special closed-to-the-public meeting the day after the special election to choose the site of the new school. Charley was the only other person privy to the meeting.

"Let's dispense with the reading of the minutes of the last meeting. We all know what happened then. Let's get right to the point of this meeting. First, I would like to express the gratitude of the whole council for the generosity of Mr. Johnson. I checked with the bank today, and I find that our account now contains 15 million dollars more than it did last month. Mr. Johnson, would you like to say anything at this time?"

"Yes, I would. I liked your explanation of where the money came from. It was better than my idea. Now, let me explain something that I'm sure has crossed your minds. How can we afford to staff this new school with really good teachers and school administrators? How about such things as athletic equipment? How about custodians and all the things they need to keep everything running? Let me assure you I haven't forgotten about these things. The 15 million I promised and delivered is only for the initial cost of the structures of the school. I will take care of any and all expenses that we incur until this town has a large enough tax base to take care of it on its own. I will deposit another 15 million when the building is completed. I suggest that you begin now to advertise the teaching and administrative positions. You will probably have to elect a school board for the actual hiring of personnel. I suggest a five person board."

"Would you be interested in running for one of those positions?"

"No, I don't want people to know where the money comes from, and if they don't know, why would they vote for a total stranger?"

"You're probably right about that. Would you consider becoming our special adviser with no special title?"

"Yes, as long as I'm not required to attend meetings that are open to the public. I don't think you people understand yet what this could mean to your small town. People will begin to move here in droves. This is a great place to raise a family. The climate is good, the recreational activities are limitless, and a good school system is the clincher. I've seen small towns like this one take off. The town of Perdido, where I first began my business, wasn't a whole lot bigger than this one when I first got there. If things go as I hope, I can promise you some help with the building of a hospital and a medical clinic, maybe some outdoor recreational parks as well."

"I can't believe what I'm hearing. Can I ask you why you chose our small town for all of your generosity?"

"You can ask, but I'm afraid you'll not receive a satisfactory answer. My wife and I passed this way once and agreed that we liked the looks of the place. At the time we had less than $200 to our name and were on the way to Mexico. All we really had was my idea about the carburetor, but we talked about coming back some day. That's all I can really tell you."

"We'll have to inform the State that we are forming a new school district. They may squawk because they don't like small school districts. They say they aren't cost efficient. They may not give us much in state aid."

"Don't worry about that. I'll make up any difference in what you feel you need and what they're willing to provide."

"And what if they say no to the whole idea?"

"Then our school will be a private school not depending on any State aid."

"You'd really do that for us?"

"Yes, I will. Gentlemen, we are going to have a school, make no mistake about that. I hope you're as excited about this as I am."

"I'm sure I speak for the council and the whole town when I say this is the most exciting thing that has ever happened in our town. Is there anything else you wish to tell us at this time?"

"Only that the architects will be here in about a week. At your next meeting I hope to be able to show you what the new school will look like. That's all I can tell you for now, and my wife is waiting up for me, so I think I'll wish you all a good night."

"Good night, Mr. Johnson.

****

Exactly one week later the architects arrived. They met at Charley's house and did all of their work from there. Charley explained to them in some detail what he wanted in the way of a new school. He let it be known early that costs were not the most important issue in the building. Beauty and function were to be the primary items. They would be responsible not only for the building itself, but also the grounds surrounding the school. This would include playgrounds, athletic fields, and parking lots for both the faculty and the students. Charley told them that he wanted the building to be in use by the next school year so he encouraged them not to waste any time in coming up with their final design. It took them ten days to come up with a design that finally met with Charley's approval. He thanked them, paid them, and sent them on their way.

At the next council meeting Charley presented the blueprint for the new school. The members to a man thought that the building would be much too large for the projected enrollment.

"Gentlemen, when I first began my business in Mexico, I had the foresight of my own benefactor. He told me from the beginning that I could not see the big picture. He was right. I had no idea just how big my enterprise would become. Now I see that you guys are in about the same position I was in. If our enrollment in the school were to remain no larger than what you project for next year, then I would have to agree that you're right. I project that the enrollment will triple by the end of the first year, and in three years you may be asking me to help you enlarge what you have. Are there any questions about the design?"

"Why is the swimming pool included in the plans?"

"Let me ask you this. Living as close as you do to such a beautiful lake, don't you think it would be a good idea if all the children had a chance to learn to swim?"

"Yes, but we have a small city pool."

"You said the magic word—small. Not everyone could possibly fit into that pool. By having it there at the school, we can make learning to swim a part of the curriculum for the P.E. classes. In the summer months we can open it to the public. We'll have to hire lifeguards, but I'll take care of that. Are there other questions?"

"We've never had athletic teams before. Shall we go ahead and hire coaches?"

"Yes, at least for girls and boys basketball. I don't know if we'll have enough enrollment for football or baseball for a while, but since we're going to have an all-weather track, I think we should include that sport from the beginning."

"How can we get games scheduled for next year? I know we can't get into a league soon enough to compete next year."

"You're probably right about that. That will be one of the first duties of your athletic director, to schedule teams for us to compete against."

"But there won't be many schools as small as we are nearby. We might have to travel all over this part of the state to find people we could compete against."

"So, what's your point? If we have to travel, we'll have a couple of good activity busses, so we'll travel. When the teams we play see what kind of facilities we have, we won't have any trouble getting them to come to our place. I suspect we'll be holding invitational tournaments before too long. In two years we'll be in a league, and in four years we'll be dominating that league."

"How can you say that with such confidence?"

"Because I can see the big picture. Families with potentially exceptional athletes will be moving here because of the facilities. It takes talent to win at any level, but I can assure you we'll have the talent. It will be up to you people to see that we have coaches who can use that talent. Anything else?"

"When will the actual construction begin?"

"I'm not sure of the exact date, but I can tell you it will be soon. I've taken it upon myself to tackle the problems with the State Department of Education. They may hassle us some over accreditation, but I think I can smooth that over. Don't be slow in electing your school board. Try to discourage anyone from running if you don't think they'll whole-heartedly support our new school. We don't want anyone with a negative attitude on the board. We'll have enough problems in the beginning without internal problems. Are any of you guys interested in running?"

Three of the five raised their hands. He asked if this would be an election based on where each of the members lived or would all positions be at-large. They could not answer that because they had not even considered the question.

"Find out quickly and try to encourage people you think will do the best job. Don't let things like friendship or family relations influence your choice. Hold the elections as soon as you can. We need an elected school board before we can attack a lot of problems we'll face. Guys, I gotta tell you, I think the job on the school board will take up a lot more of your time than serving on the council, at least for the first couple of years. Also, don't be surprised if you make a few enemies along the way. Dealing with things that affect the lives of other people's children is a serious matter. Nothing gets people more fired up for good or for bad than the things that deal with the schools. It's up to us to see them fired up for the good we're doing."

****

In less than a month the construction crew was busily at work breaking ground for the new school. It became the major preoccupation of the whole town to go down at least once a day to see what progress had been made. Even the smallest of children who would attend the school could not resist the temptation to look at the building at every opportunity. Charley could feel the stir of excitement about the school. On an almost daily basis he got calls wanting to know if he would be willing to sell any of his recently purchased land. His answer was always "not at this time." He believed that maybe in time he could part with some of the land, but for now he needed the buffer affect that the land provided.

The summer was passing more swiftly than Charley liked. Unusually heavy rains had delayed the building of the school. He could get no assurance from the builders that they could get enough of it finished in time for school to start. The newly elected school board had moved back the opening day of school until the week after Labor Day.

Most, but not all, of the faculty had been hired. Few coaches had interviewed for a job. Only a couple of first year graduates had been brave enough to think they could compete at any level with so few athletes. Charley advised the board to raise the pay for the coaches to try to attract someone with at least some experience. Still no one seemed interested. Good grade school teachers were in abundance, and when they came to interview and saw what beautiful facilities the school could offer, they were anxious to become a part of this new system.

****

Two weeks before the opening day, Charley was asked by the board to represent them in a meeting with the State Board of Education. He reluctantly agreed. He used most of that two-week period studying school law as it related to school finance. He wasn't sure what questions would be asked, but he assured the board that school would start on time no matter what the result of this meeting.

A seven-member board welcomed Charley into its executive chamber. The president of the Board introduced Charley and took his seat at the table.

"Gentlemen, I hope I can answer any questions you may have about the new school we intend to open soon. I'll take your questions now."

"Where has all the money come from that has made possible that impressive new building we're reading about?"

"Okay, I guess that's a fair question. You know my name is Charles Johnson. Do you know that I am the same Charles Johnson who invented the carburetor that put the Big Three out of business? I have spent most of my recent time in Mexico where I have become one of the richest men in the world. I'm not bragging when I tell you that almost all of the money you speak of came directly or indirectly from my own bank account."

"Then why do we hear this story about a man dying and leaving all this money to the city?"

"It wasn't only modesty that kept me from disclosing myself as the one donating the money. At that time, and to some extent still, I feared for my own safety. It was with great reluctance that I decided to try to return to my native land. I have a wife and small child. My life has been threatened many times by people who greatly resent what my business has done to them financially. Several attempts have been made on my life. I thought it prudent not to advertise my presence here in Missouri. Does that answer your question?"

"Not completely. Who are these people whom you fear so much? Surely you could get protection from the law."

"I'm not so sure about that. The people who hate me the most are rich and powerful. They include the whole of the petroleum industry, the remnants of the Big Three, and the Mafia. The authorities have never been able to adequately protect me from them, so I employ lots of people of my own for that protection."

"Are you responsible for buying most of the land in Lake Side?"

"Yes, it's true that I own a controlling share in the land companies who've bought up much of the land."

"Why have you bought up so much of the land?"

"For my own protection. The land stands between me and anyone who might want to harm me."

"I see. Do the people of Lake Side know who you are and that it was you who donated the money?"

"I think it's reasonable to assume that most of them know by now. Early on, I thought it was best to keep my identity a secret, but I'm afraid by now most everyone knows."

"Have you ever been officially cleared of the murder charges against you in the states of Illinois and New Mexico?"

"I'm not sure what you mean by 'officially.' As far as I know I'm no longer on the wanted list, and the American government long since dropped their attempt to have me extradited. That much I do know."

"Why are you so interested in establishing a school in Lake Side?"

"I have a wife and child, and I may have more in time. I want that child and all of the children in Lake Side to have the best education possible. I don't think that the long bus ride they take every morning is conducive to a great education."

"Have you any idea how much money it would take to keep a school that size going?"

"No, do you have any idea how much money I have?"

"No, tell us."

"I'm afraid I can't tell you exactly."

"Why not?"

"Because my accountants tell me my corporations make money faster than they can tally it. All I ever get are estimates."

"And what was your latest estimate?"

"It runs into billions. I don't remember how many. I don't really care anymore."

"Are you serious? You don't care?"

"Yes, I'm serious. Once you reach a certain point, the total is irrelevant. It's just a lot of zeros, nothing more."

"Why did you pick Lake Side?"

"That's hard to explain. When the wife and I were on our way to Mexico, we passed through the town and liked it. We made a vow we'd come back some day if we could."

"What do you see as the end of this experiment?"

"I see a thriving community that is fully capable of financing its own school system."

"And if it doesn't turn out that way, what then?"

"Then I'll keep funding it until the billions are all gone."

"What if something should happen to you? You've told us you have powerful enemies. What happens to the school if you're not there?"

"I've already made provisions in my will to see that the school will be able to continue long past my demise."

"What about accreditation?"

"All of the people we've hired to teach or coach are state certified. We'll accept probationary accreditation until you've had the time to check and see that all our hires meet the qualifications of the state."

"What will happen if we deny your request and refuse to grant you any state aid or any accreditation?"

"Then you will lose a school system that would make you look really good. We will simply open as a private school, and you will look foolish for not making it a part of the public school system."

"I see. You seem to have looked very closely into lots of possibilities. Do you have any questions you would like to ask us?"

"Yes, just one. How long will our probationary status last before we are given full accreditation?"

"If everything checks out, the normal time period is two years."

"I'm afraid that until we achieve full accreditation we won't see the growth we anticipate. People are leery of sending their kids to schools that might not be good enough to get their kids into college."

"Quite so. Well, if you have no further questions, that's it. We'll let you know what we intend to do as soon as we can check on the certification of all your hires. The building inspectors will have to check all of the wiring, plumbing, and safety measures before we could allow any students to enter the building."

"Then have them ready to make their inspections soon, because we anticipate opening this year on the second Monday in September."

****

The inspectors came in late August. They found that every aspect of the things to be checked far exceeded the State's requirements. The State Board sent the newly elected school board a registered letter advising them that they had achieved probationary status, but that because their decision to open this year had come so late, there would be very little in the way of State aid to the school.

Charley was ecstatic. He had already purchased five new school buses and two activity buses that were of the Grey Hound mold. He could hardly wait for the first day of school. He had the principal send him a copy of the enrollment for each of the 12 grades and the pre-school and kindergarten. The list looked like this:

Pre-scholl-11
First grade-9
Second grade-7
Third grade-8
Fourth grade-11
Fifth grade-6
Sixth grade-12
Seventh grade-11
Eighth grade-12
Freshmen-12
Sophomores-13
Juniors-10
Seniors-7

He couldn't believe all the things he'd been through for less than 130 students. He realized the numbers would be radically altered in a very short time if things went as he planned. Finally he had something to look forward to. Since he had become one of the richest men in the world, there had been very little anticipation of future events. Now, he was beginning to feel a part of this growing community, and his only wish was that he could more openly take part in future events. There was, however, that old fear that his enemies would strike again, and he knew that he was considerably more exposed to them here than he had been in Perdido.

****

The first year for the Lake Side school system was hectic. Classes were interrupted often by representatives of the State Board of Education. They did not seem anxious to give the school full accreditation. They looked continually for some small flaw in what they examined, but more often than not, they found absolutely nothing to report back to the Board.

Charley found it amusing to watch the practice sessions of the athletic teams that would represent Lake Side. There were not enough players for even an 8-man football team. Also there was no equipment. Still, the coach took the seven young men who had reported for the first day's practice out to the beautifully groomed practice field every day. They worked solely on the fundamentals of the game, running, passing, and catching. The lack of equipment kept them from any type of physical contact. It seemed pointless to Charley, but each day he devoted a few minutes to watching part of the session. One day he decided to leave his car and exchange a few words with the coach.

"Say, coach, how's it going?"

"Okay, I guess. I sure we wish could have scheduled at least one scrimmage. I know the guys get bored with all the training and repetition and no reward like a game or scrimmage to even look forward to."

"No doubt. Hey, I'm sorry about the screw-up on the delivery of the pads and other stuff. Partly my fault. I think by next year we'll have at least enough guys for an 8-man team. Have you ever coached 8-man football?"

"No, I've never even seen an 8-man game. I'll have to get some films or CD's of the game. I'm pretty sure it's mostly just like the 11-man game."

"I guess so. I never played any football, just basketball, when I was in school. I loved to watch our teams play, but I always thought it would be a little too rough for me."

"Yeah, it's a game for guys who like a lot of contact. It's really brutality within the rules. Do you think there's any chance we could still get the pads before basketball season starts?"

"I don't think so. But I can assure you we'll have'em long before next season starts. I'm just hoping we'll have the bodies to fill the pads."

"Yeah, me too. Gotta get back to locker room now to see that the guys leave it the way they found it. I want to thank you for the wonderful facilities we have. I've never seen better."

"They do look nice. Are you involved any with basketball?"

"Sort of. I'm supposed to be the JV coach, but I know we aren't gonna have enough guys for two teams."

"Well, at least you'll have a few games. I understand that we already have four scheduled and possibilities for three or four more."

"What do you think the possibilities are for a football game or two next year?"

"Pretty good. The things I'm hearing about our school tells me we'll have enough kids to play. We won't be able to be very picky about our opponents, and all the games may be away games, but I think we'll be competing."

He'd never really thought much about girls' athletics, but now having a daughter changed all that. He spent almost as much time watching the girls play volleyball. The coach was young and pretty, but he could see that she had been and still was a competitor. The athletic director had managed to schedule 6 matches. The girls won two of the six and were competitive in the others. All but one of the matches had been played on the road. It made Charley smile when he saw how much better facilities his girls had than their opposition. He hoped the volleyball coach had a least a part in the upcoming basketball season.

Eleven boys showed up for the first basketball practice. Four had at least some experience. There would be no JV games. Although the young coach preferred closed practice session, he had reluctantly agreed to let Charley visit the gym while they practiced. After the first two weeks of practice, Charley decided to have a chat with the coach.

"How's it going, coach?"

"Alright, I guess. I understand you played a lot of basketball. Is that right?"

"Well, I never played at the major college level. Wasn't tall enough. I think the game's changed a lot since I played. We didn't even the have the 3-point shot. I wish they had. Shooting from that distance was the best part of my game."

"Yeah, I suppose things have changed. What kind of defense did most teams play when you were playing?"

"Mostly zone. We never had a lot of depth on the teams I played on, so our coaches were always worried about getting into foul trouble with a man-to-man. What are you planning on playing?"

"We'll start with man-to-man, because I don't think you can play good zone defense without good man-to-man principles. What do you think?"

"I think you're right. Got any real talent for this year?"

"Nothing outstanding. If we have any success at all, it'll have to be through teamwork. There certainly aren't any superstars in this bunch."

"Sometimes that's more fun to watch than a bunch of superstars. Thanks for letting me watch some of your practice. I think now I'll run over and take a look at what the girls are doing. I'll see you later."

He walked over to the auxiliary gym where the girls were busy shooting lay-ups. He'd never spoken to a girls' coach before, and he really didn't know what to say. She was standing underneath the goal and encouraging every girl as they went through the lay-up drill. The assistant coach whom he had met during volleyball season was standing at mid-court. When she became aware of his presence, she walked toward him and met him with a smile.

"How's it going, coach?"

"Fine, I think. I can't believe this gym."

"Why not? Is there something wrong with it?"

"No, it's just that when I first heard that we'd have to practice some in an auxiliary gym, I was afraid we'd be all cramped up in a really small space. This may be an auxiliary to some, but the only thing different from the regular gym is there's no room for spectators. I suppose you hear a lot of this, but I would like to thank you personally for this gym and all the other facilities we have here."

"I'm glad you like it. It gives me a lot of pleasure to see some of the fortune I made going to such a good cause. Can the girls win any games this year?"

"Gee, I don't know. We don't have any size, and I'm afraid we're not very fundamentally sound. Bev, she's the head coach, is trying awfully hard to teach them. She gets frustrated when they can't execute things."

"What's your title?"

"I'm the JV coach and assistant head coach. I'll probably have to take over the head coach's job before the season is over."

"Why's that?"

"Because Bev is almost four months pregnant. She isn't showing yet, but I know she's having trouble with morning sickness."

"Are you married?"

"No, but I'm engaged. We've set the date for sometime this summer. Consider yourself invited to the wedding. It'll be here in Lake Side."

"I'll do my best to be there. Will it be a big wedding?"

"No, just the local Baptist church. My father died two years ago, so we're gonna have to foot all the expenses by ourselves."

"So, who'll be giving you away?"

"I don't really know."

"Can I ask you a big favor?"

"Sure, what is it?"

"Would you consider letting me give you away. My wife is an expert at these things. If you have any questions about the ceremony, she'd be glad to fill you in. I love the job you did with the volleyball girls. They really learned how to compete. What's your fiance's name?"

"Phillip, Phillip Connery. He hasn't found a place for us to live here yet. We drive about twenty miles every day to work. He's a carpenter."

"Are you really interested in finding a place here to live? If you are, why don't you and Phillip come to dinner at our house Friday night. I might be able to help you find something."

"I'll have to ask Phillip, but if he says okay, we'll be there. What time?"

"Let's say about seven. What does Phillip like to eat?"

"He's not picky, neither am I."

"Well, call and let me know if you can't make it. If I don't hear from you between now and then, I'll assume we're on for dinner."

Alice was pleased when Charley informed her of the guests who would be coming to dinner. She envied Charley his access to the things that were happening in Lake Side. He was willing to take chances on his own personal safety, but he was adamant that neither Alice nor his daughter expose themselves to possible harm. Alice worried all week that for some reason their guests would cancel at the last minute. Her worries were groundless.

Just before 7:00, the guests arrived. They were both a little overdressed for the occasion. Neither Alice nor Charley had seen fit to dress in anything but casual attire. Alice tried her best to put them at ease, but both seemed extremely nervous.

"Hey, loosen up, you guys. This is supposed to be fun. Phillip, loosen up your tie, or better yet take it off. Your wife tells me you're a carpenter by trade. I don't imagine you have to wear a tie very often."

"No I don't, but Sally thought…………..

"Well, for once Sally thought wrong. Get comfortable. Tell me a little about yourself."

"Well, I was born in Arkansas, not really that far from here. Went to school there."

"Where did you meet Sally?"

"She was going to a Junior college close to where I lived. I first saw her playing basketball."

"Was it love at first sight?"

"For me it was. Not for her, though. I had to ask her three times before she'd even go out with me. I didn't get anything but a high school education, and I could see that I wasn't even in her class when it came to brains."

"Well, sometimes formal education can be overrated. I don't have a college degree, and I've done pretty well. Sally tells me you have to make a drive every day to get to work. Why haven't you moved to Lake Side?"

"Property here is just too expensive. Together we don't make enough money to qualify for a loan."

"But you would like to live here, right?"

"Yeah, I get awfully tired of the drive every day."

"Tell you what, why don't you come to the Lake Side Realtors tomorrow morning at nine? I'll meet you there and see if we can't work something out."

"I can tell you ahead of time that I don't have enough money for a down payment on any of their stuff. We've already been there twice."

"Well, I don't know if it'll make any difference, but I own that company. I'd say your chances for financing a home have greatly improved since your last visit there."

Sally and Phillip smiled. They knew his being at the realtor's office tomorrow morning made getting financing a lead pipe cinch. Alice asked Sally if she would like to see the rest of the house. Both women headed toward the kitchen.

"Charley tells me you and Phillip are scheduled to be married this summer. Have you made all your wedding plans?"

"No, I still have lots to do. Mr. Johnson said you might be able to help me with some of the details."

"Well, I think planning a wedding could be lots of fun. My own wedding happened so quickly that I really didn't get a chance to do a lot of the planning. I didn't even have a chance to pick my wedding gown or this ring I'm wearing now."

She held her hand out toward Sally so she could see the huge diamond ring that had been the gift of the alcalde.

"Did Mr. Johnson pick it out for you?"

"No, he didn't, and you don't have to call him Mr. Johnson. He'd like it a lot better if you just called him Charley."

"Okay, I'll try to remember that. I know that you have a daughter. Where is she now? I'd like to see her."

"Maria is watching her. She's the nanny. When we were in Mexico, she helped with the baby. When we moved here, she just couldn't bear the thought of being separated from her, so we brought her along. Both of them are in the nursery. Would you like to see it? It's upstairs."

"Yes, I'd like that a lot. I'd like to see the rest of the house, too, if you don't mind."

"Of course not. We have at least twenty minutes before dinner will be served. Let's look at the rest of the downstairs before we go up to the nursery."

While the women ambled about from room to room, Charley and Phillip made small talk. Phillip seemed to relax when he found out that Charley had been an ordinary mechanic for most of his life. He had the preconceived notion that Charley was some kind of genius who had never used his hands to make a living.

"You know, Phil, I'll take credit for my adjustment. I worked on it for several years in my spare time, but the thing that's propelling most of the cars in the world today is really no work of mine. The idea came from a young man about your age. He was killed, and I inherited his patent on the thing. That's how I got to be where I am today. Mostly just pure luck. I think most of the great fortunes of today can be attributed to some kind of luck."

"Why did you settle on Lake Side? You could go anywhere in the world. Why here?"

"That's really hard to say. Alice and I passed through here on our way to Mexico, and we both liked it. I don't really know why, we just did. It hasn't really been that long ago, but it seems like a lot longer. How do you like it?"

"I love it. I like the lake because I like to swim and fish and water ski. How about you, do you like any of those things?"

"Well, growing up in Chicago, I never really had a chance to do any of those things. I think it might be a little late for me to take up water skiing, but boating, swimming, and fishing sound like fun."

When the ladies returned, dinner was served. Charley was more interested in how things were going at the school. He tried his best to direct most of the conversation in that direction. Sally said she liked the principal and the rest of the faculty, and her praise for the facilities at the new school was emphatic. The meal ended with a glass of wine and a toast by Charley that their upcoming marriage would be as wonderful as his own. The couple left early, and Charley was forced to smile when he saw them leave in a battered old pick-up truck.

"You know, Alice, she makes pretty good money as a teacher, and I'm sure he does even better as a carpenter. Why do you suppose they haven't managed a little better vehicle than the one they just drove off in?"

"I don't know, but my guess would be that they might be trying to save up for a down payment on a house closer to Lake Side. I sure hope they aren't buying gasoline for that old relic. Surely they're running on Tink's adjustment."

"I'll ask them tomorrow when we meet at the land office. You know, it was really fun tonight having them over. I had gotten used to life in Mexico, but tonight reminded me of why I wanted to come back home to the States."

"Yeah, my talk with her about her wedding was a lot of fun. I hope she'll let me have a small part in it. Are you sure it's a good idea to sell a piece of land that close to us? What do you think Hans will say about it?"

"I'm pretty sure he's not gonna be in favor of it. He'll squawk and say it's way too soon to start opening up, but it's gotta come sometime. It's people like them that I wanted to help when I first started working on my own adjustment. My dream now is to get this town really on the map."

"Aren't you afraid that putting them on the map is also gonna give away your new location to all of your enemies?"

"Sooner or later they're gonna know. I'm not getting any younger, so let's get on with it. If they're gonna make a move against me, let's go ahead and get it over with."

"That sounds pretty fatalistic to me. Are you sure you're ready for another attack?"

"I never have been ready for any of the other attacks. Why should I be ready for the next one?"

"No reason, I guess. Are you ready for bed?"

"Yes, I think the wine has made me sleepy.

****

The next morning Charley got up early and settled for a cup of coffee before he headed to the land office. He found Sally and Phil waiting in the parking lot, still seated in the old pick-up. He pulled up beside them in his Lincoln and motioned for them to follow him to the door of the office. Neither had the look of great confidence, possibly because they had already been refused by this same office.

The door to the office was still locked, but Charley banged on the door loudly. One of the land office people motioned toward his watch to indicate that it was too early to open the door. Charley banged on the door again, and this time the man inside made his way toward the door. When he recognized who was doing the banging, he fumbled nervously for his key to the door. Charley led the trio through the office to the desk in the rear of the office. He waved off the apology of the man who had detained their entry.

"Where's Albert? Is he late for work again?"

"No sir, I think he's in the rest room."

"Well, holler at him and tell him to get in here. I haven't got all day, and neither do these good people."

Albert came in and took a seat behind the empty desk. He apologized for holding them up. He was nervous, and Charley made a mental note to remind all of his employees to stop trying to make him out to be some sort of dictator who was always on the look-out to fire someone.

"So what can I do for you good people this morning?"

"Well, you can do what you failed to do the first time these people were in this office."

"And what would that be, Mr. Johnson?"

"Get these people a good piece of land here close to Lake Side, and then help them finance the building of a good house on that property."

"Give me the last name again. I'm sure the previous application is on file here in my computer."

He fumbled briefly with his computer, read what came up on the file which bore their last name.

"Well, sir, here it is. It would appear that they came in about four months ago. I'm afraid they were turned down because they didn't have enough money for the down payment. Has there been any change in that situation?'

"One very large change. I want these people to have whatever they want. They won't be needing any down payment. They're both well employed, and I see no reason why they shouldn't be able to make a mortgage payment. Also, for the first time, I'm opening up some of the land closer to my own place. I have to run now because I have some other important things to see into by this afternoon. When I speak to these people tomorrow, I want them to be able to show me where they intend to build."

He left abruptly and went in search of Hans. He found him with the latest of the labor crews that had arrived from Perdido. He informed him that he was about to open up some of the property closest to his own. Charley had already gauged what his reaction would be.

"Well, it's your funeral. Wouldn't you at least let me run a background check on these first newcomers?"

"I don't think that will be necessary for this couple. We investigated people pretty thoroughly before we hired them to teach in the new school."

"They both teach, then?"

"No, he's a carpenter. If it'll make you feel any better, I'll give you his name and current address, and you can do all the checking you want to."

"Okay, I'm pretty tired of babysitting these guys. A little detective work would at least break up the monotony."

It was two days before Charley checked in with Hans. He could have found out what he wanted to know over the phone, but he wanted to look the man in the eye when he gave him his report on Phillip.

"Well, tell me, is this guy a trained assassin or just the carpenter he seems to be?"

"As far as I can tell, he's a straight arrow. No bad habits, no political connections, no vices. His co-workers say he doesn't even cuss when he hits his thumb with a hammer. I hope all the others who'll be moving in later check out as well as this guy."

"Okay, that's really all I wanted to know. Now I gotta go see them and find out exactly where they intend to build."

He waited until school was out before he went to see Sally at practice. She didn't seem busy, and the girls had not yet taken the floor. She smiled warmly as he approached and waited for him start the conversation.

"Well, did you get the piece of land that you wanted?"

"Yes, we did. We can't thank you enough. The land we got is only about half an acre, but it's only a short distance from your own house. Phil will like it because it's so close to the lake. He wants a boat pretty bad, but he knows the house has to come first."

"When will you start the actual building of the house? Would you like me to line up some home builders for you?"

"That's awfully kind of you, but Phil is hoping the people he works for will take the job. He'd really like to have a hand in the building himself."

"Yes, I can see that. Then he wouldn't always be having to check every day to see what progress they're making. Also, he can be sure they're not cutting any corners on the materials used in the construction. Let me know if his company can't get to it. I'm sure I can find a company that would be glad to build it for you."

"Phil says he'll know in a week. I wish there were some way we could thank you with more than just words. It's really hard to imagine what we could do for the richest man in the world."

"Yeah, Alice says the same thing when it's my birthday or Christmas or an anniversary. What can you get for the man who has everything? The only thing you can do for me is what you're already doing."

"What's that?"

"Just becoming some of the best citizens that Lake Side has. I can see you're doing a great job with the girls, and from what I've heard about Phil, I think he'll make a great dad when you guys decide to start a family. You're gonna have a whole lot more girls to look after a lot sooner than you think. That's gonna make your life a whole lot more exciting."

"I'm looking forward to that. I can hardly wait for the time when our girls and guys are competitive in our own league. League tournaments, sub-states, and someday a state championship banner to hang on the wall of our beautiful gym."

"I couldn't have said it better. Let me know if there's anything else I can do to help with the building of the house."

****

The de los Santos brothers had not been idle. In spite of their failure to land a piece of their father's estate, they had thrived on the drug business of New York City. They had recouped all of the money they had spent on their fruitless attempts to somehow force the Johnson corporation to include them as partners. Carlos and Jorge had been content to give up the attempt, but as usual Diego could not let it go. When he read in the newspapers that a Mr. Johnson had taken up residence in Missouri, he couldn't wait to see how his brothers would react. He was disappointed in their reaction.

"Listen, brothers, this is our chance. He can't possibly have all the protection there that he had in Mexico."

"How can you be sure of that? He might have even more protection here than he had down there. I'm pretty sure he didn't just move up here for something to do."

"Yeah, but back there he had all the authorities backing him. Here, he'll have to rely on his own people for protection."

"True, brother, but do you have any idea how much money he now controls? I don't know how much, and I don't think anybody really does. Some people have him listed as the richest man in the world. Do you think a man like that is going to be an easy target? Besides, the only thing you could hope to get out of it would be revenge. He's never gonna let us have a piece of the pie."

"I'd settle for revenge. If you guys are content to let things stand the way they are, okay, but I'm not. I'll go it alone if you guys ain't got the balls to do something about it."

"Go right ahead, brother. It's your ass. After Hans or another of his protection takes you out, can Carlos and I have your share of the drug profits?"

"You don't think I can do it, do you?"

"No, we don't. We've seen some of your brilliant plans before."

"They were no worse than anything you guys came up with. If this guy wasn't the luckiest son-of-a-bitch in the world, he'd either be dead by now or have us for partners."

"Still, I don't see how his being a lot closer makes him any less vulnerable than he was down in Perdido."

"Well, can you guys look after things for a week? I want to go down there and see for myself what the situation is."

"Take all the time you need, brother. I'm pretty sure we can handle things until you get back."

"Okay, I'll be taking off today. Be back in a week. I'll call you if I need anything."

"We'll be here."

He packed a suitcase with enough clothes for a week. He took two pistols which he packed away, one inside his bag and the other hidden in the car. He had decided against any kind of public transportation for fear he could not get past security with his guns. He would have more freedom to look over the whole area if he had his own wheels. He might attract too much attention in his disguise if he was forced to rent a car at an airport or bus terminal.

He looked closely at a map of the area and decided it would be best not to check into a local motel. People might wonder what his business was there, especially if he stayed for a whole week. He chose a town that was somewhat larger than Lake Side and about twenty miles away. He shook his head in disbelief when he saw how the locals were dressed. Hill Billy's, he thought. He was certain his identity would never be discovered by this bunch of clowns. He picked up a copy of the local newspaper to see if there was any news concerning Lake Side. He took the paper to his room and read it from cover to cover. It contained nothing of interest to him.

He changed clothes and straightened his disguise before returning to the lobby. He asked the attendant where the local library was located. He drove there and told the librarian that he was doing some research concerning their town and asked if they kept copies of all the local newspapers. There were no actual copies, but they had all been micro filmed and were available on request. He asked the librarian if he could see all copies from the previous year.

He didn't have to look for very long to piece together what Mr. Johnson had done. He saw all of the land acquisitions of the past year and correctly assumed that they were the work of Mr. Johnson's corporation. He read two editorials by locals decrying the huge increase of Mexican population. That also pointed to Mr. Johnson. Then he ran across a series of articles devoted to the building of the new high school. It was clear that this must be the work of Charles Johnson. No one else in the world would have spent that kind of money on a school with so few students. The last in the series described the donor of the money as a recluse and hinted at the similarities between this philanthropist and Howard Hughes. He thought to himself what a clever ploy. What better way to ingratiate himself with the locals than to build this magnificent school. It also told him that Mr. Johnson had no intention of leaving this area any time soon.

He was glad that this area was big on tourism. He had forgotten to get rid of the New York license plates on his car, but with so many other states represented by the various plates, he was certain his own wouldn't attract any undue attention. He had no problem in locating the new home of Charles Johnson.

Locating his new house hadn't been difficult, but getting close to it was. No matter what sort of zig-zag course he followed, there were always locked gates that prevented him from getting a close look at the house. At four different locations he felt the presence of armed guards. He hadn't actually seen any weapons, but he was certain they were there. This smelled of the security of a man named Hans. He remembered what it had been like in Perdido. Nevertheless, he was unwilling to give up so soon. He would try some other method than a drive-by shooting. His brothers thought that he was on a suicide mission, but he had no idea of getting himself killed while exacting his revenge.

By nightfall of the second day, he had come to the conclusion that if he was to be successful, it would have to be from long range. Even a successful attempt left him no means of a speedy retreat. The roads were too winding and rough. He would need a better plan. That meant that the weapons he had brought with him were inadequate.

The next morning, he visited a sporting goods store nor far from his motel. He asked a man in the front of the store if they sold deer rifles. The salesman directed him to the back of the store. He saw several rifles hanging from the wall, but there did not seem to be anyone else around. He stood patiently until suddenly a salesman appeared.

"Can I help you, sir?"

"Yeah, I been thinking about buying a deer rifle. You seem to have a bunch."

"Yes, we do. We sell a lot of them. It isn't the season now, but it's always cheaper to buy in the off-season. What did you have in mind?"

"I was thinking maybe a 30.06. I've never hunted in this state before. Would that be a good choice?"

"It's one of our most popular calibers. Would you like to look at what we have on hand?"

"Sure, show me what you got."

He looked at four different guns before he asked, "How much is this one?"

"Well, normally during season it would run about $500, but I could let you have that one for $450 You'll probably be wanting a scope for it, won't you?"

"How much more is that gonna run?"

"I'll mount it for you for another $100, okay?"

"Okay, will I be able to take it with me, or is there some sort of waiting period?"

"Not much of one. If you'll let me see your driver's license, I have to run in it through a routine check before we can let you take the weapon out of the store."

He reluctantly reached for his billfold and extracted a rather worn driver's license. The man looked it over curiously and then said, "New York, huh? We don't get many hunters from that neck of the woods."

"Well, hunting's not that good back East. Too many people and not enough game."

"Well, it's been pretty good around here. Here's a little pamphlet that will explain all the rules and regulations of our hunting seasons. The state is divided into different zones with different seasons for each zone. Do you want some ammunition for the gun?"

"Sure, throw in a couple of boxes."

"You'll be able to pick up the gun by 10:00 o'clock tomorrow morning."

He didn't want to appear too anxious, so he waited for two days before he went back to pick up the gun. He told the clerk that he had been too busy to come by the day before. He checked all the screws on the newly mounted scope to make sure that it was secure. He asked if the man had a carrying case for the weapon. He coughed up another $28 for the case and left the store. He stashed the rifle in the trunk of his car and made a circle route in the general vicinity of the house he knew was Charley Johnson's. Once more he was convinced there was no way he could ever get past all the roadblocks to the house. Even with the range of his new weapon, there was simply no way he would ever get close enough to use it.

Then after two hours of circling the roads, it came to him. There were no roadblocks on the lake itself. Perhaps if he rented a boat, he might be able to get close enough to get a shot. He had no idea how to go about renting a boat. It was a thing he had never attempted before. He saw signs up ahead that advertised a marina. That would be a good place to start. He drove on and parked on the large parking lot. He then walked down a stairway to a large floating dock.

The man behind the desk wore an outfit that strongly suggested that he was in charge. His outfit was similar to that of an admiral.

"What can I do for you, sailor?"

"Well, I've always wanted to take a boat ride on a lake like this. Do you have boats for rent?"

"Of course we do. That's how we make a living. Exactly what kind of craft did you have in mind?"

"Well, I'm not really sure what you call it, but I'd like to have something that's really fast."

"Why? Are you going skiing?"

"No, I just would like to feel the sensation of speed out on the water. I've been a passenger in the boat of a friend of mine, but I've never gotten to drive one myself."

"Lots of people like that feeling you just described. It's a real kick. Will you be taking anybody out with you?"

"No, I'm alone here. I live in a big city up north, and I'm just down here on a little business and a vacation at the same time. How much does it cost rent one of the fast ones?"

"That depends on how long you want to keep her out. How long did you have in mind?"

"Oh, for today, no more than an hour or two. How much would that be?"

"Well, it's $100 an hour. We also insist on a three hundred dollar deposit to cover any damage the boat might incur while you're out."

"Well, here's the $300. What else?"

"I'll need to see your drivers license."

He fumbled in his wallet for the license which matched all the other phony ID he carried. The man gave it a cursory glance and handed it back to him.

"Do you have any experience at all with motor craft?"

"Not really. Is there much to it?"

"No, I'll give you a short course in about everything you'll need to know. Follow me."

He followed the man to a sleek 20-footer that was powered by twin 150 horse Mercury outboard engines. He put a key into the ignition, turned it, and smiled as the engines roared. He then showed him the forward, neutral, and reverse gears.

"Here's the choke. If for any reason you should stop, you might have to choke her a little to get her going again. Any questions?"

"No, I think I can handle it. What do I do if it should quit for some reason?"

"Here's how we handle that. Here's a cell phone with the Marina's number on it. Just dial us and we'll come looking for you. You're a little overdressed for a boat ride. Do you have any other more casual clothes with you?"

"No, this is all I brought. This suit is an old one, so it won't make any difference if I spill something on it."

"Okay. Check your watch. We'll be expecting you back in a couple of hours."

"Do you have a map of the lake, just in case I should get a little turned around?"

"Sure, I'll go inside and get you one."

He pulled away slowly from the dock and headed in the general direction of the Johnson abode. He waited until he was outside the cove of the marina before he opened the twin engines to full throttle. The man hadn't been kidding. It was an exhilarating experience.

As he approached Charley's cove, he slowed the boat down to a crawl. He had never seen this view of the house before. He had seen the landward side of the house through binoculars, but he had never seen the veranda that gave the place such a great view of the lake. He would have liked to get an even better look at the place, but he dared go no closer. In the back of his mind was always the thought that you should never underestimate the security of the man named Hans. He would come back later for a better look. He continued his cruise to fill out the two hours of his rental. He didn't want to cut it short because he didn't want the marina to wonder why he kept coming back if he didn't enjoy it enough to use up his rental time.

"Well, did you enjoy your ride?"

"Yeah, it was a hoot. I'll be coming back some time tomorrow. You can keep the $300 deposit. I'll just leave it with you."

"Fine, lots of our regulars do that. It saves on the paper work. Any idea what time you might be back tomorrow? I'll save this boat for you if I know when for certain you'll be back."

"Well, I have to work kinda late tomorrow. Is there any rule about staying a little late after dark?"

"No, we have'em equipped for night time running. You have to be careful, though, if you're not used to being out at night. It's really easy to get lost. There's lots of landmarks that are visible during the day that disappear at night. I'd suggest that you at least head in the general direction of the marina before it gets really dark."

"Okay, I'll keep that in mind. Thanks for the tip. I'm really looking forward to another cruise tomorrow. I'll see you then."

As he drove off, he was wondering how he was going to get such a bulky weapon on board the rented craft. There simply was no logical explanation he could make to the man at the marina as to why he would need a weapon of that type on board for a fun cruise. Still, there had to be a way to get the rifle on board. Otherwise, the whole idea was futile.

As he sat watching TV in his motel room, it came to him. There was no way to take the rifle to the boat, but there was a way to take the boat to the rifle. All he had to do was to stash the rifle in a place he could reach with the boat. He would explore for such a place when he made his next trip out in the boat.

About an hour before sundown the next day he returned to the marina. The old man was waiting for him when he arrived.

"Well, I was about to give up on you. Don't forget what I told you about heading back a little before it gets dead dark. Here's the key."

"Okay, I'll cut it a little short. I sure don't want to get lost out there."

He made no effort to return to the Johnson cove. That was not the purpose of this ride. What he was looking for was a lake access road in an area that was off the beaten path. He dismissed three such roads as too accessible to the public before he found one that would suit his needs. This road did not come completely down to the lake; it stopped about fifty yards short of the shoreline. There was a small sandy beach where a man could push his boat ashore without damage to the hull of the boat. He was certain it would be easy to conceal the rifle nearby and pick it up along the way.

Having found what he was looking for, he cut the trip short and returned to the marina before nightfall.

"I didn't mean to scare you about getting lost. You could have stayed at least another thirty minutes with no problems in getting lost."

"Yeah, I know. I just wasn't in the mood tonight for some reason. I had a lousy day on the job. I think I'll come back tomorrow evening and try it again."

"Okay, I'll reserve the boat for you if you're sure you'll be back tomorrow."

"I'll be back tomorrow for sure."

"What time?"

"Same as today, I'm afraid. I have to work long hours."

"What do you do, if you don't mind my askin'?"

"I'm in sales. Sometimes it's good, and sometimes it's not. I'll see you tomorrow."

It took more than two hours of driving to find the road he had discovered the night before. He drove down it as far as he could and shut down his car. He got out and looked around for a good place to hide his rifle. A natural depression some 15 yards off the trail to the lake seemed to be the best place to hide the weapon. He was glad of the case he'd bought to protect the gun from the elements. He was certain a rain shower would do the gun no harm. He left it there out of sight and returned to his car.

That evening he returned about an hour sooner than he had the previous day to the marina.

"Still afraid of the dark, huh?"

"Oh, I suppose a little bit. Is my boat ready to go?"

"Sure is. I think if you keep this up, it might be cheaper for you to buy one."

"Funny you should say that. I was thinking the same thing myself just last night. How much would a rig like this one run?"

"Oh, I'm not sure exactly. I think this one sold new for in the neighborhood of $30,000 to $40,000. I can't be for sure. I'm not the one who buys them. The man who owns the marina is the one who buys and sells the boats and motors. Sometimes he can make you a real deal on a used one that he's not gonna rent the next year."

"Well, if I decide to buy one, I'll listen to what he has to say. Thanks."

He pulled out slowly and headed in the opposite direction of the one he intended to pursue. He made a wide circle around the spot where he had hidden the rifle. He would have liked to put the boat ashore and check on the weapon, but other craft were in the general vicinity. He headed on down to the Johnson Cove and took out the binoculars he had purchased earlier that day. He tried to gauge the exact distance his bullet would have to travel to have a killing affect. At best it would be a long shot, but he could see no alternative. He let the boat drift at the edge of the cove while he kept a constant view of the veranda. He was about ready to start his return trip to the marina when he saw the door open and one person make an appearance on the veranda. He started his engine and slowly edged his way a little closer to be certain of the identity of the person on the veranda. It was Alice.

He was a little disappointed. He had hoped it would be either Charley or Hans. He turned his boat around and headed back toward the marina. There were several elements of his plan to be plotted before he tried the actual kill. The major one was the escape. He had never considered a suicide mission. Life was too good to end it on an impossible assassination attempt.

When he returned to the marina, he told the old man that he would probably be back for the next three days.

"Well, I see you're really into this thing. Have you considered what I told you about maybe buying this rig or one a lot like it?"

"Yeah, I'm givin' it a lot of thought. I'll see you tomorrow."

When he got back to the motel, he sat up in bed thinking. How could he affect an escape after he took his shot? What should he do with the rifle after the shot? What should he do with the boat? Where should he park his car to make the fastest getaway? Should he dump the car quickly and rely on public transportation for his return trip to New York? All of these things had to be answered before he could act.

The first thing he decided was that he would avoid any means of public transportation. The car would be his best bet if he made no mistakes. He would not use the road which led to the place where he had stashed his rifle. It was too rough and crooked to make a rapid escape. He would find a hard surface road that led to the lake. He would park his car there and hitch a ride to the marina. He would take the boat to the cove where the rifle was hidden and put it in the boat. Then he would head for Johnson's Cove. Once there, he would wait for his opportunity. When it presented itself, he would take his shot and then dump the rifle in deep water. Then he would motor toward his car. He would use his use and his knowledge of explosives to take care of the boat. After all, even though his brothers had been more than willing to take the credit for the blow-up of the Universal boardroom and the super tanker, he had designed the actual explosives that did the trick. He would set a timer on the boat, head it out toward the middle of the lake at slow speed, get in his car and leave at a speed that would attract very little attention. By the time the boat exploded, he would be well on his way back to New York. He turned out the light and got the best night's sleep he had enjoyed for years.

****

He could hardly wait for the day to be over. Just the anticipation of finally getting his shot at Charley Johnson made him happy. He sat around and drank coffee most of the morning. Then he took his car and had it fully serviced to make ready for his getaway. It was ironic that his vehicle was equipped with the device which Mr. Johnson had developed. That device would let him make his escape with hardly any chance of needing to stop along the way for gasoline

At about the usual time he showed up at the marina. It was a beautiful evening and promised to be a terrific full moon night. He told the marina man that he had overcome his fear of getting lost and that he would be a little later in getting back that night.

It went as he had visualized it. He motored to the point where he could retrieve his rifle and checked it out as best he could without firing it. He then headed in the general direction of Johnson Cove. When he got to the point that he thought was as close as he dared to get, he cut the engines and let the boat drift. He would not attempt a shot before the end of twilight.

The lack of a wind allowed him to remain in the position he had wanted.

It was almost 8:30 and there had been no activity on the veranda. Now the waiting was becoming almost unmanageable. He smoked two cigarettes and was about to light his third when he saw the door open to the veranda. Two people appeared. The first was Charley and following close behind was Alice. They stood and stared out into the night. All other boat traffic had called it quits for the night. He eased the rifle up to his shoulder and fixed the telescopic sight on Charley. He squeezed the trigger gently and was surprised at the recoil of the gun. He heard a distant scream as he fired up the engines and made his way toward his car. In deep water he deposited the rifle. He then began to set the timer for the small amount of plastic explosive he had attached to the section of the boat closest to the gasoline tanks. He beached the boat and got out. Then he turned the boat with great difficulty toward the open lake. He had left the engines in neutral and had tied a strong cord to the lever which controlled the gears. He pulled the cord that was tied to the gearshift lever and the boat began a slow journey toward the middle of the lake. Ten minutes later the explosion shook the whole area as Diego made his way back to the main highway.

On the veranda, Charley knelt over Alice's body. He had reached down to pick up a stray piece of paper just as Diego had fired his only shot. If he had remained in an upright position, the bullet that had struck Alice would certainly have hit him. He made a quick 911 call and then called his guards to alert them that medical people would be on the way and not to delay their passage. Then he got in touch with Hans and told him what had happened. He was there five minutes ahead of the ambulance.

"Is she still alive?"

"I think so, but the wound is pretty bad. Take a look."

He looked and slowly shook his head. "You're right, it's pretty bad. I think it missed the heart, but if I were guessing, I'd say it probably got the liver. Where the hell are the doctors?"

"You gotta remember this isn't Perdido. We don't command the same respect and attention we'd get if this had happened there."

"I know that. I've seen a lot of blood in my life, but I've never seen it running out of someone I liked as much as Alice. I hope to God they're not too late."

Alice regained consciousness briefly on the way to the hospital. The emergency team did their best to stop the flow of blood as they rushed her along with Charley to the nearest hospital.

"Hang in there, honey. It's gonna be alright."

"I'll try, Charley. I got a lot of pain. Are you okay?"

"Yes, don't you worry about me. You just save your strength and hang in there."

She drifted into an unconscious state and never did recover from it. She was pronounced DOA at the hospital. Charley had never felt such grief, not even the loss of his eldest son and grandson had affected him like this. He fell to uncontrollable sobbing and could not answer the questions of the police officers assigned to investigate.

It was Hans who took control and escorted him back to his house. He did not try to make any conversation. When they got back to the house, he put his arm around him and almost carried him to his bed. He poured him a stiff drink of bourbon and insisted that he drink it. He then helped him undress and put him gently into bed.'

The next morning Hans had fixed a small breakfast for himself and Charley. They first had coffee, and Hans waited to see how Charley was emotionally before he started asking questions.

"You got any idea who?"

"Not really, but if I had to make a bet, I'd make it on the brothers."

"Why do you say that, Hans?"

"I just think it's a lot more personal to them than your other enemies. The oldest one, what's his name? Yeah, Diego. I think he's a certifiable nut case. I should have killed all three of them when I rescued Juan. I promise you this. If I find out any of them had anything to do with this, I promise you that I will take out all three."

"I hope you take out whoever was responsible. It won't bring her back, but I won't sleep good again until whoever did this is in his grave. I got to call Billy now and tell him what's happened. He'll take it hard because he loved her almost as much as I did. He'll want to be here for the funeral, but I don't think I want him to risk it. What do you think?"

"I think you're right. It's too risky, but that doesn't mean he'll listen to you. I think you'll just be wasting your time to try to talk him out of it."

"Well, I'm gonna try."

He tried, but as Hans had predicted, it was no use. He would fly in to the nearest airport on the first flight he could catch. Luisa would stay in Perdido with their daughter, but there was no way he would miss being with his father at a time like this. He managed to control his own tears until he had finished his conversation with Charley.

Charley had hoped that the locals would not make a big deal of this, but it was impossible to downplay the death of the wife of the richest man around, also the wife of the town's chief benefactor. Charley would not allow any photographers around his house or the morgue which held the body. He refused all interviews and announced that the funeral would be a strictly private affair for close members of the family. He also announced that the burial would take place in the local cemetery

On the day after the funeral, he finally had to answer a lot of questions from the local police. He gave them no information that would have been useful in trying to apprehend the killer. The State Police were more persistent with their questions.

"Come on, Mr. Johnson, surely you can think of someone who might have wanted you dead, can't you?"

"Of course, but it's just that there are so many that I don't think they would be of any value to you."

"Why don't you let us be the judge of that. Just give us something to go on."

"Okay, here goes. How about anybody connected with Universal Oil or any of the other major oil companies. If that isn't enough suspects, try the whole of the Mafia, or any of the big shots of the so-called Big Three. Is that enough suspects?"

"Too many I'm afraid. There isn't any way you could narrow it down for us, is there?"

"Not really. Now listen, guys, you don't get to be in the position I'm in without making a lot of enemies. It just comes with the territory. Why don't you leave me a number where I can get hold of you if I think of anything. I'm really tired, and I'd like to just lay down and try to get some rest. Could we call it quits for today?"

"Sure, Mr. Johnson. Here's a card with my number on it. Call us any time if you think of anything that might be of help."

"Will do."

Billy made the trip to the Ozarks for the first time. He was there in plenty of time for the funeral and did provide some consolation for his father. His own sadness was overwhelming at times, for his friendship with Alice had become far more than the usual stepmother relationship. He remained with his father for a little more than a week before he decided that he had to return to his wife and daughter.

It was the day after Billy's departure that the sudden change in Charley became evident. Hans was the first to notice. He left his work crews to their own devices and went to visit Charley early in the morning. There was no discernable difference in his outward appearance, but the tone of his voice was something Hans had never heard before.

"I want them dead."

"Who?"

"The brothers. I'm 99% sure that they're responsible. What do you think?"

"I think you're probably right. What if you're wrong?"

"Who gives a shit. They all deserve to die. If they weren't responsible for this one, we know they were responsible for some of the previous attempts."

"Got any ideas about how we, I mean I, should go about eliminating them?"

"No, I'll leave that up to you. I would like for you to make it a priority item. The sooner I know they're dead, the sooner I'll be able to rest easy."

"Well, I gotta tell you, Charley, that this is a side of you that I've never seen before. Can I ask you something?"

"Sure. Fire away."

"Have you ever been this angry before?"

"Yes, one time."

"Tell me about it if you can."

"I'm sure you'll recognize the moment. Do you remember the night of my wedding to Alice?"

"Sure, I remember. I tried to have you killed that night. I killed that miserable sheriff for lousing up my plan."

"Yeah, that's right. After I saw Billy get hit, I went after the man who had shot him. You picked him off from long range, but I didn't know that. I had a pistol and I shot the man in the head. I didn't know he was already dead. It wouldn't have made any difference. I felt I had to do something that was completely foreign to my nature. I had to shoot that man. Now I have almost the same feeling. I say almost because I don't feel the need to actually do the killing, but I need to know that they're dead. Can you understand that?"

"Not really. I hardly ever let my feelings get mixed up with my work Most of the people I've killed were not a result of emotion."

"Are you comfortable about going after them in their home territory?"

"I don't know if comfortable is a good word. I have confidence that I can do the job. I have rarely felt comfortable on any assignment."

"Will you need any special equipment?"

"I don't think so. When do you want me to take off?"

"Well, I think they might be on their guard right now. Let's let them think they're home free before we try to hit them. I'd like for you to do a little investigation of the murder of Alice before you strike out for New York. I'd just like to confirm my suspicion before you hit them."

"Okay, I'll spend a week looking into that before I take off. Is that enough time to satisfy you?"

"Yes, that should do it. Where do you think you should start looking?"

"Well, since the shot that killed her came from a boat, I think the logical spot to start would be the marinas in this area."

"I agree. Get started."

****

It took less than three days for Hans to put together what had actually happened. When he questioned the man who had rented the boat to Diego, he was certain that he had put an end to the mystery. Of course the man who had repeatedly rented the boat had used an alias, but Hans was not deceived. There were three things that led Hans to the conclusion that the killer was Diego de los Santos. The short stature of the man, his swarthy complexion, and a just a slight trace of a foreign accent. When he reported back to Charley, it was enough to convince him that he had identified the killer. The green light was now flashing for Hans to proceed.

He had decided to use the Johnson's private jet to make his way to the north. He would be flown to Philadelphia and make that the base for his operation. The plane would return immediately to Perdido, leaving him on his own to make his getaway back to the Ozarks. He wished there was some way for him to avoid the trip to Perdido to gain access to the jet, but there was no place close by with a long enough runway to accommodate the jet. He would allow three days for the trip by car back to

Perdido to use the jet. He was afraid to make use of any means of public transportation for fear that he would be restricted in the number of weapons he could take on the trip. He took with him three pistols, a silencer, a sniper rifle with a night scope, and an M-16 with three clips of ammo. He considered explosives, but decided he wanted the pleasure of seeing the men die, something explosives could not produce.

He wasn't certain whether he would try to take out all three at once or manage it one at a time. There were disadvantages either way. It might be more dangerous to take on all three at once, but the element of surprise would certainly be on his side. Killing one at a time might be safer, but it would no doubt take longer. After the first killing, the other two would be more on guard and less likely to walk into a situation that left them at risk.

Before he left Perdido, he made certain that the pilot would understand the part he would have to play when they arrived in Philly. The pilot would have to get to the car rental place with everything it would take to rent a small car, one that would not attract attention. Then he would drive that car back to the airport where Charley would take over. Then he was to fly the plane back to Perdido where he would report back to Terry who would inform Charley as to what had happened.

The weather was good, and the flight to Philly was uneventful. The pilot had no problem renting a small car and was back to the airport in no time. He helped Hans unload his weapons from the plane to the car and quickly made ready to take off for the return flight to Perdido. Hans had worked in Philly before and knew exactly where he wanted to stay. He drove to a small motel on the outskirts of the city. He wore a disguise because he feared that someone might remember him from a previous stay. He requested a room on the downstairs and as far away from other occupied rooms as possible. He explained that he was sensitive to noise and a very light sleeper. When the motel manager seemed hesitant, he dropped a $50 bill on the desk which the man pocketed and handed him a room key. He was certain that no one saw him unload the weapons from his car to his room.

After settling into his room, Hans picked up the telephone. His call was to the same man who had given him the location of the brothers on his rescue of Juan.

"Hello, old friend. It's me again."

"Hans, is that you?"

"That's right. How've you been?"

"I've been better. You were kinda late with that payment for my information. Let me guess. You want some more information on the same bunch, don't you?"

"Right, as usual. What have you heard recently about the de los Santos brothers?"

"Are we talking the same amount for this information?"

"No, it's worth twice as much this time, and I guarantee you the payment won't be late this time."

"Well, the oldest has been going around town bragging how he pulled a hit on the richest man in the world. He says he'll be going back soon to get the billionaire bastard himself."

"Any thing else?"

"His brothers are scared shitless that you'll be here soon looking for them. They're right, aren't they?"

"One more thing. Have they changed their base of operations?"

"No, they got the same room in the same hotel they had the last time you were here. It wouldn't surprise me if they made a sudden move, but the last I heard they were staying put."

"I'm sorry I couldn't pay you in cash last time. Did you have any problem getting the check I sent you cashed?"

"Only I had to take it out of town to cash it. I didn't dare cash it here. These guys got lots of connections, and it would be my death if they found I cashed a check on any of you guys."

"Well, this one will be in cash, old friend, I promise."

He hung up the phone and relaxed on the bed for a few minutes. It was a relief to know that he would not have to spend a lot of time tracking down his quarry. Still, he had no real plan of action. This did not concern him much. He had been in similar situations many times. His ability to improvise had always been one of his best qualities. He would drive to New York tomorrow.

He chose what he considered to be his best disguise before he took off in his car and headed toward New York City. He checked into a large hotel not far from the one he knew housed his quarry. He was relatively certain that it would be several days before he dared move against them. He had binoculars for long range spying, and he was willing to spend as long it would take to establish a pattern of behavior that would help him plan a strategy.

On the first day he noticed that it was Carlos who first left the hotel. At about 7:30 he went down to a corner newsstand and purchased a newspaper. He was not out of the hotel for more than twenty minutes. It was not until almost 10:30 that Jorge went out and returned with what looked like a bag containing food from a nearby fast food restaurant. At about twelve noon he went himself to this same restaurant to see if it might provide any special opportunity for an ambush. He saw one possibility, but he knew he would have to wait for quite some time to be sure that this place was a part of their daily routine.

It was almost dark when the trio left together in a cab. He had no way of knowing what their destination was, but they did not return until almost midnight. He took down the number of the taxi, hoping to bribe the driver that next night into telling him what their destination had been. He knew that it would be virtually impossible to follow them to their destination in his own car. He had been exposed to the snarls of New York City traffic before.

The next morning it was Carlos again who went out for the morning news. The time element was almost exactly the same as the day before. The time was the same, but it was Diego who went out to the fast food restaurant. He returned in about the same time frame. None of the three made another appearance until all three left in the same cab they had used the night before. Now he knew for a certainty that he must find out where this taxi took them at this time. There were two ways to find out. He could pay the driver enough to divulge their destination, or he could take another cab and follow them until they themselves showed him where they liked to spend the night. He would try their driver first.

The next day it was Carlos again who went out for the morning paper. That pattern had been established. Hans suspected he was the only one of the three who took much interest in events other than those directly involved in gang activity and therefore the only one who ever looked at a paper. It was Carlos also who went out for their lunch. This duty seemed to rotate. Each man had gone once in the three days he had witnessed.

He was watching to see if the same cab would be there to take them for their nighttime trip. He was relieved when the cab bearing the same number showed up in front of the Hotel about 30 minutes before their usual departure. He walked up toward the cab and signaled that he would like a ride, but he got no response from the driver. He walked on up to the cab and tapped on the window. The driver rolled down the window on the passenger side part way and said, "Sorry, Mac, I'm waiting for a fare. I won't be back this way for more than an hour. You better try to get another ride."

"That's okay, I'm really not in need of a ride right now. I just would like little information."

"Well, I ain't the tourist bureau. What you want to know?"

"These guys you're waitin' for, are they the same guys you picked up here last night?"

"Who's wantin' to know?"

"Just me."

"What do you want with those guys. They're bad hombres from what I hear. My advice would be to stay away from them."

"Probably very sound advice, but I got some big money dealing with them, and I really got to get together with them."

"Why don't you just wait here until they come down and do your business right here?"

"The business I have to do isn't the type you do right out here in the open, if you get my drift."

"I think I know what you mean. Lots of money involved, right?"

"You bet, mister. You catch on quick. Listen, there could be a lot of money in this for you if you'll just let me know where they're headed."

"That money would just be for my funeral if they found out I told you where they hang out. They'll pay me a grand just for tellin' them that you were here askin' questions."

"Well, how's this? I'll give you two grand tonight to tell me where they're headed, and if I can get in contact with them, I'll give you another two grand after you've delivered them and come back here."

"Talk's cheap. Let me see the dough."

He pulled out a roll of hundred dollar bills and peeled of twenty of them. He offered them to the driver, but he shook his head no.

"What's the matter. You got something against makin' an honest dollar?"

"No, but I got a lot against wakin' up dead. It would take a lot more than a lousy two grand for me to risk my neck doin' business with you."

"How much?"

"Five grand up front and five more when you connect with these guys."

"Done. Here's another three G's. Don't hold out for any more. I could just get another cab to follow you to where they're headed and save myself a chunk of change."

"Okay, let me see the rest of the money."

He pulled another 30 bills from another pocket and handed them to the driver. He counted them slowly before he put them in a bag under the seat.

"Okay, almost every night unless there's something special goin' on, I take them to the Aristocrat Club down town. Do you know where that's at?"

"Yeah, I been there. How long do they usually stay?"

"It varies. The club closes at two, but they never stay that late. Usually they ring for me between 12:30 and 1:00. I wish I knew a little more about what kind of business you have with these guys."

"You do know what kind of business they're in, don't you?"

"Yeah, I do."

"Well, I'm a wholesaler in the same business. If you don't queer this deal for me by tellin' 'em about this conversation, you could be in line for a lot more dough than you just put in that bag."

"Okay, my lips are sealed. I got two kids who want to go to college. No way they're ever gonna get there on what I make."

"Smart thinking."

He left and went back to his own hotel room. He waited there until past the time that he thought the brothers would have taken their ride to the Aristocrat Club. Then he flagged down a cab and told him to take him to the Aristocrat Club. He despised driving in New York City.

"That's a pretty fancy place. You a member there?"

"No, I got a friend who is, and he told me he'd meet me there. You ever been inside the place?"

"Who me? You gotta be kiddin'. They wouldn't let stiffs like me inside the door. Come to think of it, the way you're dressed they might not let you in unless your friend is a big shot."

"He is, one of the biggest. I'm not a name-dropper or I'd tell you who. I'm sure you'd recognize the name."

"Maybe, I do know the names of some of the guys who go there a lot. You do business with some of the guys with long foreign names?"

"Sometimes. Listen, I don't think my friend will be driving his car tonight. How much would it cost for me to have you pick me up about 10:30?"

"Probably another $50. I get off about 10:00."

"Okay, here's another 50, and there's a good tip for you if you're waiting outside for me at about 10:30."

"It's a deal."

He wore dark glasses and a long overcoat as part of his disguise. The coat was to help cover up the pistol he carried and the silencer that was attached. The doorman asked to see his membership card, and when he admitted that he had none, he was almost summarily bounced from inside the club. He had anticipated that something like this might happen and was holding two hundred dollar bills in his left hand. He waved these at the doorman as he was escorted to the door, and their retreat ended abruptly. The doorman released his grip on Hans elbow, and stepped away from him.

"Will you be wanting a table, or will you be sitting at the bar?"

"A table for two would be nice. I have a lady friend who I think will be here shortly."

"Follow me, sir. I think I have one toward the back that would be excellent for entertaining a lady."

He watched carefully as he was led toward the back of this expansive club. He was hoping that he would be able to pick up exactly where the brothers would be sitting. He had imagined that they would be together, but the only one he was able to spot was Jorge. He was seated between two gorgeous looking ladies who seemed extremely interested in what he had to say. He was certain that neither of the three took any notice of his arrival. He took a seat at the small table and ordered his favorite drink, Chivas Regal scotch straight up. He left the waiter a $5 tip.

After twenty minutes of sizing up the club, he decided to visit the nearest of the three restrooms. It was fairly small for such a large club, and he was surprised. There was no one else in the rest room. He took a seat in one of the five stalls and waited. He hadn't really thought about actually making a hit on the brothers tonight, but gold is where you find it.

Ten minutes of sitting on the stool with the door closed and his pants still buttoned went by slowly. Then it happened. It was the sound of the voices of Carlos and Jorge. He heard them as they lined up together at the urinal and discussed the probability of getting laid that night. He slipped the pistol with the silencer attached out from underneath his coat and stood up. He pushed the door of the stall open quickly.

His first shot hit Jorge in the back of the head, and he was dead before he hit the floor. His second and third shots struck Carlos in the upper body, and he crumpled to the floor without uttering a sound. Just to make sure, he walked over to both bodies and put another round into the heads of both.

He knew that it was far too early for his cab to waiting for him, but he knew he would be able to find another. He had seen several waiting outside along side the exit. Some might be already be taken, but he was certain the tip he could offer would be enough to lure one of them into taking him back to his hotel. He smiled as he walked toward the exit. Two down and one to go.

He found a cab easily and went back to his hotel. Once there he packed his bag quickly, went to his rented car, and drove directly back to Philadelphia. He checked back into the motel he had taken when he first arrived. He was certain that it would be a good idea to lay low for a while. He also was certain that Diego would be a hard man to find for a few days when he saw what had happened to his brothers. It probably wouldn't take him long to figure out who was responsible, but he would have a hard time locating the killer. He knew the motel phone was not tapped, so he decided to call Charley. It was late to be calling Missouri, but he was sure Charley would want to know what had happened.

"What do you intend to do about Diego? He's the one who shot Alice. He's the one I hate more than the others."

"I know that. I'm pretty sure he'll lay low for a while. He'll be hard to find, but don't worry, I'll get him. The only assignment I ever failed was when I let you get away. It may take a while to locate him, but when I do, he's history. What's going on there in Missouri?"

"It's unbelievable the support I'm getting from the town's people. The funeral was supposed be a private affair, but I think everyone in town must have showed up at the church and the cemetery. I wish Billy could have stayed longer, but I know he had to get back to his own family. How long do you think it will take to finish this job? I feel a lot safer when you're closer to us."

"Thanks for the vote of confidence, but I can't say with any certainty how long he'll hide out. I also have no idea how the other people in his organization will take it. I'm not sure they even know that one of their own was responsible for Alice's death. When they find that out, and I'm sure they will, they may decide they no longer need his services. If that's the case, they'll probably do my job for me. He's known in their organization as a man who makes irresponsible decisions. That's something they try to avoid at all costs."

"Stay after it then till he's finished, one way or the other. How do you plan to get back here?"

"That's something I'll just have to play by ear. I don't know where this all will end, so I can't say how I'll make it back. Probably the safest way would be to rent another car and just drive it back to Missouri. I'll get back to you as quick as I can."

****

Hans had been right. The big boss indeed had learned of Diego's abortive attempt to hit Charley Johnson. He wasted no time in letting him know that he wanted to see him in person. Two days later he was standing in front The Man.

"I think you know why you're here, don't you?"

"Yeah, I suppose so. It's about my brothers, isn't it?"

"Not directly, no. I'll miss the service they provided for the organization, but that's not really why you're here. Did you have any authorization to make a trip to Missouri and try to kill the richest man in the world?"

"No, but...."

"No buts. Don't you know that he's aware that you work for us? Now he's already sent someone here for revenge for the death of his wife. How many of our organization do you suppose he'll have to kill before he's satisfied?"

"I don't know. I think he's really only out to kill me. I don't think he'll go after anyone else in the organization."

"Maybe not, but we never know what someone will do when someone he cares about is murdered. Often they become irrational. When that happens, no one around them is safe. I don't care much for the feeling of not being safe, do you?"

"No, I don't. Listen, I think I know who killed my brothers. All I'm asking is a chance to go after him. I'm not asking for any help. Just me alone."

"Good thing you're not asking, because you're certainly not going to get any help from us. If we knew how to get in touch with Mr. Johnson, we just might make a deal with him."

"What kind of deal?"

"Your hide for a promise not to make any more hits on the people of the organization. If I thought he'd accept that offer, I'd kill you myself. You've made too many rash decisions, Diego. We can't have people like you in our organization. Don't stand there shaking. I'm not going to kill you. I will just put out the word that you are no longer affiliated with our organization. Whatever money you have in your own private account you can keep. My advice to you is to get out of the country as fast as you can."

"Couldn't I just have one more chance to make things right. If I kill this man who murdered my brothers, wouldn't that even the score?"

"How do you figure that? That'll just piss him off even more. He'll send more and more of his people after us. When a man with that much money gets pissed, you have to be very careful not to get in his way. We don't intend to get in his way of taking his revenge out on you. If you decide to go after him or any of his people, you could bring his wrath down on us. So if you even act like you want to go after him, I'll take you out myself. Now get out of here."

He swallowed hard and headed for the street. He knew that he was finished with the organization. Now, more than ever, he wanted the death of Charles Johnson. The man had cheated him out of his birthright, killed his brothers, and now had taken away the only security he had ever known by causing him to lose his connection with the organization.

He went to the hotel room that had been his primary residence for several years. He was certain that it would be his last trip to the room. He didn't bother to pack very many clothes, but he did take a variety of pistols with him when he left the room. He had decided that a rifle would not be necessary. It was his poor shot with a rifle that had been the beginning of the end for him and his brothers. This time he would get close enough to do the job with a pistol. Never mind the consequences. If he could not survive the assault, so be it.

He knew that public transportation was out of the question. There was simply no way to take the small arsenal he wanted with him by plane, train or bus. He took a taxi to the bank which had handled millions of dollars for him and his brothers. He withdrew everything he could with no explanation. The bank was used to huge withdrawals since the nature of the drug industry thrives on cash. He took the briefcase filled with $100 dollar bills and flagged another taxi to a rent-a-car agency. There he rented an inconspicuous small motel for a week and then headed for Lake Side, Missouri.

It was two days later when Hans finally confirmed that Diego had been banished from the mob. It was late in the second day when he learned of the car rental by Diego. From there he scurried to make a flight back to Lake Side to try to intercept the suicide attack he anticipated. He called Charley to warn him of what might be coming his way. The only advice he could give was to make no public appearances and to tighten what security he could around his own residence. He wished that Terry could be there until he could get back, but he knew that Terry could not get there any faster than he could.

He was a little surprised when he got back to Lake Side to find that Charley himself had arranged a perimeter defense that was solid. There was little for him to do except to stay close and be certain that Charley did not relax and take any unnecessary chances. He didn't think Diego was a man of much patience, and he was certain that no more than a week would pass before he made his attempt.

****

Four days passed without incident. Two false alarms had been set off when well-meaning council members had tried to make impromptu visits to add their condolences to Charley on the death of his wife. They were also nervous about whether her death might cause Charley to lose his enthusiasm for the new school or Lake Side in general. They were stopped unceremoniously and hustled away before ever getting close to their chief benefactor.

It was the night of the fifth day that Diego decided to make his move. He had scouted for the preceding three days, looking for a weakness in the perimeter defense. He had witnessed the changing of the guard at a key location the last two nights. He had noticed a certain laxity on the part of the guards who were coming on duty. He believed if he could eliminate these three, he would be able to get within range of his quarry. He smiled when he remembered how close he had gotten to Mr. Johnson on that morning when he had mistakenly killed Tink, believing him to be his youngest brother, Juan. He would not make the same mistake again. This time the range would be so short that there could be no mistake.

He crawled to within 15 yards of the three guards. He paused behind a huge oak tree to gather his thoughts. He waited until one of the guards walked past the tree to relieve himself. As he walked past, he grabbed him around the neck to cut off any sound he might try to make. Before he could attract any attention from the other two guards, he stabbed him twice with a stiletto and waited for the body to go limp. Then he laid the body down gently and resumed his vigil behind the tree. He knew now that his chances were greatly increased with only two men between him and his goal.

He reached inside his coat and pulled out a silencer which he attached to the largest of the three pistols he was carrying. It was almost ten minutes before another of the guards walked in his general direction. When the guard was no more than five yards away, he fired twice and the man went down without a sound.

The third man waited at his post for another 10 minutes before his curiosity got the better of him. Why neither of his fellow guards had not returned from a call of nature was strange, strange enough to require an investigation. He saw Diego with his pistol pointed at him just before he fired the first of three shots. He made one feeble cry before falling to the ground.

He felt these guards were the last obstacle between him and Charley Johnson. There would be no more crawling. He walked slowly, using the shadows of the huge trees to cover his movement.

Back at the house, Hans gave Charley a shake to awaken him "Hey, get up. Something is wrong. Something is going down. I can feel it."

"What do you mean?"

"I just tried to make contact with checkpoint number 6, and I got no response."

He shook head twice in an effort to wake up, then cautiously got to his feet. "Let's go try it again. They may have been just takin' a crap or something."

"I doubt it. My gut feeling tells me something is wrong. Didn't you instruct the guards that someone had to be on the alert at all times?"

"Sure, but you know how men are. Sometimes they listen, and sometimes they don't."

"How far is that checkpoint from the house?"

"About a half a mile, I think."

"That means if someone has breached that point he could be here in a very short time. Here's what I want you to do. Tell the guards here at the house to take the rest of the night off. Then make your bed so that it will look like you're are still in it. Then I want you to go to the room fartherest away from your bedroom."

"Where are you gonna be?"

"In that closet right over there."

"I got one request. If you can with no danger to yourself, take him alive."

"Why?"

"Because I'd like to be the one who pulls the trigger on that worthless son-of-a-bitch."

"Are you sure you can do it?"

"Oh, yeah. Don't worry about that. I can definitely do it."

They tried twice more to reach one of the guards at the checkpoint and got no answer. They double-checked the equipment to make sure there had been no electrical malfunction. There had been none. Hans was certain that this would be the night that Diego would make his move. He told Charley to take his place in hiding and to be ready with a pistol of his own just in case.

As he approached the house, Diego could not believe his good fortune. There were no lights inside the house, no guards that he could see, and no watch dogs. He was prepared to jimmy any type of lock that he might find on the door. He was amazed to find it would not be necessary. He was starting to imagine that Mr. Johnson was not at home. With Hans in charge of security, there was no way it could be this easy for him to gain entrance into the house. Once inside, he waited for his eyes to adjust to the diminished light. He checked the two downstairs bedrooms and found no trace of anyone having slept in either. If he was in the house, he must be upstairs. Experience told him that stairs often squeak, but there was no choice but to climb slowly and hope he could escape detection.

At the top of the stairs, he found two small bedrooms unoccupied. He slipped past what he perceived to be the master bathroom and edged toward what seemed to be a larger bedroom. The door was partially open, and as he slowly increased the opening, he could see the outline of a man sleeping in the bed. He was glad he had reloaded the large caliber pistol with the silencer. This time there would be no mistake. He moved two steps closer before he opened fire. He stood over the bundle of clothes that had been arranged to give one the impression of a man and continued to shoot until a click told him the gun was out of shells. It was the click that Hans had been waiting for. In a single motion he opened the closet door and delivered a blow to the back of Diego's head. He crumpled to the floor while Hans stood over him to see if he was indeed unconscious. He reached into his pocket and produced a pair of handcuffs. He rolled the body over onto its stomach and cuffed the man's hands behind his back. Then he yelled as loud as he could, "It's all over, Charley. You can come on up here and show me if you have the balls to finish the job."

He climbed the stairs two at a time with his pistol drawn. As he entered the bedroom, Hans turned on the overhead lights to give Charley a clear view of what was lying on the floor.

"Well, are you ready to do it?"

"Not yet."

"Why not?"

"I want to wait until the lousy bastard is conscious. I want him to see that it's me that's about to end his miserable life."

"It could be awhile before he wakes up. I hit him a pretty good lick."

"Would it speed things up to dump some cold water on him?"

"Probably, but what's your hurry. You should savor this moment. Things like this only come about once in a lifetime."

"Go get some water. I can hardly wait."

Hans was back in a few minutes with a large pitcher of cold water. He stooped over the prone body and poured generously onto the head. There was a slight groan but no movement at first. Then gradually the eyes opened, and he struggled to free his hands. When he could not, he began to curse, first in Spanish and then in English. The first face he could distinguish was Hans, but he became aware of Charley's presence.

"Hans, help this stupid son-of-a-bitch to his feet."

Hans grabbed him by the hair and pulled him to a sitting position. The he grabbed him underneath both arms and literally threw him against the wall. His knees were shaking but he managed to remain upright.

"So we finally meet again. I guess I haven't really seen you since just before your father's funeral. You know, my first impression of you was that you were mean, vicious, and stupid. I can now see that my first impression was correct. Did you really think I was stupid enough to let an idiot like you come into my house and shoot me while I was asleep?"

"Yeah, I thought there was a good chance. What the hell do you know about security? If it weren't for this asshole standing beside you, you'd been dead a long time ago."

"Possibly, but I was smart enough to get this man to come over to our side early in the power struggle."

"Yeah, I guess you do have to get some credit for brains. Your invention got the Japs over here, and you screwed my family out of a share of the profits. That did take some brains. The one thing you've always lacked is balls."

"I take it then that you have more balls than me."

"Damned straight."

"Not any more."

He put all six bullets into the groin area. Blood spattered all over but Charley never flinched. He stood over the body, relishing what his eyes showed him. Hans allowed him to stand there silently for several minutes before speaking.

"You know, you've just done something I never did."

"What the hell are you talking about? I know you've killed dozens, maybe hundreds of men. I remember all those teenagers coming to Perdido that I hear you stood over and finished off if they showed any signs of life. I was close to you when you killed Toyota Man and that Japanese assassin, so why tell me now that I've just done something that you've never done?"

"That's not what I meant. I confess I've killed lots of men, but none I ever killed gave me the satisfaction that I just saw on your face. All of those men were nothing more than a job. I was paid to do what I did. There was never any real emotion in the killing. I never stood over a man I killed with such joy."

"You've never lost a wife, have you?"

"No, I've never been married. My line of work would make a thing like marriage impossible. I guess that's why I can't identify with what you're feeling."

"What do you think we should do with the body? Should the authorities be notified?"

"Before we decide on that, I think we should run out to the checkpoint and see exactly how much damage he created in getting here. If we find what I think we'll find, there'll be three more bodies to worry about. It would be a lot easier to explain his body here if we link him to the bodies we'll find out there. If for some reason we don't find any bodies out there, I think we

137

should just bury him in a spot where he's least likely to be found. I'm sure no one is gonna come looking for him."

"Do you want me to go with you to the checkpoint?"

"No real reason to, but I don't think you want to stay here alone with that body. Maybe you better come along with me."

They rode to the checkpoint in silence. Hans made a quick check of the electrical system and found everything in working order. It took even less time for him to discover the three bodies. He walked back to the car and was not surprised that Charley was visibly shaken. His hands were shaking so badly that he could not roll down the window of the car.

"Try to relax. I know it's gonna be hard, but you gotta try. I found the three bodies, just as I thought I would, one stabbed and the other two shot. I think we better call the authorities. If you want me to, I'll take the responsibility for shooting Diego. I'm sure it will be a justifiable homicide."

"No, I want the world to know that Charley Johnson is the one who got rid of this vermin. I think there's people out there who think I couldn't possibly do something like this. I'll let you call the police when we get back to the house."

"I don't think we should go back to the house right now. Let's just drive into town and tell our story to the police in person."

There were only two policemen on duty when they arrived at the station. One was asleep, and the other was reading a detective magazine. Their knock on the door awakened the one who had been sleeping. He was the superior officer. He jumped to his feet as they entered.

"What brings you boys around at this ungodly time of night?"

"Serious business, I'm afraid. There's been several homicides we'd like to report."

"Say, who are you? Wait a minute, I know this other guy. He's the one who donated all the money to build the new school. Who are you?"

"My name is Hans, and I'm the chief of security for Mr. Johnson. Do you want to hear what we have to say?"

"Sure, go ahead."

"A couple of hours ago, our security was breached by an individual who murdered three of our guards. He then broke into Mr. Johnson's house and tried to kill him, but Mr. Johnson shot and killed him. His body is still lying there in the house, and the three guards are still by their posts. We can take whoever investigates to the spot where they'll find the bodies."

"Then what you're saying is that we got four dead bodies to be looking at. Wow! We've never had anything like this before. I'm afraid this is more than we can handle. I think I better get in contact with the State Police."

"You're probably right. How long do you think it will take them to get here?"

"My guess would be that they got somebody close enough to get here in less than an hour. Hey, Zack, what is that number they gave us to get a hold of them in an emergency?"

He dialed the number, told the man who answered that they had an emergency, and asked how long it would take someone to get there. The man on the other end of the line replied that it would take him a minute to see who was closest to Lake Side. After a two minute pause, he told him that an officer would be there in about 30 minutes.

In slightly less than 30 minutes, two uniformed officers of the State Police knocked on the door. The one in charge seemed to recognize Charley and nodded in his direction and then walked on toward the deputy.

"Can you tell me a little more precisely what the emergency is?"

"I think these gentlemen could do a better job of that than I could."

Hans stepped slightly in the direction of the man in charge. He hesitated briefly before starting his explanation.

"My name is Hans Van Braun. I am the chief of security for Mr. Charley Johnson. Perhaps you've heard of him."

"That's right, we have. That's him standing behind you, isn't it?"

"Yes, it is. You must have heard that Mr. Johnson has lots of enemies here in the U.S. The events of tonight are living proof of that."

"Go on."

"Well, tonight one of those enemies breached the security around his residence and killed three of the on-duty guards. When we couldn't make contact with the guards with our surveillance system, we suspected correctly that we were about to be attacked. We set things up to look like Mr. Johnson was asleep in his bed. When the killer got to the bedroom, he emptied his pistol into what he thought was the sleeping Mr. Johnson. Then Mr. Johnson came from out of hiding and struck his assailant on the head and knocked him unconscious. Later, Mr. Johnson shot and killed the man."

"Did either of you recognize the assailant?"

"Yes, his name is Diego de los Santos. He is the oldest son of the man who at one time was the senior partner in Mr. Johnson's corporation."

"What reason did he have to try to kill Mr. Johnson?"

"Greed and revenge. When his father was killed in Mexico, neither he nor his brothers were allowed to share in their father's inheritance. All three tried several time to have Mr. Johnson killed, but they failed. Recently this man's two younger brothers were the victims of a shooting in a nightclub in New York City. This man may have thought that Mr. Johnson was somehow responsible for the death of his brothers. It's hard to say. All three were members of the Mafia, and shootings of that type are common to those who deal in drugs."

"I see. Well, let's go to the house and start there. I'll radio for the crime scene boys to join us as quickly as they can."

Hans got behind the wheel. He knew Charley's nerves were in no condition to drive. He chuckled as he said, "There's one thing I'm glad of."

"What's that?"

"I'm glad I took the cuffs off him before we left. It's gonna be pretty hard to explain how you shot him six times in self-defense."

"Yeah, I suppose so. What do you think they'll do?"

"Impossible to say. If there's an ambitious prosecuting attorney in this state, what better way to show off your skill and zeal for the law than to try to convict the richest man in the world of first degree murder?"

"Do you really think I'll have to stand trial?"

"Possibly, but I wouldn't worry. You're pretty popular around here. All of the jury pool will know about the death of your wife. I don't think you'll have any trouble establishing the fact that he was the one who shot Alice. Besides, there's another important thing you got going for you."

"Yeah, what's that?"

"Money. You can get the best lawyers in the world to represent you. You saw what they did for O.J. Everyone in the world knew he was guilty, and still he walked."

"That's true. Do you think I'll have to take the stand?"

"I have no idea. Your lawyers will have to answer that for you if it comes to that."

When they got back to the house, Hans led the troopers to the upstairs bedroom. Diego's gun was lying close to his body. The troopers whispered to each other, and Hans could not make out what they were saying. The man in charge then turned to Hans and said, "Have you guys touched or moved anything since the shootings?"

"No, sir. It's just exactly the way it was. We left right after the shooting to go check on the guards at the checkpoint."

"Well, as soon as we get this crime scene roped off, I think we better head out to the check point and rope it off before somebody moves something. We'll just take a minute."

Shortly thereafter, Hans directed them to the checkpoint by leading the way. He showed them the electronic warning system that had given them a reason to suspect that an intruder was on the way. Then he showed them the location of the three bodies. This time the two officers were forced to rope off a much larger area with the yellow crime scene ribbon. When they finished that, they were ready to return to the house.

At the house, the officer in charge said to Charley, "I'm sorry Mr. Johnson, but I'm going to have to ask you to give me the weapon that you used. I'm sure it will be a part of the investigation. Do you have any other weapons?"

"No, that's the only one I had. I put it away down stairs. I'll have to go get it for you."

"And how about you, sir? Do you have any weapons?"

"Yes, I do. I have several and a permit for every one of them. If I'm not charged with any crime, I don't think there's any reason for you to want me to surrender them to you. My job in security makes those weapons necessary."

"Nevertheless, until we sort all of this out and decide if anyone is going to be charged, I'm going to ask you to surrender those weapons."

"I'll do so if you'll post some of your own men around Mr. Johnson's property for his protection. This man is dead, but he by no means represents all the potential enemies that Mr. Johnson has. I'll insist on some sort of police protection if I have to give up my weapons."

"I'll see what we can do."

****

It was hard for Charley to get used to all the uniformed security he now had. He had been surrounded by security in Perdido, but it had never been like this. Most of the security there had been covert, but here it was obvious. Anyone who wished Mr. Johnson harm had to realize that getting to him would be difficult.

It was a week before a decision was made. The officer who came to place Charley under arrest read him his rights but did not bother to handcuff him. At the station he was photographed and finger printed and allowed to make a phone call. His battery of lawyers was there in less than 15 minutes. They were from the most prestigious criminal law firm of the day. The firm was James, Williamson, Abrams, and Kelly.

Arraignment was scheduled for the following day. His lawyers were shocked when the prosecutor asked the judge to deny bail. His reason was that Mr. Johnson might well use his huge wealth to flee the country. The judge set the bail at ten million dollars which was posted within the hour.

An hour after his release, he sat discussing the case with his lawyers. He had decided to tell them most of the truth. The only item he failed to mention was the handcuffs that Diego had been wearing when he was shot.

"So what do you guys think? Can I make a good case of self-defense?"

"That's hard to say. We're not sure exactly what the defense will be. We'll wait until the prosecution shows its hand by showing what they have in the way of discovery. I've got to tell you that self-defense may be hard for the jury to swallow since the man was shot six times."

"What other defense is there?"

"I think we're going to have to look into temporary insanity. You aren't the first man to lose control when confronted by a man who you were certain killed someone very dear to him. If we decide to go that way, you'll have to be prepared for lots of questions from our psychologists as well as theirs."

"Will I be required to take the stand?"

"That depends on how the case is going. If I think we are way ahead with the jury, I'd rather you didn't, but if things are shaky, you might have to tell the jury what was on your mind when you shot him. Do you think you could stand up to an intense cross-examination?"

"Yeah, I think so. What are some of the questions you think they'll be most likely to ask?"

"Your feelings about the man you shot. They'll no doubt go back to the animosity you two had for each other since the time of his father's death and he and his brothers were left out of the will. They'll also blame you directly or indirectly with the death of his brothers. What can you tell us about that?"

"You want the truth don't you? Well, here it goes. After Alice was shot and killed, I had my chief of security look into the matter. It didn't take him very long for him to show some pictures of the son-of-a-bitch to the marina operators. One of them gave him a positive ID of Diego."

"So what happened then?"

"I sent Hans to New York City with instructions to take out all three of the de los Santos brothers."

"And he was only successful with two. What happened next?"

"I can't verify any of this, but from what my chief of security learned, Diego was dumped from his mob connections. They were afraid that I might declare war on the whole organization, and they weren't ready to go to war with me. They know how many soldiers I could buy if push really came to shove. I think they dumped him to try to appease me. From that point we began to prepare for some sort of suicide attack."

"Why did Hans kill the other two if your main quarrel was with Diego?"

"This wasn't their only their attempt on our lives. They collectively hired a bunch of mercenaries to attack us from the air. We blew their aircraft out of the sky before they even got to Perdido. They were also instrumental in leading a bunch of disgruntled out-of-work auto workers down to try to do as much damage as they could."

"Would that also have been a threat to your life?"

"I think so. It might not have been the main thrust of their attack, but I'm sure if I had been a target, I wouldn't have been spared."

"Anything else?"

"Yes, Diego himself came alone after we abandoned my adjustment for the current system of powering vehicles down the road. We think he might have come to try to assassinate his youngest brother who was and still is our CEO. He got closer to my house than we thought he could because he knew the land so well. The young man who invented the process that powers nearly all cars now was taking a morning stroll and wandered too close to where he was hiding. He killed the young man who we called Tink. He was about the same height and build as his brother Juan. It was still pretty dark, so we're pretty sure he thought it was his brother."

"So how did you come to be in control of his invention?"

"When he came to us seeking financial help for his invention, I insisted that he make me his sole heir if something should happen to him."

"And why did you do this?"

"Because we were in the middle of negotiations with the Japanese to move their plants to Perdido. We couldn't afford to let things get bogged down in court over his patent. His share of the profits from the Japanese move to Perdido would have made him a very wealthy man, but he was told of the risks."

"Well, that may come up. I'm pretty sure they'll try to get in all the dirt they can about the death of your lawyer and your former boss. They'll also bring up the deaths of your son and his family. You were once wanted by the authorities on murder charges, and they tried to have you extradited from Mexico to face those charges. What happened?"

"There was a meeting between the State Department of the U.S. and that of Mexico. My former partner, Juan de los Santos, acting as my attorney, completely squelched all the charges against me. They gave up on the whole process when they saw they really had no case against me. I guess it might look pretty bad when you consider how many people around me have been killed."

"You haven't mentioned how your first partner, Mr. de los Santos, met his demise or why you were his sole heir."

"Well, it was a cooperative venture. My invention, or patent if you will, and his capital. Neither of us could have succeeded without the other. We agreed in writing before we even started out to make each other the sole heir if something should happen to either of us."

"Why didn't he leave anything at all to his sons?"

"He'd been unhappy with all four of them since not one had been willing to come back to Mexico to help him run his business."

"And just what was his business?"

"Well, I didn't know it till just before his death, but I found out too late that he was in the business of growing marijuana. All of the tenants who farmed his land were growing it as their principal crop."

"How did you find out about it?"

"My son who was dating his niece found a huge supply of it one night in the barn of one of his tenants. When he asked her about it, she told him it was one of the worst kept secrets in Mexico. Almost everyone knew, but no one seemed to care. The old man was a throw-back. He was held in high esteem by most of his countrymen. He was extremely proud of his heritage and the de los Santos' name."

"And how did he die?"

"When we began to make considerable progress with my adjustment, he had vision enough to see what it could lead to. He wanted out of the drug business. He knew if he stayed in it in any way at all that the Japanese could never be persuaded to move to Perdido. The problem was that the people he supplied wanted his tenants to keep on growing the stuff for them. When he refused to insist that his tenants continue to grow the stuff, the members of the de las Rosas family arranged for a parlay at night on neutral territory. There they set up an ambush, and he was killed."

"Were there any other people killed at this parlay?"

"Yes, Hans was there because he suspected the rival family might try something like that. He killed some of their family. Since both families had lost some of its members they decided to end the feud."

"Tell me more about your head of security."

"That's a really strange story. Are you sure you want to hear it?"

"Of course we do. We can't give you the best defense unless we have all the facts. We definitely don't want there to be any big surprises once the trial starts."

"Okay, here goes. The major oil companies were really pissed when they saw what might happen if my adjustment was a success. They sent Hans down to try to kill both me and my partner. He was given a certain time limit to do the job, but luck was on my side, and he failed. For fear that he might tell the authorities who had authorized the attempts to kill us, they sent another hit man nick-named Toyota Man down to Perdido to assassinate Hans. He knew of this guy's reputation at never failing to kill whoever he went after, so he surrendered to us to save his own life. Most everybody thought we should execute him, but my partner thought he might be useful in the way of security. Boy, was he right. Later when Toyota Man came after me, Hans saw through his disguise and killed him. He saved me more than once."

"Can you give me another example of his expertise in security?"

"I can give you several if you want them. When the brothers hired French mercenaries to come and attack us, he found out what they were up to and shot their asses right out of the sky. When a mob of unemployed auto workers came down and opened fire on the plant, he surrounded them and managed to kill all but a handful. Diego was the only one who escaped."

"Any others?"

"Yeah, I took him to Japan with me to prove to them that my adjustment would not harm their cars. We never were completely sure who hired the guy, but an assassin tried to get us while we worked. Hans recognized that the man was different from the waiter we'd had the day before. When he approached close enough to kill me, Hans finished him off with a single shot to the head."

"What part did he play in Diego's death at the house?"

"It was him who thought we should disguise my bed to look like I was asleep there. He sent the rest of our security home so that Diego could gain easy entry into the house. He advised me where to hide myself to be in position to nail him if he took the bait."

"Why didn't he handle the job himself? It would have been logical to let a man of his experience in these things to take care of Diego."

"Because I insisted that I be the one who took care of the miserable bastard. He killed my wife. Can you understand that?"

"Yes, I can. Let me ask you this. Did you intend to kill him that night, or were your intentions just to turn him over to the police?"

"I'm not really sure about that. We talked about turning him in to the police, but I'd be lying to you if I didn't say that I hoped he'd try something so I could kill him."

"What exactly did he try?"

"He made a lunge at me while I had my pistol aimed directly at him. He said I didn't have the balls to shoot anybody. He said he had a lot more balls than I did."

"Is that why all of your shots were aimed at his balls?"

"Yeah, he was so proud of those balls. I don't regret for a minute what I did."

"I can understand that. You see, what we have to do is make the jury believe that when he made a move toward you that you felt threatened and fired your gun. Once you began firing, you simply couldn't stop. I hope they don't attach any significance to the shots to the balls. That might signify your hatred of the man. We won't try to hide that hatred, we just don't want to emphasize it. What can you tell me about the blow-up of Universal Oil's board room and their super tanker?"

"Not a whole lot. I really didn't have anything to do with either one. Both of them were arranged by my partner. I didn't even know about them until I read about them in the papers."

"Who actually set the charges for the blow-ups?"

"He never really said, but I do know it was one of his three sons. They didn't want to do it, but he threatened them with something, and they agreed."

"You don't know what he threatened them with?"

"No, I heard them arguing over the phone, but their conversation was in Spanish, so I couldn't understand what they were saying."

"Okay, then you're sure there's no way they can link any of this directly to you. That's good. How about the youngest brother, the one who's currently your CEO. How did he get involved in all this?"

"I had never met any of the brothers until they came to Perdido for their father's funeral. I knew that Juan was his favorite. He was the only who hadn't run off to the States to become a part of organized crime. Juan was making his way to the top in legitimate business in South America. The other three hated him for the preferential treatment he'd received during their childhood. He understood business negotiations because that was what he did for a large corporation. He was the only one who wasn't bitter about not being remembered in his father's will. He knew his brothers wouldn't take it lying down, that they'd try something, so he agreed to join with us. I think more to spite his brothers than anything else."

"And how has that worked out?"

"Great. He has his father's knack for compromise. That has been his greatest asset to our company. It was him who convinced the Japanese to come to Perdido. Did I tell you that his brothers actually kidnapped him and dragged him off to New York?"

"No, you didn't. What did they want for his ransom?"

"They wanted a piece of the corporation."

"You obviously didn't give them that, so how did he wind up back in Perdido?"

"Hans rescued him from right under their noses. He always regretted that he didn't kill all three of them that night when he had the chance. He was afraid the noise might interfere with their getaway."

"We've heard in a roundabout way of protestors that were headed for Perdido on a bus. What can you tell me about that?"

"Not much, I'm afraid. Hans told me he stopped the bus to make sure the protestors were unarmed. They weren't, and there was a shoot-out. What became of the bus and the protestors I never knew. Don't ask, don't tell. Isn't that the way it goes these days?"

"Right. In political circles it's called plausible deniability. It gives the man at the top an out when his subordinates do things he knows about but doesn't want his name mixed up in what they did. This Hans seems like a most remarkable man."

"He is. He's one of the most resourceful men I've ever been around. I know we'd be out of business if it hadn't been for him."

"Will he take the stand in your defense?"

"Of course, but he may have to take the fifth if they ask too many questions about his dealings with the oil companies when he was employed by them. I don't want him put in any danger of having charges brought against him."

"We may have to tread carefully around some of the issues to avoid perjury charges, but I'm sure we can do that."

"How long do you think it will be until the actual trial begins?"

"I'm going to ask for a continuance that will set the date back for at least six weeks. Can your son and your CEO be counted on to be here and testify if they're called? We can't subpoena them since they are not residing here in the States."

"I'm sure they'll both come voluntarily. My son Billy would already be here if his wife wasn't having a tough time with her second pregnancy. Juan will need a little more time to get everything lined up business-wise. How long do you think the trial will last?"

"There's really no way to know about these things. It could be three days, or it could be three months. Have you any idea just how big this trial is going to be? I don't think you do. America loves trials that involve celebrities, and like it or not, you are a celebrity. There most likely will be television cameras in the courtroom. I think a lot of it may depend on how much latitude the judge will allow the prosecution to go fishing for something in your past that will paint a picture of you as a murderer."

"How much coaching will it take for the witnesses on our side take?"

"We don't like the word "coaching." We prefer to think of it as instruction. Coaching has a really negative connotation."

"I see. How much instruction then will they need?"

"Not a whole lot with Billy and your CEO, but we'll have to be careful with Hans. His background as an assassin for the oil companies is something we'll skirt around as best we can."

"I'm really tired. Can we call it quits for today?"

"Sure, just remember that you're out on bail. Don't take any sudden trips to Perdido or any place else. The prosecution has already made the statement that you might flee the country, so don't give them any opportunity to have your bail revoked."

"I'm not going anywhere."

"I don't think you realize yet what a circus this thing might become. I don't think this will last nearly as long as the OJ trial, but we never know about these things."

****

His lawyer had been correct. This thing did have circus potential. A billionaire on trial for murder, the Mafia knee deep in the whole affair, a man known to be a killer now in the roll of hero, maybe the whole truth about the oil companies and their collusion with the Big Three------what else could the American public wish for?

Hans had spent more time with the lawyers getting his "instruction" than Charley had. He was never told exactly how he was to answer certain questions, but there was a long list of questions that he had been told to answer with "I'll take the fifth." A lot of these centered on his activities when he had been employed by the Oil Companies, especially Universal. He was to answer only in general terms about his destruction of the French mercenaries, the break-up of the auto workers who invaded Perdido, and the destruction of the teenage gang and the buses in which they were riding. He was to vehemently deny any responsibility for the death of the two de los Santos brothers in the New York City night club. Charley had arranged an airtight alibi for him for the time frame in which the brothers had been shot.

****

Charley could not believe the huge crowd that had gathered outside the courthouse. This was the county courthouse some forty miles distant from Lake Side. The State Police were on duty outside to keep the crowd from breaking into the courthouse. There were huge arguments among the media for the limited space that had been provided for them.

"I tried to tell you it was going to be like this. It will get worse on a daily basis. Most of the media here are from Missouri. I see Kansas City, St. Louis, and Jeff City. By the third day, we'll see lots bigger towns than those here. I'll be surprised if the prosecution doesn't ask for a change of venue. He'll claim it's to avoid overcrowding, but the real reason is that they know they won't be able to find twelve people out of this jury pool that would convict you after they're told what you've done here in Lake Side."

"I hope you're right."

"I get paid to be right. Did you notice that they've added a couple of big time prosecutors to their team?"

"Do you know these guys?"

"Yeah, I know them, and they know me. We've locked horns several times before."

"How have you done against them?"

"I think 7 out of 10. They're good, but my team is better."

"You make this sound like some kind of game."

"It is. Didn't you know that? You really don't think cases like this one are settled by truth and justice, do you?"

"I've often heard the expression that one gets as much justice as he can afford. Is that really true?"

"Generally speaking, yes. And if that's true, you certainly are going to be well blessed with justice."

"I think by the time I pay my legal fees you guys will be pretty well blessed as well."

"True, but consider yourself lucky in that regard."

"How so?"

"We usually base our fee on a percentage of the net worth of our client. If what I hear is true, the 10 million were charging you is chicken feed."

"I guess if you look at it that way, you're right. Have you had a chance to analyze the prosecution's witness list?"

"Sure. I don't see any big surprises yet, but I'm pretty sure they'll try to slip someone in before it's over."

****

The selection process of the jury took more than a week. The prosecution had indeed asked for and received a change of venue, and the trial had been moved to Kansas City. While the courtroom there was several times the size of the previous one, it still could not accommodate the media or the crowd of would-be onlookers. Court TV had the largest contingent of reporters in attendance. It seemed to Charley that every legal mind of any stature was there to give an opinion on the progress of the case.

Both sides used all their peremptory challenges in the jury selection process. When it was all said and done, it was likely that neither side was completely satisfied with the jurors that had been selected. Four alternates were chosen should anything happen to one of the chosen 12.

It was time for opening arguments. The prosecution began with the tallest of the four men at their bench.

"He's not their best," Charley's lawyer confided to him. "They'll save him for their closing argument. This guy is good, but sometimes he turns a jury off by being a little too long winded."

"I would like to begin by congratulating the members of the jury on their selection. I'm sure each and every one of you will do your best to see that justice is done in this case. What is at stake here is an opportunity to prove to the rest of the world that here in Missouri, no matter how much money you have, you are not above the law."

"The man on trial here today is in some respects a remarkable man. He invented a process which revolutionized the present day means of automotive travel. Even after that, he made that process obsolete with another revolutionary type of propulsion. Everyone who drives today owes something to this man. With the world running short of oil, he searched for and found a way for Americans to still be able to travel. Yet with all his accomplishments, we are forced to look closely into this man's character."

"After first obtaining a patent for what he called the "adjustment," it wasn't long before the lawyer who helped him get that patent was mysteriously killed. No one was convicted of that crime. Then soon after, his boss at the garage also was murdered. His boss was the man who had introduced him to his lawyer. He was probably the only other person who knew the details of their contract. I say that because the lawyer and his boss were cousins. Again, that murder was never solved."

"Shortly thereafter with no notice, Mr. Johnson set out for what seemed like parts unknown. He advised both of his sons to meet him in New Mexico at the home of their aunt. Three days after their arrival, his oldest son, daughter-in-law and grandson were found murdered not very far from the aunt's residence. Once again, murders that were never solved."

"The United States Justice Department investigated and issued a warrant for his arrest. I concede that the evidence against Mr. Johnson is purely circumstantial, but he was the only one with connections to all five murder victims. Mr. Johnson fought the extradition and with the aid of the powerful political influence of his partner, Juan de los Santos senior, he never came back to the United Stated to answer the charges against him. He claimed that he couldn't get a fair trial here in the United States, yet here he is today facing American justice, seemingly unafraid. My how things have changed since he became one of the richest men in the world. Perhaps he thinks his inventions, patents, and wealth will absolve him of all responsibility for all these unexplained events."

"Now let's get back to some other unexplained events. Mr. Johnson has always suffered paranoia about the American Oil Companies."

"You honor, I object to the term paranoia. I was not aware that learned council was also an expert in the field of psychiatry."

"I'll withdraw that term, your honor, and replace it with unreasonable fear."

"I'll object again to the word "unreasonable." I think future events proved that Mr. Johnson's fears were fully justified."

"I'll reserve my ruling on the word unreasonable until the man has a chance to explain why he was so afraid."

"Mr. Johnson has never denied that he stole a vehicle in his flight to escape the United States. He was almost stopped short of the Mexican Border by the Texas Rangers, and when he refused to obey their lawful order to stop, he was wounded in a shootout. Shortly thereafter, he went into a partnership agreement with Juan de los Santos senior."

"Almost immediately the violence escalated. First there was a mysterious explosion in the boardroom of Universal Oil that took the lives of most of their board of directors. Not too long after that, a super tanker of the same company exploded with the loss of the total cargo and the lives of twenty-three crew members. The company had reason to believe that Mr. Johnson was responsible for both actions, though they could never prove his part in these explosions."

"Next, we ask you to think about this. There were two busloads of Mexican teenagers who were coming from Mexico City for a peaceful demonstration about the hiring practices of the Johnson Corporation. Once again, they mysteriously disappeared. Neither the buses nor the teenagers were ever seen again. The tally that time was 50 dead as far as we can tell. Quite a coincidence, wouldn't you say?"

"After luring the Japanese auto-makers to Perdido, there was an explosion of an airplane not far from that town. The plane was of Costa Rican registry. According to their records, the plane had been leased to a bunch of vacationers wishing to visit Mexico. Mr. Johnson's Corporation insisted that the plane was filled with French mercenaries who were sent to destroy his plant. There was so little left of the aircraft that it was impossible to tell who really was on board. According to Costa Rican records, there were thirty people on board, no survivors. The number of dead people just keeps on growing and growing."

"Your honor, I'm going to have to object to about everything the prosecution has said. I wasn't aware that my client had been charged with anything but the murder of Diego de los Santos."

"I only include these facts, your honor, to show the jury a pattern of behavior."

"I'll overrule the objection for now, but I'll be waiting to see if any of these things you've described have any basis in fact."

"I'll continue. A large group of unemployed United States auto workers made a pilgrimage to Perdido to protest the loss of their jobs in Detroit. They were surrounded and annihilated with automatic weapons before they ever got a chance to protest. Only two of twenty-five survived."

"Now let's get back to the United States. Just recently two of the de los Santos brothers were shot and killed in a nightclub in New York City. The prime suspect for the shootings is Hans Van Braun, the number one hit man for the Johnson Corporation."

"Once again, your honor, I object. Hans Van Braun has never been charged with anything to do with the death of the de los Santos brothers in New York City. Like all the rest of his opening statement, the prosecution is filling the jury with scraps of truth surrounded by rumors, innuendo and downright falsehoods. How long must we listen to this before we finally get to the only charge made against my client?"

"I think your point is well taken. I'll ask the prosecution to move expeditiously toward the charge we are supposed to be trying."

"I was just about to get to that, your honor. Now let me tell the jury something important."

"It's about time."

"Gentlemen, gentlemen, let's stop this bickering right now before we go any further."

"As I was about to say before I was so rudely interrupted, the prosecution is not going to tell you that Diego de los Santos was a good man or a decent human being. We readily admit that he was a member of organized crime. We know he was big into drug trafficking, and that he had "made his bones" as those in the criminal world like to say about a man who has killed another human being. Nor do we deny that he might very well have gone to Mr. Johnson's residence with the intention of killing him."

"We recognize the right of self-defense, but there are limitations. After it appears that the victim had emptied his gun into the trap the defendant had set for him, the coroner's report was that he had been struck on the head, probably with the barrel of a gun. The wetness on his head indicated to the investigating officer that someone had poured water on his head, probably in an attempt to bring him back to consciousness. Red marks around his wrists also indicated that he might have been handcuffed. Now comes the interesting part. Supposedly, he made a sudden movement toward the defendant, whereupon he shot Diego de los Santos six times, including six times to the area of his groin. Six times is a bit much for self-defense, wouldn't you agree?"

He paraded past the jury with a perplexed look on his face as if to say he couldn't possibly see how the defense could claim self-defense

"Is the defense ready for their opening statement?"

"Yes, we are, your honor."

"Then proceed"

"Ladies and gentlemen of the jury, like the prosecutor, I would like to extend my congratulation to you one and all for your selection. However, the congratulations may have to be tempered with condolences if you are forced to sit here day after day and listen to the garbage that the prosecution has just put before you. Virtually nothing in his opening statement had anything to do with the guilt or innocence of Charles Johnson concerning the case you were chosen to decide."

"The one and only thing you have to decide is this. Was the killing of Diego de los Santos justified or not? That is all. None of the other incidents, no matter how tragic, have any relevance in this case. Mr. Johnson was aware that this man hated him and very likely might be in the vicinity the night of the shooting. It's true he laid a clever trap for the man. He arranged for the security around his house to be absent that night. He left the door to the house unlocked so he would have easy and noiseless access to the inside of the house. He arranged his bed to look as though he were asleep in it, while he hid himself in the closet."

"As he suspected, the man was out for blood. At close range he emptied his pistol into the pile of blankets that he thought was Charles Johnson. When he stopped shooting, Mr. Johnson stepped out of the closet and struck the intruder a blow to the head with the barrel of his own gun. That blow rendered the assailant semi but not completely unconscious. When he recovered enough to get to his feet, Mr. Johnson told him he was about to be arrested for the murder of his wife. He lunged forward toward Mr. Johnson, at which time Mr. Johnson began to fire his own weapon. He didn't stop firing until he was out of shells in the gun. I suppose that considering the circumstances, if the gun had held nine or even twenty rounds, he would have kept on firing till the gun was empty. I'm sure he didn't count how many times he fired at the man. I also maintain that not being a professional killer, as the prosecution has admitted that his assailant was, he was not an expert in aiming a pistol. Where the shots hit Diego de los Santos is really of no consequence. When a man who is known to be a killer makes a lunge at you, you simply react. He wanted to have this man arrested and tried for the killing of his wife, nothing more. If he had intended to kill him, why would he have hit him over the head to disable him? Why not just shoot him in the back? The reason is obvious. He wanted only for the man to stand trial for the murder of his wife."

"In spite of all trumped up charges made against him, Charles Johnson is a decent man. Prior to his discovery of the "adjustment," he had nothing more serious than a couple of speeding tickets on his record. He has no record of violent behavior. He is simply a man who loved his wife and family. To people like Diego de los Santos he had already lost a son, a daughter-in-law and grandson, and most recently his wife. I think you could understand if he had shot Diego in the back instead of trying to apprehend him and turn him over to the authorities. He didn't because that is his nature."

"If you are not convinced of what Mr. Johnson is truly like, we'll let you hear from some of the people of Lake Side. They'll be glad to tell you what he's done for the town where he's chosen to make his home. Thank you for your attention."

After that, the judge announced that there would be a recess of about an hour. Television cameras went into action as all of the experts were asked how they thought the opening statements had gone. Opinions varied as to which side had scored a victory in the opening round.

An hour later the judge announced that court was now in sessions. It took several raps of the gavel to bring the court to order. When the noise finally subsided, he asked, "Is the prosecution ready to begin?"

"We are, your honor."

"Then call your first witness."

"We call Nate Newell to the stand."

"Your honor, I object. I can't find this man's name on the witness list."

"Counselor?"

"Your honor, we didn't even know this man existed when we made out the witness list. There was no way his name could have been included. He only notified us yesterday that he had information that might shed some light on these proceedings. We weren't even certain that he could make it here for the beginning of this trial."

Defense counselor leaned forward and whispered into Charley's ear, "Do you know this guy? What can he possibly be here to testify to?"

"No, I never saw him before in my life. I have no idea why he's here."

"I'll allow this man to testify if I find that he has anything relevant to say. I'll have to be the sole judge of what is and isn't relevant. Swear him in."

After the oath was taken, the DA approached the witness and asked., "Would you state your name, please?"

"My name is Nathaniel James Newell. Folks call me Nate."

"Where do you live, Nate?"

"New York City."

"And what do you do there?"

"I drive a cab."

"Do you see anyone in this courtroom that you recognize?"

"Yes, I do."

"Would you point him out?"

"He's the guy sitting just behind the guy on trial?"

"Let the record show that the witness has just pointed out Hans Van Braun as the one person in court that he recognizes. Will you rise and face the jury? Now, are you absolutely certain that you recognize this man?"

"Yes, I am."

"You honor, I object. What possible relevance can there be as to whether this man can identify Hans Van Braun? Hans Van Braun is not on trial here."

"Your honor, Mr. Newell's testimony is intended to show that there was a great hatred by Mr. Johnson for Diego de los Santos. It will show that Mr. Johnson had intended to have him killed long before the night of his death."

"I'll overrule the objection, but I must admonish you to get to the point."

"Thank you, your honor. Now, Mr. Newell, how is it that you recognize this man now identified as Hans Van Braun?"

"He rode in my cab one night in New York City."

"Only once, you say?"

"That's right. I'd never seen him before, and I never saw him again until now."

"Why does this particular fare stick in your mind?"

"It was the night two of the de los Santos brothers got whacked inside the Aristocrat Club."

"Tell us what you remember about that night."

"Well. I was parked outside the hotel where the de los Santo brothers lived. Sometimes they have me take them to the

Aristocrat Club. This guy, yeah the one sitting behind the guy on trial, he comes up to my cab and wants to know where the de los Santos brothers go in a taxi every night."

"And what did you tell him?"

"At first I didn't tell him nothin', but later I told him that they usually go to the Aristocrat Club."

"What's so special about that? Why does that stick so strongly in your mind?"

"This guy offers me a whole bunch of money to tell him where they go at night."

"By they you mean the de los Santos brothers, right?"

"Yeah, that's right. He offered me two grand not to say anything to the brothers about him askin' where they go."

"Did you take his offer?"

"Naw, I held out. I could see he wanted to know real bad so I decided to see if he'd make me a bigger offer."

"Did he?"

"Yeah, he gave me five large in hundred dollar bills."

"Why did he say he wanted to see the de los Santos brothers?"

"Well, he really didn't really come right out and say it, but he hinted that he was in the same business they were in."

"And that would be?"

"Dealin' drugs."

"And you're absolutely sure that the man sitting behind Mr. Johnson is the same man who gave you the five thousand dollars?"

"Yes, I am."

"I have no further questions of this witness."

"Cross examination, counselor?"

"Yes, your honor. Mr. Newell, how many passengers do you deal with in a normal day?"

"It varies. Sometimes on a good night maybe 50, on a real slow night, only a dozen."

"So it stands to reason that you might see hundreds or even thousands of fares in a year's time, right?"

"I suppose so."

"And you're absolutely sure about your identification of Han Van Braun?"

"Yes, I am."

"Let me ask you, what time of day was it when he came up to your cab to ask you about the de los Santos brothers?"

"I'm not sure of the exact time, but it was just starting to get dark."

"That's not exactly the best light is it? Isn't it just possible that the man who gave you the money just looked a lot like Mr. Van Braun?"

"Naw, that's him alright."

"Does he look exactly today the way he looked on the night in question?"

"No, he had a beard and mustache and his hair was a lot longer, but that's him alright."

"Was his hair the same color?"

"No, it was kind of a reddish color then, but I think he may have been wearing a wig."

"And what makes you think that?"

"I don't think the color of the beard and mustache matched exactly the color of his hair, that's all."

"Weren't you afraid that giving this man the location of where the de los Santos brothers could be found might be a risky proposition?"

"Of course I was. That's why I held out for more money."

"And why are you not afraid now?"

"That's an easy one. In case you haven't heard, the de los Santos brothers are all dead."

"I see. No further questions."

"Any redirect?"

"No, your honor."

"The witness may step down."

The next witness called was John Appleby. He was dressed in the uniform of an officer of the law. He strode to the stand with an air of confidence. He was sworn in and took the stand.

"Will you state your full name for the court."

"Johnathan Edward Appleby."

"And what is your occupation?"

"I am a deputy sheriff in Lake Side Missouri."

"Are you familiar with the defendant in this case?"

"Yes, I am."

"Will you tell the court why you know this man?"

"Well, almost everybody in Lake Side knows who he is. They've all seen his picture in the paper and read about all the things he's done. The only time I met him personally was when he and that guy sitting behind him came to the station one night to report a shooting."

"The guy you refer to is Hans Van Braun, right?"

"I guess that's his name."

"Describe that incident for us."

"Well, it was after midnight when they came to the station. The other guy did most of the talking. He said there had been a shooting close to where a bunch of men that he was responsible for had been working. He led us to the body. We found that the man had been shot with what later proved to be a high-powered rifle. We found one empty shell casing which had been fired from the gun next to the body."

"And what did that seem to indicate to you?"

"Well, it would appear that he and whoever shot him had exchanged shots, and he got the worst of it."

"Did you question all of the men who were working nearby?"

"Yes sir, we did."

"Tell the court about the interrogation."

"Kinda strange, really."

"In what way?"

"Well, we questioned quite a few men about everything that went on that night, and we got exactly the same answer to every question. It was almost like they had been rehearsed."

"I'll move to have that last remark stricken from the record, your honor. It calls for a conclusion on the part of the witness."

"I agree. Strike it."

"Did you make a thorough search for the weapon that had fired the shot which killed the man?"

"We did, but we never could find any trace of it."

"Did you identify the victim?"

"Yes, that was easy. He was a local. His name was Henry Walker."

"Tell us what you can about the man."

"He had a reputation for being a loudmouth with a bad temper."

"Had he ever had any altercations with anyone connected to Charley Johnson?"

"Yes, earlier he and a couple of his buddies tangled with Hans in a local bar."

"What caused the trouble?"

"Well, he didn't like the idea of all the Mexicans in the Lake Side vicinity. He claimed they'd be selling dope if the people didn't do something about it. He and his two buddies jumped Hans when he came in to get some beer for the men that were workin' for him."

"Tell us what happened after they jumped him."

"From what the bartender told me, he kicked their asses pretty good. I've been told that he's good at the martial arts."

"I see. Then he very well might have been harboring a grudge against Hans and the Johnson Corporation, right?"

"I suppose he might have."

"Objection again, your honor. Calls for a conclusion, by the witness."

"I agree, although it does seem logical. The jury will disregard the last statement

"I have no further questions."

"Cross examination?"

"Yes, your honor. Were any of these men who attacked Mr. Braun seriously injured in this so-called altercation?"

"No, as far as bar room brawls go, it was pretty tame. No blood, no missing teeth, or broken bones. He actually only tangled with two of the men. The third turned and ran when he saw what happened to the other two."

"What made you suspicious of the way the men answered your questions when you interrogated them?"

"Well, they said the same thing. They had all been drinking beer and having fun. Hans had too much to drink and passed out on a blanket on the ground. They all made a special point of saying he never left the camp or was out of their sight at any time."

"Do you have any real doubts about their testimony?"

"Not really. It just sounded like a recording."

"No further questions."

"The prosecution calls Hans Van Braun."

There was a smile on his face as he walked the short distance to the witness chair. He was trying hard to exude a confidence he did not really feel. For all the criminal activities he had ever taken part in, he had never before been called to the witness stand.

"Will you state your name please?"

"Hans Van Braun."

"And what is your present occupation?"

"I am chief of security for the Charles Johnson Corporation."

"Mr. Van Braun, have you ever killed a man?"

"Yes, I have."

"Really? You don't seem to show any remorse for such a thing."

"Why should I? I was a member of the French Foreign Legion. I saw action on two continents, and there were several occasions that required me to defend myself and my regiment."

"I see. Well, other than your service in the Legion, have you ever killed a man?"

"I'm afraid I'll have to take the fifth on that one."

"Can you tell me how you became the chief of security for so large an organization as the Johnson Corporation?"

"Yes, if you want me to."

"I do."

"Well, I was employed as a trouble shooter for one of the major oil companies. They sent me to Perdido, Mexico, to try to have Mr. Johnson and Mr. de los Santos taken care of."

"By 'taken care of" you mean killed?"

"That's right. I was given a time limit to complete the task. When I failed to do so, they sent their best hit man down to take care of me as well as the other two. He was known to the underworld as Toyota Man. I knew that he never failed on an assignment like that, so I sought refuge in the only place where I would be safe. That was the jail in Perdido. I confessed that I had been sent down to assassinate both Mr. Johnson and Mr. de los Santos."

"And after your confession, they made you their chief of security?"

"Not right away. Mr. Johnson wanted me to be summarily executed, but I convinced Mr. de los Santos that I could be quite valuable in countering whatever moves the oil companies might try next. I told them how Toyota Man tried to have me killed by blowing up the jail where I had been locked up. When the jail blew up as I had predicted, I think they realized what I could do for them."

"So you avoided becoming a victim of Toyota Man?"

"That's right, but he didn't avoid becoming one of my victims."

"You say that with a sense of pride."

"I am proud. He was considered the best in his field of endeavor, and I took him out. It not only saved my life, it gave me the job I have today."

"What can you tell us about the plane that exploded close to Perdido?"

"My connection warned me that the de los Santos brothers had hired a bunch of French mercenaries to fly to Perdido and attack the plant. I got together a small fleet of helicopters to guard against the attack. We saw it coming and shot it out of the sky with a SAM missile."

"There seems to be some disagreement about what was on that plane. There wasn't really enough of the plane left to verify your claim."

"I know there wasn't a whole lot left of the plane. The reason for such a huge explosion was no doubt the amount of explosives and ammunition they were carrying on board. Nevertheless, we found enough fragments of powerful weapons to convince the embassies of three different countries that our version of what happened was the truth."

"What can you tell us about two bus loads of young Mexican teenagers who disappeared on their way to Perdido?"

"Nothing really. We were told they left the City and were headed our way for a huge protest. They never got there. My own suspicion is that the painted the buses another color and sold them. I also think they were paid to do more than protest, so they just took the money and ran."

"And not a single person who was on that bus was ever seen again. Don't you find that very strange, Mr. Van Braun?"

"Not really. From what I've heard, they were a notorious gang there in the City. Unless they were arrested for something, I can't think of any reason why anyone would know what became of them."

"Tell us about your encounter with the Japanese who sneaked into the plant one night."

"Six members of a Japanese gang breached our security one night and attempted to plant explosives to blow up the place. The night watchmen disarmed two of the six, I took care of two, and two escaped."

"And did they succeed in planting explosives?"

"Yes, they did, but our dogs smelled out the location of the explosives, and we managed to defuse them before they went off."

"When you say you took care of two of them, do you mean you killed them?"

"Yes, I did. They refused to halt so I had no choice but to shoot at them, or they too would have escaped."

"You must be a good shot."

"Yes, I am."

"What do you know of the Universal Oil boardroom blow-up and their supertanker?"

"Nothing, nothing at all. I was employed by the oil companies when all that happened. That's one of the reasons they sent me to Perdido."

"Do you have any idea who was responsible for those two explosions?"

"I have no direct knowledge, but I do have my suspicions."

"And what might they be?"

"I think that Juan de los Santos senior had one of his sons in the States arrange for the big bangs. He didn't take kindly to being threatened himself or the people around him. I'm sure he knew it was the oil companies who were his most threatening enemies."

"And just how did he know?"

"I'm not sure, but he had connections. I'm sure that he knew."

"What other business was Mr. de los Santos in before he hooked up with Mr. Johnson?"

"Once again, I have no direct knowledge, but I'm told he was on the wholesale end of selling marijuana."

"How would you describe this Juan de los Santos senior?"

"In some respects he would be considered a dinosaur. He was quite old fashioned in some ways, but he was both feared and respected in most of Mexico. I found that out the hard way when

I attempted to kill him. He had protection from both the State Police and the Federales. He was a man of vision. He could see that Charley's adjustment could be worth millions. He was the one who got the Japanese interested in moving to Perdido. It was his youngest son who actually closed the deal that brought them to Perdido, but it was his idea."

"You seem to admire the man, right?"

"Yes, he saved my life. If it hadn't been for him, I'm sure the others would have lynched me as soon as I surrendered to them."

"Did Mr. Johnson send you to New York to 'take care of' the de los Santos brothers, once and for all?"

"No, he did not."

"Did he ever send you to New York for any reason?"

"Yes, once they kidnapped their youngest brother to hold for ransom. I used one of my former connections to locate them, and managed to make my getaway with him while they were asleep."

"Are you aware that we have a witness who can place you very close to the Aristocrat Club on the night they were shot and killed?"

"And as you are aware that I have several witnesses that can place me a thousand miles away from there the night they were killed?"

"Are these the same witnesses who were so well rehearsed on your alibi the night the Walker man was shot and killed near your camp?"

"Your honor, once again I object to the word 'rehearsed'. There has been no proof that any of their testimony was rehearsed."

"Objection sustained."

"Are these the same men who provided you with an alibi for the Walker killing?"

"I couldn't say for sure. Some of them may be the same."

"That's all the questions I have for now, but don't get too far away. I may want some re-direct."

"Cross examination?"

"Not at this time, your honor. I'd really like some time to spend with my client. Would the prosecution agree to an early adjournment for today? If so, I'll save my cross for this witness until tomorrow."

"I have no objection, your honor."

"Then court is adjourned until 9 tomorrow."

Charley had suggested that all his legal team accompany him back to his home. He wanted to show them exactly how things had gone that night he killed Diego de los Santos. When they were all seated around the dinner table, Charley asked, "Well, how do you think it went today?"

"I'm satisfied that they didn't make any real headway toward proving you murdered the man. I'm sure several of the jurors are going to be sensitive to the fact that Diego killed your wife. I purposely got two jurors who are widowers and were married to their wives for a lot of years. They'll understand the sorrow that goes with losing a loved one. I'm sure they'll empathize with you."

"Were you surprised at anything that happened today?"

"A little bit. I didn't think the judge would give them such latitude as he did in their quest for a pattern of behavior. That didn't help us any, but I don't think it hurt us all that much. Right now I'm thinking you may have to take the stand to answer some of the garbage he brought up."

"That's okay, I'm not afraid to take the stand."

"Have you ever taken the stand before?"

"No, but I think I can hold up under anything they can throw at me. I think tonight we better go over whatever things he might ask that would cause me trouble."

"You're right. We'll go over that right after dinner. Where did all that delicious smelling food come from?"

"I got a Mexican nursemaid for my daughter. She's also a great cook. She keeps the house clean, too. I couldn't do without her."

After dinner, two of the law team wanted to smoke, so Charley invited them to go out onto the veranda. He showed them where Alice had been standing the night she was shot and killed. He told his lead counsel, who had followed him outside, about Han's investigation of all the marinas to find out who had rented a boat the night of the killing. When one marina operator definitely identified Diego, he told him then that this was the point that he had decided that all of the de los Santos brothers had to go.

"I gotta come clean on this. I did send Hans there to kill all three. He got the other two, but Diego got away. Don't worry, I've got an airtight alibi for Hans. He won't crack under pressure."

'It's not Hans I'm worried about. It's you."

"Why me? I'm sure I have all the right answers."

"It's not the answers that bother me."

"What then?"

"It's a nonverbal thing. It's facial expressions and body language and the tone of your voice. These things are sometimes extremely difficult to control."

"I never thought of that."

"I know, some people never do and sometimes it's too late. They betray themselves and never know how they did it. That's why a lot of lawyers are extremely careful about putting their clients on the stand."

"You got any advice on how I should project myself while on the stand?"

"Don't lose your temper. That's the number one thing. If he can get you to lose it, you may say things or do things that will influence the jury in a negative way. Answer all the questions slowly. That gives you a chance to think before you speak. If you're in doubt as to what answer you should make, ask him to repeat the question. Don't forget to smile once in a while. Don't use a permanent smile, or the jury may think you're not taking this as a life and death matter. It really is."

"How about content? How about the truth?"

"The only time truth is important is if they catch you in a big untruth. That destroys your credibility. If they catch you in a lie, the judge can instruct them to disregard the rest of your testimony."

"What question do you think they might ask that would be the hardest for me to answer?"

"I don't know exactly how he'll phrase it, but I'm sure he's going to ask you if you hated Diego de los Santos."

"And how should I answer that?"

"Calmly in the affirmative. I think the jurors will be able to understand the hatred if you can present it in a calm and cautious manner."

"What else do you think he might ask me to try and get me going?"

"He'll try to do something with your wife."

"Like what?"

"Look, you may not know it, but I did considerable research before we accepted the case. I'm pretty sure your wife was a working girl before she became your wife. Just bringing up that possibility might be enough to make you show some anger. He also might say you just used her death as an excuse to go after the de los Santos clan. He might try to say that their anger against you stemmed from the fact that you somehow cheated them out of their birthright by having their father make you his sole heir. You'll have to stay calm when you explain why you were the sole heir and why none of the sons were asked to share in his new found wealth."

"I think I can handle that alright. Are you gonna call Juan Junior to the stand?"

"Yes, I think he'll be able to say that a lot of the animosity toward you was really directed at him. Tell me a little more about him."

"Well, he didn't inherit anything from his father either. The old man was really pissed at all four of them. He wanted to retire, but he couldn't get any of them to come back to Perdido. They all came back for his funeral. That was the first time I met any of them. He was the only one who didn't raise hell because the old man didn't leave him anything. The other three took off in a huff and didn't even stay around for the funeral."

"Why did you decide to take him on?"

"Well, in both looks and mannerisms he reminded me a lot of his father. Also, he had a lot of successful experience working for a big company in South America. His job there was acquiring land for his company to build roads. Even at a young age he'd already made a big splash in the company. They were grooming him for a position as president of the company."

"I see. Anything else?"

"Yeah, when the old man died, we were right in the middle of negotiations with the Japanese to move their operation to Perdido. I felt he was the best chance to finish those negotiations. I've never been sorry that I made him CEO of our corporation. He's a wealthy man now, but I trust him to stay an honest one."

"You say there was already a lot of hatred between the other three and him. Why so?"

"I think it went far beyond normal sibling rivalry. There's no doubt he was the favorite of both his mother and father. They didn't even try to make it a secret. Also physically, he was the spitting image of the old man. I think from what he told me, they made his childhood pretty miserable."

"Can he be counted on to keep his cool if I put him on the stand?"

"Oh, yeah, he's cool. He's been in a lot of pressure situations, and I've never seen him blink."

"He's not here. He's in Perdido?"

"Yes, I need him there to take care of things. He's actually been running things there for quite a while. I'm just a stamp for most of his decisions. He can be here by the next day if you decide he can be useful."

"Send for him then. I want him here to reinforce what a terrible person his brother was. It doesn't sound like he'll have any trouble doing that."

"I'm sure he won't. I'll call him tonight. Will he be needed for tomorrow?"

"No, I don't think the prosecution will call him, and the ball is still in their court. I'm not really sure who they will call, but I think they'll try to put you on the stand next. I know it will be hard, but try to get a good night's sleep."

"Okay, do you need to see me before court is in session tomorrow?"

"No, I think we covered about everything we needed tonight. I'll meet you in the conference room just before court is in session."

****

His lawyer had been right. It was indeed Charley who was called first to the stand. As he walked forward to take the oath, he tried to remember everything the lawyer had told him about nonverbal communication. He tried to remain totally emotionless, but he knew he could not maintain that attitude indefinitely.

"Will you repeat your full name?"

"Charles Everett Johnson."

"What is your residence, and what do you do for a living?"

"I now make my home in Lake Side, Missouri, and I am president of the Charles Johnson Corporation."

"Have you ever denied you are the man who shot and killed Diego de los Santos?"

"No, I haven't. I shot and killed the man after he came into my house and tried to kill me."

"And how many times did you shoot him?"

"Six, I'm told. I really don't remember."

"Why did you shoot him six times? Was he still a threat to you when you continued to shoot until the gun was out of shells?"

"I guess I thought he was. I'm not sure I thought anything after the first shot. It was just a reaction after he made a move toward me."

"A reaction toward a man you hated, right?"

"Yes, hated and feared. If you know a man is a killer, and you have just been his target, I don't think there's any doubt that a normal person would feel some fear."

"I see, but you don't deny the hatred, do you?"

"No. I swore to tell the truth."

"Come now, didn't your hatred far outweigh the fear you had of this man. Remember now, you swore to tell the truth."

"I'm not sure that's something you can weigh. Fear and hatred aren't something you can weigh on the scales and see which one is the heaviest."

"But you hated this man for a much longer time than the fear you felt on this occasion, right?"

"I suppose so, but consider this man killed my wife and...."

"Let's talk about that for a minute. You say you loved your wife, and her murder by this man is what brought your hatred of him to a head."

"I don't recall saying that."

"Well, did you love your wife, or was her death just an excuse to go after the man you'd hated for other reasons for a long time?"

Charley glared at the man and was about to make a bitter comment when he remembered what his own council had warned him about. He tried to take away the look that was on his face and replace it with a look of no expression at all. He felt the muscles in his face relax before he tried to answer the question.

"No, my love for my wife far outweighed, as you put it, anything else he might have done before that night."

'Tell us a little something about your wife. We have it on good authority that she'd been nothing more than a common street walker before she married you, is that right?"

Charley's face grew red and he pondered a reply. He remembered his lawyer's advice to ask the man to repeat any question he wasn't sure how to answer. He didn't want to repeat the question to reinforce the sound of it to the jury or the onlookers. Before he could form a reply, his lawyer leaped to his feet and said, "Your honor, I strenuously object to that last question."

"On what grounds?"

"Unless council has had personal contact with this woman practicing her profession, his so-called good authority is nothing more than hearsay."

"Objection sustained. You need not answer that question."

He hesitated briefly, but before the prosecutor could ask another question, he said in a calm voice, "I'd like to answer that question. It's true, what he just said. Before I met her, circumstances had forced her onto the street. An abusive stepfather had raped her and she fled to the street to avoid him. She became addicted to cocaine with the help of her pimp. After I met her, she gave up that life to follow me to Mexico. She was the only person who stood beside me when powerful forces were trying to kill both of us. I loved her dearly."

"So her death at the hands of this man did trigger the already festering hatred you'd had for this man and his brothers?"

"It wasn't *my* hatred that brought this man into my house on that night. It was *his*."

"But you will admit that you made the entrance into your house a very easy matter, won't you?"

"Yes, but I didn't plan to shoot him. I thought when he saw the hopelessness of his situation, he'd give up and wait to be arrested by the authorities."

"Really? Is he the type to give up? I don't think so. I think you knew he'd do exactly what he did and that you'd have the chance to blow him away. Isn't that right?"

"I think I've already answered that question. Do you want me to answer it again?"

"No, I think we've gone far enough down that road. Let's move ahead. Was your wife's death the reason you sent Hans Van Braun to New York City to kill the de los Santos brothers?"

"I never sent him to New York for that purpose. The only trip he ever made there on my behalf was when he went to rescue Juan Jr. after they kidnapped him. He could have probably killed them while they were sleeping if that was what I sent him there to do."

"Then why do you think a witness came all the way from New York City to identify him as the man he talked to on that night of the killings?"

"You'd probably know more about that than I would. I certainly didn't pay his way to come here and testify."

"Are you implying that the prosecution paid the man to come here?"

"If the shoe fits, wear it. I can't think of any other reason he might have come here. According to his own testimony, he sold out the location of the de los Santos brothers for cash. I don't see why he'd turn it down now if the stakes were high enough."

"I'm done with this witness."

"You may step down."

"Your honor, the prosecution would like to request a recess until after dinner."

"Any objection from the defense?"

"Request granted. Court will reconvene at 1:00 p.m."

****

As he sat in the conference room with his defense team, Charley seemed more relaxed than he had been at any time since he found he would be on trial.

"Well, how did I do?"

"You did great. I know it was hard to keep your cool when he attacked your wife. I thought for just a second that you were going to lose it, but you regrouped and did just fine. That last shot you gave him about suborning testimony from the cabby was great."

"Is that what I did? Accuse him of suborning perjury? I'm not even really sure what that means."

"It just means you pay someone to give false testimony. I think he was planning on grilling you further, but that sort of took the wind out of his sails."

"What's next?"

"He's probably got a few more witnesses that will testify that you hated Diego, but we've already admitted that you hated the man. I don't see how it's much to their advantage to keep hammering on that theme."

"Are you still thinking the trial might drag on for a long time?"

"Not really. Things are going well. I'm gonna call several of the locals from Lake Side to tell the jurors what a fine fellow you are. I've got several from the school you financed lined up to testify and several more from the city council to tell about the hospital that I hear is under way. Other than that, I'm going to call you back to the stand. I won't have many questions, but I want the jurors to hear one more time that you killed Diego out of fear and not out of hatred. The prosecutor may hammer away at some of the same stuff you've already been through, but I'm convinced now that you can handle anything he throws at you."

"How about Juan? You thought you might call him. Have you changed your mind about that?"

"I'm not certain. I'll just have to see how things go."

****

Things went well. Every member of the city council was anxious to take the stand and tell those present what a great guy Charley Johnson was. No amount of cross examination by the prosecution could get any of those witnesses to say anything negative about the man who put their town on the map in a big way. Not one person could assign any ulterior motive to his generosity.

Those people who manned the new school, which he alone had financed, were also quick to sing his praises. He had not tried to influence any of the decisions the school board had made. He was a tremendous backer of their scholastic, athletic, and all extra curricular activities.

At the conclusion of their testimony, lead council decided to put Juan on the stand. There was little he could say about the night of the killing. A large portion of his testimony was nothing more than an effort to show the jury what a despicable man his older brother had been. He dug back deep into his childhood memories to illustrate the nature of all of his siblings, but more especially of Diego. There were several objections by the prosecution as to the relevance of these somewhat sordid tales, but for the most part the judge allowed the defense the same latitude he had allowed the prosecution. Then Charley was recalled.

"You know that you are still under oath?"

"Yes, I do."

"I really don't have many questions. I think you've already answered most everything we need to know. We have already established that you hated Diego de los Santos for very good reasons. You have been accused of sending Hans Van Braun to New York City with explicit instructions to kill all three of the de los Santos brothers. What do you have to say to that accusation?"

"I say if they really believed those accusations, there would have been charges made. I've never been charged with anything, so I'd say their accusations don't hold much water. Hans has several people who can account for his whereabouts on the night of the shootings. The only man who testified to the contrary has admitted he can be bought if the price is right. I think it's up to the jury to see who they believe."

"Tell us once again why you let Diego get so close to you that night."

"It really wasn't my idea. My chief of security, Hans Van Braun, was the one who thought we could take him alive by making him think I was in my bed when he got up to my room. I really thought it would be better to see this man arrested and sent to prison for the rest of his miserable life than to have him dead there in my house.

When he made that move toward me, it was only natural instinct to stop him."

"But why did you shoot him six times?"

"Simply reflex action. When it was all over, I couldn't have told you whether I'd shot one time or a dozen."

"Is there any significance to which parts of the body that your bullets struck?"

"The only thing it shows is that I'm not a very good shot. I really don't have any experience in this sort of thing.

""Then this is the first person you've shot?"

"Sort of."

"What does that mean?"

"Well, on the night of my wedding, we were shot at as we left the church. My son and the best man were hit by a shooter. The shooter himself was hit by someone else's shot and was lying dead beneath the car. Juan senior threw me his gun, and I shot at the body under the car. I wasn't aware that the man was already dead. It was a very dark night."

"And would you say you fired at the shooter out of hatred?"

"No, just a very strong sense of self preservation, very much like I felt when I shot Diego."

"No further questions."

The prosecutor tried unsuccessfully for most of the rest of that session to trip Charley up with a series of questions designed to make him look bad, no matter what his answer might be. He had only marginal success. When he had finished, Charley's attorney said, "The defense rests."

****

Charley did not sleep well that night. He knew that tomorrow would be the day of the final arguments. He was also aware that no matter how strong the defense was, the prosecution always got the last word. He thought his defense team had done a good job, but he had been warned that the prosecution always saved their big gun for the final argument.

Until the prosecution had enumerated all of the people who had lost their lives directly or indirectly as a result of the adjustment, he had not bothered to think along those lines. Many of those who had died were not his fault. Still, he had left an impressive line of corpses along the way. He wasn't sure how the jury would react to all those whose lives had been lost as they became tangled in his affairs.

What little sleep he got was of the variety that provides no real rest for the body. He got up earlier than usual, determined to dress in such a way as to put his best foot forward. He put on his best suit and picked out a tie that would go well with the conservative look he wanted. He wasn't sure how the jury would react. He met with his lawyer for about thirty minutes before court was in session.

"Is the defense ready for their closing argument?"

"Yes, your honor."

"Then proceed."

"Ladies and gentlemen of the jury, I would like to thank you for your attention to all the testimony you have heard in this case. Throughout this case you have heard the prosecution try their best to paint Charley Johnson as a sinister character, numerous stories of the people who died close to him. But I want you to consider, were any of those who perished really the fault of Charley Johnson? I think not. There can be little doubt that his partner, Juan de los Santos senior, was a man who was used to violence. His life showed that if he felt challenged, he would resort to violence. Before he became the senior partner in the Johnson Corporation, he was a major dealer in the marijuana trade. No one has accused Mr. Johnson of any part of that operation. He had no knowledge of the blow-up of the Universal boardroom or their super tanker until after the fact."

"Let's look closely at four different events brought up by the prosecution. A notorious gang of Mexican teenagers supposedly leaves Mexico City to make a "peaceful" protest in Perdido. They disappear mysteriously. Somewhere between the City and Perdido something sinister is supposed to have happened. We are never told what. The prosecution has used innuendo to suggest that Mr. Johnson was perhaps responsible for their disappearance. Isn't it just as likely that this group of miscreants simply stole the bus and disappeared? I think so."

"Now let's examine the "Japanese Six" who broke into the plant under the cover of night and killed two guards along the way. Hans Van Braun, along with two other guards, was responsible for foiling their attempt to blow up the whole plant. The prosecution made a big point of how Mr. Van Braun killed two of the six. He gave them warning to stop before he fired his pistol at them. That was his job. That is what a chief of security is supposed to do in a situation like that."

"Now, about the French mercenaries. The prosecution would have you believe that Mr. Van Braun shot down a plane full of tourists on their way to Mexico City. Nothing could be farther from the truth. True, he discovered the plot in advance of their coming and was ready for them. Under his direction, the plane was blown out of the sky. Much was made of the extent of the explosion, such a big bang that it was impossible to tell what had really been on the plane. Impossible they say. Not so. An extensive search of the area where the remnants went down produced enough evidence that the people on the plane had not been vacationers on their way to Mexico City. What was found were dog tags, and the remains of offensive weapons, including fully automatic weapons, bazookas, mortars, and proof positive of plastic explosives. It is no wonder there was such a big bang. When that missile hit the plane, it no doubt detonated the explosives and ammunition for the weapons. Three different nations had a chance to lodge an official protest with the Mexican government or the United Nations. None of the three did so."

"So how about those peaceful protesters who had lost their jobs in Detroit? It's true that Mr. Van Braun continued to do his job. He found out what their real intentions were. He knew they possessed automatic weapons, mortars and bazookas. This group fired on the plant and did extensive damage, as well as killing and wounding several of the employees in the plant. However, this group was poorly led and had no real chance to succeed. When they were surrounded and ordered to throw down their arms, they continued to fire at the defenders of the plant. All but two were killed in the fire fight that ensued. The only one of the invaders who escaped without harm was Diego de los Santos."

"So now we come to the night that two of the de los Santos brothers met their end in a night club in New York City. Once again we have some very doubtful testimony that Mr. Johnson was somehow responsible for their deaths. I'm sure he had every reason to wish them dead, and he certainly didn't shed any rears when he heard about their demise. But the only person who testified that Hans Van Braun was anywhere close to the Aristocrat Club on the night in question is a man who confessed he sold the brothers out for cash. You also know that people in the drug industry are in a high risk occupation. It's just as likely that their deaths were the result of a drug deal gone sour. You must also consider that this cab driver conceded that the man he talked to on that night did not look exactly like Hans Van Braun. He thought the man might be disguised with a wig and fake beard, but he admitted that the light was failing at that time of day. Not exactly proof that Han Van Braun had anything to do with the deaths of the de los Santos brothers."

"So now I want to ask you, why did Charley leave the security of Perdido to move to this place where he was far more open to attack? I think the answer to that is easy to figure out. He never wanted to leave the United States in the first place. He was forced to flee for his life. It's true he made a great fortune from that move, but fortune has never been the main concern in the life of Charley Johnson. He worked for years trying to figure out a way to help working people in his own country afford to take a vacation. With the price of gas soaring, and the greed of the oil companies obvious, he worked tirelessly on what he later described as his "adjustment." If all he had wanted was to be a rich man, he could have taken the offer of the oil companies and lived handsomely for the rest of his life. This wasn't what he wanted. He was warned by his lawyer that to go against the oil companies was dangerous. He was skeptical. It was not until his lawyer was murdered in cold blood that he realized the danger he was in. When he found a note pinned on his door that read "You're next!" he knew he couldn't be safe anywhere in this country. He fled to Mexico with the agents of the oil companies hot on his heels. His only companion was the lady who was later to become his wife. She was the only one he could trust. He didn't want his sons to get involved in this for fear they would be harmed by the oil company thugs. He was right. His oldest son, his daughter-in-law and grandson were all murdered close to the home of their aunt in New Mexico where he had sent them for protection. The same people who murdered his family then tried to make it look like Charley had done the killing. They tried to have him extradited, but they failed because they had no real evidence against him."

"The so-called shootout with the Texas Rangers is another fanciful tale told by the prosecution. It was a one-way shootout. The Rangers did all the shooting. Charley was hit in the arm and would have bled to death if it hadn't been for the courage of Alice, his wife-to-be. She got him to a doctor who patched him up, and later she got Juan de los Santos senior to agree to take them in. The paid assassin tried again to shoot Charley, but his luck held. The only thing their failed attempt did was to make Juan de los Santos angry. He took great pride in protecting anyone under his roof. Their attempt to kill someone under his roof was a great insult. It was because of this attempt that he enlisted the help of his sons in the States to make a show of strength that would cause the oil companies to back off. They hesitated at first, but finally agreed to the bombing of the Universal Oil company boardroom and later the blow-up of one of their super tankers. How they were induced to perform these acts is something we will probably never know. Neither of these actions was done with the knowledge or consent of Charley Johnson."

"It was Juan de los Santos Senior who saw the great potential of Mr. Johnson's adjustment. He agreed to finance the beginning of the company for 50% of the profits. He insisted that each of the partners make the other partner the only heir to the company if anything should happen. He didn't want to see the company tied up in the courts while a family argument kept the Japanese in Japan. Maybe, he just didn't want to share any of his good fortune with his sons. True, they had helped to discourage the attacks of the oil companies, but all of them had refused to return to Perdido to help him run his marijuana operation. It was this same connection to marijuana that caused his own death. A rival family, the de las Rosas, ambushed him when he refused to continue doing business with them. That left Mr. Johnson in complete control of the company."

"At the old man's funeral, Charley met all four of the brothers for the first time. He took an instant dislike to the older three, but there was something about the youngest that set him apart from the other three. He could tell in an instant that there was no brotherly love lost between Juan Junior and the other three. He liked what he saw and offered him a job as chief negotiator with the Japanese car manufacturers. His success in that role led to his promotion as CEO of the company."

"After the move of all the Japanese car makers, a young man came along with an idea for the propulsion of the automobile that was even bigger than the "adjustment." It's what more than 70% of all cars are now running on. As he'd done with Juan Senior, when he agreed to finance this young man's innovation, he made this youngster, who went by the name of Tink, agree to make him the sole heir to the patent should anything happen to him. Shortly after the successful conversion by the Japanese from the adjustment to Tink's invention, Diego de los Santos stalked and killed this young man. There is reason to believe that for Diego it was a case of mistaken identity. He had no real reason to shoot Tink. It was the belief of Mr. Johnson that Diego had mistaken Tink for his youngest brother, Juan Junior, whom he hated with a passion. He was also extremely jealous of his success in the company and angry at his failed attempt to get a piece of the company by kidnapping him."

"After the death of his brothers, Diego set out to kill Charley Johnson. He thought that Charley had somehow cheated him and his brothers out of something that should have been theirs. His attempt was what caused the death of Alice, Charley's wife. He tried sniping from long range from a boat. He missed Charley, but his shot hit Alice, and she died from the wound. Because of this, it has been from the beginning, the contention of the prosecution that Mr. Johnson sent Hans Van Braun to New York City to eliminate all of the de los Santos brothers. This contention of theirs has not been substantially backed up with any hard evidence, only the word of a taxi driver whose voice we know from the past has been for sale."

"Let's face it. Charley Johnson has since become one of the richest men in the world. He could have moved into seclusion like a modern Howard Hughes, but he chose to come back to the country he loves to try to help his fellow man again. You've heard the testimony of many of the citizens of Lake Side that Charley Johnson has been more than generous. He's built a modern school that is the envy of every other school district in the state. He's also got an ultra modern hospital almost completed. He is financing low cost housing for almost anyone who wants to move to Lake Side."

"So now we are faced with an overwhelming question. Did Charley Johnson lure Diego de los Santos to his house so that he could have his revenge, once and for all? That's what the prosecution would have you believe. Frankly, I'm not sure what exactly was on his mind that night. None of us can really know. I can tell you this. There is a thing called reasonable doubt. You've heard Charley tell you what his intention was on that night. Whether or not you believe it, you must admit that what he says is entirely possible. He said he wanted the man who shot and killed his wife to suffer for the rest of his life in a maximum security prison. He wanted that a lot more than to just see him lying dead on the floor of his house."

"In closing, let me say this. Charley is a good man. Diego de los Santos was a killer and a drug dealer. Think about the message you send to the rest of the country before you decide on a verdict. Thank you."

The judge rapped twice to bring the court to order. Another member of the prosecution team walked toward the jury. He was the man Charley's lawyer had warned him would make the closing argument. Until now he had not seemed to be a part of the trial. He had taken notes from the beginning, but he had not questioned any witness from either side. The judge rapped one final time before he began.

"Ladies and gentlemen, you have a hard decision to make when you all are in the room set aside for you. It's always difficult when a man of good reputation is responsible for the death of a man who is frankly, not a very good person. This is precisely what you are being asked to decide. Does the fact that the man with presumably a good reputation and billions of dollars have to be as answerable for his actions as the other would be if the trial was to see if Diego de los Santos had killed Charley Johnson? I hope your answer to that is yes. Money is not the deciding factor in this case. As jurors, you can go a long ways toward dispelling the old saying that a man gets as much justice as he can afford."

"There is no denying that Charley Johnson is a remarkable man. He began as an ordinary auto mechanic and has used his ingenuity to become one of the richest men in the world. You have heard from both sides in this case that a lot of men have died who were very close to Charley Johnson. The defense claims that none of these deaths are really his fault. Still, that leaves a whole lot to coincidence, doesn't it?"

"There's been a lot said about hate in this trial. The prosecution says that hate was the primary motive for Charley to lure Diego de los Santos into his house so he could empty his pistol into his body. Consider once again. He shot the man six times with all of the shots to the man's groin. He says he isn't an expert with a pistol, but how much of an expert does one have to be to hit a man standing a mere arms length away? Mr. Johnson said he would have kept on firing at the man until he was out of shells even if the gun had held 30 rounds instead of six. The prosecution agrees with that statement. The hatred he felt for this man would never have let him stop shooting so long as the gun kept on firing."

"Was the hatred he felt for this man justified? No doubt it was. The man had tried to wipe out his corporation by hiring six Japanese intruders to plant explosives in his plant. No one testified to this, but we have it on good authority that Diego hired a young man to try to sneak explosives into the plant in the trunk of his car just before his father's funeral. He hired mercenaries according to the defense to attack the plant. He personally led a group of out-of-work auto workers to attack the plant. He led them to their death while he escaped unharmed."

"Then came the final straw. He tried to assassinate Mr. Johnson from long distance with a hunting rifle fired from a boat. His aim was faulty, and his bullet struck and killed Mr. Johnson's wife. The hatred this last act engendered is only human and completely natural. The prosecution does not blame Mr. Johnson for the hatred he felt for Diego de los Santos. We understand that. But the law does not permit those who have good reason to hate someone to take that hatred out on them in the manner in which he took care of Diego de los Santos. To lure someone into a situation where his murder can be justified is still the crime of murder."

"The manner in which the trap was set was obvious. He dismissed his personal security around the house when he determined that Diego was on the way. He turned out the lights and unlocked the doors to his house. He placed blankets on the bed to resemble the body of a man asleep. He hid and waited for the man to use up all of his ammunition firing into the blankets on the bed. Then he struck the man on the head with what appears to be his pistol. The investigating officer said that the body appeared to have had water poured on his head, probably to awaken the man. If, as Mr. Johnson claims, his only intent was to have the man arrested and tried for murder, why didn't he call the police while the man was unconscious and no threat to him?"

"The answer to that question is all too obvious. His hatred for the man had caused him to plan the execution of Diego de los Santos. There is no justification for a person to allow himself to become the judge, jury, and executioner of another human being. That is why we have the law. It is the duty of law enforcement people to arrest people like Diego de los Santos, and the duty of people like myself to see that they are appropriately punished. It is not the privilege of the very rich to be allowed to settle things for themselves. They are under the same constraints of the law as you and I are."

"Nor can the good deeds a man performs such as building schools and hospitals be a defense for the crime of murder. However laudable these acts may be, they do not entitle a man to take the law into his own hands. That is precisely what Charley Johnson did on the night he shot and killed Diego de los Santos. When you have thoroughly considered the matter, I'm afraid you will have no other choice but to find Charley Johnson guilty of murder as charged."

He then with a slight swagger walked back to his seat and smiled at the jurors. The judge then instructed the jury concerning the law and had them escorted to the room where their verdict would be made. Charley's lawyer leaned over and said, "I told you he was good. He's one of the best. He's almost as good as I am."

"Well, what do you think? How long will it take to decide?"

"I think it will take quite a while. Don't worry. I think at worst it'll turn out to be a hung jury. There at least three people who will never vote to convict."

"What happens if it turns out to be a hung jury?"

"Then the State has to decide if it's worth all the time and the money for a new trial. I'm certain they won't try to convict you again."

"Does that mean I'm found innocent?"

"Not really. What the jury finds in a case like this is you're not guilty. Innocent is not the same as not guilty, but either way it's a lot better than being found guilty. What it really means is there is reasonable doubt."

"How long do we have to wait if they want another trial?"

"It varies, but I'd bet dollars to doughnuts they won't try it again. My guess is they'll drop it in less than a month."

****

Charley sweated for the greater part of five days before being told that the jury was returning to the courtroom. He couldn't see anything in the faces of the jury to indicate what the verdict might be. His lawyer's face betrayed his own uneasiness. Charley sat almost at attention as the judge asked, "Has the jury reached a verdict?"

"No, your honor. I regret to inform the court that we are hopelessly deadlocked. We cannot reach a verdict."

"I hate to hear that, but I am going to release the jury. Since you cannot agree and by your own admission hold no prospect of ever reaching a unanimous decision, I shall declare a mistrial and release the defendant on his own recognizance. Court is adjourned."

"See! I told you not to worry. Congratulations! You're a free man!"

"You didn't look all that confident when the jury came in. Do you guys remain on retainer until we're for certain that they're not gonna try again?"

"Yes, we do. We'll be heading back to our own home base tomorrow, but we'll be back here in a flash if were needed."

****

The feeling of elation lasted for only a few hours. It was followed by a sharp pang of sorrow as he returned to the empty house. With Alice gone, there was no one there to share the joy he had felt briefly. Only his housekeeper and his young daughter were there for him when he returned. Billy had left immediately after the trial's climax to return to his own family. Hans had decided it was about time to have a few drinks, and he had left the courtroom in search of the nearest bar. He would return to Lake Side the following day.

Back home again, Charley sat and tried to figure out what he would do now. He could not really relax until he was notified that his trial was over. Once again he went over in his mind what the lawyer had told him. Unless there was new evidence, there would be no second trial. His mind searched for anything that might be considered new evidence, but he could think of nothing. He wondered if his status in Lake Side had been permanently damaged by his trial. He was certain there were some that would shy away from him because of it. It would take time to erase from their memory the trial and the verdict.

It was late in the evening of the third day when he heard the doorbell ring. He was surprised to see Sally standing there alone when he opened the door. In a quiet voice she asked, "May I come in?"

"Of course you can. Where's Phillip?"

"He had to work late. He works late almost every night. I'm afraid we haven't had much time together recently. He takes all the overtime he can get to help pay for the wedding and all the things we'll need to set up housekeeping."

"Is there anything I can do for you?"

"Not really. I just stopped by to tell you how sorry I am about Alice. I had really looked forward to having her help me plan my wedding."

"She was looking forward it, too. She got to plan very little of her own. My partner, Juan de los Santos, was a powerful man and by most people's standards a rich one. Alice loved the old man in her own way. He was about as close to a father as she'd had since her own father committed suicide. He asked her to wear the wedding gown of his own deceased wife, and he asked me to marry her with the same ring he'd used for his wedding. We really couldn't deny him since he was picking up the tab for everything. Our engagement didn't last but a couple of days since he was in a hurry to see us married. She had almost no say in the wedding, not even the church where the ceremony was to be performed in a language she didn't even understand. To top things off, a gunman tried to kill me on the way out of the church. My son was hit and also the best man, but both recovered. She was hoping that somehow helping you plan your wedding would in some way make up for what she'd missed on her own."

"I'm sorry I couldn't be at your trial. I followed as close as I could in the papers and on TV. Everyone in school, and I think the whole town, was hoping and praying that everything would turn out alright for you."

"Well, it may not be over yet. They may decide to try me again, but my lawyer says it's highly unlikely."

"I hope so. I miss your visits to practice. I've had to take over as head coach since Bev is having so much trouble with her pregnancy. I thought I was ready to be a head coach, but now I'm not so sure. Would you be kind enough to explain a few things to me?"

"If I can, I'll be glad to. I've never really had anything to do with girls' athletics."

"I don't think there's really that much difference between girls and boys. I know we can't run as fast or jump as high, but I think it's really the same game."

"If you'll sit at the table, I'll pour us a cup of coffee. I'll grab a note pad and try to answer any questions you have."

"Oh, I didn't mean for you to do it tonight. I just meant when you have time."

"Well, I may never have more time than I have right now. If you'll take a seat, I'll pour the coffee."

She sat down at the table as he got down two cups. He was careful not to use the cup with Alice's name on it. He intended to put it away soon to make sure that it was never accidentally broken.

"Do you take cream or sugar?"

"No, black is fine. Where are your daughter and your housekeeper?"

"Both upstairs. It's about her bedtime."

He sat down beside her after pouring the coffee. He laid down a notebook and a couple of pencils and waited for her to ask him a question.

"Well, I guess the first thing would be how we can best break a press. We're having a devil of a time getting the ball in position to run our offense. What can you show me?"

"Well, there are really two ways to do it. One is to dribble the ball through it if you have someone who is really good at dribbling. If you don't have someone with great ball handling skills, you gotta pass the ball through it or over it."

"We don't have anyone who dribbles all that well, so how should we set up to pass the ball through or over the press?"

He scooted his chair over closer to her and put the note pad between them. Then he drew a picture of a basketball court and drew a bunch of X's and O's to represent the offense and defense of two teams. Then he asked, "Are you trying to break a zone press or man-to-man? Maybe I should say girl-to-girl. I should have asked you that before I drew my X's and O's."

"It's mostly zone. Hardly any of the girls' teams play a man defense."

"Well, is your problem getting the ball in bounds or how to avoid a double team after it's in bounded?"

"Some of both."

"Well, set up this way. Have this person set a screen for the person you want to handle the ball. Then have this player break to the open spot. The trick to breaking a zone trap is to pass at angles, like this, never in a flat line, like this."

"Could you come to practice some day and show the girls first hand what you just showed me? I'm afraid it might lose something in the translation."

"Sure, just tell me when and I'll be there. I don't really have much to do right now."

"Could you come tomorrow at 3:15? We have the big court to practice on this week while the guys are using the auxiliary."

"Okay, I'll be there."

He was a full hour early to basketball practice. There was no one in the gym when he arrived. He found an old ball outside the coach's office, took off his shoes so as not to scuff the beautiful hardwood floor, and shot free throws for a short while. A custodian who heard the ball bouncing became curious about the noise and went to investigate. From a distance he did not recognize the man who was shooting the ball, but when he got closer, he stopped, turned around, and went back to his regular rounds.

Sally got to practice 15 minutes ahead of the time she had told him to be there. She said, "I've got to change. I'll open up my office so you can get comfortable till I'm back. Have you been here long?"

"Not really. I'm a little nervous about this. I've never coached anyone except my own sons. I'm a little leery of how girls will take to the coaching of man who was just tried for murder. I'm sure they know all about the trial. I know they've read all the newspaper accounts of it."

"Don't worry about that. They've all been rooting for you. I'll be right back as soon as I get changed."

She ducked into the bathroom that had been built in the coach's office. It reminded him of how well the building had been planned and constructed. The gym in which he had practiced had neither a dressing room nor a coach's office. When she got back, he couldn't help but notice that she had powdered her nose and was looking as fresh as a daisy. He wondered if he didn't look out of place in what he was wearing.

"I've had a chance to look over the notes you gave me, and I think I understand where all the girls are supposed to be, but if I make a mistake, I want you to stop what we're doing and have them get it right. It won't embarrass me if you change something we're doing wrong."

"Okay, shall I just stay here in the office until they finish their warm-up drills?"

"You can if you want to, but I'd really like for you to see what we're doing and see if there's anything else we should be doing."

"Okay, I'll peek through the door and watch. Do they have any idea that I'll be at practice today? I don't want to scare anyone."

"Yeah, they know. I told my first hour class and you know how word gets around, especially with girls. They're pretty excited about it. Here they come now. I gotta go into their locker room. I'll holler at you when we start to work on the press break."

They came out looking nearly as well groomed as their coach. They passed a ball around until all had left the locker room. Then they began running laps without being told. After that it was lay-up drills for the next 15 minutes. When the drill was finished, Sally went to the center of the court and was surrounded by the team. She motioned for Charley to join them. She waited till he had reached center court before she introduced him to the team. He said, "Girls, I'm tickled to death to be here today. Your coach tells me you're having some problems breaking a press. I hope I can show you a couple of things that will help you. Set up the way coach wants you to be when you're in-bounding the ball from underneath the opponents' basket."

He watched patiently as the girls tried unsuccessfully to get the ball to center court. After three fruitless tries, Sally blew the whistle and asked, "Well, what are we doing wrong?"

"A couple of things. First, you're not looking up the floor. You have people open up the court, but you're dribbling with your heads down, so you can't see the open player. Also, you're not anticipating the double team. When it comes, you have to see what direction it's coming from. There will most likely be an open player in the direction the double team comes from. You girls on the receiving end of that first pass have to step toward the pass. That cuts down the distance the pass must travel and makes it a lot harder for a defender to get between you and the pass. Now, let's try it again."

They set up again, and almost immediately they began to have some success. He stopped play three or four times to illustrate how they could improve. He shouted encouragement when twice they not only broke the press, but also got easy lay-ups at the other end.

"That's the way to go, girls. That's the best way to break a press. Score a couple of easy baskets, and they'll give up the press. A poor press is the worst defense there is."

Sally chimed in. "Good job. Now everybody get a drink of water and let's shoot some free throws. We'll hit the press break again in about ten minutes"

As the girls drifted off toward the water fountains, Sally said, "You are a natural born teacher. I saw more than a 100% improvement in the short time you worked with them. I've got an idea if you're willing to listen."

"Shoot, what's on your mind?"

"Well, since Bev is having such a hard time with her pregnancy, we really don't have an assistant coach. What would you think if the school board offered you the job?"

"You're kidding, right? I don't have a degree in anything. Don't you have to have one to be a coach?"

"No, you don't. As long as someone has a degree, that would be me, the assistant doesn't need one. Would you be interested?"

"Boy, it's something I never even thought about. Do you think the school board would really consider it?"

"Consider it? No. They'd just do it if I asked them to. After all, where can they get a coach at this time of year who has played the game and won't come asking for a raise if we have some success?"

"Yeah, I guess they know I don't need the money. I guess it can't hurt to ask them."

Two days later the Lake Side school board was in session. Sally had asked permission to address the board. She gave them no hint as to why she had made the request. Some feared she was about to announce her resignation. She wasted no time in letting them know her purpose.

"Members of the board, I have come to this meeting tonight to ask you a huge favor. You know that Bev is having great difficulty with her pregnancy. As of now, we have no assistant basketball coach. Two days ago I asked Mr. Charles Johnson if he would come to our practice to give us some pointers on basic basketball strategy. He agreed, and I can't begin to tell you the progress the team made due to his help. The man is a born teacher. The girls responded to him far better than I thought possible. I'm asking you now to make him my assistant coach. He wants no compensation for his work."

"What qualification does he have for the position?"

"If you're asking does he have a college degree, the answer is no. What he has is very practical experience. He was a star in high school as a player, and he played two years of junior college ball. I'm told that only his lack of height kept him from playing major college ball. He taught both of his sons to play, and they both had scholarships to play."

"What do the girls think about his trial? Would it be a distraction to know their coach had just been on trial for murder?"

"No, I don't think so. They kept up with the trial, and they were rooting for him to be acquitted. They know the details of how his wife was killed and how the man who was killed had tried to kill him. I think really he's a gentleman, but he has a sense of toughness that I hope he will pass on to the team."

"Well, if you'll allow us to go into executive session, we'll have to put this to a vote. If you'll wait outside, we'll call you back when we're finished."

The discussion lasted about ten minutes. There was only one dissenting vote. They called Sally back into the room.

"We have decided to grant your request. There is only one stipulation. No position of coach can be taken without some form of compensation. He will be paid the same salary as any other assistant coach. If he chooses to use the money in some way to benefit the team or the school, well, that will be left up to him."

"I thank you, gentlemen. I'm sure he'll be pleased with your decision. He'll be on the job regularly then starting tomorrow. Don't be surprised if we win a few games. Good evening."

She couldn't wait until the next day. She called him on the phone to give him the news. He sounded quite pleased and thanked her for the call. He asked what time he should report to the gym tomorrow. She said he should be there an hour before practice was scheduled to start. She wanted him to look over her practice schedule to see if he had any suggestions about how to utilize their practice time.

He was well dressed for the job when he made his way onto the court. He had purchased some new Nikes and some great looking coaching shorts. He'd gotten a shorter haircut than he'd had during his playing days. When the girls arrived, he was certain he looked the part of a coach.

He noticed a small but significant change in the attitude of the girls. They obviously had been informed of his new status as assistant coach. They gathered around him after they had run their preliminary laps. Sally had not come out of the coach's office yet, but the girls seemed anxious to get the practice started. He started the lay-up drills and kept them at it until Sally arrived.

"Sorry I'm a little late. I had a discipline problem this afternoon, and I had some paper work to finish for the office. I'm glad you didn't wait for me to get here."

"I didn't think you'd care if we ran our laps and did the lay-up drill. I think we should spend a little more time on the girls working with their left or weak hand. The strong hand seems to have pretty good form, but from the other side we look pretty awkward."

"I know, but it just seems there's never enough time to work on all the things you need to. What seems to be the biggest problem?"

"I'd say a lack of confidence or a lack of strength. Do any of the girls work out with weights?"

"Only two or three. Somehow they think it's unlady like, or they're afraid they'll look muscle bound if they hit the weights."

"Yeah, I know. Times have really changed in that regard. It wasn't too long ago that guys felt the same way. Coaches didn't encourage work on the weights until they'd gotten a good licking from those who did. I haven't even had a chance to look at the weight room. How is it?"

"Like everything else in this school, it's top notch. I'll bet there isn't a school we'll play that has anything like it."

"Is there any reason we can't push them to use it a little more?"

"All of our staff have pretty full schedules, so we don't have anyone to supervise full time."

"How about before school? I could come early, if there's enough interest to justify opening early."

"I'll check with the principal and see what he says. Could we open it up for both the guys and girls? I think the guys' coach wouldn't mind seeing his guys getting a little stronger."

"Sure, do we have enough equipment to accommodate anyone who wants to lift? I think we'll have to open it up for even those who aren't out for sports. What do you think?"

"Yeah, I think you're right. We can't offer credit for the class because.....

"Yeah, I know, because I don't have a degree in weight lifting. Well, I hope they'll lift for more than just a PE credit."

Charley found the weight lifting class to be a blessing. It gave him a reason to get up in the morning. Hans hated it. He still felt it was absolutely necessary to accompany him no matter the time or destination when he left the house. He never went inside the school. He just waited outside in the car until Charley was finished with the class.

Another thing Charley liked about the class was that it gave him an opportunity to learn the names of a lot of the students. He had picked up on the names of most of the basketball girls, but in the informal setting of this class, he was able to pick up on the nicknames of boys and girls alike.

He picked up several good publications on weight training. The one he had chosen to implement was called "Bigger, Faster, Stronger." It was well illustrated and easy to follow. The girls were less enthusiastic than the guys at first, but they soon overcame their shyness when lifting with the boys.

The season opened with a three game tournament. It was invitational, and Charley suspected they had been invited late to the tourney just to provide an easy win for the other schools. Neither the boys nor the girls were able to win a game, however the girls did show a big improvement, and by the third game they were competitive.

The losses did not dampen Charley's enthusiasm. He was becoming more than just a coach. He was the head cheerleader. It had been so long since he's watched a game closely that he had almost forgotten how really bad some of the officiating can be. He narrowly missed being whistled for two technical fouls in the last game when he voiced his opinion about two calls that went against Lake Side. It was Sally who had to calm him down, and at the conclusion of the game, he apologized to both Sally and the girls. The captain of the team said, "That's alright, coach. We like the way you stand up for us."

Sally said, "I'm proud of the way you guys played tonight. You didn't give up. Even though we got way behind in the first half, you hung in there and competed. That's what it's all about. If we continue to play hard, we're gonna win some games."

She was right. They won five games while losing fourteen. Charley and Sally were both looking forward to their next season. Only one of their starters would not be back. Charley's enthusiasm was tempered by the realization that he probably wouldn't be back as an assistant coach.

"They'll probably hire another full time assistant for next year, won't they?"

"Not if I have anything to say about it, they won't. You made a big difference in the team. The girls really like you, and they listen to you. You do want to come back, don't you?"

"Yeah, I do. I think I would have gone crazy sitting around that empty house every day. This gave me something to look forward to. When is your marriage gonna take place?"

"June 23, and you better be there."

"Why are you guys putting it off?"

"He doesn't think we have enough money yet. It's one of those male ego things, I think."

"Is he too proud to let me pick up the tab for the whole affair and to give you away?"

"I don't know. He is a proud man, and it rankles him somewhat that he doesn't have a college degree. He makes more money than I do, but that doesn't seem to matter to him."

"Well, this is just the middle of March. That makes it a long time till June 23. Would you speed it up if he didn't object?"

"Yes, I'd marry him tomorrow if he'd agree to it, but I'm not sure he would."

"Would you be upset if I talked to him about it?"

"No, but don't be surprised if he turns you down flat."

At first he wasn't at all interested in accepting Charley's offer, but Charley was persistent. It was during their third discussion that Charley began to see his resolve weaken.

"Come on, guy, there's nothing wrong with letting somebody help you get started. I got more money than I'm ever gonna need. Why don't you just let me speed things up a bit? Nobody is gonna think less of you for getting a little head start. That gal is crazy about you, and she can't wait to be your wife. She hasn't sent out invitations yet, so you could move the date up to whatever you two could agree on. What do you say?"

"Well, I'll talk to her about it. If she really wants to speed things up, I guess I could be ready to move things up."

"Now you're talking. Have you agreed on where the marriage will take place?"

"Yes, she wants it right here in Lake Side. There's a Baptist church there that she goes to most of the time."

"How many people will she invite?"

"I'm not sure. I think about a hundred, but I'm not sure a lot of them will make it. Most of her folks live a long way from here."

"And how about your own folks?"

"I think there might be as many as thirty or forty who might come. They don't have enough money to rent rooms, and I can't put all of them up."

"Don't worry about that. I can put them up."

"Is that place of yours really big enough to put up that many people?"

"No, I didn't mean that. It would take care of twelve to fifteen, but that isn't what I meant. I'll just reserve the whole Lake Side Inn. They just expanded to more than a hundred rooms, so I'm sure they could handle all of her folks and yours, too."

"Yeah, I know. I helped build a lot of those rooms."

"Where are you planning on holding the reception? I don't think the church has room for as many as you're planning on."

"No, they don't. Do you have any ideas?"

"Yeah, here's one. How about the gymnasium at the high school? I'm sure it's big enough. We had larger crowds in it than your guest list during the season. Do you think she'd agree to use it?"

"Yeah, I think she would, but I'm not sure the school board would agree to make it available."

"Well, I don't know if you know it or not, but I do have a certain amount of pull with the school board. I don't think we'll have any trouble getting their permission to use it if we agree to clean it up after it's over."

"Okay, I'll ask her tonight if she would agree to have it there. If she says yes, we'll start mailing the invitations right away."

"I can let you know about the reception as soon as she agrees to have it there."

The wedding was moved up. It was the largest in the history of Lake Side. Charley bought a new tuxedo in honor of giving the bride away. He felt almost as good about being able to help a young couple get started as he was the building of the school.

Charley felt lost as soon as school was out. He missed his son and granddaughter, but he couldn't persuade Billy to move back to the States. His wife was adamant in her refusal to accompany him if he decided to go. She often reminded him of what happened to Alice when he brought up the subject.

Charley became the poster boy for loving fathers. He spoiled his daughter to the extent that even her nanny had to tell him to slack off. He could never leave the house that he didn't feel obligated to bring her a present back when he returned. Her hair and eyes were strictly Alice. The joy he felt each time he saw her was always tempered by a pang of grief over the death of her mother. Her bedroom was soon filled with every conceivable type of stuffed animals and dolls. No matter how busy he might be, there was never a day he didn't find some time to spend with her.

****

The spring and summer slipped by with no real problems. The de los Santos were no longer a threat, and even the Mafia had decided that attacking Charley Johnson was too dangerous to be attempted. The oil companies and the Big Three were trying desperately to find some new way to make it back to the top.

Hans couldn't believe it. His only real duties these days were to make sure that the daughter arrived safely at the nursery school and to see that he was always there to bring her back to the house. He couldn't believe that she called him Uncle Hans. Never before in all his life had he gotten hugs and kisses from a child.

Charley could hardly wait for the beginning of basketball season. He had read every coaching magazine that was published. He had sent away for videos of all the most successful coaches of women's basketball. He was particularly impressed by the coaching philosophy of the coaches of Tennessee and Connecticut. He supported wholeheartedly the football and volleyball teams and never missed a game, at home or away, but he could hardly wait for the coming of basketball season.

His prediction about the growth of both the community and the school had been correct. The population of both the town and the school had almost tripled since the opening of the school. Construction crews worked year round to try to supply the demand for new housing.

The football team won three games that fall and the volleyballers achieved a .500 record. There were twice as many girls out for basketball as there had been the first year. Several transfers from larger schools in the vicinity now made up a good portion of the roster. There would be enough girls to field a junior varsity team, and Charley was looking forward to coaching those girls.

His JV girls went 13-4 and gave the varsity some good competition in every day practice. His success as a coach left him almost euphoric. He regretted he had no degree, and forever would be barred from being a head coach in name as well as actuality. He knew that in the next two years there was a very good likelihood that Lake Side would have a chance at going to the State championship.

He was right again. They went to State that year and finished fourth. More transfers and the return of two star players made next year seem even more promising. That made the news that he would not be returning next year as the assistant coach even more devastating. It was the decision of the board that the school would be better served by hiring someone with a college degree, preferably another woman. His interest never waned, but he never attended another practice session. He never missed a game, and he continued to be the biggest fan and booster of all Lake Side activities.

With no more time spent at basketball practice, he had lots of time to spend with his daughter. She seemed to Charley to resemble her mother more and more each day. She was wearing out lamp-shades by shooting nerf balls at them. She seemed to have excellent eye-hand coordination, and Charley decided to have a small hard surface court built there on his own property. He had installed an adjustable goal with a starting height of about six feet, and as she grew older and stronger, he would raise the height of the goal until it reached the regulation height of ten feet. The ball she would start with would be small enough for the size of her hands and would be increased as her hands grew.

It wasn't enough. Even though he had taken up fishing in an effort to fill his empty hours, it wasn't enough. He had a good boat and the best guide in the state to teach him how to fish, but it never completely satisfied his desire to compete. He brooded more and more each day. Juan kept him informed and business was still booming, but he really didn't care. He gave money to almost every respectable charity and kept most of his generosity a secret. The expenses of maintaining the school increased each year, but he had never looked closely at the budget. His initial anger at the board's decision to drop him as the assistant coach had gradually melted away. He knew he could have pressured them into keeping him on as the assistant coach, but he had decided early on not to become involved in the board's decisions.

He took to reading to fill the void in his life. It was something new. He had never been an avid reader. He had always preferred working with his hands. Now he became fascinated with reading about the efforts of scientists who were actually experimenting in controlling the genetics of unborn children. With animals, they had already been successful in controlling such features as color of hair and eyes, and overall size. These people were anxious to extend their experiments to include human beings. The barrier to their experiments was a severe lack of funds. Many in high places thought that such experiments could lead to an attempt at creating a "master race." The religious right was the most vocal of those opposed to the experimentation. They were quick to accuse those who worked at such things of trying "to play God."

One afternoon Charley put in a call to Juan. His CEO was accustomed to such calls, but invariably they dealt with something to do with business. He was taken by surprise at the nature of this call. After the customary inquiries about the business, Charley made a request that caught him completely off guard.

"Say, Juanito, I want you to do me a favor."

"And what might that be?"

"I want you to get in touch with the scientific community that is interested in controlling the genetics of the unborn."

"What? Say again!"

"I think you heard me. I want to be in touch with those scientists who think they can control the genetics of unborn humans."

"To what purpose, if I may ask?"

"I would like to meet with some of them to see if they might be interested in some funding I could give to their efforts."

"Could you at least give me the names of those you want to see?"

"Yes, the most prominent in this field are Dr. Rosenblat and Dr. Williams. They have a phone number listed at 791-874-4681."

"What exactly do you want me to tell them?"

"That I'm interested in their project and that I might be willing to finance some of their experiments. Be certain they know who I am. Sometimes these eggheads are so wrapped up in their own affairs that they might not recognize my name."

"Assuming they're interested, where would you want the meeting to take place? I know you don't do business over the phone."

"You're right about that. I think since I'm picking up the tab, they can at least come to my place. You can arrange their flight and pay for the tickets. If they're interested, set up for ASAP. Let me know if they're coming and when. I'll have someone pick them up at the airport."

"Okay. I'll let you know as soon as I know anything. Is there anything else?"

"No, that's about it. I'll be waiting for your call."

He didn't have to wait long. Juan called him back that same day. Both men were anxious to travel to Lake Side to meet the famous Mr. Johnson. They would arrive at noon the next day.

****

It was Hans who was assigned the duty of picking up the men when they arrived at the airport. He carried a large sign with the names of the two scientists on it to help the men locate the limo that would take them to their destination.

Charley couldn't help but smile when he saw them for the first time. Dr. Williams looked the part of the egg-head professor, while Dr. Rosenblat more resembled the mad scientist.

"Gentlemen, I can't tell you how glad I am that you accepted my invitation to visit Lake Side. Welcome."

"And we can't tell you how glad that we are that a man of your prominence is interested in our field of endeavor. Is there anything we could tell you at this time about how far we have progressed?"

"Well, I've read extensively about the nature of your research. Have there been any recent breakthroughs?"

"I'm afraid we've hit the wall recently. We have some new ideas we'd like to try, but we just don't have the resources to...."

"Well, then let's get right to the point. I'm interested in what you're trying to do. How are the facilities you're now using? Are they adequate for what you're trying to accomplish? Can you tell me how much you'll need to continue to make progress?"

"I can't tell you how much we'll need to complete our work, but we would be eternally grateful for any financial help you could give us."

"If I decide to fund this project, there is one stipulation that must be agreed to before I invest a penny in your work."

"And what might that be?"

"Complete anonymity for myself. I don't know how you'll explain the sudden huge amount of money that you'll have, but if my name gets mixed up in it, I'll withdraw my support."

"Leave that to us. I'm sure we can find some way to explain it. Have you any idea how much support we can expect?"

"Well, let's start with a hundred million. If that falls short of what you need, let me know, and I'll arrange for more if I see progress."

"Are you serious? That's more generous than we could have dreamed. When would we receive the money?"

"Would tomorrow be soon enough? I can't guarantee the actual money will be there, but you'll have that much credit. I'll give my CEO the word, and he'll have your credit extended to the amount I just mentioned. He'll notify you when the arrangement has been completed. Will you gentlemen want to spend the night here, or will you be returning immediately?"

"This is sudden. We thought there might be a lot more to say to try to persuade you to...."

"You mean to persuade me to be more generous. Right?"

"Yes, I suppose that might be an accurate description."

"When is your return flight scheduled?"

"The day after tomorrow. Is there anything we can tell you that might be of great interest to you personally about our work?'

"There is one thing. Have you been able to identify in the genetic code exactly how the height of a person is controlled?

"We're working on that, and the funds you have promised might very well be enough to give us the answer to that question."

"Another question. Have you done anything about the probability of multiple birth?"

"Very little, but we could put you in contact with some of our colleagues who are on the cutting edge of that phenomenon."

"I'll let you know if I decide to encourage their research as well as your own. You gentlemen are welcome to stay here at my house until your return flight is ready, or I can get you a new return flight if you're anxious to get back to work."

"I hope you won't take it as a sign of ingratitude if we opt for the latter. We would really like to get back to work as quickly as possible. There's so much to do, and now that we have the funding, we should push on as rapidly as we can." ...

"Okay, I'll get you on the first flight back. Thank you for coming to my place. I hope you'll unravel all the mysteries of the genetic code."

****

Things drifted along peacefully for the next two months. Charley was kept informed of the progress being made by the two scientists. Then one day the phone rang, and Charley was surprised to hear the voice of Dr. Rosenblat. It was usually Dr. Williams who made the calls to keep Charley informed.

"Mr. Johnson, how are you?"

"I'm okay. How's everything going?"

"Very well. I think we have good news for you. We have isolated in the genetic code to identify which factors will decide the height of an adult while it is still an unborn child. I thought you'd like to know."

"Yes, I'm glad to hear that. Could you come to Lake Side again? I have a project I would like to discuss with you."

"Well, we are never too busy to ignore a person who has been so generous to our endeavors. When would you like us to be there?"

"As soon as you can make it. This weekend would be nice. If that fits your schedule, I'll have the airline tickets ready for you and a car waiting at the airport."

"I'm sure that will be fine with us. Can you give us any idea exactly what you want to know?"

"I could never discuss serious business over the phone. There may not be much to discus and you may be getting a turn-around flight back if that proves to be the case. Don't worry. This has nothing to do with funding. You are still on my list of good charities. If the project I have in mind is feasible, I'm ready to extend funding to whatever the additional costs may be."

"If there's anything we can do for you, we'll be glad to give it our best efforts. We'll look forward to seeing you this weekend."

****

So they arrived the next Saturday morning, not having a clue as to why they had been asked to make the trip. Hans picked them up as before, and once again there was no conversation between the three on the way to Lake Side.

"Welcome again, gentlemen. I hope you had a good flight. If you like, you can plan on staying here at my house until our business is concluded."

"Our flight was great. I speak for both of us when I say that we will be glad to accept your hospitality if we are to have an extended stay."

"Great. Can I get you anything to drink? I have about anything you could ask for."

"Yes, I'll have a scotch and soda. How about you Dr. Williams?"

"Yes, that would be good. Make it two."

"Okay, Juanita, will you mix two scotch and sodas for these gentlemen? Have a seat and make yourselves at home."

"I understand your reluctance to talk serious business over the phone. Much of what we do is that way as well. Can you tell us now why you wanted to see us?"

"I like the way you get right to the point. Yes, I can tell you. I'm excited that you've found a way to isolate the gene that controls the height of an individual as an adult. I'm considering becoming a father again. I would like to have some guarantee that my progeny will be taller than I am. Is there any way to guarantee a thing like that?"

"That depends on what you mean by guarantee. One of the biggest factors would be the height of the mother. How tall would she be?"

"I have no answer for that one."

"Really? Then you're not married?"

"Not even engaged. I have no idea who will be the mother of my children. The only thing I can tell you about her is that her genetic make-up must be such that she will give birth to tall children."

"Well, to be truthful, there is no way we can give you a lead pipe cinch on the height of the unborn. There is only the statistical probability of such things."

"I see. So what is the statistical probability of what I want if the mother is considered to be right?"

"With what we have done so far, and this is only with animals, not humans, we are 94.4% correct in predicting the height of the offspring. Would that satisfy your definition of a guarantee?"

"I guess so. There's nothing more certain than that. Now here's the tricky part. Can you help me locate a woman who would be right for this thing?"

"You mean you want us to find a mother for your children?"

"Yes, that's exactly what I mean."

"Can you qualify further what you want in this woman, other than just her genetic make-up to produce tall children?"

"Yes. There are certain other factors. She herself need not be a beauty queen, but I don't want someone repulsive to look at. She doesn't have to be a genius, but I don't want a moron, either."

"And how about race?"

"Caucasian would be nice."

"Is there any inducement we can offer a woman to come here and be your wife? I assume you mean to marry this woman."

"I hadn't really thought about it, but now that I do, I think you're right. I really should marry this woman. I'm kind of in the public eye here, and I think it would go better if the woman was my wife."

"Is there anything else you would like to know about our work?"

"Yes, have you done work in the area of multiple births?"

"Well, of course, but not with humans. We've never gotten to the point where we could have a human mother try such a thing. Are you interested in becoming the father of twins?"

"Yes, twins or triplets, or more."

"But why? If things work out, she could have a single child more than once.'

"I'm sure that's right, but you have to consider my age. The mother could be quite young, but I can't."

"True, but men much older than you are quite capable of producing children. That's not really a problem."

"There's more to being a father than just producing sperm. I'd really like to be around long enough to give their lives a little direction. I've already raised two sons, so I know a little about it."

"So really what you're asking us to do is to find a woman that we think gives you the best chance of giving you sons in multiple birth, and then somehow induce her to come here and be your wife. Is that it?"

"I think you've got it. Now, you seem to think the matter of inducement will be the hardest part of whatever you have to do. It could be, but what I've learned since I became rich, is that marrying a man of my considerable wealth is really the goal of most women. Will this woman, if you find her, be much taller than I am?"

"Not necessarily, but it is a distinct possibility. There is such a thing as a recessive gene, but we think it is far more likely to display itself as a dominant one. How tall can the woman be and still be acceptable?"

"That doesn't really matter. I was just curious."

They stayed two days, but there was really very little to discus after their first conversation. They seemed relaxed, and when they were not with Charley, they joked about the union of a man who had a wife considerably taller than he was. On the third day they told him they were ready to begin the search for the mother of his children.

****

It was more than two months later before Charley received a call from Dr. Williams. He sounded excited.

"Mr. Johnson, I think maybe we have found a woman to be the mother of your children. We've found three so far that could probably meet your criteria that you laid out for us, but only one that stands out."

"I know we don't like to talk business over the phone, but could you tell me a little bit more about this woman?"

"I could, but I'd rather tell you in person. We're both a little tired after this exhaustive search. Could we get a little R and R at your place this weekend?"

"Sure, why not. The tickets are on the way and Hans will pick you up as usual."

Hans wasn't really sure what this was all about. He was about to make his third trip to the airport to pick up these same two men. They never spoke to him in the limo, and Charley had never spoken to him about their purpose in visiting Lake Side. He wondered what it was all about, but he was certain Charley would have told him by now if he wanted him to know. A subtle change had come over Charley since he no longer coached the girls' basketball team. He spent most of his time alone, seemed to be in deep thought, and was less talkative than he had ever been. He hoped that whatever these two men brought to Charley would help him regain some of his good nature that had disappeared with the death of his wife.

Charley waited anxiously for Hans to get the men to his house. He paced the floor nervously until he heard the knock on the door.

"Gentlemen, come in. I can hardly wait for you to tell me what you've found. Can I have Juanita pour you a drink?"

"Yes, that would be great."

"Juanita. Pour these two gentlemen a drink. Scotch and soda, right?"

"Right."

"Well, let's get right to it. What can you tell me about the woman you think will be the right match for me?"

"Okay, here goes. She lives in a remote part of Russia. She is twenty-three years old, and she has never been married."

"Go on, go on. How tall is she? What does she look like? How about her intelligence?"

"Well, she has brown hair and brown eyes. Why don't I just let you look at this picture of her?"

He handed Charley a photograph of a woman standing between two men. She was several inches shorter than they were.

"I figured she'd be taller than she looks in this picture."

"Looks can be deceiving. Those two guys she's in the picture with are her brothers. Both of them are a little over 6' 10". She's only 6'6"."

"How about her intelligence?"

"Better than average as far as we can tell. She has the equivalent of what we would call a high school education. She played volleyball, but they had no basketball team."

"Have you contacted her to see if she might be willing to come here? Would she be interested in becoming Mrs. Johnson?"

"We have contacted them through her brothers. If you'd like to visit them, they would be glad to hear what you have to say."

"Would it be her decision or her brothers? I mean, to come here or not?"

"I'm not really sure about that. The family has very little in the way of money. I'm sure a generous offer would receive serious consideration."

"Here's the address. They don't have a phone or a computer, so you won't be able to call or E-mail them. If you think you don't want to wait for a letter to get there, I'd suggest you just fly over and see what they have to say. There's no airport closer than 60 miles from where they live, but you could probably rent a car and drive to the town where they live. Before you leave I'd find out what the exchange rate is for dollars to rubles. They might not understand what you're offering in dollars."

"Would I have to take an interpreter? You say they don't speak any English, so how can I make an offer they'll understand?"

"I think it might be advisable to take an interpreter. I hadn't though about it, but I think you're right."

That conversation set things in motion. Charley called Juan that evening and asked him to see if he could find an interpreter who was fluent in both English and several Russian dialects. Money for his service would be no object. They would leave for this small Russian town as soon as the man could make his way to Lake Side.

The interpreter arrived in Lake Side three days later. He was a friendly and talkative man, short of stature and long on laughter. He was amused by the purpose of the trip to his native land.

"I never thought I would be used as a marriage broker. Perhaps I should take another look at 'Fiddler on the Roof' before we take off."

"I hadn't thought of it, but you're right. You will really be trying to strike a deal with her family if I like what I see. Were you born in Russia?"

"Yes, I spent the first 35 years of my life there. I graduated from the University of Moscow in 1981."

"You speak English with very little accent. Did you learn that at the University?"

"I suppose, but I have been in this country for 25 years. I have worked for several years at the U.N. I speak six other languages as well."

"What can you tell me about the place that we'll be visiting?"

"I can tell you if things haven't changed radically in Russia in the last few years, you wouldn't be allowed to visit where we'll be going at all. It's a very isolated area, and one which the Russians have always feared might be infiltrated by spies."

"Will we be closely watched while we're there?"

"You can count on it, especially if the people you talk to suddenly show up with lots of rubles. I'm afraid someone might think they have sold some secrets to you, although I'm not sure what secrets they might know that your country would like to have. Russians have always been a little paranoid, especially where it concerns the United States."

"Why do you suppose that is?"

"Well, for one thing, you are the only country in the world that has ever used the atomic bomb on another country. Other countries have these things, but they have never used them."

"I guess I never thought of it in those terms. Will we run into a lot of "red tape," no pun intended, if the lady agrees to leave the country to be my wife?"

"That's hard to say. There is really only one way to avoid the red tape."

"And what's that?"

"Rubles. Lots of rubles. Don't be surprised if you have to grease a lot of palms to get what you want out of this?

"I think my credit is good for about any amount that I'll need."

"I'm sorry to inform you that your credit won't be worth a damn where we're headed. These people only understand cash, so I advise you to take lots of it with you. Also have access to a lot more than you carry. You may need it. I'll send a message to some of the people I know that might make things a little easier. It will take two or three days for me to contact them and wait for their reply. If you were not an international personality, I'm sure it would take a lot longer to get permission to visit there."

"Am I really that well known?"

"Oh yes, anyone with the financial resources you have is certainly well known internationally. Be sure to take along American dollars as well as lots of rubles. Sometimes the currency rate is volatile and people prefer dollars to rubles."

"Will I have any trouble getting permission to take along my personal bodyguard? I never go anywhere without him."

"The bodyguard will present no problems if he has proper credentials. However, he won't be allowed to carry any weapons with him. He'll have to go through metal detectors, so firearms are out."

"He won't be happy about that, but I think he'll go along for the ride. How long will it take for you to arrange our little trip?"

"Oh, I think a week should just about do it. It might not take that long, but if I were you, I'd plan on that length of time. Can I stay here while we get all the details worked out?"

"Of course. I have plenty of room here, and in the meantime, maybe you can tell me a little about the customs of the place we'll be visiting. I don't want to do anything that would embarrass me or them. What do you call the money that I'll offer the brothers for the hand of their sister?"

"Well, I guess the closest English equivalent would be a dowry. I could give you the Russian word for it, but you'd forget it, so why worry about it. I'll be doing all the talking, so don't worry about it."

"Okay, so what happens if the brothers like the idea, and she doesn't like the looks of me?"

"Well, I'd be surprised if they let her objections be the deciding factor in the decision. Usually the father would have the deciding vote, but in his absence the brothers will make the ultimate decision."

"How much money do you think I should offer them for her....hand?"

"I really don't know. I'm sure you have more than enough to satisfy their greed. If I were you, I'd take a gaudy diamond ring for the engagement. That might make a good impression on her."

"Take a look at this one. This is the one I used when I married my last wife. What do you think of this one? Is it gaudy enough?"

"Well, in size it's a beauty. It's really an old fashioned style, though. Where did you purchase it?"

"I didn't. My partner, Juan de los Santos gave it to me just before my wedding. He'd used it to marry his wife. Their union had been a happy one, so he asked me to use it in my own wedding."

"And was yours a happy one?"

"Indeed it was. Until her death, we were two of the happiest people on earth. So this ring is two for two in that regard. Will it impress her?"

"I should think so. I don't imagine she's had many opportunities to look at diamonds to compare it to. I'll need the use of both your E-mail and telephone for the next few days to try to arrange our arrival."

"Anything you need here or anything I can get you will be yours for the asking."

****

It was a full ten days before all the details of their trip could be arranged. Hans was less than thrilled to be assigned bodyguard duty with no weapon at his disposal. It was only two days before their departure that Charley revealed to him the purpose of the trip. His first reaction was one of disbelief.

"Have you lost your mind? Why in the hell could a man with everything you've got be traveling to Russia to propose to a woman he's never even met before?"

"It's hard to explain. I just think she'd be a great mother for my children."

"Does this have anything to do with those two weird guys I've picked up three times at the airport?"

"Yes, indirectly it does. I'm not going to try to explain what part they play in this thing, but they are a large part of it."

"Will they be making the trip with us? They kinda give me the fidgets."

"No, only the guy who's been here for a week will be traveling with us. He'll be my interpreter."

"I've never been to Russia."

"Neither have I. It'll be an educational experience for the both of us."

****

Indeed it was. Neither could have imagined the "red tape" involved in getting permission from all the authorities. Charley wondered if it would have been possible without the aid of the interpreter.

They flew into Moscow because there was no airport close to their destination with a runway long enough to accommodate the type of plane that took them there. From Moscow they boarded a much smaller plane. They made two stops to refuel before they arrived at their destination. It was very cold with light snow falling when they finally touched down on the bumpy runway.

There didn't seem to be anyone there to meet them, but shortly after their landing, two very tall men pulled up in a very old car. Neither got out of the car, but one of them motioned for them to come toward the car. The interpreter spoke briefly through the window of the car before he opened the back door of the sedan. Then all three men piled in and watched as the driver sped down a crooked road that became less visible as the snowfall increased. The ride took almost an hour before it came to a bumpy stop.

The house was not impressive. It was an old two-story affair that looked as though it might fall over if the wind continued to blow. None of the three passengers had brought a suitcase, only a small overnight bag. The driver had not offered to open the trunk for their baggage, so the space the bags occupied had added to the discomfort of the three men riding in the back seat. The passengers were more anxious to get inside the house than either of the men in the front seat. They waited outside the door for someone inside or one of the two men still in the car to open the door for them.

When the driver got to the door, he produced a key from his pocket and unlocked the door. The three visitors were surprised to find that the inside of the house was not appreciably warmer than the outside. It did block out most of the howling wind, but some of it still whistled through the cracks in the walls.

Charley was disappointed that she was not there to greet them. He assumed correctly that she was somewhere upstairs. The interpreter spoke to what appeared to be the older of the two brothers, and he yelled loudly, "Annika!"

She came down the creaking stairs with a grace that surprised all three visitors. She was wearing a dress that came almost to her ankles. The light inside was dim, and Charley could not tell if she was wearing any make-up. Her hair was long and beautifully groomed. His first impression was that the picture he had seen of her did not do her justice. While the older of the brothers talked to the interpreter, Charley and Hans stood almost entranced as she approached them. She gave each of the men a smile and a small curtsey. She stepped back away from where the men were seated and seemed to say by the way she waited that she really had no idea what the purpose was that these men had in coming. The elder of the brothers continued in an interchange with the interpreter that looked as though it might become heated. After some 15 minutes, both men smiled, stood up, and shook hands.

"The interpreter turned to Charley and said, "It's done if you agree to take her as your wife."

"Does she know what this is all about?"

"Not really, but that doesn't matter. Her brother will explain it to her, and she really has no choice in the matter."

"I see. So how much will this cost me?"

"Not nearly as much as it would if they knew how much you're worth. They know you're rich, they just don't know how rich. The cost will be about $200,000 in American currency. Do you have that much with you?"

"Yes, I do. When will her brother tell her what this all about?"

"Right now, if you like."

"Yes, I'd like to see the expression on her face when he tells her."

The interpreter spoke softly to the brother. He then got up and pulled his sister aside and almost whispered in her ear. Then she smiled.

"What did she say?"

"She said she is glad. You are more handsome than the other two."

Now it was Charley's turn to blush. "Ask her brother if she can go home with us, or if she'll have to wait for the paper work."

"I think if I pull the right strings and grease the right palms that she can go back with us."

It was the coldest night that Charley had ever spent. His bed was in the northwest corner of the downstairs, and the wind whistled through the wall. No amount of cover could keep off the chill. He was relieved when the morning came and was the first one up. He dressed and went into the kitchen, hoping it would be warmer there. It wasn't. He stumbled in the semi-darkness and banged into the stove. The noise awakened both of the brothers. They peered into the kitchen wearing their long underwear. They both laughed at the way Charley was dressed. He had not anticipated the cold and was totally unprepared for the biting air. His first thought was that if the interpreter couldn't pull the right strings, he would freeze to death before he could return home with his bride-to-be.

The laughter of the brothers awakened the rest of the house. Hans and the interpreter made their entry, followed by Annika, dressed in a long robe.

"Coldest damn night I ever spent in my life. How about you, Hans? Ever seen it so cold?"

"If I did, I can't remember it."

"You two Americans are soft. I grew up in this area. And believe me last night was far from the worst I've ever seen."

"Maybe you're right. Can you get started today trying to fix it so we can get out of here?"

"I can start, but they'll have to get me to a telephone. If I can reach a couple of people, we should be back in Moscow by nightfall. That's the best I can do.

"Well, if we can get back there, we can surely find some place warmer to spend the night. I wonder how much stuff she'll have to take with her. Women never travel as light as a man, and they never throw anything away."

"I'll have to take your word for that. I was never married."

"Trust me. Only once in my life did I find a woman who could travel light."

"Who and when was that?"

"It was when Alice and I were making our escape to Mexico. She left a lot of her stuff when we left hurriedly. I wasn't rich then, and she had no idea how she would ever replace what she left."

Annika fixed breakfast which consisted of scrambled eggs and a cold black bread. There was strong black coffee to wash down the food. She cleared the table when they had finished and washed the dishes. Charley noticed that she had to heat the water for the dishes since a hot water tank was a luxury her brothers could not afford. When she finished the dishes, her oldest brother spoke to her, and she left the room.

"What did he tell her?"

"He told her to start packing, that she might be leaving today."

"How far will you have to travel to get to a phone?"

"I'm not sure, but I think there's a line we can use not more than an hour from here."

"These people don't seem to be the type that can be rushed, but do what you can to get the thing started."

He spoke to the youngest who merely nodded his head. He left the room in search of the eldest and came back nodding his head in the affirmative.

"Good news. He says we can start in about an hour. We should be back about noon if everything goes as I hope."

"Will both of them go with you?"

"Of course not. One must stay here to guard the virtue of their sister."

"She looks big enough to guard her own virtue from someone the size of me."

"Probably, but they don't take many chances."

They got back shortly after noon. There was a smile on the face of the interpreter, which told Charley that they would be leaving soon. The eldest went straight to his sister to tell her to start packing her clothes. At first she showed no emotion, but shortly thereafter, she began to cry. Her brother put his arm around her and talked to her in a soothing voice. She dried her eyes and went upstairs to pack.

Only one brother took them to the small airport that would get them back to Moscow. One brother stayed at home since there was not enough room for six people and the baggage which had to accompany them. There was little conversation until they reached Moscow. They took three rooms from the best hotel, one for Hans and Charley, one for the interpreter, and one for Annika. The warmth of the modern room was enjoyed by all, but especially by Hans and Charley.

The next morning they boarded a huge airliner that took them all the way non-stop to New York City. They decided to spend the night there and take the last leg of their journey the following day. Before they booked a flight to Missouri, the interpreter pointed out something that Charley had not considered.

"Did you see the clothes she packed?"

"I didn't really look at them. What's wrong with her clothes?"

"Nothing, I guess, if she were about to become the wife of Santa Clause. She'll burn up in most of them. They're just not right for Lake Side."

"Will we have time for a shopping spree while we're here in New York?"

"Yes, I think so. Here in the big city, I'm sure you'll be able to find some attractive clothes for a woman her size. That's something you won't find in Lake Side."

Hans decided to stay in the hotel until they returned from their shopping spree. The interpreter told her they were shopping for some new clothes for her. She seemed pleased but said nothing. They went directly to a nationally famous store for big and tall women. It was obvious that he had never seen such a variety of beautiful clothes in sizes she could wear. She almost whispered to the interpreter, "How much can I spend? How many clothes will he let me buy?

"I think it does not matter. You can buy as many as we'll have room to take back to his home."

She bought more than a dozen outfits, not including shoes and undergarments. The total when she had finished was more than $3000.

When they got back to Lake Side, Charley was surprised to see the interpreter getting ready to leave. He had assumed that the man would be with them until he could find a permanent interpreter.

"I'm sorry, but I can't stay. I have other clients. I am already late, so I must leave you now."

"Surely you can stay until I find someone who can begin to teach her some basic English. It's gonna be a mess around here if we can't communicate at all. How much will it take to keep you here until I can find someone to get her started?"

"I think a thousand dollars a day would be enough for me to disappoint those who will be waiting on my services."

"Okay, but I gotta tell you, that makes you a bigger crook than some of the people that Hans has to deal with."

"Surely you jest. I can probably get someone for you in a couple of days. How much are you willing to pay for a permanent interpreter?"

"Whatever it takes. I want a woman, one who is not too old and decrepit to help take care of the children when they come."

"Okay, what if I tell the candidates that salary is negotiable. That way they will be the ones holding you up, not me."

"Okay, sounds alright to me. You'll stay then until I've hired a permanent replacement?"

"Yes, for the amount I mentioned."

"Deal. How long do you think it will take to find a suitable replacement?"

"Maybe only a day or two, maybe as much as a week. No more than that."

"Could you maybe get her started a little bit, you know, just our names and maybe the names of some of the more common things around here."

"Perhaps, but if I get into a teaching mode, it may take me longer to find a replacement."

"Yeah, and I bet that would really tear you up to have to stay for a lousy thousand dollars a day, wouldn't it?"

"Oh, to be honest, not really. You have a very comfortable abode here. What's your beef if I stay a while? You'll never miss a paltry thousand dollars a day."

"True, it's just the principal of the thing. I know you don't make that much on a regular basis."

"Also true, but this is not a regular situation. How many multi-billionaires are in the process of marrying someone who doesn't even speak a word of the language? Not many, I warrant you. Unusual situations often call for unusual payment."

"I guess I can't argue about that. How soon will you start the search for a permanent interpreter and teacher? I want her to understand not just the words we use, but also some of the customs. I'm sure they'll be a lot different than what she's used to."

"You're right about that, but time and time alone will make her familiar and comfortable with your customs. That's not something someone from a radically different culture can pick up in a few days."

****

She was 42 years old with slightly graying hair. Her name was Diedra Ustanov, and she spoke three other languages, as well as English and a couple of Russian dialects. The amount she said she would work for was $50,000 a year. She was surprised when Charley offered her $75,000 a year, free lodging, and health and life insurance to boot. He told her he expected more than just teaching of the English language. He wanted her to understand American customs and traditions. He asked her when she could start, and she told him it would take a couple of days to move her belongings into his house. He offered to hire the movers that might speed up the process. He was anxious to get things off on the right foot, and he feared their relationship might go sour if there were too many initial misunderstandings

All of her things arrived in slightly less than 48 hours. Before she arrived to stay, Annika spent much of her time in her own large bedroom. She tried on the new clothes she had bought in New York several times. She still could hardly believe her good fortune. Her husband-to-be was not only a rich man, but also a generous one. He was older than she, but not nearly as old as some of her friends' husbands. She had worried all her life that she would never get a husband. She had learned early that men are not attracted to women who are several inches taller than they are. The only two men in town where she lived who were not intimidated by her height were her two brothers.

The first thing Annika learned was how to address her husband-to-be. Diedra suggested that she call him Mr. Johnson until they were married; then she could call him Charley. The two women would call each other by their first names only. Hans would also be called by only his given name. Charley had Diedra tell her that she was never to leave the house unless accompanied by Hans.

Diedra helped prepare her first meal in America. It was nothing more than hamburgers and fries, but it gave her the opportunity to begin to learn the names of everyday items for the table, including condiments. Everything she touched she was told the name of and asked to repeat several times. Both were pleased that she seemed to learn rapidly and retain what she had learned.

It was a week before Charley had Diedra ask Annika what she would like in the way of a wedding. She wanted a church wedding, but since there was no Eastern Orthodox in Lake Side, she would have to settle for Roman Catholic.

She wanted to know if her brothers could come to the wedding. Charley agreed to pay their way if they could make the trip to Lake Side. Charley sent them a telegram with the invitation and wired them enough money to send him a return telegram with their answer. The answer came two days later and was an acceptance of Charley's offer. Annika was ecstatic, for there would be no one else there at the wedding that she would know.

Charley got the young woman with whom he had coached basketball to give Annika some help with planning the wedding. Diedra had to translate for the pair as they planned it. It was hard for Annika to understand the meaning of the word honeymoon. Such a thing was not common in the region where she had lived her whole life. Only the very rich ever had the opportunity for a vacation of any kind.

The priest who would perform the ceremony also had need of Diedra's service. She had listened to what he said and nodded as Diedra translated. Charley was familiar with most of it, although there were some slight differences from the Mexican service that had joined him and Alice.

Annika's natural shyness gradually disappeared. As she became more familiar with her circumstances each day, the beautiful personality, which had remained hidden, emerged so all could see. Her language lessons with Diedra progressed faster than either Charley or her teacher could have imagined. She was beginning to put short sentences and phrases together, and when she made a mistake, she smiled and corrected it. She seldom made the same mistake twice. The wedding would take place in six weeks.

Annika picked out a wedding gown, or at least a picture of one, from a bridal wedding magazine. It could not be purchased as it was shown in the magazine; it would have to be sewn to accommodate a bride of her height.

Charley was glad that he was a very rich man, for he had decided to extend an open invitation to the people of Lake Side to attend his nuptials. He was certain that the church where the ceremony would be performed would not contain all the curious who came to either the wedding or the reception. He had gotten permission from the school board to use the gymnasium for the reception. He really had no idea how many to plan for at the reception, but he decided to err on the side of caution. He told the caterer to be prepared for 600.

****

The population of Lake Side had gradually become accustomed to the sight of Hans escorting an extremely tall woman around the growing town. She loved to shop for groceries, and Hans had gotten used to the idea of taking her to two or three different stores several times a week. She could hardly believe the incredible variety of foods that Americans had at their disposal. At first she had trouble with American currency, but she quickly learned. She could hardly believe that there was nothing in any of the stores that she could not have. Charley had arranged for her to simply sign for anything she wanted, eliminating the necessity for carrying large sums of cash.

The wedding was the social event of the year for Lake Side. The church was filled to overflowing. Annika looked splendid in her white wedding gown, and Charley looked better than he had at any of his two previous weddings. He hadn't really wanted to wear a tuxedo, but he could see that anything less would look tacky next to the splendor of the bride.

The reception completely filled the gymnasium. The food was plentiful, and the champagne flowed until the wee hours of the morning. A twelve piece band provided the live music, and it was only when Charley escorted the bride to the dance floor that he discovered how graceful she was. She danced with Charley almost exclusively. The only exceptions were the few she danced with her brothers. Her brothers got gloriously drunk, preferring the vodka to the plentiful champagne. It was well past three a.m. when Charley managed to corral them both and get them back in the house. They were scheduled to return to Russia later that same day.

Charley had already decided what must come next. He had thought about the consummation of the nuptials for a long time. Diedra had told him that Annika had admitted to her that she was indeed a virgin. His first wife had also been a virgin, but that was different. He simply could not picture himself having sex with this beautiful, young and extremely tall woman. He had no idea what position would be the best. There was also the fear that she would become pregnant before he had a chance to arrange a meeting with his two scientific friends. He had decided to use the old fashioned rubbers as a means of contraception.

It wasn't nearly as bad as he feared. He found the missionary position to be quite satisfactory. He had remained celibate since the death of Alice, so sex was a welcome release from the pent up energy. He wasn't certain how she would react, but there was no sign of disappointment from the bride. Things went on as usual for a month. Charley twice made contact with the scientists. He found that they were ready to try to accomplish what they had told him was impossible. They would need to see Annika twice, once to remove the ovum and again to replace it in the womb. They wanted to know if she would be aware of what was happening.

Annika was learning English at an astounding rate. She was glad when Charley told her they would be taking a trip. He told her they would be seeing some doctors to examine her to see if she was ready to become a mother. She was pleased, although she wondered what the doctors could really tell about her chances of motherhood.

Timing was everything. Charley had to use Diedra to find out about Annika menstrual cycle. Charley's vacation would be to the upper Midwest, which would include Minnesota. That is where the doctors did all their work. They would plan on being there for a couple of days on their way back from Niagra Falls. Annika liked the thought of being in Minnesota because the snow reminded her of home.

When they arrived at the clinic, the doctors told Annika that she would be sedated for a short time with a general anesthetic while they performed their examination. While they were there, Charley made his sperm donation. They had to come back in a month for the results of the exam.

****

For Charley the month went by slowly. He had trouble concentrating on anything other than the upcoming trip to Minnesota.

"Annika, will you be ready for another trip to Minnesota in a few days? We have to go back there to get the results of your tests."

"I like Minnesota. Does it ever snow in Missouri?"

"Yes, but it doesn't stay on the ground for long. Did you ski a lot when you were in Russia?"

"Not a lot, but some. I had chores to do, and I looked after my brothers and tried to keep the house clean."

"What have you heard from your brothers?"

"They say they miss me, but I really think they miss my cooking and cleaning more, but I love my brothers. They are all the family I have. Are you anxious to have children? I know you have already had three. How many would you like to have?"

"It really doesn't matter as long as they're healthy. How many would you like to have?"

"Lots. I like children."

"Wonderful."

****

The stay in Minnesota was for a single day. Annika was told that she would need to be sedated again to re-run one of the tests. She had no objection since the first time had been painless.

In private, the doctors told Charley they were extremely confident that everything had gone well. She was in great physical shape for the ordeal that multiple birth might require. They also told him they would advise a Caesarian section, rather than natural birth if a multiple birth was forthcoming.

The following month, Diedra informed Charley that Annika had missed her period. Annika was more than two weeks overdue when she finally got the nerve to tell him herself. She was nervous about what his reaction might be. She was relieved to find him in such high spirits at the news.

By the end of the second month, Charley was taking her to see a local pediatrician. She looked forward to seeing this young doctor who had recently arrived in Lake Side. He had taken up his practice here largely as a result of the influx of young couples who had moved to Lake Side. The beautiful new school had already begun attracting people who had school age children and who might have more.

By the end of the first trimester, Annika was not showing any more than a woman who was expecting a single child. Early in the second trimester, the pediatrician called Charley in for a conference after his routine examination of Annika.

"Folks, I have some exciting news."

"And what would that be, doctor?"

"Well, it looks likely that Mrs. Johnson is expecting triplets. I say that's exciting. This will be my first experience with a multiple birth, but I've had lots of training. I'm also glad that Mr. Johnson is a very rich man. Any type of childbirth is expensive, but I'm told that multiples are outrageous. Sometimes the manufacturers of baby formula and diapers pitch in and help out, but I don't think you need any of their help."

"Are you sure about triplets?"

"No, not really, but I'm sure there is more than one heart beat, probably more than two."

"What facilities do you have here in Lake Side to take care of something like this. What should I do in the meantime to be ready?"

"Well, considering your means, I'd get started building a nursery. Then I'd try to line up some full time help for Mrs. Johnson to take care of the babies. She won't be able to nurse them all, so you'll need lots of formula.

"How much assistance will you need in delivering the babies? Is the hospital itself ready for so many babies at one time?"

"Well, I may have to ask for a little help with the births, but I can have all that arranged in advance."

"Thank you, doctor. We'd better be on our way now and start trying to get ready. I do have one question, though."

"What's that?"

"Would you recommend natural birth or Caesarian for something like this?"

"Well, that could well depend on the size of the babies. I'd hate to make a decision like that at this time."

Charley was almost as happy as Annika. She could hardly wait to start shopping for the baby clothes. Charley began immediately to prepare for the arrival of his sons. He called the scientists who had made this possible and told them what the doctor had told them. They were excited and wanted to know if he could bring her to them so they could make their estimate of how successful the experiment had been. He agreed and set up an appointment with them in two weeks.

During the two weeks' waiting period, Charley watched as a full construction crew began the work on the nursery. They would be paid overtime since it was imperative that the construction be completed before the arrival of the babies.

He wondered if he would need an explanation about why they were going back to see the men who had first examined her. He only told her they were the best experts at multiple births. He told her the examination would not take as long as the first two. She didn't seem to mind since she loved Minnesota.

"Welcome, Mr. and Mrs. Johnson. It's good to see you both again. How are you feeling, Mrs. Johnson? Congratulations on your pregnancy. We hear from your husband that you will be the mother of more than one child. The only thing our examination will do is let you know exactly how many you will have."

"But my doctor at home has already told me there will be three. Do you think he is wrong?"

"Well, sometimes these things are harder to predict if you don't have all the equipment we fortunately have. If you are far enough along, we can also tell you the sex of the children if you really want to know."

"Yes, I would like to know. It would make buying clothes for them much easier if I knew whether they were boys or girls."

"Then step this way with Nurse Williams. She'll take you back to the examination room."

The examination took about forty-five minutes. Annika got back into her clothes and accompanied the doctors back to the reception room where Charley was anxiously waiting. The doctors had told her nothing. They wanted to see how both would react together to their news.

"Well, doctors, what's the good news?"

"The good news indeed. Mr. and Mrs. Johnson, you are about to experience something that is extremely rare. Less than one in twenty million parents will ever know the potential joy that is about to come your way. Mrs. Johnson, in a few months you will be the mother of five baby boys. From our examination we can tell that all five seem in very good health. If you carry them to term, and I have no doubt that you will, their size will be enough for you to take them home in a shorter period of time than usual. Usually, in cases like this, the infants require a longer period of time before they weigh enough to leave the hospital. I don't think you will have to wait too long."

"But my doctor said only three. Why could he not tell there were five?"

"Well, very few doctors have all the equipment that we have to predict these things. Your doctor is no doubt a good man. It is not his fault that he could not detect the presence of all five babies at such an early stage. I'm sure that by now he will be able to mark the progress of all five of your sons."

"I'm glad he's not at fault. I like him very much. He is a kind man, and I think a good doctor."

"Good, it's important for people top have confidence in their doctors. We specialize in multiple births. If you develop any problems, you can be assured that we will offer your doctor any assistance that he might need."

"Do you anticipate any problems?"

"No, but things like this are so rare that we can't be sure. We have never dealt with quintuplets before. We have had lots of triplets and three sets of quads, but no quints. That is why it is impossible to say what problems might occur."

"Do you think the facilities in Lake Side will be enough to handle something like this?"

"Probably, but we would like to be there just in case something should go wrong. Would your doctor object if we were there just as observers?"

"I don't think so. He told us this is his first experience at multiple births, so I would think he would be thrilled to have people like you there just in case. He's a young doctor, so I think this experience will be really valuable to him in dealing with future multiple births."

"Then you'll let us know if he agrees. We would like to be there for the final week of the pregnancy."

"We'd be glad to have you stay at our house for that week."

"You'd be welcome."

"If your doctor would like, we'll be available to answer any questions he might have at any time during the pregnancy."

"Thank you, Doctors. I think it's about time we headed back to Missouri."

****

It was Diedra who brought Charley back to reality. She had never scolded him before, but she wasted no time in telling him what was on her mind. He had hardly set foot back inside the house when she opened up on him.

"Sir, I think you may have forgotten something that is very important."

"And just what might that be?"

"Sir, you have a daughter. I know this upcoming pregnancy is extremely important, but you seem to have forgotten about your daughter. She has lots of toys, but she really has no one to play with or anyone to talk to. I know you are a busy man, but you should really spend more time with her. She has no mother, and at times it seems as though she has no father."

"I'm sorry. I'll try to make it up to her somehow. Where is she now?"

"She's in her room. I don't think she's gone to bed yet. Please go and talk to her and read her a bedtime story. I can see the sadness in her face. She really needs you now. I hope that Annika will not get so caught up in her own children that she forgets about her."

Annika chimed in, "I'm sorry, too, Diedra. I have neglected my duty to her, and I take so much of his time that he has neglected her, too. We'll start making it up tomorrow. What do you say, Charley? How about a what you call a "picnic" tomorrow?"

"Sure. Where do you suggest that we have it?"

"I think right down by the lake would be good. She really likes the water. If she wants, I'll swim with her at the little beach. Would you join us?"

"Maybe if the water isn't too cold, I just might take a dip. If it is too cold, we have the heated pool here inside."

"I know, but it's not the same. Oh, heavens! I forgot. I have no swimsuit that will fit me now. How can I go swimming with no suit?"

"Just wear a pair of shorts and a top. It won't make any difference. I don't know if I even have a suit, but it won't stop me from going into the water."

He went up the stairs to her room and quickly slipped inside. When she saw him, she gave a squeal of delight and jumped into his arms. He held her in his arms while she smothered him with kisses.

"Are you going to stay at home now, or will you be leaving again?"

"I think I'll be home for quite a while now. Would you like for me to read you a bedtime story?"

"Yes, I'd like the one about the princess who married the handsome prince. Do you like that one?"

"Yes, it's one of my favorites."

He began the story, but he had hardly finished "Once upon a time" when she was fast asleep. He kissed her gently on the cheek and tucked her neatly in the bed. He went back downstairs and found the two women sitting at the kitchen table.

"I started to read her favorite story, but she fell asleep. I tucked her in. She reminds me more of her mother every day."

"She's beautiful, Charley. I hope our sons will look as good as she does. Her hair makes her look like an angel."

"Her mother was beautiful, too. I hope our sons resemble you as much as she resembles her mother. I think you're beautiful, too."

"Why, thank you, Charley. You never told me that before. It makes me feel good."

"I'm glad Diedra reminded us about her. We just got so caught up in the pregnancy that we forgot. Now I'm reminded that I have another son and granddaughter that I've been neglecting. I think I'll call him now and see how everything is going with them."

He excused himself and went into the den to talk privately. Billy seemed surprised when he heard his father's voice.

"Gee, Dad, it's been a while. What's been going on?"

"Not a whole lot. How's everything in Perdido?"

"About like always. Juan keeps everybody happy, and the money just keeps rolling in."

"That's great. So how's the family?"

"Okay, I guess. Really? It doesn't sound like everything is okay. What's the matter?"

"Well, you know I'm sick and tired of life here in Perdido. I'd love to be back in the States with you, but you know Luisa won't even consider it. She's never really gotten over the way Alice got killed. I don't think she's afraid for herself, but she's afraid for our daughter."

"I can understand that. How is my granddaughter? I miss her a lot. I wish you guys could be here with us."

"She's growin' like a weed. Looks a lot like her mother, but she does have my eyes. How's your youngest?"

"A lot like your own. Prettier every day and lookin' more and more like her mother. I do have some news, though. Annika is pregnant."

"Really? When is she due?"

"She's in the second trimester. That's not the really big news, though."

"What is it then?"

"She's expecting quintuplets. All boys."

"Good God, dad, are you kidding?"

"No, I'm not. I've never been more serious in my life. We're pretty excited about it. I wish you could be here when the boys arrive. Is there any chance you can talk Luisa into making the trip for the big event?"

"I don't know. I'll give it my best shot, and if she won't come with me, I'll make the trip by myself."

"I'd really like that son. I really miss you, and I'd give almost anything to have you here with me. It's really kinda funny, isn't it?"

"What's funny, dad?"

"Well, you wind up with a Mexican wife and I wind up with a Russian. Don't you think that's just little strange?"

"Yes, but life's been more than a little strange ever since you came up with the adjustment."

"You're right about that. Let's try to keep better in touch. You tell me if there's anything I can do to persuade Luisa to make the trip with you."

"Will do, dad. Tell everyone "hi" from me."

He went back to the kitchen where the women were still talking. He smiled and sat down to join them.

"Did you talk to your son?"

"Yes, I think he may be here when the babies come. His wife is afraid to come with him, but I think he'll come by himself."

"Is his wife afraid to fly?"

"No, she just remembers that my first wife was killed here, and this frightens her."

"Does your son like living in Mexico?"

"Not really. He only came there because I was there. He was a big help to me when our business was just getting started. He was shot and almost died when he attended the wedding of Alice and me. He fell in love with the niece of my business partner. I think when they married, they thought I'd be content to stay in Mexico for the rest of my life, and for a while, I thought so, too. But after all the success we had, and all the money we made, I grew homesick for America."

"I see, and now he would like to come home, too, and his wife won't come with him. That is sad. I liked him when I met him at our wedding. Is there any chance he would ever leave his wife and daughter to move back here?"

"I don't think so, but you never can tell how things will work out. I could never have predicted that I would get you to be my wife, or that I would be the father of five sons. Life is strange sometimes."

"Yes, and I never could have imagined that a very wealthy man would come all the way to my small home town and take me away to America. Life is strange. I felt the babies move today."

"Really? When?"

"When we were on the way home. I never thought to tell you then, but the next time I feel a move, I will let you feel it too."

"Yes, please do. I've had the pleasure of feeling the movements of all three of my other children. How are you feeling? Will you be up to a picnic tomorrow? I certainly hope so."

"Yes, I feel good. I'm going to have fun, especially if we go swimming."

"What's the weather supposed to be like tomorrow, Diedra?"

"I think the weatherman said it would be sunny and nice, but he's been wrong several times recently."

The weatherman was right for once. The weather was beautiful and the picnic was a huge success. Even though the water was quite cold, Annika could not be restrained from going into the lake for a dip. She explained that she was used to going into water much colder than that. Neither Charley nor his daughter got past putting their toes in the water before retreating back to the towels lying on the beach. Charley paid more attention to his daughter than he had at any time in previous months.

"Are you cold, Sweety?"

"No, Daddy, I'm fine. This is lots of fun. Will we have time for picnics when my brothers are born?"

"Sure, Sweety. We'll always have time to have fun together. Do you look forward to having brothers?"

"Yes, I think it will be nice. How much longer do we have to wait until they're born?"

"Not too much longer. Are you about ready to call it a day, Annika?"

"Yes, but I think Diedra will have to fix supper tonight. I don't feel like fixing anything."

"What if I just order some pizza? Will that be alright? Are you hungry for anything in particular?"

"No, pizza is fine. I feel like I could eat a large all by myself."

Things grew hectic in those last few days before the arrival of the quints. The doctors were amazed at the enormous size Annika had become. They were certain that each of the babies would weigh more than three pounds. The prognosis was for a live and healthy birth for all five. The doctors advised Charley that Caesarian birth for all five would be easier on Annika, but they warned him she might never be able to give birth again if they decided to go that way. He decided to leave it up to Annika. She opted for natural birth.

It was in all the newspapers. There was simply no way to make a thing like this a private affair. Charley tried his best to stay far in the background of all the publicity, but his name was already a legend, so his attempts to stay out of the limelight were futile. Like it or not, he couldn't help being on the front page of every paper in Missouri and many national tabloids.

The first of the quints to be born was also the largest. He weighted almost three and a half pounds and was named Jack. The second weighed three and a quarter pounds and was named Jerry. The third was Joshua and weighed three pounds and two ounces. The fourth was Joseph and weighed three pounds and one ounce. The last was John and weighed an even three pounds. Annika came through the ordeal with a courage that made Charley proud of the fact that she had chosen natural over Caesarian birth.

Three weeks in the hospital were all it took for the quints to reach the minimum weight that would allow them to leave the hospital. The addition to the house, including the nursery, had been completed for a month. Three women had been hired to help with the babies and the housework. Each woman would be on duty for 8 hours each day, and, if any problems should arise, the women would work double or triple shifts.

Charley had turned down all the efforts of companies who specialized in baby products to give him their products for his endorsement of their company. He simply did not want the publicity. He had never sought the limelight, even when the popularity of his adjustment was at its height. Now more than ever he was content to stay in the background. While Annika and the three nurses supervised all the activities of the babies, Charley devoted most of his time to his daughter.

****

The first three years were wild. The boys grew at an astounding rate. No one would ever have guessed that these five brothers had not been born individually. Charley hired even more help to take care of the boys. He wanted them to be able to play outdoors, so he had hired a trio of young men to supervise their activities. He watched with interest as the boys were introduced to such activities that would maximize their eye-hand coordination. Whiffle-ball was fun, and tossing around a plastic football had its moments, but Charley was more interested in their play with a small basketball and a goal which stood about six feet high. Charley provided a new concrete slab so the boys could learn to dribble the ball.

Jack, the eldest, quickly became the best at bouncing the ball. He took his role as the eldest seriously. When disagreements came up, he became the arbiter, using physical force to impose his will on his brothers when necessary. John, the youngest, soon proved the best at putting the ball through the hoop. Joshua and Joseph by this time were a good two or three inches taller than the other three. They resembled each other more than the other three. The only way Charley could tell them apart was that Josh was left handed. Jerry, the second born, really did not excel at any one phase of their little games, but he was the best all-round at whatever they did.

No mother had ever been prouder of her offspring than Annika was of her boys. She would have liked to have had other children, but Charley was careful to practice birth control. She spent sufficient time with the boys to be sure they were learning her native language. Charley had made little effort to learn that language and was often confused when the boys used it. Sometimes he was sure they did it just to aggravate him. His only restriction on the use of it was that English would be the only language spoken at the table.

One morning after breakfast, Charley heard loud voices coming from the living room. The voices grew louder, and he detected a sense of anger that he had not perceived from the boys before. He headed in that direction to see what was happening. When he got there, he was surprised to see Jack sitting on top of Joseph and pummeling him with his fists. Although Joseph was taller and heavier, he could not manage to extricate himself from the position he was in.

"Hey! What the hell is going on here?"

"He says he wants to be the leader when we exercise today. I told him that was my job. He said it was his turn, but it's not."

"Does he get a turn?"

"Sometimes I let him, but it's my job. I'm the oldest."

"Does being the oldest make you the leader all the time?"

"Yes, it does."

"Let him up. We have to have a talk. Jack. I know you're the oldest, but I think we're going to have to talk about who gets to be the leader. Besides being the oldest, what else makes you the leader?"

"I'm the strongest. You can ask any of them and they'll tell you that I'm the strongest. When we wrestle, I always wind up on top."

"Well, that may work for some things, but from now on we're going to take turns. Joseph, you'll be the leader today. Jack, I'm going to let you be the one to tell your brothers when it's their turn. Everybody will get to be the leader for the same number of days. Jack, you'll be responsible to tell the others whose day it is to lead. If you try to cheat one of them out of their days, I'll keep you in that day, and you won't be allowed to go out at all that day. Do you understand what I'm telling you?"

"Yes sir."

Charley thought to himself as they went out side. If we play baseball, Jack will be the pitcher. If we play football, Jack will be the quarterback. If we play basketball, Jack will be the point guard. It really hasn't taken very long to see who will be the leader of this group.

****

When the boys became kindergarden age, Annika for the first time opposed Charley on a serious matter. He wanted to enroll the boys at the school he had personally created. She was reluctant to see the boys leave the house and wanted them to be home-schooled by tutors that would come to the house each day. In the end, Charley had agreed to let her have her way.

The tutors were amazed. For children only five years old, they were remarkable. They could count to a hundred easily, they knew their alphabet; and they could read at the fourth grade level. Not only this, they were bilingual as well.

Classes began at 8:00 and ended at 3:00 Four and a half hours were devoted to studies, one and a half to physical activity, and the rest to meals and snacks. It was one of the happiest years ever for the Johnson family.

As the boys approached their sixth birthday, Charley had decided to insist they be enrolled in school. He knew they couldn't get a better education than the one they were getting at home, but he realized their social development would be sadly lacking if they didn't learn to mix with the rest of the kids their own age. Over the tears and objections of their mother, Charley enrolled the boys in Lake Side Elementary School.

It was awkward from the beginning. The other children stared at the quints as objects of curiosity. The teacher found it increasingly difficult to find any material that would challenge them, and on the playground, the boys had to play with children several grades older than they were. Even against older kids, the quints usually came out on top if they were allowed to play on the same team.

Charley and Annika attended every Parent-Teacher meeting. They were called in on more than one occasion due to the behavior of the boys. All five were willing to settle disputes with their fists, and Jack, though not the biggest of the five, was easily the most aggressive. If any of the other children hurled an insult at any of the five, it was always Jack who was the first to react. Two larger and older students had been sent to the school nurse from fighting with Jack. Charley had been quick to pay the medical bills of those who quarreled with any of his sons.

Charley lectured the boys about fighting, but it seemed to have no affect. By the third grade, he was convinced that his sons would be getting a better education if they resumed home schooling. He re-hired his former tutors, and once again the Johnson quints were confined to their home ground.

The boys often watched all manner of sports on TV. Charley did not encourage the boys to pursue football or baseball, but he did like soccer. He thought that learning to use their feet would definitely improve their basketball skills.

In order to provide competition for the boys, Charley allowed them to invite some of their older friends over to play with and against his sons. Things usually worked out well with little or no fisticuffs, unless the argument was among the quints themselves. Jack and John were usually the ones who mixed it up if there were any serious disagreements about the rules of any game. It was bad when they were forced to compete against each other, but sometimes it was even worse when they were on the same team. Both always wanted to be the captain of any team they were on. Charley listened to this exchange one day.

"Yeah, I know you're the oldest, but that doesn't make you the best."

"Oh yeah? Who says so?"

"I do. I can run faster than you and jump higher, and I can certainly shoot the ball better than you."

"Well, how are you with your fists?"

"You want to try me?"

The answer was a looping right hand punch which connected just above John's left ear. He went to the ground, but he jumped back to his feet and tackled Jack. They rolled around on the ground until Jack wound up astride his brother and got in two good punches before John threw him aside. Both got to their feet and sparred in a circle before one of the tutors broke it up.

At supper that night, Charley decided it was time to do something to keep the boys from fighting with each other.

"I want all five of you to listen to this. But Jack and John, it's especially for you two. Now I saw what happened out on the basketball court today. I'm not gonna have you guys fighting among yourselves. I know both of you want to be the captain of any team you're on, but it isn't worth fighting over. So, here's the way it's gonna be. Starting with today, neither of you will be allowed to play any kind of sport for a week. If it happens again, it will be for two weeks. Punching each other in the face could cause either one of you to lose sight in one of your eyes."

It had the desired affect. Both of the boys could hardly stand being kept inside away from the playground for a whole week. Each blamed the other for their confinement, but by the fourth day, being isolated with only the company of each other, they seemed to have settled their differences. Charley noticed that each had mellowed since their banishment from the basketball court. He called them aside after the evening meal.

"Boys, I think I see a better attitude today than what I've seen before. I'm going to let you back outside tomorrow, but if this happens again, I'll add on the two days I'm letting you off of, and they'll go with the two weeks you'll spend inside. Do you understand what I'm saying?"

"Yes sir!"

From that time on, Jack and John found it was easier to share the role of captain than to fight over it.

****

It was just before the start of the fourth grade that Charley began a most ambitious project. It followed the wettest fall season that Lake Side had seen in years. The quints had become troublesome since they were not allowed to go outside and play in the rain. At one point the rain had kept the boys inside almost exclusively for ten days. As the weather continued throughout the fall to be too wet for outdoor play or exercise, Charley had decided to take action. He contacted the firm that had constructed the gym in Lake Side High and asked them to give him a bid for another gymnasium.

"Could you be a little more specific, Mr. Johnson? Will the gym be part of the already existing complex?"

"No, it won't. This structure will be on my own personal property, not in any way connected to the school."

"Will it require much in the way of seating?"

"No, it will mostly just be a practice facility. There won't be much in the way of spectators."

"How about dressing room facilities?"

"Just enough for the guys to shower after a practice."

"How about the dimensions of the floor itself?"

"Regulation, just like the one at school."

"How about heating and cooling?"

"Just like the one in school."

"Well, I couldn't begin to give you an accurate estimate, but I can tell you it's gonna cost you a hell of a lot of money."

"That's not a real problem. How soon can you give me an accurate estimate, and how long will it take to get a look at the blueprint?"

"Well, I'll have to send a team down there to get a look at the lay of the land where you want it built. As soon as they get back to me, I'll get their info to the guys who'll do the blueprints. I'd say we can get back to you in ten days or two weeks. Is that gonna be quick enough?"

"Yeah, the faster the better. The weather here has been miserable for so long that I'm sure it will probably slow down the construction. Do you guys work through the winter?"

"If the weather will let us. Can the team I send down there stay at your place until they finish their estimate?"

"Sure. They'll be welcome. How many will there be?"

"Four or five. I'm not sure how many we can spare at the moment. We're pretty busy, but we're never too busy to do business with you."

The crew arrived two days later. They went right to work and spent only three days to accomplish their objective. The weather stayed nasty for the whole three days. When they finished, they assured Charley that he would be able to see a preliminary blueprint in about a week.

True to his word, the blueprint arrived by express mail in six days. It showed a full size gymnasium of regulation length with four side goals. The floors would be hardwood. There would be two locker rooms with showers in both. There would be a single row of seats on both sides of the gym. Projected costs: 11.5 million dollars: projected time to complete the project: three to four months depending on the weather.

Charley had told the boys they soon they would have a place to play no matter what the weather might be outside. They watched with enthusiasm as the structure began to take shape, but they really had no idea of the scope of the whole thing. Each day they made a trip down to the site to see if they could detect any progress.

"One day John said to Jack, "Brother, can I ask you something?"

"Sure, go ahead."

"I know you're the oldest. So I guess maybe you know more about some things than the rest of us."

"Holy cow, John, I'm only a few minutes older than the rest of you. So how can I know any more than the rest of you?"

"I know, but you are the oldest, and Dad talks to you more than he does to us."

"What did you want to ask me about?"

"Where did Dad get all the money he has to build things like this building just for us?"

"I'm not really sure. He never talked to me about it, but one time I asked Mom about it, and she said it had something to do with an invention he made that got him all the money."

"What did he invent?"

"She wasn't certain, but it had something to do with helping cars get lots more miles to a gallon of gas. He still owns lots of stuff in Mexico. His other son Billy runs things for him. Dad said one time he wished Billy would move back here. I wonder if he loves him more than he loves us."

"Naw, I don't think he does. You know how much he loves us. Look at all the stuff he's given us. Look at this huge building. You know he's having it built just for us. How could he love anyone more than that?"

"I don't know. I just wondered. What do you think of our sister?"

"She's not a real sister. She's just a half-sister. You know Dad had two other wives, don't you?"

"Yeah, I know. I heard they both died. I know the first one got sick and died, but Dad never would say what happened to the other one. He never likes to talk about it. He says our sister reminds him a lot of her."

"Do you think he loves Mom? I don't think they sleep together much any more."

"I know, but that doesn't means he doesn't love her. I think it means he doesn't want any more kids."

"Why not?"

"Well, stop and think. He already has seven. Don't you think that's enough?"

"Yeah, I suppose so."

"Do you think he'd tell us about how he got all his money if we'd ask him?"

"He might. I'll try it next time we're alone. I'd really like to know. Some of the kids at school said he was famous. I'd like to know if that's true."

"I'll ask him tonight after supper if it looks like he's in a good mood."

He was in a good mood, and the question was posed at the table. He hesitated for a moment before he began to explain.

"I won't go into a lot of details, but here goes. I found a way to adjust carburetors to allow them to get a lot more miles to a gallon of gas than they were getting before. I got a patent so no one could steal my idea. The people who make the gasoline didn't want me to start using my adjustment because they knew they couldn't sell nearly as much gas. This was when I lived in Chicago. I had a lawyer who helped me get the patent, but the oil people killed him. Then they killed the guy I worked for. They said I was next. My first wife and I ran away to Mexico. There I met a man who was rich and powerful. They sent people down there to try to kill us, but they failed. One of the people they sent was your uncle Hans."

"You mean Uncle Hans was sent to kill you?"

"That's right, he was. I'll tell you all about it when you're older, but not now."

"Aw, please, Dad. Tell us now."

"Not now, I said. Now, do you want me to go on with the story or not? Well, this rich and powerful guy was named Juan de los Santos. He and I became partners, and we got all the Japanese carmakers to build their cars there. That was the start of how I got my money. I let the Japanese use my adjustment, and they put most of the American car companies out of business. Then a young man named Tink came up with an even better idea of how to improve gas mileage. He and I became partners after Mr. de los Santos died and left all the company to me. All of the cars now use his idea, but my company gets most of the money for using his idea."

"How did Mr. de los Santos and Tink die, Dad?"

"I told you I wasn't going to go into a lot of details. Maybe some day I'll tell you more of the details, but not now."

"How did your first wife die, Dad?"

"She got sick and never recovered after she gave birth to Billy."

"What happened to his older brother Jack?"

"I don't want to talk about that. Maybe some day when you're a lot older, I'll talk about it, but not now."

"How about our sister's Mom? How did she die?"

"That's another thing I don't want to talk about. Have you guys finished your homework?

"No, Dad."

"Then I suggest you leave the table and get after it."

After finishing their homework but before retiring to their bedrooms, they got together to discuss what they had learned at the table that night.

"Why do you suppose there are things Dad doesn't want to talk about?"

"I think it's because he may have done something illegal, and he doesn't want us to know."

"No, I don't think that's it. I think it's because it might have something to do with violence, maybe even murder, and he doesn't want us to know about it. Maybe we should ask sister. She might know."

"Yes, she might, but I think the one who could tell us everything would be Uncle Hans. I can't believe he was really sent to Mexico to try to kill dad. Do you guys believe that's true, or is Dad just joking with us?"

"No, I don't think he would joke about anything like that. He might tell us unless Dad made him promise not to."

"Jack, you're the oldest. Will you be the one to ask Uncle Hans to tell us what happened in Mexico?"

"How come when there's something unpleasant to do, you guys always bring up that I'm the oldest. Any of you guys could ask him the same as me."

"Come on, Jack. Please."

"Okay, but if I get him to tell me, you guys owe me one."

The next day Jack managed to separate himself from his brothers long enough to have a chat with Uncle Hans.

"Uncle Hans, could I talk to you for a minute?"

"Sure, Jack. What's on your mind?"

"I really don't know how to start this."

"It's not about girls, is it?"

"No, we know all about that. Last night at the table Dad told us that a long time ago in Mexico that you had been sent down there to kill him. Is that the truth?"

Hans hesitated briefly before asking, "Did he really tell you guys that?"

"Yes, he did. Is it true?"

"Well, if he told you that much, he probably won't mind if I tell you the rest of the story. Yes, it's true. I used to work for the oil companies. They knew if your Dad ever put his adjustment on the market, it might be the end for them. They sent me down there to try to kill your Dad and Mr. de los Santos. When I couldn't do it, the oil companies sent another guy down there to kill me. I surrendered to your Dad and Mr. de los Santos. They hired me to try to help them defeat the oil companies."

"What happened to the guy they sent down to kill you?"

"I killed him. He was disguised, but I recognized him and shot him just as he was about to shoot your dad."

"Wow! I wonder why Dad wouldn't tell us about that. I'm not sure whether my brothers will believe what you just told me. I'm afraid they'll just think I made it up."

"Yeah, I know. It sounds kinda like a fairy tale, but it's the truth. What else didn't he tell you?"

"He wouldn't tell us how Sister's mom died."

"Well, I'm gonna leave that one up to him. It doesn't have anything to do with me, so I'll wait and let him tell you about it."

That night before bedtime, Jack gathered his brothers around his bed and told them everything that Hans had told him. Their initial reaction was exactly what Jack had anticipated: a story he made up to make them think he had actually talked to Uncle Hans when he really hadn't had the nerve to ask him. Then Jack used the phrase " I swear" which is what they had long ago agreed would be a sign that a story was absolutely true. Then the other four pointed at John and told him he had been appointed to ask Sister about the death of her mother.

"Why me?"

"Because you're the youngest, and you look so sweet and cuddly. You're the baby of the family and no one can refuse you."

"Okay I'll try, but I bet she won't tell me. She may not even know what happened. Dad doesn't like to talk about it, and she wasn't very old when her mother died."

"Ask her anyway. I'd like to know some of the family's secrets. You know, sometimes I think we may be the strangest family in America."

"Not just America, maybe the whole world."

It had been two days. And John had not found an opportunity to question his sister about the death of her mother. He really didn't know how he would begin to ask her about something so sensitive.

It was Saturday, and his four brothers had headed down to the construction site to check on the new gym's progress. Charley and Annika had gone to town to shop for groceries, leaving only Uncle Hans to look after the boys. John suddenly found himself alone in the dining room with his sister.

"Sister, can I ask you something?"

"Sure, John, what is it?"

"I really don't know how to start."

"Come on, I've got some things to do. Ask me whatever you want."

"Can you tell me what happened to your mother?"

"Well, I don't know all the details, and Dad won't talk about it very much, but here's what I do know. Mr. de los Santos, Dad's partner, had four sons. Three of them were really mad when their father died and didn't leave them anything. The fourth son was like you, the youngest. He went to work for Dad and still does. His name is like yours, too. It's Juan which is Spanish for John.

Dad never really told me a lot of what I'm going to tell you, but I overheard him telling it to your mother."

"The three oldest sons of Mr. de los Santos tried several times to kill Dad or have him killed. Finally, Diego, the oldest and meanest of Mr. de los Santos' sons came by himself to try to kill Dad. He rented a boat and shot at Dad from the lake, but he missed and hit Mom instead. For Dad, that was the last straw. He sent Uncle Hans to New York to try to kill all three of them. He failed, but he did get two of them, all but Diego. Diego came after Dad and got into the house. Dad shot and killed him. Later, Dad had to stand trial for murder because he had shot him so many times. They found him not guilty."

"Did Dad really shoot and kill him? It sounds more like something Uncle Hans would do."

"I know, but Dad never denied he was the one who killed him."

"Gee, that's really hard to believe. Our Dad really shot and killed a guy and was charged with murder. I'm not sure my brothers are gonna believe this."

"I know it's hard to believe. Dad is such a gentle man. Have you ever watched the way he treats your mother?"

"Yeah, he lets her have anything she wants. Did you notice they hardly ever sleep together?"

"Yes, I noticed."

"Do you think he still loves her?"

"Yes, I do. You gotta remember that we're not around all the time. I think maybe they ....you know? When we're not around."

"How much do you remember about your Mom?"

"Not very much. I just remember that she loved me, and she loved our Dad. They say I look a lot like she did when she was my age."

"I gotta go now. My brothers are gonna think I'm a big liar when I tell them what you told me."

That evening she went to her father after supper and asked him if he had time to talk. It was something she rarely did, and he could see there was something serious on her mind. They went upstairs to her room.

"What's on your mind, Sweety?"

"I had a long talk with John today, Daddy."

"Really? What did you guys talk about?"

"He wanted to know what happened to my mom."

"And what did you tell him?"

"I told him how Diego tried to kill you and hit mom instead. I told him that Uncle Hans had killed Diego's two brothers and how Diego got into the house and tried to kill you. I told him you had to stand trial for murder and that they found you not guilty. I hope you aren't mad at me for telling him too much. I know you don't like to talk about Mom's death."

"That's right. I don't, but they had to find out sooner or later. Is there anything else you'd like to talk about?"

"Yes, I have a question I'd like to ask."

"Okay, go ahead."

"Dad, I know you're really interested in the boys and how they play basketball. How come you never tried to get me interested in sports?"

"I really don't know, Sweety. You never seemed to have much interest. I thought you preferred music and dancing lessons to basketball or volleyball. Are you thinking about going out for any of the team sports?"

"No, you're right. I never had much interest, and I still don't. I'd rather spend my time practicing piano or my ballet then being around a lot of girls working up a sweat. I don't think they like me because you have so much money. They call me a spoiled brat because I have better clothes than they do. They call Uncle Hans my bodyguard, and I don't know what to say when they do. Is he really my bodyguard?"

"I guess in a way he is. I still have lots of enemies, and I'm still afraid they might try to kidnap you. They know I'd pay anything to get you back safely if they could grab you. Just try to ignore the hateful comments. If you make friends, you know they'd be welcome here in the house. I think a lot people just don't have the courage to try to get to know you. It's easier to make fun of people than to try to get to know them."

"Could I have a party here next week?"

"I think so. What kind of party would you like?"

"I think they call it a slumber party. I don't know why. It doesn't sound like much fun if all you do is sleep."

"Well, I think they call it a slumber party because the girls spend the whole night and eventually everyone goes to sleep. How many girls would you like to invite to the party?"

"Seven or eight. I don't know if they'll come, but I'd like to invite that many. Would that be okay?"

"Sure. Will I be expected to be the chaperone?"

"I think I'll have to tell the girls you'll be here or their parents won't let them come, but I don't like the word chaperone. It sounds like you'll be watching our every move."

"Yeah, I know, just tell 'em I'll be here. That's all they need to know."

"Thanks, Dad. I got homework to do now."

"You just let me know the exact date of the party, and I guarantee you I'll be here."

****

Annika wasn't much help in planning the party. She'd never organized a party for young girls and had no idea what refreshments should be served or what activities the girls would want to make a party a success.

Diedra was much better at a thing like this. She suggested cake, cookies, and soft drinks in abundance. She helped her pick out the most popular CD's for dancing and helped her roll back a thick Persian rug to make dancing easier. A large TV was made available in case the girls wanted to watch a late night movie.

The party was a huge success. Seven girls accepted the written invitations they received. They came more out of curiosity than anything else. Hardly anyone in town had ever seen the inside of the house where the Johnsons lived.

It didn't take long to figure out that the main topic the girls wanted to talk about was boys. Some admitted that they had a crush on some of the boys in school, and three even admitted they had been kissed. When she commented that she'd never been kissed and hardly ever even thought about boys, she received a new name. From that time forward she would be known as "Charley's Angel."

When the girls departed the next morning, Charley could tell that the party had been good for her. She was smiling when she gave the girls a good-bye hug at the door.

"Well, how did it go?"

"It was great, Dad. Most of the girls weren't as bad as I thought. I think some of them might even become friends."

"So, what did you talk about?"

"Gee, Dad, it was mostly just girl talk, you know."

"No, I don't know. I never attended a slumber party, and I have no idea what "girl talk" is all about. Boys, I suppose."

"Yeah, that's some of it. They named me Charley's Angel because I have no interest in boys. Is that an insult to me, or what?"

"No, they're just having fun. When the time is right, you'll have plenty of interest in boys, I suppose."

"Thanks, Dad, for the party and this chat."

****

The gym was completed. The boys were ready to begin the sixth grade, but boys that young were not eligible to participate in inter-school athletics. Charley had long ago decided not to wait until the boys were old enough to represent Lake Side before giving them some experience at team play. Already they far exceeded boys of their own age in all the fundamentals of the game, but they had no concept of team play. He had tried at times to teach them the three-on-three game by becoming a participant himself, but it was difficult to come up with sides that were equal. At least they became aware of what a pick-and-roll game was all about.

The nearest AAU competition was fifty miles away. It was a summer league competition for boys and girls of all ages. Charley was anxious to find out how his boys stacked up against some of the better players in their age group. He had decided to do the coaching himself and had picked up five other boys to fill out the roster of his team. The team name would be Lakers, of course.

It was incredible what can be accomplished when one has his own personal gymnasium to practice in. For Charley, it brought back fond memories of the days he had been an assistant coach for the high school girls' team of Lake Side High. Practices were held five days a week and usually lasted about two hours. All practice session were open to the public with all parents of players urged to attend.

Three of the five Charley had recruited were good enough to push the quints for playing time. Charley felt that was a bonus, not because it would help them win games, but because he could substitute them for his own boys if they played poorly or did not follow his directions. He was harder in practice on his own than he was on the others. He felt it had to be that way so there would be no whining by the others about favoritism.

Until the first game, Charley was not aware how much bigger his boys were than other boys of their age group. There was a heated discussion before the game between Charley and his rival coach. His rival insisted that some of Charley's boys must be too old to play against his team. Charley had to promise to bring the birth certificates of all his players to the next game before the game began.

It wasn't much of a game. Any practice the Lakers had would have been more beneficial than what they got out in a lopsided 63-19 win. The quints played less than a half or the score could have been much worse. The rival coach could not believe the execution of the Lakers so early in the season. He had no idea that they had their own gym and had practiced far more than his team.

Charley had the game video-taped so his players could see the mistakes they had made in their first game. He used this to deflate the egos of the Lakers who thought they had played an error-free game. He pointed out the poor plays of their opponents and warned them not to expect such mistakes later in the season. Practices became even more intense before the next game.

True to his word, Charley produced birth certificates for all the Lakers at the next game. He even had copies made to give to all the coaches of the other teams. He didn't want the age thing to become a distraction for his team.

The next game was a little closer, 58-35, but the Lakers were never pushed, and the quints still only logged about half of the playing time. The competition was much better in the second game, so Charley still found plenty of mistakes by his team that would need corrections.

"Boys, first let me congratulate you on the win. There were times when we looked pretty good out there, but there were other times when we stunk. I'm afraid you're gonna see a lot more of the stinking in the video than you did of us looking good."

"Offensively, we did a good job, but on defense we made a ton of mistakes. We didn't play through their screens the way we should. We switched men way too often, rather than fight through the screens. Switching men should be the last resort, not the first option. A better team will use the pick-and-roll and shoot lay-ups against you when you switch men. I'll show you at least ten times they had you beat when you switched men if they had executed well. I'm telling you, we've got to improve that part of our game. Now, before we shower, are there any questions?"

"Yeah, coach, are we gonna eat at McDonalds on the way home?"

"Yeah, Artie, I think a couple of Big Macs are just what you need to improve your quickness on defense. Use some soap in the showers. I don't want to smell you guys on the way home."

****

It was Hans who drove the team to and from their games. Charley did not ride with the team. He drove his own car with Annika being his only passenger. Charley noticed that not many people from Lake Side had attended their first game, only parents and a few close relatives, but at the second game there was a sizable crowd cheering for the Lakers. Not surprising, Charley thought. Everybody loves a winner.

As the summer progressed the competition got tougher and tougher, but the Lakers didn't seem to notice. They improved even faster than their competition. They went through the season undefeated and were never really seriously challenged. Three of the quints were voted first team All-Stars with John and Joseph named to the second team.

****

When the school year began, there was not nearly as much time for basketball practice as there had been during the summer months. Still, the Lakers continued to practice regularly twice a week.

The growth rate of the quints was phenomenal. Joshua and Joseph both stood 6'3" with feet that required size 14 shoes. Jerry was 6'2" and Jack and John were an even 6'.

When football season ended, Charley had an idea that might improve the quality of Lake Side High's basketball team. He invited the Junior High coach to send his team to Charley's gym to practice before the season began. The State Activity Association did not allow practice on school property before a specified date, but there were no restrictions on other facilities.

For the first time in their lives the quints were challenged. Boys from the 7th and 8th and 9th grade showed them what their father had tried to teach them was true. They no longer held a significant height advantage over their opponents, and their quickness was challenged at every turn. Charley taped every session of practice.

"I hope now you see that what I've been trying to tell you is the truth. We get beat on the screens because we don't move our feet properly. I know these guys are older than you guys, but it shouldn't make that much difference. The one thing we can do to improve on this is to anticipate. You gotta talk to each other and tell each other when a screen is coming. That way you have a chance to avoid the screen or fight through it. If you can't fight through it, one of the other guys has to rotate over and pick up the screener. Do you need me to draw it up for you again?"

"No, Dad, we understand it. It's just that it's hard….."

"Damn it! I know it's hard. If it was easy, anybody could do it. I don't expect you to be able to beat these guys, but we oughta be able to give 'em a better game."

By the time regular basketball practice was about to begin, the quints were close to being able to holding their own with any of the Junior high players, regardless of age. It made Charley anxious for the year to begin so the boys could begin their careers as players for Lake Side High. He hardly ever thought of all the events that had led him to his present position in life.

It was during that year that the phenomenal growth of the quints became apparent. Joshua and Joseph were the first to reach a height of 6'5" The sudden growth spurt was not without the usual onset of clumsiness that accompanies such a thing. It seemed that Charley had to buy new shoes monthly as they outgrew what they had been wearing.

The other three did not lag far behind. Jack and John each measured 6'2" and Jerry was 6'3". It was now that a new weapon was added to the quint's arsenal—the dunk. Joshua was first, followed closely by Joseph. Jack was third and John was anxious not to be the last one to be able to dunk. He ignored all other aspects of the game until he managed to successfully dunk a ball. It was more than a month before Jerry joined the club.

As the quints prepared for their first season as representatives of Lake Side Junior High, Charley decided to have a chat with the man who would be their coach.

"Hi, Coach. Are you getting ready for practice next week?"

"Yes, I am. Can I help you with something?"

"Not really. I just thought we might have a little conversation."

"What's on your mind?"

"Well, I don't really know where to start. It's about my boys. I don't want to sound like a typical parent who comes to the coach to tell him he knows more about the game than he does."

"Mr. Johnson, I know that having five sons to worry about gives you a little more room to talk than the average parent. Just tell me what's on your mind."

"Well, I'm sure it hasn't escaped your notice how big the boys have gotten since last year. In fact, two of them are measuring 6'5" and from the size of their shoes, I'd say they still have some growing to do. I think that might turn out to be a problem."

"What kind of problem?"

"Well, you got 9th grade kids that are looking forward to being starters on your varsity this year. They're gonna be real disappointed if they get beaten out of a job by a bunch of 7th graders."

"How do you think I ought to handle a situation like that? I've always tried to start my best players, regardless of what grade they're in."

"I'm not really sure I can answer that. At first I wouldn't start all five of them as a team. I'd like to see them compete against each other for playing time. Also, I'd like their time on the varsity to be limited to one quarter a game. That may be difficult because I'm sure a lot of JV games will get out of hand. You know what I mean, scorewise. I know from watching you coach that you don't like to run the score up on kids."

"Then I take it you're not gonna come crying to me if they don't get a ton of varsity time. I saw some of their summer league play, so I got a pretty good idea how good they can be. I don't know how I'll be able to keep the score down in the JV games if they play a lot. They're just too big and too talented for kids anywhere close to their age to compete with them. I wouldn't be surprised to see some coaches try to hold the ball against us just to keep the score respectable."

"Neither would I. I hate that because the boys can't develop their other skills just playing a game of keep-away. It's just something to think about. I'd be willing to talk to you about this at any time you want to."

"I'm glad to hear you say that."

"One more thing. They've already had considerable coaching, so they have a set way of doing things that may not be the way you want things done. Insist on your way. If they don't want to go along with your way, put their butts on the bench."

"Thanks again. We'll be talking."

****

The first game was against Hillsdale, a town no bigger than Lake Side. The two quints the coach had decided to start were Jerry and Joseph. That left the other three bewildered: John angry, Joshua stunned, and Jack seething. You could see the disappointment in their faces as they sat down on the bench. At the quarter, the coach inserted the other three into the game. The score was already 14-2, and by halftime it had ballooned to 35-5. As the third quarter was about to start, the coach looked over his shoulder to where Charley was sitting. When the coach's gaze turned into a stare, Coach shrugged his shoulders as if to say he had no idea who to start in the third quarter. He went back to his original line-up, but they only played about two minutes. At the start of the 4th quarter, he subbed in the other three for a couple of minutes and then benched them for the rest of the game. The final 55-17.

The varsity game was close until the 4th quarter. At the start of the 4th, the coach put the Johnsons into the game for the first time. They trailed by six points at the start, but the deficit didn't last for long. The huge size differential was just too much for Hillsdale. The boys had too much adrenaline flowing for their shooting to be accurate, but they simply kept rebounding and shooting until they scored. It finally came down to a series of free throws by Jack. He made the first which tied the game but missed the second which would have given them the lead. Joseph tipped the rebound out to John who got off the game-winner at the buzzer.

While the boys showered, Charley chatted with the coach in his office. "Well, what do you think? Did I manage the playing time alright?"

"You did fine. I have no complaints, but you'll have to be ready for a different way of handling things with every game. If we're safely ahead, I'd rather you didn't play them together all at the same time. They need to learn to play with the rest of their teammates, not just with each other. How much resentment do you think you'll get from the varsity guys who didn't play in the 4th quarter?"

"I don't have any idea. Winning is a good antidote for griping. I'm a lot more likely to hear griping from the parents than I am from the players."

"So how do you handle that?"

"The way I handle all complaints, I ignore them."

"Tell me, do you think we have a chance to win the league this year?"

"I didn't think so before tonight. I think it all depends on how much you'll let me play your guys."

"I think later in the season they should get to play as much as you think they should. By tournament time, I'll leave it strictly up to you."

"You know, it's funny, but in a way it's scary. I get the feeling right now I have potentially the greatest basketball team that ever took the floor. If I handle them right, by the time they finish their high school careers, they just might reach heights in the college and the pros that have never been reached. I see every one of them growing right before my eyes. I don't let them do it in practice or a game, but I know every single one of them can dunk a basketball. We probably won't see a single player playing against us this year who can dunk a basketball, and we've got five! I know they're having growing pains, but the clumsiness will wear off. It's already starting to go. Do you know what I really see?"

"No, tell me."

"By the time these guys are 9th graders, they could probably beat any senior high school team in the state."

"You're kidding. That's pretty high expectations."

"Think about it. If they continue to grow, and judging from the size of their shoes. I think they will, you could have two seven footers playing side by side. Not to mention a power forward who is 6'10" and a pair of guards at 6'5" or 6'6". I know that with their own private gym to work year round, they'll just get better and better. Their footwork and jumping ability will be out of sight. No team will be able to play keep-away. I see a team that will be able to press a team of any size. The only two things I could see that could mess them up is a bus wreck or...."

"Or what?"

"Some idiot coach like me messing them up. Believe me, it puts a lot of pressure on me."

"You know, I really hadn't thought about it in those terms. I just thought it was a tremendous opportunity for a coach. I never though about the pressure you're talking about."

"Right now, it's just fun, but later on if I lose a single game, it'll be grounds for my dismissal, and I like it here."

"So do I. I'll talk to you later."

****

The rest of the season was predictable. It became harder and harder to deny the quints their playing time. They never started a varsity game, and their playing time in the JV games had shrunk to less than a half. The varsity had lost only one game and finished in a tie for first place. They were seeded second in the season-ending League Tournament.

They won their first two games with the quints playing no more than a half. In the finals they would play the only ream that had beaten them in the regular season. Charley had already told the coach to play his guys as much as he wanted. He thought all the hard work the guys had put in should give them a shot at being champions.

They were nervous at first, never having started a varsity game. They had never experienced the thrill of having their names pronounced by the man on the PA system as they were introduced as starters.

They suffered a bad case of the jitters in the early going. They were tentative and turned the ball over several times before settling down at the start of the second quarter. From that point on, the crowd was treated to the best showing they had ever seen by a junior high team. The final score was so lopsided that neither Charley nor the coach could believe it. He pulled his starters one at a time midway through the 4th quarter so that each could get a round of applause from the huge home crowd.

Charley was on a real high. He could hardly believe that Annika did not share his elation. She was a big fan and never missed a single minute of any of her sons' games. After the boys had turned in for the night, Charley found Annika reluctant to talk about what they had just witnessed.

"What's the matter, Hon? Didn't you enjoy watching your sons win a championship?"

"Yes, I did."

"Then what is it?"

"I know you love the boys as much as I do. Would you love them less if they had lost the game tonight?"

"Why, that's a foolish question. Why would you ask such a thing?"

"I don't know really. It just seems to me that their whole lives are about winning. I'm afraid they should learn a little about losing. Life isn't just about winning. I know now that you and the doctors set things up for me to give birth to the quints. That's alright. It got me out of Russia. I just think you should make it clear to the boys that your love for them goes beyond winning basketball games. Why does it seem so important to you?"

"That's really hard to explain. I was a really good player myself many years ago, but I was often told that I was too short to ever be a really great player. Then my first two sons came along, and they were told the same thing, too short. After I found the adjustment and made all that money, Alice and I were happy, but I wanted to come back to the States. I don't think she really wanted to come back, but she would have followed me anywhere. It's really my fault she was killed. My life was empty after her death. I had all that money, but I really didn't have any way to use it that would make me happy. I gave a lot of it to charity, but it just kept piling up. I'm sure you don't have any idea how much money I really have."

"You might be surprised. I think I could guess a number as close as you could as to what you're really worth."

"Really? How could you make an accurate guess?"

"I know how to use a telephone, and I have the numbers of Juan and Billy. They don't know exactly what you're worth, but they have a pretty good idea. I know what the numbers are, but I can't imagine what they mean. I can't think in terms of billions."

"I know I should have told you sooner about the doctors, but I was afraid you wouldn't let them do whatever they did."

"Do you love me, Charley?"

"Yes, I do. I'm not in love with you the way I was with either of my first two wives, but I've learned to love you in a different way."

"Can you tell me about this love you have for me?"

"I'm not sure I can express it. I love the way you take care of my house and children. You've always supported everything I try to do. There's a comfort I feel in being around you. You have made my house a home, and that's something that no amount of money can do. You gave up the life you had in your country to take a chance and move here and marry me. I don't think I've ever told you that you're beautiful."

"No, you haven't. Are you telling me now?"

"Yes, I am. You are beautiful. And right now I would like to make love to you."

****

He was relieved that she accepted the fact that the quints were the product of the doctors she had visited. He had feared she might be so hurt and angry that she might threaten divorce or worse yet, taking the boys with her back to Russia.

The 8th grade was a far cry from the 7th. There would be no holding back the quints. This year they would play as much as their ability warranted. They would start and play until the score became embarrassing to their opponents. They would learn to press any opponent who tried to hold the ball. Once a comfortable margin had been established, the press would be called off.

Huge crowds attended every game. The only thing in doubt about any of the games was which quint would be the leading scorer. During the course of the season, every one of them would take scoring honors. The gymnasium was filled beyond capacity for every game. Twice the fire marshal had warned the school officials to limit the number of those who tried to force their way into the gym. People from surrounding towns abandoned their own teams just to come and marvel at the show the quints put on.

By midseason, Both Joshua and Joseph were listed at 6'10". Each had developed a hook shot that would have been almost unstoppable even by players of their own size. The outside shooting of John and Jerry was equally impressive. Jack could have been the leading scorer in any game, but he preferred to pass the ball to his brothers and build his own reputation as a point guard.

Much of the clumsiness associated with the rapid growth was diminishing. More than shooting, passing, or rebounding they practiced agility drills. More than an hour each day was devoted to footwork. It was an hour the quints had come to dread. They much preferred working on their shooting to the seemingly endless exercises to promote agility.

One day at practice it was Joseph who complained, "Gee, Coach, how much longer are we gonna have to keep doing these stupid drills?"

"So you think they're stupid, huh? I've tried to tell you why they're important, but you guys sometimes think you know more about coaching than I do. Well, let me tell you Mr. know-it-alls. If it weren't for all the agility drills you guys have been through, you'd just be a bunch of oversized yahoos. I hoped that you guys would realize that with the special talents all of you have, you could be great if you'd spend the effort it takes to be great. I think you need to re-think the situation. Maybe if we stopped these "stupid" drills, you could think more clearly. So, here's what were gonna do. Put the balls away. Now, we're just gonna run for the next 45 minutes, and then you can tell me what you think of my agility drills."

The groans were audible. The quints and the rest of the team began to run. The run was not confined to the gym floor. The stairs became a part of the track. Jack slowed down as he passed Joseph on the stairs.

"Why the hell did you have to go and bitch to the coach about the drill? We'd still be shooting the ball if you'd kept your mouth shut."

"Yeah, and I suppose you never complain about anything. You're the biggest griper on the whole team."

"Yeah, but the coach doesn't hear my griping. I'm too smart to let him hear me say anything like you just said."

"Too smart? Or too gutless?"

When he heard the word gutless, he gave his brother a shove that sent him flying down the last three stairs. He rolled on the gym floor twice and then just lay there. Fearing that his brother might be seriously hurt, Jack went over and stretched out his hand to help him to his feet. Joseph took the hand, scrambled to his feet, and all in one motion delivered a haymaker of a right hand that landed solidly on the side of Jack's head. The punch caught him completely by surprise and sent him toppling to the floor. He got up with clenched fists and headed toward his brother. Before another punch could be thrown, the coach jumped between them.

"What the hell is the matter with you guys? Have you lost your minds? What started this?"

"He started it. He pushed me down the stairs."

"Yeah, I pushed him after he called me gutless. I didn't realize how much he needs the agility drills till now."

"Why did you call your brother gutless, Joseph?"

"I'd rather not say, Coach."

"How about you, Jack? Why did he call you gutless?"

"Because I wasn't the one who went and complained about the agility drills. I told him his complaint was stupid, and then he called me gutless."

"Okay, the rest of you guys take it in. Joseph and Jack have earned a little extra time."

They ran side by side for the first 15 minutes. Finally it was Joseph who broke the silence. "I'm sorry, Jack. I shouldn't have called you gutless."

"That's okay. I know you didn't mean it. You were just mad at Coach for all the drills."

At that point they stopped and shook hands. They embraced each other and looked in the direction of the coach.

"Okay, boys, it looks like you got things worked out. That's good. Now hit the showers. You're gonna be late for supper."

Charley had already picked up the other three and taken them back to the house when Joseph and Jack finished showering. He sent Hans back for the other two and started supper without them. At the table he tried to get them to tell him why their brothers were late. They just said the coach said they needed some extra running. They gave him no details.

When the late arrivals sat down to supper, Charley waited till they had finished eating before asking them why they were late.

"Oh, it really wasn't anything, Dad. We just had a little argument."

"Now, Jack, I want to know what happened. Coach didn't keep you guys after practice just for a little argument. What were you arguing about?"

"Oh, we just got a little tired of the agility drills. He didn't like our attitude so he made us run."

"How about it, Joseph? Is that all there was to it?"

"Yes sir, that was about it."

Charley just shook his head and decided not to press the issue. He was sure the coach would give him the details if he asked.

He was wrong. When he asked why the boys had drawn extra running, the coach just shrugged and said, "Oh, it really wasn't anything big. They complained a little too much about some of the drills, so I just thought some extra running would do them good." He made no mention of the fisticuffs. Charley was pretty sure he wasn't getting the whole story, but he decided to let it drop.

There was never another incident that left the quints at odds with one another. The precision they had developed at both ends of the floor amazed everyone who watched them, including their coach. Anyone who didn't know would have thought they were watching a tremendous high school or a good junior college team. The growth rate had slowed down, and with it had come the agility the coach had predicted would come. It was almost embarrassing to watch them devastate every opponent that took the floor against them. They finished the season undefeated and unchallenged.

****

At the start of the 9th grade season, Charley was wishing that Lake Side used an 8-4 system instead of the 9-3 system. That meant they would have to spend another year competing against kids their own age. There was little to be gained in this. Charley's greatest fear was that they would become complacent and satisfied if they weren't challenged. He had pushed them hard during the summer months, getting them involved in AAU tournaments, but even against that level of competition, they were never really challenged.

The basketball season itself was little more than a repeat of the previous one. The only noticeable difference was the number of college coaches who came to see a junior high game. Several coaches wanted to talk to Charley about the advantages of attending their institution. Charley invited several to his house and let them speak to the quints there, but he warned them not to make direct contact with the boys. He told them it was much too early for them to be thinking about college when they hadn't even begun high school. He told them when they had finished their junior year, he would see that they got good seats to any home game. Then they might entertain thoughts of a college scholarship, but for right now, they had a lot of growing up to do. He also told them there was very little chance that the boys would split up and attend several different colleges. He couldn't be certain of that, but the boys had never mentioned anything except staying together.

****

Excitement ran high in anticipation of the basketball season. The coach could hardly wait for the attention he knew would be directed toward the team he would coach this coming season.

The biggest challenge came not from the opponents on the schedule but from a case of the flu which infected all of the quints. Though they were able to play, their energy level was so depleted that not one of them could stay on the court for more than a couple of minutes. They were a mere shadow of what they had shown before, but the coach staggered their playing time so that they always had at least two of them on the floor. That, with the wise use of timeouts, was enough to preserve another undefeated season.

****

The excitement generated by back-to-back undefeated seasons in junior high was nothing compared to the level of expectation that permeated Lake Side as another basketball season approached. Though the league tournament had not been scheduled to be hosted by Lake Side, a majority of the league schools had voted to move the tournament there. The seating capacity of the gym Charley had ordered built was far larger and better equipped to host a tourney than any of the other league schools. It was already conceded that none of the league schools would have a chance against Lake Side, regardless of where the tourney was played, therefore, the schools had opted for the benefits that would accrue to each of the schools with a sellout of every session of the tourney.

The junior high coach had been promoted to the head coaching job in the high school. The school board had been split down the middle on the issue of the change. Some felt it was unfair to relieve the high school coach of the head coaching job, while the others felt that the school would be best served by the continuity of the only coach the quints had ever known. Charley had been asked to attend the school board meeting that would decide the head coaching job. He listened attentively as both sides presented their arguments.

"I don't care what the other side says. There is just no reason not to keep the coach we already have in the high school. I know that Mr. Johnson is the one responsible for building the gym, and the whole school, for that matter. But the high school coach has done a good job. There just isn't any reason to let him go."

"We're not sayin' he did a bad job, it's just we think we can do better. The junior high coach has dealt with some difficult situations, and he's kept a level head on the kids. What do you say, Mr. Johnson?"

"Well, I know that personnel decisions are made in closed sessions, not open to me or anyone else not on the board. I agree that the present coach has done a good job. I can find no fault with his program. Now if you're asking me who I'd rather have as the coach for my boys, I like the idea of continuity."

The grumbling over the last statement forced the board president to pound his gavel three times to restore order.

"Let me finish what I have to say. I think at this late date it would be really unfair to let the present coach go. Therefore, this is what I propose. If he will agree, I would like for him to stay on as the assistant coach with the same pay he had as head coach. If he wants to be a head coach at another school, I would propose we give him a year's pay as severance at last year's salary. I'd like to see him stay. I think he would be a pretty good insurance policy if something should happen to the head coach. I think the coaches are pretty good friends, and I think they could work together. That's the offer I would recommend."

"Since it's your idea, would you be willing to present to him what you just proposed to us?"

"Of course, if that's what you want."

"If he wants out, where is the severance money gonna come from?"

"Don't worry about that. It's my idea, so I'll put up the money if that's what he wants."

"Okay, let's put it to a vote. How many in favor of having Mr. Johnson make his proposal to the current coach?"

Six of the seven hands went up. The meeting was adjourned shortly thereafter, and Charley went directly to the house of the current coach. It was after 9 o'clock, but the lights were still burning brightly. He knocked on the door and waited for some sign of life inside. The coach's wife answered the knock.

"Hi, Mrs. Bell. Is coach still up?"

"Yes, but he's in his pajamas. Would you like to come in?"

"If you don't mind."

He went to the den of the newly constructed house and found the coach in front of a large screen TV.

"Sorry to come calling so late, Coach, but I just left the school board meeting, and I know you want to know what they decided."

"I got a pretty good idea. I'm gonna be lookin' for a new job, right?"

"Not necessarily. Ask your wife to come in here and hear what I have to say. I think she'll have to help you make a decision."

"Honey, come on in and hear Mr. Johnson has to say."

"Well, the board has authorized me to come here and make you an offer for the next year. For the sake of continuity, the board has decided to move Fred up to the head coaching position at the high school for the next year. No one, including myself, has found any fault in the job you've done there. Here's two options the board is offering. If you want to stay on as assistant coach, you'll receive the same salary as the head coach. I know you guys get along pretty good, and you can be sure Fred didn't come asking for your job."

"What's the other option?"

"If you decide to leave to pursue another head coaching job, the board will give you the amount of last year's salary as severance pay."

"How the hell can they do that? There's nothing in our contracts about severance pay."

"There's also nothing in there about letting a good man go for no reason. Look, I told them I'd put up the money if that's the way you decide to go. I'd really like for you to stay. You're at least familiar with the way Fred does things. A new guy wouldn't have any idea what he's trying to accomplish. I know you're aware of the great things everyone is predicting for Lake Side for the next four years. I hope you'll stay to be a part of that."

"How long do I have to think about it?"

"They didn't put a time limit on the offer, but you're gonna have to give them time to find somebody else if you decide to leave."

"Well, she and I will have to talk it over, but I'll let you know by this time tomorrow."

"One more thing you might want to consider. If Fred should decide to move up when the boys graduate, I can guarantee you he'll take you with him to whatever college the boys choose to attend. If, God forbid, something should happen to Fred, you automatically resume your duties as head coach of Lake Side High."

"Okay, I'll let you know."

At noon the following day, the coach knocked on Charley's front door. Charley was surprised to see him standing there, and couldn't guess from the look on his face what his decision would be.

"Come on in, Coach. I wasn't expecting you quite this soon. Have you made your decision?"

"Yes, I have. The wife and I think we'll be better off here than we would be with a move. I guess the hardest part is the blow to the ego that comes with a demotion to assistant after the time I've spent as head coach."

"Well, I think I can understand that, but I think you're making a good decision. Have you talked to Fred yet?"

"No, but I think I'll head over his way today and see what he has to say. Are you sure he's not gonna resent me lookin' over his shoulder?"

"I haven't talked with him about it, but I'm pretty sure he'll have no objection. I think he'll just be tickled pink to have the head job under any circumstances. Let me ask you something."

"Fire away."

"You watched the quints play quite a lot last year, didn't you?"

"Like everybody else, yeah."

"Tell me, how far do you think they can go?"

"I think the sky's the limit if they don't run into ego problems."

"Have you got any idea where they're gonna want to go to school?"

"I'm pretty sure they're not going to want to split up. I think they'll want to stay pretty close to home. I know they'll have a chance to go about any place they want to."

"Well, I'm glad you decided to stay. Let me know how your chat with Fred goes."

Charley sat wondering why such a thing as who would coach his sons was such a big thing. For the better part of the rest of the day, he sat engaged in thought about a multitude of events that had had a far greater impact on his life than the choice of a basketball coach.

The discovery of the adjustment was the foundation of all the major events of his life. It had led to his meeting with Alice and the death of his lawyer and his boss. It had brought him together with Juan de los Santos and the formation of the world's richest corporation.

Sitting comfortably in his own home, his thoughts turned to all the close calls he'd had since the adjustment. The note on his door had read "You're next". He had eluded those who followed him that night, and he considered that the first real threat to his life. The second threat was when he had been stopped by the phony highway patrolman on their retreat to Mexico. He had no doubts that if they had not abandoned the Interstate Highway for the back roads, they would have been found dead.

Then his mind shifted to the times he had actually been shot at. The first was by the side of the road after they had crossed the border into Mexico. He remembered the blood oozing from his arm as they sped away in the stolen pick-up. Then he thought about how his luck had held when he had stooped to pick something up in the house of the alcalde. The stooping action had caused the assassin's bullet to sail over his body.

Then there was the incident at the church on the night of his wedding to Alice. His son and best friend had been wounded, but he had once again escaped unscathed. Next through his mind came the incident at the doctor's office where he had taken Luisa and Alice to check on their pregnancies. The shooter had been captured and confessed that he had been hired by the de los Santos brothers.

Next he thought of other attempts to get rid of him. There was the gang called the Fuegos from Mexico City. He shrugged with disgust as he thought about the manner in which Hans had eliminated every trace of the whole gang. Then there was the gang of Ningas who came to plant explosives to blow up the whole plant. Once again it was Hans who had foiled the attempt. There were the French mercenaries and the unemployed auto-workers who had made the final assault on the plant. Hans had destroyed both.

One of the closest calls had been on his trip to Japan to convince them that his adjustment was not harmful to the engines of the cars he adjusted. Hans had shot the would-be assassin between the eyes just before he made his move against Charley.

Next he thought of Diego's abortive attempt that led to the death of Tink and left him in sole possession of the invention which now drove most of the cars in the world. That had made him the richest man in the world.

Then he reflected on Diego's next attempt that had been the death of Alice. That had sent Hans to try to eliminate all of the de los Santos brothers. His failure to get Diego had sent him back to try once again to get Charley.

He smiled as remembered the feeling of exhilaration he had experienced as he emptied the pistol into Diego. The feeling didn't last long as he remembered the close call he'd experienced as he stood trial for murder. All of these things outweighed the choice of a basketball coach, but somehow he couldn't get the choice out of his mind. He was guided back to the present by a knock on the door by Hans.

"Come on in. It's unlocked."

"I can remember a time when it was always locked. What have you been doing? I've been trying your cell phone for most of the day."

"Nothing much. Just sitting around and thinking about all the close calls I've had. What would you say was the closest call you had a part in?"

"Two come to mind. The one in Japan is certainly there, but I think the one that got Toyota Man was the closest."

"You know, I hadn't even thought about that one, but I'll have to agree that was the closest. What would you say was your closest? Toyota Man?"

"No, I think I felt the closest to death was when I surrendered at the Perdido jail. I was pretty certain the old man was gonna have me executed. He would have if he'd listened to the rest of you guys."

"Yeah, you're right about that. Anything in particular you wanted to talk to me about?"

"Just one thing. You daughter is going on a field trip next week. She'll be traveling by bus with the rest of the kids in her class. What I wanted to know is do you want me to shadow the bus just in case something goes wrong?"

"She hadn't said anything about it. I didn't know there was a field trip. She usually lets me know about these things."

"She probably couldn't get your attention. Nobody else could. You've had your head up your ass for quite a while over that basketball coaching thing. Has that finally been decided?"

"I think so. What do you think? Is it safe for her to go on any kind of trip without you being there?"

"I don't know. We haven't had any close calls for quite a while now, but I just can't relax knowing there are still folks out there who aren't very fond of us."

"Then I guess the answer is yes. If you think there's any danger, by all means keep an eye on things. Don't forget that I care about her every bit as much as I do the quints."

"I haven't forgot, but I think you should show her your love in a more tangible way."

"What do you have in mind?"

"Well, now that she's old enough to get a driver's license don't you think she might be wanting wheels of her own?"

"I'll give it some thought, maybe a reward for some good grades. I can't believe she's really old enough to drive a car."

"Well, believe it. She's fast becoming a young woman. That's something you're gonna have to get used to."

"Go ahead and shadow the bus, just don't let her know that you're there. She told me once that she appreciates your protection, but it kinda gives her the creeps to know she's being followed."

"Okay, I won't say anything about it. I'll be on my way now. I got a few things to take care of."

Charley couldn't help but notice his daughter as she prepared to go on the field trip. The skirt she wore was a little too short for his liking, but he said nothing about it. He hadn't noticed until recently how much make-up she wore. She was practically a spitting image of her mother.

Hans dropped her off in front of the school. Then he disappeared out of sight to wait for the bus to take off. He knew exactly where the bus was headed, so he made no effort to keep it in sight. He wanted to honor her wishes about being followed. As long as she didn't know he was there, she wouldn't complain.

The huge farm where the bus was headed was some thirty miles from the school. Hans dared not follow close enough to be seen before the bus reached its destination. He parked about a quarter of a mile away and remained there for an hour. He let the car run to take advantage of the air conditioner and dozed off for a few minutes. He then decided he had best get a little closer, just to be sure that everything was under control.

Everything was not under control. He knew something was wrong as soon as he pulled into the area where the bus was parked. Students were scurrying in and out of both the huge barn and the farm house. He got out of the car and grabbed one of the students by the arm as he was running by.

"What the hell is going on? Why's everybody running around like chickens with their heads cut off?"

"They got her," he managed to say breathlessly.

"Got who? Now slow down and tell me what happened."

"They grabbed her, Mr. Johnson's daughter. They pushed her into a four-wheel drive pick-up and headed out across that field. They turned on a dirt road and headed north."

"How many of them were there?"

"Three."

Did you get a good look at any of them?'

"Not really. They were wearing ski masks. The only thing I could tell you was they were white men. I could see their necks under the masks."

"Where's the owner of this farm?'

"He's in the house. He already called the police. They should be here any time. He doesn't know whether they should call her father yet or not."

"I'll tell them not to bother. I'll tell him myself."

"Who are you? Do you work for Mr. Johnson?"

"Yes, I do. I'll use my cell phone to let him know."

"Are you really the man she calls Uncle Hans?"

"Well, you can believe that I am Uncle Hans, but beyond that, you can believe whatever you want to."

He pulled out his cell and dialed Charley's number, but he got no answer at the house. He tried Charley's cell and was relieved to get an answer.

"Charley, we got a problem."

"What's going on?"

"Three guys grabbed her and took off in a four-wheel drive pick-up across a field. They took a dirt road for a short distance and then hit a hard surface road running north. The police have been notified, but they haven't got here yet. Wait a minute. I see them headed this way now. I'll call you back as soon as I have a talk with the police."

He introduced himself to the three men in the squad car. He relayed the information he had got to them.

"I don't want to tell you guys how to do your job, but if it were me, I'd get an expert here as quick as possible to find out what kind of tires made these tracks across that field. It might give us a clue as to the owner of the truck."

"Probably a waste of time. The truck was probably stolen."

"Well, you won't know till you find out. If it's stolen, you'll want a list of all the stolen pick-ups recently that might fit the description we have."

"You seem to know a lot about these things. Do you work for the State Police or the FBI?"

"No, I work for Mr. Johnson. I'm the one they call Uncle Hans, and that girl is my responsibility. I'd be obliged if you'd keep me informed if you get any breaks in this. My feeling is we'll be hearing from the kidnappers soon. I have no idea how much money they're gonna want. The voice you hear might be a record."

"We'll be in touch."

****

It was about noon the next day that the ransom call came. The man on the other end had a high, squeaky voice.

"Mr. Johnson, we got your daughter. If you ever want to see her alive again, play close attention to what I have to say. The price to get her back alive will be cheap for a man like you. We only want ten million out of all the billions you have. For you, that's chump change. We want the money in unmarked hundred dollar bills. We're gonna give you a whole day to raise the cash. We'll call you again tomorrow to tell you where we want the money delivered. Don't try to keep me on the line to get this call traced."

"I'm not trying to stall, but before I start trying to raise that much cash, I want to hear my daughter's voice. I'm not going to pay that much money just to get back a dead body."

"Here she is. Say hi to daddy."

"Hi, daddy. It's me."

"That's enough. Are you convinced that's her. If you are, get the money. If not, you'll never see her again."

He hung up the phone and turned to Hans with a perplexed look on his face. "What do you think, Hans? Should I start trying to raise that much cash?"

"Raising the money isn't what's gonna save your daughter. They already know whether they're gonna release her alive or not. Whether or not they get the money is really no factor. The key thing that will keep her alive for a while is whether they think they'll get the money. I've dealt with kidnappers before. Most of the time they don't want to run the risk of having to get rid of that person."

"Then you think it's hopeless?"

"Not necessarily. If we can get a handle on where they're holding her, there's always a chance I can get her out."

"Did we even get a partial fix on where the telephone call came from? That would be a start, wouldn't it?"

"It would, but I don't think they were on long enough for us to get a trace."

"They're gonna get in touch tomorrow, so maybe we can get some idea…."

"Don't count on it. If these guys are professionals, they won't stay on the line long enough for a trace."

"Well, then what chance do we have?"

"I think most of the time kidnappers screw up when they try to actually pick up the pay-off. They take all kinds of precautions, but eventually someone has to come and get the money, and when they do, that's our chance."

"Have you any idea where they might take her?"

"Just a hunch, nothing more."

"So what's your hunch?"

"I think it's some place pretty close. I don't think they would risk a long ride in the getaway truck. Too easy to spot. Also too big a risk to try an airport or bus terminal. So that leaves someplace close to where they grabbed her. That doesn't narrow it down much, but that's what I'm guessing. If they had waited another day before contacting you, I would have said they were a lot further away."

"So what should I do about the money?"

"That's up to you, but if it was me, I wouldn't worry about it. I told you the money will make no difference. Could you even raise that by tomorrow if you tried?"

"I'm not sure. I've never tried to raise that kind of money on short notice. People think that just because your net worth is huge that you have ready access to unlimited amounts of cash. It isn't true."

"We can make it look like you have the cash. You're probably not going to like my next suggestion."

"What's that?"

"Leave the police out of this. They'll just get in the way. Once we find out where they want the money delivered, we'll try to set something up that will get her released. Here's the way I think it will go. They'll want the money soon. Once they tell you where to deliver it, try to put them off for a day. Tell them you're having trouble raising that much on short notice. Tell them the money has to come from Mexico. They might buy that because they know about your corporation."

"What happens if they agree to wait a day?"

"Then it'll be up to me to get to the place before they do and try to set up a rescue."

"Okay, but I gotta tell you that I'm really scared. Tell me what you really think. Are these guys professionals or just three amateurs trying to make a huge score?"

"It's hard to say, but if I had to guess, I'd say amateurs. I'll be able to tell when they give you the arrangement for the money."

"What's her best chance to survive this?"

"Amateurs. Be sure to make them let you speak to her again when they call again. If they refuse, I'm afraid there's no hope. If I get a chance, there'll be no trial for kidnapping for those three. Once she's free or dead, that will be the end of those three. I can assure you they will repent this caper."

"Hans, I appreciate that, but I don't want you to expose yourself unnecessarily if she's...."

"I know what you mean. The only thing that frightens me is the long amount of time I've had since my last real work. There's a fine edge in my line of work, and the long layoffs can cause you to lose that edge. If you don't mind, I'll stay here until we hear from them again."

****

The call came at noon the next day. Charley picked up the phone and waited for a voice that seemed disguised. After a short silence, the high pitched voice said, "Mr. Johnson, are you ready to meet our demand?"

"Yes, I'm ready, but I haven't been able to get all the money,"

"You're lying. We know that what we're asking is chicken feed to a guy like you. You're just stalling."

"No, I'm not. Listen, you surely know my corporation is in Mexico. That's where the money has to come from. I can get it here by tomorrow, but that's the very soonest. Can I hear the sound of my daughter's voice again? I won't settle for "Hi daddy." That's something you might have recorded. Put her on now if you want me to continue to try to get the all cash together."

"Okay, here she is."

"Please hurry, Daddy. I'm really scared."

"Have they harmed you?"

"No, but ....."

"That's enough. Satisfied?"

"Yes."

"Okay, here's how we'll handle the pay-off. Do you know where the Lighthouse Marina is located on the Lake?"

"Yes, it's only thirty miles from Lake Side. Is that where you want the money delivered?"

"Shut up and listen. No, we don't want the money delivered there. About a mile straight east of the marina there will be an amphibious airplane floating there, waiting to take off as soon as we get the money. We'll expect you at midnight."

"Then how will I get my daughter back after you take off?"

"Here's how it will happen if you don't try to drag the cops into this. As soon as we get the money we'll take off. She'll be wearing a life jacket, and we'll toss her into the lake. I'm sure that whoever delivers the money will be able to find her. She tells me she's a good swimmer. It won't do any good to try to trace this call. We won't be anywhere close to where this call is coming from. Also, only one man in the boat. If we see more than one, we'll shoot her and take off. Got it?"

"Yeah, I got it."

"Okay, be on time with the money. My partners are getting impatient."

Charley hung up the phone and turned to Hans. "Well, what do you think?"

"Amateurs. I think they'll make a fatal mistake. You know I want to be the one to deliver the money. I've already got a bunch of cut up newspapers in a trash bag to make it look like we're gonna pay them off."

"What if they look inside the bag before they release her?'

"I'll manage that somehow, don't worry. These guys are gonna be awfully anxious to take off in that plane and make their get-away. I don't think they'll look too closely before take-off. We'll put some hundreds at the top of each bundle. I don't think they'll look any further than that."

"Do you think I should tell the boys what's going on?'

"No reason to. They'll know soon enough. Try to relax. I know that's an impossibility, but try. Under no circumstances tell the police about any of this, especially the State Police. They'll try to get in the middle of it and louse up any chance we have of a rescue."

"I guess the only thing we can do now is wait."

****

Hans was up early and headed for the Light House Marina. From there he found that there were no rental amphibious aircraft within a 100 mile radius. That left one of two possibilities. Either the aircraft was coming from a longer distance than he had projected, or it might be a privately owned plane.

He went ahead and rented a boat for the night. He took it for a spin to be sure there would be no engine failure at the crucial time. He spent the rest of the day just loafing around the general area, waiting for nightfall. He wished there was a place where he could make sure the submachine gun he had not fired for so long was in good condition.

At 11:45 he headed out to the place where he had been told would be the meeting place. He never opened up full throttle. He wore the military glasses that allow one to see in the dark. He was beginning to doubt that the plane would be there when he heard the start of its engine. He slowed his own engine to a crawl as he approached the plane.

"Ahoy, out there! Do you have the money?"

"I do if the girl is alive and well. Let me see her before I get any closer."

One of the men pushed her out onto the edge of a wing where she was clearly visible and then shouted, "Here she is."

"Why isn't she wearing a life jacket? That was part of the deal."

"I'll put it on her as soon as you hand over the money."

"Sorry, but I'm not the trusting type. Put it on her now, or I'll just head on back to home base."

"Without her? I don't think so. Her old man would shit if you come back without her."

There was a lull in the conversation while the three tried to decide if he really wouldn't give them the money if they didn't put her into a life jacket. Hans was aware that there was a difference of opinion. He waited patiently until she appeared once again, this time wearing a life jacket.

"Satisfied now?"

"Yes, how do you want me to get the money to you?"

"Just ease your boat along side the plane and toss it to me."

He slowly edged the boat into position to toss the bag, filled mostly with cut-up newspaper. He could see a man standing on the wing with her. He could see that her hands were tied behind her back. He tossed the bag as high as he could into the air and yelled, "Jump!" just as the man who had been holding her reached with both hands to grab the bag. She leaped into the dark water and kept herself afloat by kicking her legs and with the aid of the floatation device.

Before the man on the wing could react, Hans opened up with his automatic weapon. The man fell into the water as the pilot sent the plane as fast as it would go for a take-off. Hans fired the rest of the clip in his M-16 at the moving aircraft, but he could not prevent it from taking flight. He watched as the plane disappeared into the darkness of the night. Then he pulled the frightened and shaky girl from the water and into his boat. He untied her hands, and she gave him a hug that she was reluctant to relinquish. Finally he told her to loosen her grip so they could get started back to the marina. He picked up the bag that had contained the ransom before he headed to shore.

Charley was there waiting for them. He'd heard the shots and was frantic to know the outcome. In spite of his protests, the quints had insisted they be allowed to come with him.

"Thank God," was all Charley could say when he saw his daughter was alive. He had feared the worst from the time he had heard the gunshots.

Each of the quints took his turn at a huge hug from their half-sister. Charley, like his sons, could hardly wait for the details of the rescue. Hans was reluctant to fill them in, pointing out that it would be best to notify the authorities now. He knew that the longer they waited, the more difficult it would be to apprehend the other two kidnappers.

Charley took his family home before he accompanied Hans to the police station. Hans told in brief fashion the events of the evening, including the approximate location of the dead body floating in the lake. Before they could make their get-away from the station they were surrounded by both the print media and the cameras of a local TV station. The police chief want Hans to remain for more details, but Charley threatened to have him fired if he didn't let them go immediately.

On the way back home, Hans turned on the radio. Already the story of the rescue had become the news of the day. In the middle of what was supposed to be an in-depth story of the kidnapping, the announcer suddenly exclaimed, "We have some breaking news in conjunction with our lead story this morning. Some sixty miles from the lake where the rescue took place, an amphibious aircraft has crashed to the ground. The plane is believed by the authorities to be the one used by the kidnappers. At the time of this report, there were no bodies in or near the wreckage of the plane. More on this as the news comes in."

Charley turned to Hans and asked him, "What do you make of this? Got any ideas?"

"There is one thing that comes to mind."

"What's that?"

"Well, do you remember several years ago when a skyjacker collected a huge sum of money and then parachuted into a remote area. He was never found, but the authorities claimed he must have died out there in the wild. I was never convinced of his death."

"And you think they may have planned something very similar?'

"Well, look at it this way. They had everything planned pretty well, so it stands to reason they didn't run out of gas. They probably had checked the plane out for any mechanical problems beforehand. If you concede those two things, what other explanation can you make for the crash and an absence of bodies? My guess is they probably had a vehicle, most likely an off-road type, in the area. If they don't find any trace of those two, my guess is it will take a long time to find them."

"You gonna pass your suspicion on to the police?"

"It wouldn't do any good. They don't like for civilians to come up with ideas that make them look bad."

After two days of no new clues, Hans reluctantly explained his theory to the State police. They pretended to be disinterested, but as soon as he left, they began a search in the area for signs of an off-road vehicle somewhere in the vicinity. Only three miles from the crash, they found the tracks of an off-road vehicle. There was no road leading to the tire tracks. It had been driven several miles through rough terrain to reach the spot where it had been parked. Experts concluded that the tracks had been made about two days before the crash of the aircraft. The clincher came when a thorough search of the area produced part of one of the parachutes. There was never a mention by the State Police that the idea for this type of escape had not come from one of their own.

As things quieted down, interest returned in the upcoming basketball season. People in general were interested in whether the change of head coaches would affect the team. Opinion had been almost evenly split over the change.

The hardest part of the job for the new coach was telling the upperclassmen that they might see very little playing time in the upcoming season. Those who had endured riding the bench during their junior high years were already accustomed to such a thing. They didn't like it, but at least it gave them an opportunity to be a part of something that might make history. Every day in practice they were overwhelmed by what they saw from the quints.

It wasn't just their size that made an impression on those who watched them. It wasn't the dunks, the hooks, the mid-range jumpers, or the three pointers. It was the speed and agility of people so young and so big that impressed them most. They played mostly zone defense, but they were capable of man-to-man pressure if the need should arise. Hard work on the weights had made them difficult to rebound against.

The first game was on the road, and the small gym had been filled for an hour before the start of the JV game. The team they faced was awestruck from the opening tip. They never managed to score in the first quarter and trailed 23-0. The quints did not play again until the start of the fourth quarter. The final score was 63-26. The losing coach was quick to come over to shake the hand of the winner. "Thanks," he said, "for not making it any worse. Our kids have been dreading this."

The second game was also away from home for the Lakers. The start of the JV game was delayed as the fire marshal made several of the standing room crowd leave. Several college coaches tried to get seats, but no provision had been made for them. The Lake Side coaches made a point of telling them that they would be given priority seating at the first home game. The outcome of the game was similar to that of the first. Lake Side fans had taken to booing when the quints were taken out of the game

The first home game was the largest crowd yet for the Lake Side gymnasium. No one had had the foresight to even imagine the gym would be too small for the crowds that would attend the games that year.

The opponent for that game might well have been the favorite in the league if it hadn't been for the quints. It was thought they could provide the only real competition for Lake Side.

They couldn't. The quints played a little more than they had the first two games, and the final score was 75-41. It was after this game that the television stations of St. Louis and Kansas City began to cover the Lake Side games. From that point on, any Lake Side game became more than an event; it was a happening. Tailgating before the games had become a massive traffic problem as the people from miles around flocked to Lake Side to get a look at what was already being called the greatest high school team of all times.

Charley sat in the coach's office after the third game. He waited there for the coach to finish his wrap-up with the team. When he came in, Charley asked, "Well, what do you think?"

He shrugged his shoulders and hesitated before replying, "I just don't know. How can I possibly assess how good we are against competition no better than we're likely to see this year. What do you think?"

"I think you're right, but I do have one idea, though."

"What's that?"

"Well, there an invitational tourney at the State level this year. It's gonna be called the Tournament of Champions. It will feature what the writers are calling the best eight teams in the State from all classes. No one has to attend. It's optional. If we get an invite, would you be willing to give up part of your summer vacation to coach the boys in mid July in St. Louis?"

"Of course. Do you really think we'll be invited?"

"I have no doubt. We been getting lots of pub lately in the big city papers. I'm sure there'll be lots of college coaches who can't wait to get a look at the boys. I don't think you ought to mention it until after our own State Tournament. It might be a distraction."

"Okay, I'll not say anything until after that. If we should stumble in the State, my guess is we won't have to worry about being invited."

"You're probably right, but I don't see any way we can lose a game if we can just stay healthy."

"I hope you're right."

****

The rest of the season was predictable. What had started as local publicity had long since switched to regional and later national acclaim. The team had never really been challenged, and it was the opinion of most experts that there was no high school and very few college teams that could provide worthy competition.

When the school year ended, the coach and the quints took off for two weeks before they began training for the Tournament of Champions. A new element had been added. A national Tourney of Champions had been scheduled with the winner of the State Tournament of Champions to be given an invitation.

Lake Side was easily the smallest school to make it to the Tournament of Champions. The tourney itself was almost a re-make of the movie "Hoosiers." Everyone seemed to be rooting for David against all the modern day Goliaths. They did not disappoint. Only the final game was close. Leading by only a single point with less than two minutes to play, the quints cashed 11 straight free throws to hold on for an 8 point victory.

There was no let up from that point on. Two-a-day practices were a daily thing. Only Sunday was a slight respite. A voluntary shoot-around was made available on their day of rest in the gym Charley had built earlier for the quints.

As the opening day of the National Tourney was approaching, Charley made arrangements for all of his family to attend. Billy and his family had agreed to visit him before the tourney began. They would fly with the whole team on Charley's private jet to the Big Apple. The coaches and their wives would also be on board.

As the Lear Jet took off, Charley peered out the window as the plane was crossing the lake that the town had been named after. A mere speck below, he spotted the Light House Marina and thought about the rescue of his daughter. His mind had been occupied recently with the details of the trip they were taking. He never dreamed it was all about to end.

Down below stood the two men who had failed in their kidnap attempt. One of them had just released a SAM missile in the direction of Charley's plane. The explosion lit up the sky, but only a few witnesses realized what they had just seen.

The first of the kidnappers turned to his accomplice and said, "I bet that rich son-of-a-bitch now wishes he'd just paid the ransom."

Back in Perdido, it was Juan de los Santos who smiled when he heard the news. He had finally managed to outdo his illustrious father. With the death of the Johnson family, he had become the sole heir of the Johnson Corporation. He now held the titles of the richest and most powerful man in the world. His father would have been proud .

THE END